A Half Moon Adventure

A Mystery-Adventure Novel

by

Evadeen Brickwood

As if growing up in the seventies wasn't difficult enough, teenager Isabell Bertrand is also too rebellious for her parents' liking. A novel treatment with hypnosis appears to be the perfect remedy and Dr. Albrecht regresses Isabell to her early childhood and even further back. She experiences previous lifetimes and then one in particular: could this beautiful young woman in a silk sari, who was forced to choose between two men, really once have been her? Years later, Isabell is invited to a wedding in Pakistan and memories of a forgotten love come flooding back - with dangerous consequences.

For Peter

"A Half Moon Adventure"

This book was first published in paperback by
Evadeen Brickwood at CreateSpace

Paperback Copyright © 2018 by Evadeen Brickwood
E-Book Copyright © 2018 by Evadeen Brickwood

All rights reserved.
No part of this publication may be reproduced, stored in a retrieval system or transmitted in any form or by any means, electronic, mechanical, photocopying, recording or otherwise without the written permission of the publisher.
The moral rights of the author have been asserted.
This is a work of fiction. Names, characters, places, brands, media and incidents are either the product of the author's imagination or are used fictitiously. The author acknowledges the trademarked status and trademark owners of various products referred to in this work of fiction, which have been used without permission. The publication/use of the trademarks is not authorized, associated with or sponsored by the trademark owners.

First edition 2018 by Evadeen Brickwood at CreateSpace
Second edition 2018 by Evadeen Brickwood in South Africa

CreateSpace ISBN: 978-1973744917
NLSA ISBN: 978-0-9946919-6-5

Cover Design by Yvonne Less, www.art4artists.com.au
Image Source: 'Depositphotos.com' licensed
South African edition printed in Cape Town
Book Layout: Birgit Böttner
Marketing: Alphalogic International

<u>Other Titles by Evadeen Brickwood</u>

In the Time Travel Youth Series:

"Children of the Moon" ("Remember the Future 1")

in the German Edition:

"Kinder des Mondes" ("Erinnerung an die Zukunft 1")

"The Speaking Stone of Caradoc" ("Remember the Future 2")

"The Secret of the Bird God" ("Remember the Future 3")

Other Novels:

This book in the German Edition:

"Abenteuer Halbmond" (An Adventure Mystery)

"Singing Lizards" (A Mystery-Adventure set in Africa)

"Singende Eidechsen" (German edition)

"The Rhino Whisperer" (A Crime Mystery)

"Der Nashorn Flüsterer" (German edition)

"Charlie Proudfoot Murder Mysteries" (Series)

Special Thanks and Acknowledgements

Many thanks to my late husband Peter, to Franciska Griesel, Svenja Böttner and Kim Hunter of Tango with Text for their enthusiasm, constructive editing, proofreading and constant support. Cobus Griesel for lending his technical know-how, Dr. Brian Weiss for his books on hypno-therapy that greatly broadened my horizon and Katerina Baumann for proof-reading the Greek dialogues. A special thanks also to all my test readers, author-friends and the family in Punjab, who so kindly welcomed me as a teenager a long time ago.

"I haven't told half of what I've experienced.
For nobody would have believed me."

Marco Polo

CHAPTER ONE

A warm breeze carries me gently here and there. Silence. Nothingness. Only warmth. A voice, calm and firm reaches out to me, pulls me back.

Dr. Albrecht's voice reached me from afar. I remembered now: he had hypnotised me. "Three, you are coming back.Two, you will wake up now. One, you open your eyes. You can remember everything."

The pictures behind the nothingness faded away. I had seen myself as a younger version of who I was now: dark blonde, slim, medium height, with full lips and blue-grey eyes. Young and vulnerable. Had I really looked so sad back then?

Actually, I liked myself the way I had been at the age of twelve.

"You did rather nicely, Isabell," Dr. Albrecht praised me and switched off the tape recorder. I opened my eyes and took a deep breath.

He checked his watch and then the wall clock. Just to make sure that the time was correct. The cosy warmth seeped away and the smell of floor polish hit me. The Lazyboy I'd been lying on for the past half hour felt no longer comfortable. "Mhmm." I wanted to stretch myself.

It always took me a while to get used to reality again. Reality – that was the summer of 1977, in my home town of Karlsruhe in Southern Germany.

At fifteen, I was an ordinary teenager; in my opinion at least. I did sports, loved pop music, had the odd zit on my face and, on occasion, defied my parents. That's the reason why I was here. My parents were convinced that I was too difficult, too rebellious. Shocker. And it was Dr. Albrecht's job to fix me.

Traffic noise echoed up from the street. There was the dank smell of a cold cup of coffee on my shrink's broad desk and the tick-tocking of the clock on the stark white wall across the room. It was 2:30 pm. A tram bell downstairs was ringing wildly. I knew I was back.

This novel treatment with hypnosis had lasted for the whole of two months now and it had dredged up a great deal from my early childhood. In the seventies, new treatment methods were all the rage - anything that was considered modern was all the rage. I didn't really mind that.

"We still have some time left and I'd like you to listen to the most important sections on the tape. I also have a few questions for you..."

"Of course, Doc," I said in a perky tone.

I sat up and watched him work the tape recorder. As far as I could tell, Dr. Albrecht was ancient. Thirty... at least.

His thinning hairline and the crows feet around his spectacled eyes were a sure sign of his advanced age. What's more was that he always wore a white coat and acted so damn polite. The picture of a scientist. He somehow reminded me of an Albert Einstein poster. Just that his hair wasn't as crazily tousled as that of Einstein. I thought by now that this new therapy was quite a smasher because Dr. Albrecht was the only grown-up who actually listened to me.

At first, I hadn't been keen on all that mumbo jumbo, but then I got used to it. Under hypnosis, I could live through stuff that had happened way in the past. Just that now I was in control. We always discussed what I'd experienced after one of these sessions. This time, my memories had begun with a phone call to my father when I was twelve years old.

'Daddy, she's just lying in bed and doesn't say anything. She just stares at the wall. I'm afraid. Please come home!'

'Are you sure that she's not just in one of her moods again? I've got so much work to do here. Were you cheeky to her?'

'No, of course not, I wasn't. We weren't naughty at all.'

My older sister Evelyn began to wail and my younger sister Paula crawled under the dining room table.

'Did she take something?'

We didn't know. She always took so many pills.

Soon, Daddy came home and shortly after, an ambulance took my mother away. As usual, we felt guilty because Daddy didn't speak to us. It clearly was all our fault. My mother then stayed at the health resort for two long months.

During this time, the health department had sent a stout valkyrie of a caregiver to our home to look after the family. Her head was topped by an old-fashioned beehive and she ordered us around in a shrill voice...

Dr. Albrecht paused the tape.

"How did you feel about your mother's absence?" He asked.

"Hmm, guilty I guess... and I didn't like this caregiver. I liked her even less than my mother," I said and answered another three or four questions. I had learned to put my feelings into words and that wasn't all that bad.

"Alright, I think that's enough for today," the good doctor said at last.

I gave the wall clock a baffled glance. It was just after three and high time. The psychologist wrote down some last notes, and as always at this stage, he went to plant himself on his leather chair behind the desk.

"Well, we have nearly reached the end of your therapy," he said abruptly and tossed his pen into the glass tray. "A great success, I'd say. You should be proud of yourself, Isabell. All we need are one... maybe two more sessions."

"Okay fine. I have to go now," I said. "We are writing an important test tomorrow." Eager to leave, I wriggled impatiently down from the Lazyboy.

Dr. Albrecht pushed his gold-rimmed glasses up the bridge of his nose. He didn't seem finished with talking. So I plunked myself onto the wooden chair in front of the big desk, fidgeting while I looked up at him.

Hardly anyone knew about this therapy of mine and I never even spoke to my family about it. That would have been way too awkward. Anyway, the girls in my class were too immature to dig something like hypnosis. They would have made fun of me for sure. Only my best friend Renate knew, and she was okay with it.

'Swell, I'm seeing a real psychologist,' I had reported back to her after my first session.

'What the hell do you need a psychologist for?' She pronounced the word as if it was rotten food or something.

'Well, you know... my mother and all that crap.'

'Why doesn't she go to a psychologist herself, then?'

'Maybe, because she's a grown-up?' I'd said.

Maybe, I shouldn't tell Renate so much about my mother. She might think that I was just as bonkers as the old bat. 'And that's the only reason? Are grown-ups always right or what?'

'What else is new?'

'That's so daft. I'm glad, my Mum's kinda normal.'

Her mother was divorced and worked part-time. Renate was a latchkey-kid and all full-time mothers felt sorry for her.

'Yes, you are a lucky fish.'

'Remember, you can't trust anyone over thirty,' Renate had warned me. 'Don't take all that stuff for real - whatever that guy's telling you.'

But I trusted Dr. Albrecht no matter what she said.

Renate was slim with long hair that she dyed pitch black. Totally awesome. The only girl in our class, who dared dying her hair. Her dark eyes were too large for that small cat face of hers and her thin lips were often curled up in a cynical sort of way. That's just how she was dealing with an uncaring world; cynical was good and Renate wasn't half as bitchy as the other girls. Only a bit aloof, maybe. It gave our friendship just the right amount of distance.

'Mrs. Beilstein is in the waiting room,' the intercom on the desk rasped. Dr. Albrecht pressed one of the buttons.

"Thank you, Elizabeth. Just one minute, please." The doctor told me something in this 'one minute' that had me stumped. That I was such a good subject and what not and that's why he wanted to continue with the sessions. Unofficially so to speak.

Come again?

"You would be ideally suited for my experiment, Isabell. What I would like to do is to further regress some of my patients as an extension of my work. Perhaps you've heard about something called regression."

I contemplated the word. "No, what's that supposed to be?"

In a nutshell, the explanation was short and sweet, since he only had a minute to squeeze it in. What he said made me nervous and I kept fidgeting on my chair. "You mean – the time before I was born?"

"So to speak. I will write a book about all of this."

"So to speak? But that's - impossible! We only live once – right?" A while ago I had seen myself briefly in a sari while I was under, but Dr. Albrecht had quickly brought me back. I remembered that I'd had curves then, but that was all. Was he talking about that, maybe?

"That's precisely what I would like to research further. With your help. There are several documented cases in the United States by Dr. Stephenson for example. You are still a minor, but we could change your date of birth and your name. Just for the sake of research."

Wow, a secret! That was an interesting turn of events. Dr. Albrecht had probably read every conceivable book on the subject. He then told me about a woman who had actually remembered a previous life. And that I could do that too!

"What if you've lived, let's say, in…Timbuktu. Do you then also speak …"

"Arabic? Possibly. That's something called xenoglossy, if someone speaks a foreign language under hypnosis that he or she has never learned." Xenoglossy – a chunk of a word. Fancy that!

"Hmm, I'm not sure. Sounds a bit odd. I have to study for school and all that," I weakly protested.

"Of course, the decision is up to you. If you don't want to participate, I'll find somebody else. Your school work comes first. That's quite normal. I completely understand."

How I hated the word 'normal'.

"But why on earth me? Didn't you ask your other

patients? I'm only number 13 on your list of 'difficult teenagers'." It was meant in an ironic sort of way, the reference to the number 13.

"Yes well, I'll also ask my other patients, of course. But in my opinion, you would be best suited for this." In his opinion!

"Smashing, I'm your best guinea pig."

"So to speak."

"I have to give it some thought."

"Naturally. Take your time, Isabell. Just don't take too long. I'll see you next week. Elizabeth, you can now —" The whole conversation had taken a lot longer than one minute. More like ten.

I was best suited for this and my mother would have kittens if she knew. Hah. "Okay, I've thought about it," I said quickly. "I'll do it."

The shrink needed me. Not as a patient, but as his best guinea pig. Not the others - ME. Fifteen-year-old Isabell and I would be in his book. I felt proud somehow at the thought of it all. I'd have a different name and would be older, but I wasn't fussed about stuff like that. Nobody was supposed to know about it, anyway.

We made an appointment for Thursday next week at the same time. I squeezed past beefy Mrs. Beilstein and dashed down the stairs. In the street, I fumbled the lock on my bike open and was about to jump on the seat, when I had to think about the body of my alter-ego.

I looked down at myself. What I saw weren't exactly curves or even well-rounded boobs, but a slim body with two tiny molehills. Other girls my age were a lot more padded than that. Never mind. It was great for doing sports!

I contemplated the whole thing, while I pedalled home through afternoon traffic. I started giggling and nearly went over a red light. A tram kept ringing its bell at me until I was out of earshot.

Dr. Albrecht had done his utmost to coax early memories out of me. At last, somebody gave a hoot about my thoughts and feelings. This thing with hypnosis was really awesome, although I had been totally against it at first. The bicycle tyres clattered over the kerb. I took a familiar shortcut and rode closely past an old lady, who was taking her dachshund for a walk. Too closely. "Hey, you lubber!"

"Sooory!" I called back and was gone.

There were only flats in our area, but I had a thing for the ancient sandstone buildings along the broad avenues, where the rich people lived.

Inside, the rooms had to be large and elegant with huge windows leading out to the verandas. I was sure that they were fitted with expensive carpets and furniture that I could only dream of. My family, on the other hand, lived in a small council flat in a more affordable road, because my parents had three children to feed.

At that point, I turned into our road and wondered for the hundredth time, who'd had the idiotic idea to paint house number 8 that ugly mustard yellow. When you looked up, lacy curtains fluttered almost imperceptibly as if moved by an invisible hand. I put the chain around my bike's rear tyre and climbed up the stairs, two steps at a time.

"Isabellshe!" I nearly blundered into Mrs. Speidel, the nosy gossip from the top floor. She always added a -she at the end of my name. Actually, at the end of everyone's name that she regarded as a child. Mrs. Speidel was a member of the club of adults, whose sole purpose it was to make my life miserable.

"Isabellshe! Wait a little while, darling..."

She had to spend half her life somewhere on the staircase, judging by how often one bumped into her all day long. The staircase was just like the main street of a vertical village and Mrs. Speidel knew just about everything about all her neighbours. Nah! She knew everything about everybody in the entire street and about every celebrity, too.

"Oh, I'm very sorry, Mrs.Speidel. Bye for now." I managed to jump onto the next landing. It would be easier to bolt if she could no longer see me.

"Well... did you just come home from school?" The chatterbox called up after me.

"Yes."

"Well you know... back in my day..." I quickly slammed the door to our flat shut. The smell of stew.

"Did you have something to eat?" My mother asked from the kitchen. She wanted to have a chat with me. "Yes," I lied and edged into the children's room.

There was no way I would discuss my therapy session with her. Not only because I really didn't feel like it, but I couldn't fill my parents in on Dr. Albrecht's new experiment. No point in talking to them, anyway. In my opinion, they were bone-headed, totally conventional and narrow-minded.

At the tender age of fifteen, I had a pretty good idea what that meant. Everybody knew about conventional people.

My parents were Walter and Hannelore Bertrand and they were not a perfect couple.

Daddy worked at the Technical University in town and came home for lunch every day. After hours, he usuallly went out to make an extra buck, repairing TV sets. He was forced to moonlight because three children cost a pretty penny. He blamed his receding hairline on his existence as a father and my Mum's cooking was responsible for his corpulent girth. Königsberger Klopse, meatballs in a white caper sauce, were his favourite dish. When I was younger, I'd also liked them, but then I had changed my mind because we had to eat them so often. What I wanted to eat now was muesli.

Dad's official job description was 'technical employee' and he was the most important employee at the university for sure. When we were little, my sister Evelyn and I had been allowed to accompany him to his place of work once in a while. Daddy even had a parking space in the underground garage and his own big office with a workshop in the basement. Cables of every colour, some with clamps on them, were hanging down the sides of shelves. These shelves accommodated stacks of tools and screws and all sorts of stuff.

He would patiently explain to us what his important work entailed. Daddy could do just about everything, it seemed, and people called him often to come and help them.

The two of us would then take turns on his desk chair, spinning it around to the left and right. Then we'd buy ourselves Coca-Colas for 50 cents from the vending machine in the passage with the polished floor. The large swivel-mounted magnifying glass above the desk was our favourite toy. You could switch on a tiny lamp on its side and get a close-up look at everything from cigar butts in the ashtray to screws and postage stamps. Daddy used to enjoy our company and sometimes it still felt like he did a little.

When he wasn't the most important man at the university, he loved working on his garden plot, where he'd created a large flower bed with plants from the nearby Black Forest. Apparently, they resembled the Masurian plants in East Prussia. Daddy had grown up there and often longed for his home, for his native province and always mentioned how much the Black Forest reminded him of Masuria.

My mother was a housewife. She wore preppy aprons and always cooked or cleaned the four rooms in our flat. Her blonde hair must have been full and shiny at some stage, but all the perms that were mandatory for a true housewife had turned it into lifeless curls. The result looked to me like sheep's wool.

Sometimes when I came home from school, I found the lounge locked.

'You kids are just going to mess everything up and I worked myself to the bone the entire morning cleaning the lounge suite,' she would say with few variations, followed by something like 'Isabell, take down the rubbish bin and then wash the dishes. Come, get a move on! Come, come, don't dawdle.' This she said in so many variations that I didn't feel like listening anymore. She also loved to polish the family-façade, because of her 'what will people think?' credo. As if anybody ever gave a hoot.

Mum had not always been a housewife. She mourned her glory days as the matron of the prestigious spa-clinic in Baden-Baden. Of course, for our benefit, she described this period in every single detail.

'Oh yes, I can count Emmerich Kalman among my famous patients. He gave me the vase over there to thank me.' Our gaze followed her index finger. 'The one with the fishes on it. Only the richest and most famous people would come to the spa-clinic in Baden-Baden.'

We had no clue, who this Emmerich Kalman was or most of the other people, whose names she would drop all the time.

Our mother also loved to listen to boring radio music by Tschaikowsky or the Wooden Clog Dance, while she ordered us around in a stern voice, urging us to do our chores. I hated window-cleaning the most, but she didn't tolerate back-talk!

Whenever we dared to fall ill, we had to stay in bed for days on end and endure her nursing. This usually meant that we had to slurp chamomile tea and eat runny porridge and that visiting hours were limited. It was way better to remain healthy.

I knew by now that my mother was like that because of her difficult childhood. Apparently, there was an agreement with Dad that he would support her against the children in every possible way, no matter what.

Whenever she threw a wobbly, little Isabell went to hide in some cupboard or pantry or under the bed. That's probably why I still suffered from stomach cramps and headaches. I started to hide even when she was in a good mood. I guess I simply didn't trust her.

Then I grew older and began to rebel.

'You have every right to stand up for yourself,' Renate had confirmed when I'd show her a particularly blue bruise. 'Why should you have to clean the windows when you are too tired and have to study to boot with?'

And that's exactly what I did. I stood up for myself. In other words: I fled.

At every opportunity, I'd ride my bicycle to the park by the castle and enjoyed the endless freedom it offered. Peace at last! The park embraced me with its green arms to soothe me whenever I was down. I just loved the peace here, I loved the grounds, the lake and the colourful azalea bushes. It was here that I had the courage to play my guitar in front of an audience. 'If I had a Hammer' and 'Blowing in the Wind' and songs like that.

Afterwards, I always felt stronger and would jump on my bike and ride home with my guitar swinging on the handlebars. It would have been my absolute favourite thing to live in this park. I'd have a beautiful home, a lot smaller than the castle, of course. In one of the small tea houses, perhaps. Size didn't matter, but it would be my proper home.

My sister Evelyn was one year older than me and already as moody as our mother. Paula was three years younger and a spoilt brat. I looked nothing like either of them. They had very fair, freckled skin and light-blonde hair. Exactly like our mother.

No wonder then that I was 'different'. My looks were different and I was obstinate and defiant and by now the black sheep of the family. A teenager, unable to adapt to rules. A rebel.

We argued often, just like our parents, and we fought unfairly, stoutly hitting each other and sometimes pulling out strands of hair. No wonder then that whenever I managed to run off to the park by the castle, I would day-dream that one of these days I'd have my own home; quiet and peaceful and of course no fighting allowed. Eventually, I had the brilliant idea to move out of this war-zone and into my grandmother's small bedsitter, two houses down the road.

Grandma Bertrand was Daddy's 82-year-old mother. A dignified Calvinist widow who always wore long, black dresses under grey aprons. Grandma Bertrand was so old that she seemed like a dinosaur to us children. She wore her thin white hair done up in a severe bun that she secured with long hairpins and her skin was all wrinkled and covered in liver spots.

But I loved her.

It didn't matter to me how she looked. What mattered was that she liked me and often mentioned how much I resembled her husband's side of the family. The husband who'd been killed in action during the war. How could I not love her for saying things like that?

'They were French Huguenots, my child. Nobles they

were and the Prussian king Friedrich Wilhelm II gave them a large stretch of land in East Prussia a very long time ago. Then we had to leave all of it behind when we had to flee from the Russians.'

I knew the story of the escape over the frozen Bay of Gdansk by heart.

The Bertrands were supposedly of a rather good-looking as well as noble lineage. Daddy resembled a young Marlon Brando. At least, that's what everybody said. And I looked like him.

Grandma Bertrand would smile her toothless smile and sigh, whenever she reminisced about her late husband whom she had given ten children. She was almost beautiful, then.

Meanwhile, the war of the Bertrands continued at home.

"Oh no, she will not move in with your mother. Over my dead body. You promised to raise her according to my faith and Isabell is far too young to move out just yet."

One night I was eavesdropping in the passage as I often did, listening to my mother's hissy fit. My heart sank.

I was not allowed to move in with Grandma Bertrand!

"Well alright, Hannelore, whatever you say." Daddy was obviously not in the mood to argue any further. "In that case, she will not move in with my mother."

"Perhaps she has a brain tumour."

I gasped.

"Hannelore, it's called puberty. It's completely normal to be a little rebellious and school is also taking its toll on her. The syllabus is getting more difficult by the year."

Daddy carefully folded his newspaper and put it next to the ashtray. Oh dear, were they going to get into a fight again?

"But Evelyn and Paula do manage their school work and Magda's daughter has no problems with school, either. Such a good girl."

Magda Pfeiffer worked at the post office and was a total drip. She was my mother's only friend and probably never disagreed with her. This was also Daddy's usual plan of action.

"Didn't you see how angry Isabell looked at me today?" She continued. There was no stopping her now. "After everything I do for the children. Let no good deed go unpunished. She actually said that Adam and Eve just have symbolical meaning in the Bible. Can you believe it?" My mother kept nagging. "Where does she hear things like that? Perhaps I should make a doctor's appointment for her straight away. Tomorrow."

This probably wasn't so much for *my* benefit but for *hers*, because Mum had a soft spot for doctors.

"Well then, if you think it absolutely necessary to take our Isabell to another one of those quacks, then go right ahead and do it. You never listen to me anyway." Dad lit a cigar and the cloying smoke wafted out into the passage.

"Walter, how can you even say a thing like that? I do listen to you."

"I just told you that I don't think there is anything wrong with the girl, only because she has a different opinion. That doesn't mean she has a brain tumour. Perhaps you should let her be and I'm sure her headaches will improve all by themselves."

"Are you saying, it's my fault? Isabell always manages to drive a wedge between us. So here we are, fighting because of her again. I work myself into the ground for you and the children and I surely deserve some respect for that." My mother sobbed wildly.

We were moving toward dangerous territory. I had to do something or they would be fighting for hours on end. I barged into the room and began to rant like a trooper.

"Can't we have one day without you two going at each other? Bloody hell, how am I supposed to study with all that noise?"

They looked at me gobsmacked.

"There... there you hear it, Walter," my mother cried. "She swears and shouts as if I was her servant girl. She truly deserves a hiding for that!"

My Dad sent me out of the room with a movement of his chin. Now he had to console her. The sobbing stopped instantly. My intervention was taking effect. At the very least, their conversation would continue at a more normal pitch.

"I'm not sure that a hiding would make a difference. Truth

be told, I believe it would make things worse."

"Oh, and why is that? It didn't do *me* any harm as a child."

My father cleared his throat. He knew better but it was useless to start another discussion with her on that point.

"Obviously. I might as well talk to a brick wall," he said. "I need some peace and quiet now if you please." Dad took his cigar, went outside and settled himself in his chair on the balcony. As so often, he sat on this chair watching the stars, while my mother pottered around in the kitchen.

A few days later, my mother got her way, allegedly because she was 'at the end of her tether'. Once again, I had to trek to the clinic for yet another check-up. My patient file must be bursting at the seams by now. My intolerable behaviour just didn't improve despite all the proper spankings.

What's worse was the fact that I had retaliated this time, and even Dad couldn't tolerate that. And just because of that stupid book!

My mother had found a book with the title 'The Good Marriage' in our fridge. Evelyn had shown me a chapter on sex in the books and I had quickly shoved it into the fridge when Mum walked into the kitchen.

Sex was an absolutely taboo topic in our home and that's why we urgently needed other sources of information.

'Why don't you just apologise to her?' Evelyn nagged me. 'You're so daft, being stubborn all the time.'

Pretty, blonde Evelyn mostly bottled her anger and pain up only to let it out on me. Preferably in front of her girlfriends.

'What's so wicked about reading a book. A book that belongs to HER?'

'That's so not the point. You were cheeky to her. She'll tell Dad to give you a hiding when he comes home tonight. Is that what you want?'

'I'll explain it to him. You can back down if you like, not me!' I insisted and Evelyn gave up once again with a tormented sigh.

'Oh come off it. Just leave her,' Paula had offered her five cents. 'She's too barmy for words.' This was the Paula who had a habit of blaming her older sisters for her own 'sins', for which we then had to take the rap.

'You're one to talk, you bitch,' I raged helplessly. We were too old for a good scuffle, but I stared daggers at her.

Come evening, our mother went off the deep end again. She didn't even wait for Dad to come home from work to do the deed and I just couldn't put up with it anymore. For the first time in my life, I hit back and of course, they didn't leave it at grounding me.

To top it all, I had stupidly forgotten to take the book out of the fridge and it disappeared never to be seen again. But this didn't mark the end of our secretive sex education. Evelyn had already discovered another book on Mum's shelf. This time it was about the Borgia-popes. Morally wrong perhaps, but exciting. My mother had no clue what kind of reading material she had lurking in her living room. 'The Good Marriage' was a children's book by comparison.

Then she had made the appointment at the clinic, where the paediatrician couldn't find anything wrong with me. "Headaches and stomach cramps you say, Mrs. Bertrand? Perhaps the symptoms are more of a psychosomatic nature. And aggressive behaviour in teens is not exactly a novelty these days. Why don't you take Isabell to the Centre for Parent Counselling? I'm sure they will give you advice."

"Yes, of course, doctor. If you say so," my mother purred. "You must know what you are talking about."

As expected, she did what the charming doctor had told her and I received my summons to appear before a social worker at the centre.

She specialised in 'difficult teens' and didn't quite fit the bill of a social worker the way I had imagined: namely stern-looking with a pinched mouth, in a formal suit with her hair pinned-up. This social worker resembled a cool folk singer like Joan Baez. She was dressed in a flowing kaftan with long blonde hair and thin jingling brass bracelets.

At first, I had to see the woman alone in her office. My mother sniffled and acted all offended, but then she took my father's hand and sat obediently down on a chair in the rather plain waiting room.

"Isabell," Joan Baez addressed me after a brief introduction, "can you try and tell me when you began feeling really angry for the very first time."

"No idea," I said in an obdurate tone. Why did she ask me that and why should I even trust her?

"Does that mean you don't know or you can't remember?" She scribbled something on my form. Then she eyeballed me over the rim of her large spectacles that made her look like an owl.

"I just told you, I don't know," I said in an even more truculent tone.

"No reason to get upset —" she tried to calm the difficult teen and wrote something else down. The movement let her bracelets jingle like crazy. Then she got up and called my parents into her office.

The grown-ups discussed me as if I wasn't even in the room, so I switched off until the diagnosis was pronounced: beginning depression caused by an undefined early-childhood trauma. Or something to that effect. Joan Baez recommended a reputable psychologist, who practised an innovative therapy with hypnosis. Dr. Albrecht or something like that.

A shrink? Don't tell me I had inherited my mother's problems! Was I doomed to become just like *her*? I panicked quietly and my stomach ached.

"You are not alone in this, Mr. and Mrs.Bertrand." The social worker peered over the rim of her owl-glasses with an encouraging squint. *She should get herself a new pair of spectacles*, I thought.

"We are here to help you. I know this sounds a bit strange -hypnotherapy - but times are changing. There are simply too many rebellious teenagers now and the old methods seem well... inadequate. We must find better ways of dealing with this growing problem."

Pah, growing problem, blah, blah, blah! Do you need a shrink for every little thing? I rolled my eyes and crossed my arms in a defiant gesture.

"Oh, I'm not so sure that a new and expensive hippie-method is right for us." My mother finished the sentence with a deep sigh. "All we want is the best for our daughter, you know. If Isabell could just learn to fit in properly."

What a hypocrite! Apparently, it was the easiest thing in the world to feign the nice and caring mother in front of strangers. My father studied the colourful Miró print behind the woman and as usual, said nothing.

"But of course, Mrs. Bertrand, we understand your problem. I can assure you that Dr. Albrecht has much experience in dealing with teenagers." The brass bangles jingled applause. "This new method is quite reputable and has nothing to do with hippies. We are still in the beginning stages but the successes we've had are very promising." The social worker squinted at us with a serious expression. "We have been able to help twelve teenagers so far and with some luck, we'll adopt the treatment long-term into our programme."

That made me number 13. *Lucky number 13*, I thought with some sarcasm and 'hypnosis' sounded sufficiently controversial.

"I would love to go to hypnotherapy," I piped up, just to stick it to my mother. The grown-ups turned around and looked at me all astonished. Maybe they had forgotten that I was there.

"Really? Oh and your medical aid will, of course, cover the expenses," Joan Baez stammered. That clinched the deal. My parents nodded their consent and the ball started rolling.

"Yes well, if *you* think that it is the best treatment… You surely know what you are talking about. All we want is the best for our Isabell."

Oh, how cross I felt at her for giving me up so quickly! I wasn't that serious about the whole thing.

"Mrs. Bertrand, I can promise you that Dr. Albrecht will take good care of your daughter." Alright then.

I started the treatment on that Monday after school. Initially, I was unfriendly toward the shrink and made no bones about it. He was on my parents' team after all. 'We understand your problem' the social worker had said. Pshaw! Then I slowly allowed him to win me over. His method wasn't half bad. A grown-up wanted to find out how I was feeling! We just talked and Dr. Albrecht scribbled down notes.

Soon, we started the hypnotherapy. During the very first session, I had produced a goddam memory-firework, which was a big surprise for both of us. It had taken Dr. Albrecht a couple of minutes or so to put me under. It took almost immediately and I found myself to be a toddler again.

'I'm three,' I said in a squeaky voice. 'Mummy has locked me into the small room by the kitchen. I can hear that the front door is closing shut.'

It was cringeworthy, having to listen to myself in the recording.

'What do you see? You can remember everything.' Dr. Albrecht's voice was calming and monotonous. *And his voice was my invisible friend in the background while I, the toddler, rolled and pounded red playdough into the shape of an elephant.*

'Evelyn is at nursery school. I'm bored and I find large scissors in the table drawer. Mummy needs them for sewing, but I can make the curtains look more beautiful with them. The curtains are sprigged with flowers. Mummy will be so proud of me. The scissors are heavy, but I manage to hold them up.' I was laughing as I watched myself cut broad fringes into the thick fabric. It was a difficult job, but soon the curtains were decorated with a droll fringe all around the bottom.

'Mummy comes back and doesn't like the fringe. She threatens that Daddy will be angry. I'm frightened.'

'You may leave the scene. Would you like me to wake you up?'

'No.'

I'd stumbled headlong into my next memory. The TV is on and I'm alone at home. Black and white flowers are opening and closing in fast forward." I had obviously 'landed' somewhere else.

'How old are you?'

'Two and I'm bored. A group of dancers is now on TV. They are wearing wide trousers and coloured shirts. Green and shimmery.' I watched them for a while. Pretty. 'The women have a red dot between

their eyebrows.'

'An Indian dance troupe?'

'Maybe, I don't know that. I'm too small. But I also want to dance with them. I climb out of my high-chair. There is Mum's lipstick! I also want a red dot like that. I smudge a bright red dot on my forehead with the lipstick and put it back into her dressing table. I waddle into the passage. Here I can see myself in the long mirror and I'm dancing to the music on TV.'

'Why are you smiling, Isabell?'

'I'm so happy just dancing like that in front of the mirror.'

'Good. Enjoy feeling joyful for a while... what happens next?'

'I'm listening and I'm afraid. There are steps on the stairs outside. The key is turning in the lock. I flee to my highchair, but I can't move fast...'

'Everything is fine. You are leaving the scene now. Visit another pleasant memory, if you like.'

'Yes, my mother is laughing with us and she sings nursery rhymes. She is reading a story from a picture book. My father is teaching Evelyn and me how to read and he draws faces and rabbits to make us laugh. We are picking sweet cherries in the garden. I am happy. Mummy doesn't look so pinched and bitter.' I reminisced about these pleasant memories.

'That's good, very good.' Dr. Albrecht let me enjoy myself for a moment.

'My sister Paula is still a baby,' I suddenly said. 'Evelyn and I are sent off to a nunnery in the Black Forest. I hear Bad Dürrheim.'

'Are you... three?'

'Yes. My mother has to recover and take care of the new baby. We have to stay there for six weeks, take salt baths and eat porridge.' I shook myself. 'I'm put in the group with the 'Little Ones' and I don't see Evelyn often. I don't like the nuns. They tied one of the boys to a chair and put him in the passage because he is homesick and crying. He sits on that chair and sobs the whole night.' I had tears in my eyes.

'I trip and fall and my head hurts. The nuns take me to the kitchen and bring a large knife. They want to press it against the bump on my forehead but I scream as loud as I can and want to run.

Run away from them. I think they will stab me with it.'

I remembered that a lonely tear had been running down my cheek and I'd turned my head left and right to get away from the nuns.

'You are leaving this scene now. You are safe and nobody can hurt you.' I'd calmed down. 'I will count backwards. You will wake up as soon as I reach one. Three, you are coming back…'

It had taken me a few moments to grasp that I was no longer a toddler. The tape was rewinding and the discussion had begun.

"So – that was more than enough for starters, Isabell," the shrink said.

"Wow, I can still remember everything," I marvelled. "Just like you said I would."

"Yes, it's usually like that. We will talk some more next time."

From that day forward I hadn't felt quite so angry and helpless anymore. It was really working. Dr. Albrecht was some kind of a sorcerer.

When we started the secret regressions, I was already an old hand at this whole thing, just that this time it was different.

He seemed impressed with me. "You spoke in a foreign language here and there. Perhaps you could explain one or two things to me."

"Really?" I said dreamily. "Okay."

I already knew that people could sometimes speak medieval French or Quechua or Chinese under hypnosis and I was proud of myself for doing just that. As always, Dr. Albrecht played the tape for me. The images returned before my inner eye and took me right back. I had tears in my eyes, listening to my own dreamy voice.

'I'm wearing a… a uniform. We have arrived in Warna. I'm still young, eighteen maybe, and I have brown hair. My name is Adam…'

After a short life as a British soldier who suffered from a broken heart and had deliberately put himself in the line of fire during the Crimean War, I suddenly found myself in an even stranger place.

There were hills covered in sparse tufts of rough grass all around, but not where I was standing. Here, I was surrounded by magnificent flowers, trimmed lawns, fountains and trees.

I saw the young woman again with her light brown hair in a braid. She was beautiful and a little unusual-looking with her green almond-shaped eyes and high cheekbones. The young woman's name was Nusrat. I just knew that. I also knew that I was Nusrat at some level.

She sat on a bench made of carved wood next to a clear fish pond that mirrored the leafy shade of the trees. Mandarin ducks floated across the water. The garden was enclosed by high walls.

At the age of fifteen, I didn't actually like the way I looked, but I just knew that this was also me, the woman who sat on that bench. I could feel the wood and I smelled the spicy scent of resin.

There was a certain resemblance between the two of us. My hair was light-brown like hers, but my eyes weren't green. They were a greyish blue and not one bit almond-shaped. Unfortunately, I also didn't possess her ample curves. Mine was the body of a slim teenager, who loved sports. Especially rowing.

Nusrat's body was wrapped in a brightly-coloured garment of embroidered silk and she wore rather expensive-looking jewellery. I, on the other hand, possessed jewellery only in the form of a cheap pendant made of green glass that hung from a thin leather strap. Expensive baubles meant nothing to me. I simply liked the way the sand and the ocean waves had ground the glass into an organic shape.

I tried to concentrate on the recording again and the room disappeared into the background. *'I can hear Rajput. Rajput,'* I said in German. *'Imran is a childhood friend. Sometimes we secretly play outside the village walls with our bows and arrows. I'm a girl and he is different to our caste, but we are still so young. Not easy… the servants are watching, but we are shrewd.'*

I could feel myself smiling inside, as I spoke these words. 'My father is generous. He doesn't have a son and even teaches me how to handle a khanda sword. My horse is called Kalyan. We belong to an important branch of the clan.'

There was a long pause. I was talking to this young man whose name was Imran – and I just knew what was being said.

'We are speaking to each other. There is a problem. I'm sixteen and must get married soon. It's about honour and family. I am the only daughter.' She was only a year older than me but looked almost grown-up. And Nusrat had to get married!

'What does Rajput mean?' Dr. Albrecht asked on the tape.

'I'm not sure... our family, our clan... warriors... aristocrats from Chandra Vamsh,' I stammered, then I heard myself speak in this foreign-sounding language again.

'The villa belongs to my father and servants are standing in the shade of the trees to keep an eye on me. The shadows are growing longer.'

I was speaking Outlandish again. Dr. Albrecht didn't know what I had said because he couldn't understand a word of it.

"Do you understand what you were saying here?" Dr. Albrecht stopped the recording and looked at me expectantly. I told him.

"Don't know if you can call it 'understanding'. I just know."

I couldn't explain it any better. The words sounded guttural. There were feelings of sadness and a sore heart ... They gave me a lump in my throat. My therapist didn't have to know about these things. It was too embarrassing to talk about all my feelings.

The tape carried on playing. *'...cannot see you any longer,' I uttered in a tormented voice. 'My father has permitted this last meeting with you.'*

The young man wore a simple white turban, which befitted his station, a long white silk shirt, a dark vest made of brocade and wide trousers. There was this feeling of unfulfilled passion...

"Imran comes from a good family. Moghuls. And we are in love. That's what we think we are," I explained to Dr. Albrecht.

I blushed. What did I know about passion? At least Renate had some experience when it came to kissing. Dr. Albrecht noticed my discomfort and paused the tape. "Would you like me to continue or is this getting too difficult?"

"I'm not sure. It's not easy to translate in detail what's going on."

"That's not necessary. I only want to know more or less what it is you experienced. Do you want to tell me?"

"Yeah sure. I cannot see him any longer, because I'm getting married."

"I see." Dr. Albrecht scribbled and scribbled. The recording played silently for a while. I could hear myself breathe and then there was Imran's voice. *I will die if your father insists.' Imran's tone was angry. His hazel eyes flashed.*

We have no say in the matter. You know that. Our customs are different. You are Muslim. We cannot marry. I am betrothed to Mansour and I must obey the law of our clan.'

What do you see now?' Dr. Albrecht wanted to know on tape. 'Try and describe the scene.'

The words didn't make that much sense anymore. 'I am not sure. He is very angry.' I continued to speak in German. Then there was silence, while I was busy talking to Imran. The tape whirred.

'Then I will have to challenge Mansour – to a duel,' Imran said angrily. 'I will not give up on you. Not for a man you don't love.'

Hey, that was so romantic. A duel!

'No, Imran, Mansour is a good man. They will kill you. And that will cause a blood feud. Is that what you want?'

'Then I will have to leave and die of loneliness.' Imran put his hand on my shoulder and glared at one of the servants by the name of Pratap. Pratap was always nearby to protect me. To protect my honour, as he had done since I was a child. The grey-bearded man moved farther back into the shade of the tree...

Swish, click. The shrink paused the tape and asked me what I had been seeing, while he scribbled on his notepad.

"Most interesting. That you can still understand this...," he marvelled. "My first case of xenoglossy! I must look this word *Rajput* up in the dictionary – you keep mentioning it. Then there are *Moghuls* and this *Chandra Vamsh*. This could be in India... most interesting."

I had never thought about India before. Wasn't that somewhere close to China? Where exactly was China...?

"Do you know this young man, Imran?"

"No, I don't know him," I answered firmly.

This question was normal for this type of hypnosis.Dr. Albrecht meant the possibility that I might recognise Imran as someone I knew in the present. For example, I had simply known that one of my comrades from the Crimean War was one of my teachers in the present. One of two teachers I sort of liked. I cannot say whether it was in the eyes or in the facial expression... I just knew somehow. It would be awkward when I saw him again at school. Unfortunately, I didn't know this Imran yet. Pity, because he looked really handsome.

I was deep in thought when I left Dr. Albrecht's office. As agreed, Renate was waiting for me at Café Wolf downstairs.

"That's totally awesome!" She was amazed by what I was telling her. Renate didn't know yet that I was doing regressions, but I just had to tell someone. "Totally. I'll go back next week. He wants to find out in what country this could have been. Then we'll carry on," I told her cautiously.

"Why don't I ever get to do cool stuff like that? I'd love to be a fly on the wall and watch how you speak in a foreign language and all that."

"Apparently, it's called Rajput. Have you ever heard of it?"

"No, but I can look it up at the library."

Renate was a little too enthusiastic about this for my liking. Hopefully, she'd keep her mouth shut. All I needed now were stupid remarks at school! I decided to play things down. "Better not. What if it's not even true. Maybe I remembered a movie about something like that."

"Of course, there are plenty of movies about Rajput on the box all the time." The corners of Renate's mouth curled up as always when she was in a strop.

"Hey, you never know."

Obviously, Renate would do what she wanted anyway. During the next session, I found myself in the same place again and began to speak Outlandish. This time, Dr. Albrecht stopped me immediately. *You are leaving the scene. You can speak German... You can —'*

I watched Dr. Albrecht fast-forward the tape. That was okay because not even I could properly understand what I was saying.

'*I don't see Imran again.*' In the recording, I actually did speak German. '*Oh, oh, he challenges my fiancé. But one of his own cousins stabs him before the duel takes place. Nobody tells me about this… only much later. My mother-in-law stirred things up between them. I haven't met her yet. Mansour's family lives elsewhere. I am heart-broken because I thought Imran had left. I had no choice but to do my duty.*'

My voice was barely audible at this stage and Dr. Albrecht forwarded the tape. It made a shrill squealing sound.

'*…not hurt anymore. Move forward to the next significant experience in this life,*' the shrink's gentle voice droned. '*What do you see now?*'

'*I marry Mansour and in time I learn to love him. He's also Rajput and we do not eat meat. Mansour is named after the man who once saved my father's life. He was a Muslim. I want for nothing and my life is good. I bear my husband three handsome sons. The elders of the clan had made the right decision. I can understand that now. We also have a glorious garden with red flowers I love…*' The red flowers distracted me for a while.

'*Can you hear or see the name of the place or a date?*' The good doctor interrupted my gush of words. '*Anything that might indicate where you are?*'

'*No, nothing. It's a long time ago,*' I answered.

'*Go ahead in time now to the last day of your life as Nusrat. To the day of your death.*' The scene appeared immediately.

'*I'm lying on a pile of pillows and I cough so much,*' I was wheezing and my chest hurt.

'*Your breathing is normal. Observe the scene from above, if it is easier for you.*' My breathing gradually became calmer.

'*They've placed a bed on the veranda. I am old… there are wrinkles on my face and age spots … I tell the servants to prune the climbing plants. I love flowers. I glance at the dense green branches, winding themselves around the pillars. The afternoon sun feels nice and warm. My sons and their families are here.*' I still remembered how I could see all that from above. '*They all look terribly serious. Birds twitter in the frangipani tree. The blooms smell so good, but it hurts when I breathe. My head hurts. Everything hurts.'*

'You no longer feel any pain, you are able to breathe normally again,' I heard the doc's instructions on the tape recording. 'Describe what you experience now.'

'I float upward. I'm so light. Everybody is crying. I levitate up… and leave them behind. I look up and see dark blue, a beautiful dark blue sky. Somebody is here waiting for me… a light grows larger and brighter.'

Then Dr. Albrecht counted backwards and I had woken up. The tape recording was about 20 minutes long. Phew, that had been incredible!

"Did I really die?" I demanded to know.

"It seems like it. Almost everybody reports seeing a light and that somebody is waiting for them on the other side," the doc explained.

"Hmm."

Pity that I didn't know the name of the country or the village. Not even the year. All I knew was that I must have lived close to the Himalayas. The villa was in a valley in the foothills. From the veranda, I could see snow-capped mountain peaks towering above the village roofs.

"Fascinating," Dr. Albrecht said and scribbled.

"Is it possible that I was actually there?" I blurted out. "I mean that I used to know somebody, whose name is Imran and… that I used to be rich and beautiful and then… I died?"

Dr. Albrecht looked a little perplexed. He scratched behind his ear as so often when he didn't know an answer to my impulsive questions. "I'm not entirely certain. It seems to help with health problems."

"What? What health problems? How do you know that it's all true? Maybe it's just my imagination."

"You spoke a foreign language and could understand it even later on. It's doubtful that this was a figment of your imagination. Perhaps you'll be able to remember more details next time around. I'm sure we will explore this lifetime some more."

"Can I speak this language now and have a conversation and stuff like that?" I asked.

"I don't think so. They seem to be just memories. But you might be more interested in such things from now on."

"Yes well, I don't know anybody who speaks this language anyway."

I stared at Dr. Albrecht, while he paged through his many notes. He looked up. "Would you like to discuss anything else?"

"Well yes, I wish I could help my sister Evelyn. She's also going to therapy now. Went to the advice centre all by herself because she keeps burning her arm with cigarette butts. Evelyn showed me the red scars."

He scratched behind his ear again. "I wish I could help you but my hands are tied." He proceeded to wring said hands. "You are my patient and your sister is already seeing another therapist. If it was you burning your arms with cigarettes, that would be a different story."

I didn't quite understand why that was supposed to be a different story. Adults were always so complicated but at least my own life was beginning to change. For starters, the hidings stopped. No doubt that it had something to do with Dr. Albrecht's final report. And I didn't have to fight so hard for everything anymore and my marks at school were improving. My mother was proud of her great achievement of having found the right medicine for me at last.

Then during the summer holidays, I also had my first kiss.

The Municipal Youth Committee organised a six-week trip to France, and I was going. It was easier to make new friends, and far away in the Haute Savoie, I almost forgot that my mother had given my beloved guinea pigs to the zoo just before we left.

'You never look after those critters properly. They are better off at the zoo,' she'd said with a laconic expression.

'How could you do that? They'll feed them to the snakes at the zoo.'

'I've had enough of all that mess. It's better that way.'

'I hate you, I hate you!' I yelled and knew that there was nothing I could do about it.

In France, I didn't have much time for dark thoughts. Our

young, long-haired minders kept us on our toes. We learned self-defence, ikebana and how to make casts of our faces with white plaster bandages. There were hikes down to the river and a trip to the marketplace in Annecy. Then it happened during one of our weekly discos: I got my first and somewhat wet kiss from a sixteen-year-old French boy by the name of Jean-Paul.

He looked so worldly-wise with his tousled brown hair and open laugh that I almost didn't mind the wet kiss. I had never been so close to a boy before, but finally, I'd been kissed as well.

From now on for some reason, even at the good old rowing club, boys seemed to notice me. Last year, one of the girls in my class had asked me to join her rowing club on the Rhine harbour. My parents were delighted and paid the small annual fee without question. I'd even received a t-shirt in the club colours and new tekkies.

"Sport will keep you out of mischief," Dad had said. "And far away from boys. Boys are nothing but trouble."

I had no clue what mischief he was talking about and had never really met any boys. But one year on, I had suddenly become visible to them.

Then things got even better. I was allowed to move in with my Dinosaur-Grandma Bertrand. By now, she was living in her own world that teemed with late relatives, celebrities and aristocrats from women's magazines and TV shows. We lived in separate worlds but it didn't bother me.

A birthday present in the form of a small radio-recorder became my other roommate in our setup. I would rush home from school, not to miss the beginning of my favourite music show 'Pop Shop' on Channel 3. I sat down on a chair in the tiny kitchen and listened to golden oldies for an hour and laboriously recorded song after song on cheap tapes. This music then surrounded me like an invisible bubble for the rest of the day.

'Ha, ha said the Clown', 'Bridge over Troubled Water' and 'Ticket to Ride'. I sang my favourite songs full blast in the afternoon while cycling all the way to the rowing club when nobody was listening.

The rowing club in the Rhine harbour was a close second-best place of refuge right after the castle park. There was a funny smell that came from a mayonnaise factory nearby but I quickly got used to it and the positive side took over. I loved the rowing boats, the way they glided elegantly over the water and I loved the peace and tranquillity of the harbour. Sometimes I skulled past a duck family and sometimes I had to dodge one of the big waves that followed the ships.

My effect on boys remained a mystery to me, despite my grand kiss with Jean-Paul. I was painfully shy and turned a bright shade of red as soon as one of them so much as looked at me.

During a club-party, I was introduced to Werner. Werner was slim and tall and twenty. He didn't mind that I blushed the moment he spoke to me. He kissed with experienced lips and patiently listened to my sad stories about school and parents and annoying sisters.

"Why is your name Isabell," he wanted to know. "Isn't that French?"

I thought it was just swell that he was interested in my name.

"Yes... well, my father comes from a Huguenot family. Apparently, I'm named after some great-aunt. My sisters are also named after great-aunts: Evelyn and Paula. I have a pretty big family on both sides."

"A great big family of great-aunts," Werner joked.

"Hah, exactly," I laughed cheerfully. "And Isabell is still better than Irene. My mother's first choice for a name. Do *you* have any siblings?"

"Yes, a brother, his name's Dieter. He's quite a bit older than me, but I hardly know him..."

Werner became my best friend and after a while, the stupid blushing stopped. We rode our bikes into town when the park was in bloom and we lingered on sunny street corners, leaning against our bicycles, chatting about sophisticated things.

Soon I trusted Werner enough to tell him about Dr. Albrecht. He thought it astounding that this kind of therapy was being recommended.

"This Dr. Albrecht is far ahead of his time," he marvelled. "Hypnosis! But it seems to work. From a psychological point of view I would say that your mother suffers from some form of bipolar disorder," he explained as we sat on someone's low garden wall.

Werner loved to talk about things like that because he studied medicine and knew a lot about it. Other boys played football and raved about the Bay City Rollers - and *my* boyfriend studied medicine. Werner had plans to specialise in psychiatry. A true expert, then.

"Is there nothing to be done about it?" I asked.

"Your mother takes medication, doesn't she?"

"I think so. She never ever talks about it."

"Typical. That must be difficult for you."

"She often tells me that I'm not normal and that she's the only normal person she knows. My mother is very controlling."

"Oh dear! That doesn't sound good."

"I guess I'm used to it by now."

"Don't let her get you down."

"I won't. I don't see her that often. Now, that I'm staying with my grandma and I go rowing at the club and so on."

After we had such discussions, we'd fly to the park on our bicycles and kissed in a dark, quiet corner. When the holidays drew to an end, Werner had to go back to university in Ghent. Ghent was in Belgium. I was devastated. Why did I have to be so young? Only fifteen! I was too young to travel to Belgium and visit Werner. Damn! And now my mother was hopping mad at me because her friend Magda had seen us together in the street, holding hands.

"What did I tell you about boys?" She confronted me roughly.

"Boys? That they're just interested in one thing?"

"Do you always have to be so vulgar? No male acquaintances until after you have an education! You have to think about your reputation here. What are people going to think?"

Did she want me to die a sad old spinster or what? "What

male acquaintances, please? I'm only fifteen and I don't have a reputation yet. Holding hands doesn't mean I have to wear a scarlet letter."

"Scarlet? What is that supposed to mean? I want only the best for you."

"Yeah sure." I was tired of our conversation. "You'll be pleased to hear that Werner is back in Belgium. That's where he studies."

"He is a student? Isabell, you are fifteen!"

I kept my mouth shut and walked to Grandma Bertrand's flat. A tear rolled down my cheek, then another one. I missed talking to Werner.

In time, I missed Werner less and I still had good old Dr. Albrecht. Other teenagers only cared about boring rubbish like 'Saturday Night Fever' and discos, tight clothes and boys, and not interesting stuff like hypnosis. Okay, to be honest, I was also interested in boys by now.

Soon, I turned sixteen and there seemed to be problems at home even without me being around. Evelyn was being punished because she had been kissing a boy in public. She envied my independence, the rowing club and just about everything else I seemed to have.

"Everything is always my fault and you, you always get what you want. I wish I had your guts!"

"I think you're forgetting who the black sheep of the family is," I defended my honour. "It's not as clear-cut as it looks."

Paula was still the spoilt baby of the family and only interested in herself. I couldn't tell any of them about my life. My precious private life that had to be kept private at all cost.

During the regressions that Dr. Albrecht guided me through, I'd had a brief glimpse of Adonia's lifetime. Adonia, a young Greek woman who had lost her life in a devastating flood in 1563 B.C. I knew the exact date this time but Adonia faded into the background after a single session, just as the young soldier Adam had faded. I never spoke anything but German during those sessions but Dr. Albrecht was enthusiastic nevertheless.

"I will dedicate an entire chapter in my book to our sessions, Isabell," he told me. It made me feel proud.

The whole thing was turning into a hobby of mine just like rowing, and I began to show some vague interest in other countries. When our school team won the regional regatta, we were invited to the nationwide 'Youth Training for the Olympics' championships in Berlin. It was so exciting to fly in an aeroplane for the very first time and I became more worldly-wise by the minute.

Alas, the girls in our dorm gossiped endlessly about boys and clothes and make-up, especially when I wanted to sleep. So I had no other choice but to join in.

"Oh, just check out that cute mini-skirt, Nicole. It really matches the orange t-shirt," Tina rejoiced.

"Wicked! You have to wear it tonight. So totally. We are meeting the boys at the 'Eierschale' club at seven tonight. You need something dinky for that." Nicole popped a chewing gum bubble.

"Should I use the blue eyeshadow or black kajal?" Tina asked.

"Both!"

"I don't own any make-up," I said feebly.

"Oh, Isabell. You have to wear eyeshadow these days! Here, you can have some of mine."

Nicole and Tina took me under their collective wing as if I was a poor relation from the province. I allowed them to take over but when it came to clothes, I put my foot down. No way would I be wearing a bright green mini-skirt. We went shopping and partied at discos that didn't require an ID document. After hours, sport was an after-thought at best.

When we returned from Berlin, Dr. Albrecht's hypnosis-experiment began to bore me out of my skull. I wanted to be uncomplicated and do all those down-to-earth things that other teenagers did.

Reincarnation was everything but uncomplicated.

"We should find out why we keep returning to your lifetime as a Rajput." Dr. Albrecht had hit pay dirt at the library by now. Rajputs belonged to one of the higher Hindu castes in northern

Hindustan somewhere between Afghanistan and Pakistan.

"There must be a reason, why this lifetime is so important to you. Perhaps it will help us find the cause for your stomach-ache."

"Yeah maybe," I answered half-heartedly, "but at the moment, I just don't have time for stuff like that."

Dr. Albrecht looked gutted. Well, what did he want me to do about it?

"I do understand. Let me know when you are ready to continue, Isabell. It would be a pity if we didn't finish this experiment."

"Sure thing, doc. Thanks for everything." Actually, I had no plans of coming back but you never knew what might happen. Soon, I got bored with rowing as well. The daily training-regime was exhausting and I refused to move up and into the national squad like some of the girls in my age group.

"Chrissie and Daniela made the squad." Heinz smoothed his long, blond hair back. He was also a rower and we were hanging out at the club disco.

"That's why they are beginning to look like a pair of wardrobes," the somewhat petite Tina giggled. "I'm glad that the trainer didn't choose me for the squad."

"Phew, right you are," I moaned. I studied Chrissie, who was standing at the bar with a Coke. Her shoulders were almost as broad as Heinz's.

"I'm really not up for that. All you do is train, train, train and drink protein shakes and garbage like that. Then on the weekends, it's just driving to regattas. No free time at all. Rowing can't be the only meaning in life."

I, for my part, wanted more from life.

My latest crush were the 'Beatles' and I stuck a 'HELP' poster on the wall by my bed. Then Renate and I started to go out at night. Grandma Bertrand tolerated my late outings and the Beatles-phase with great patience. Maybe she didn't quite notice what was going on. She was almost deaf by now and watched TV all day long with her headphones on.

'All you need is love… Hey Jude… A ticket to ride…'

John and Paul were so sensitive. They understood me and sang their songs for me. Pity that I could barely understand English. That didn't stop me from giving the songs a try whenever I played my guitar in the park.

"Do you always have to talk about them?" Renate preferred a different kind of music. "That's so yesterday! Have you never heard of Gerry Rafferty or Foreigner?"

"Yeah sure, I've heard of them. I also like Fleetwood Mac - and Pink Floyd. But the Beatles are just brilliant. Too bad they split up, don't you think?"

"No." Renate stood in front of the mirror and carefully applied blue shadow to her eyelids.

I was busy rubbing smelly setting lotion on my hair and blow-drying it into a fabulous new hairstyle. The hairdryer roared noisily but Grandma didn't even look up.

"Oh come on now, I could listen to 'Ticket to Ride' for hours on end," I said stubbornly.

"Not me. Are you ready or what?"

"Just now." I switched off the hairdryer.

"Bye Grandma, we are going out." Grandma Bertrand patted my hand and continued to stare mesmerised at the TV screen.

"Does she know what you just said?" Renate wondered.

"Don't know, she's getting very old."

"Do you have your keys?"

"Yip."

We usually took a stroll up and down Kaiser Street, ate Italian ice creams cones or we went to 'Burger King' for a Coke. Sometimes on weekends, we dared each other to take a peek into one of the discos, but we never really went in. Discos were expensive.

In September we moved to another high school. From our fancy girls high school to a co-ed school. It was me who had a reason to move and Renate did so out of solidarity.

My reason was that our Latin teacher Mr. Konrad had begun to torment me. I had been top of the log in Latin for some time now but since I had started rowing in the afternoons, there wasn't much time to study. Mr. Konrad became seriously miffed at me and the whole class had to know.

"Open your books. 'De Bello Gallico' page 32, third paragraph. Isabell, we are all dying to hear the translation you did." Ever since the 'incident' – a D in a test – I had fallen from grace and been deployed to the first row. This enabled me to look directly at the unforgiving teacher's bearded face. His flaming-red beard scarcely disguised the contempt he was feeling for me. Only later did I realise that I had smelled alcohol on Mr. Konrad and not aftershave.

"I only managed to do the conjugation of the verbs. I wasn't here when you told us about the translation —"

"I've heard better excuses."

"But…"

"No buts. You could have asked one of your classmates. Marion, wouldn't you just love to share with Isabell what homework I gave you if it pleases her to ask?"

"But of course, Mr. Konrad. It would be my pleasure." Marion grinned in my direction. At least I could feel it on the back of my head.

As soon as Mr. Konrad turned around to write on the blackboard, a paper missile smacked me on the shoulder. Then another one.

Eventually, I'd had enough. Not that the new school was much better. The teachers were harsh and cynical, but at least I no longer had to deal with Mr. Konrad and those paper missiles.

I could deal with harsh and cynical if I had to.

There were nice boys in our class. Walter had a hooked nose and squinted a little. He was tall and gangly, but also helpful and pleasantly normal. Tarek was German-Algerian, handsome, fashionable and reserved - and probably confused because he liked other boys. He lived with his mother in a flat across the Federal Constitutional Court. It was quite close to school and we often spent our free periods there.

A girl named Angie also joined our group. She lived with her grandmother who was dead-set against modern clothes and the psychedelic fashion trends of the seventies. Angie was dumpy, wore an outdated pair of glasses and wanted to move out like yesterday.

"I remember seeing some Cola in here somewhere." Tarek rummaged around the fridge in the narrow and very clean kitchen. He'd already placed four clean glasses on a tray.

"Apple juice is fine," Angie said good-naturedly.

We often sat in his rather tidy room and chatted about our teachers and how annoying they were. The teacher, who had allegedly been Adam's (my) fellow soldier during the Crimean War, had sadly transferred to another school. I would have loved to learn more about Tarek's culture and tell him about my Rajput adventure. But Tarek told us that he didn't want anything to do with Algeria and I don't think he would have been interested in reincarnation, either. The four of us soon formed a clique and Renate wanted no part of it.

"Nope, I'd rather do my own thing," she said when I told her about the way we spent our free periods.

"As long as you don't bite my head off if we can't see each other all the time," I said.

"Don't be silly," she grumbled and stomped off.

I mentioned our group at home and regretted it immediately. Apart from the subject of boys, another matter got my mother's back up even more. "I'm glad that you make friends but why does it have to be Muslims?" She referred to Tarek, of course.

"Why not?" I rolled my eyes at her.

"They are so… different to us."

"In your eyes, everybody is different. But I'm not like you. I don't care about stuff like that. If you must know, Tarek is not an orthodox Muslim. His Dad is a doctor in Hamburg and his mother is German." Then I felt like biting back a little. "Even if he was… no sweat, I won't get married to one anytime soon and embarrass you in front 'the people'," I teased her. "Although, at seventeen I'm allowed to get married to whomever I like."

She'd been lamenting more often of late that people might talk about this and talk about that. Paula who was listening, snorted with laughter, overdoing it on purpose and Mum looked all huffy.

"Are you giving me cheek again, Isabell? You know that's not what I meant."

"Ah whatever... not to worry," I played the issue down. "Must be on my way now in any case."

I was talking about going back to Grandma Bertrand's flat. There, I could be exactly who I wanted to be. Grandma never asked questions about my friends and she was happy to have me around.

Then, just when I had finally settled into my new school, something totally unimaginable happened: Daddy fell sick and died.

CHAPTER TWO

The winter funeral turned into a foggy swirl of unreal activities. Aunts and cousins made a big fuss of my mother. We, the children, were roundly ignored and had to be nice to everyone. This left not much time for grieving.

The week before Daddy passed away, I couldn't shake this awful feeling that something horrible would happen. He still lay unconscious in his hospital bed and we were assured that he was on the mend.

After one of our hospital visits, my uncle drove us home. "What are you going to do with the car, when he dies," he asked my mother in an offhand manner. What did they know? Something they had kept from me?

I felt scorching hot lava-fury surge up inside me. "Where the heck are you getting off, saying things like that?" I snarled at him. "He isn't dead yet. You're all so damn materialistic! All you think of is money and stuff. How can you be so cold-hearted?"

My mother looked at me with a guilty expression and her brother didn't quite know what to say. My sisters kept silent as usual and this just made me even more furious. "Stop the car! I want to get out of here right now," I demanded.

Before my mother could reprimand me, I was already outside, standing in the slushy snow. I started walking and didn't care how numb I was from the cold as I rushed along snow-covered streets towards the park.

My old, favourite place of refuge.

The slush on the lawns had been melting a little and had turned the ground into a field of mud. I didn't care. I cried a lot while I waded through the muddy grass. It was best to be alone and cry.

I returned home half-frozen and Grandma Heydenreich,

my grandmother on my mother's side was there pottering about the kitchen. She silently placed a bowl of hot soup in front of me and nobody mentioned the incident in the car. The Heydenreichs were a taciturn lot, but on the plus-side, there was always food around.

The phone rang. We heard voices speaking in hushed tones outside in the passage. It was the hospital. Daddy had just passed away…

The following morning I set out again for the castle park, but I didn't linger there. I walked on through the forest and then across snow-covered fields. Snow had fallen again during the night and I plodded through the soft white blanket that kept comforting me all the way.

After that walk, I was able to cope better with my grief.

To my family's dismay, I had been out walking for hours. My mother was not coping very well, so I made myself scarce until the actual funeral. I saw even less of my sisters and nobody spoke to us. Only my ancient Grandma Bertrand and I were there for each other, far from all the aunts and cousins. The idea that I could speak to Dr. Albrecht never occurred to me.

Grandma Heydenreich was friendly and pragmatic. She had seen many a relative buried in her time. So this had to be a matter of practice for her, then. Unfortunately, her generosity did not quite extend to people of a different faith to her own and as it turned out, especially not to my father's family.

Whenever she came to visit from her small village near Heidelberg, she had either been on a pilgrimage to Lourdes or was busy planning one. She brought special sweets for her grandchildren that a clever businessman was peddling off to pious pilgrims, and her purchases were always rounded off with a bottle of holy water.

She would tell us stories about old ladies sitting in wheelchairs, who had been healed by the water or about popes and saints and stigmata.

But Grandma Heydenreich had a past.

At the age of seventeen, she had worked for a wealthy

Jewish family in Frankfurt as a domestic help. Many young country women did this before they got married, in order to learn the art of keeping house. During this brief episode, the unspeakable had occurred and resulted in my mother's birth. This had led to all kinds of abuse that my mother had to endure in their small village and which had prompted Grandma Heydenreich's acts of lifelong repentance.

She'd soon married the first man who was willing to have her and who was deemed suitable enough to help resurrect her damaged reputation. This man had turned out to be abusive and, apart from giving her the gift of a new son after each furlough, he perished on the battlefield. She had six sons in total, which earned her a Mother's Cross of Honour in silver. Whenever Grandma Heydenreich did not polish her saint's halo, she ruled from the shrine of her kitchen.

"Hanne, you simply cannot have the memorial service at a Protestant church. That's out of the question," she told my mother and tolerated no objections as she stood at our stove, stirring her hissing pots.

"But what about Grandma Bertrand..." my mother sighed.

"Ah balderdash, Grandma Bertrand and her... family!" Grandma Heydenreich made the sign of the cross. "They can either come with us to a proper church or I don't mind if they stay away altogether."

"I must also respect her wishes, shouldn't I? Walter was her son after all," my mother tried to negotiate.

"Respect? What do these people know about respect for our Lord? I was against this marriage to Walter – God rest his soul – from the word go." The two of them soon went shopping as the needs of our mourning relations had to be catered for. I was ordered to hold the fort, in case more of them showed up.

The doorbell rang. I expected to see some aunt or cousin, who had the sudden desire to kiss me. It was, however, an elderly customer of my father's, who stood in the doorframe. She just wanted to let us know out of the goodness of her heart that crematoria were completely unreliable these days - and perhaps we could also invite her to the wake.

"You must know that one can never be certain that the ashes of the right person are in the urn you're given." Had I heard her correctly?

"I see…" I stood there, speechless.

"You've got to know," she continued eagerly, "that when the father of my friend Else was cremated, she was convinced that body parts of another person were also in there… an arm or a leg... who knows? They simply mix everything in, these undertakers, without a care in the world."

I could barely keep up with her torrent of words that didn't make sense to me. Why did this stranger think it was okay to harass me like this?

"How could Else know for sure that her father was really in that urn they gave her, I'm asking you?"

I'd found my voice again. "Yes, well... I'm very sorry, but I have to go now. There's so much to do. Thank you for your visit." I literally had to push the woman out the door. Then I leaned against it and began to sob.

Some rich great-uncle had paid for cakes and coffee at the wake after the Catholic service. My father's relatives were conspicuously absent.

My mother acted all disappointed by my refusal to view my father's body in the casket in the sanctuary, but I insisted that I wanted to remember Daddy how he'd been alive. My mother didn't want to cause a scene at the church, but I could see that she wasn't happy.

The priest then gave a vacuous speech. Of course, he hadn't had the pleasure of meeting my Dad in person, so he knew nothing of the flowerbed and his longing for Masuria or his many frustrations in life. Most of the churchgoers didn't seem to have known him or our family. Dammit, I had barely known him myself.

I kept thinking that everything felt so wrong. That this was not the way a funeral ceremony should happen. Although I had no experience with funeral services - none whatsoever - I couldn't shake the feeling that something was lacking. Shouldn't there be a proper ritual somehow? A procession maybe, a funeral pyre or appropriate singing?

'*Ram nam satya hai...*' The monotonous words thrust themselves upon me and I had no idea what on earth they meant. '*Ram nam satya hai...*' Yes, not bad... I softly hummed the melody during the entire service.

On my way to the tram station, I took great care not to step on broken paving stones. If I had no control over anything else, I wanted to have at least the freedom of stepping on whole paving stones. *Ram naja...*

"Sounds like some sort of a hippie tune," my latest friend Doris said. We'd arranged to meet after church at a coffee shop in town.

I had long since grown out of my Beatles phase. "What kind of a hippie tune would that be? Have you heard it before?"

Doris was different somehow. Intellectual and edgy, she kind of resembled Morticia Addams from the Addams Family - and I liked her.

In my circle of friends, it was only Doris who didn't mind talking about death and funerals. She liked discussing morbid topics: spiders and contagious diseases and stuff like that. Quite the opposite of the others.

"Hmm, maybe it was in 'Hair' or wait - 'Ougenweide'. They always use such funny lyrics in their songs. Like the 'Merseburg Incantations': Eiris sazun idisi..." She hummed the tune for me.

We had been to a concert by the folk group 'Ougenweide' last autumn. Totally awesome, and I liked going to the record store to listen to their LPs. I didn't have the money to buy myself folk records, after all. Ougenweide, hmm. I was impressed by her explanation.

"You might be right there. I must have heard the song somewhere." Just that deep down I didn't quite believe it.

"I hate funerals in winter," I complained to Doris. "Everything's dark-grey and cold and so wet. That makes it all so much worse." I swallowed a couple of tears. "Why does it have to be so morbid? Everyone behaves holier than thou and pretends to care."

"Funerals are always like that. It's so beastly morbid, but fitting somehow," Doris said soberly.

I told her about the old woman and her crematorium story.

"That so totally sucks. Why would this woman tell you a thing like that?" My new friend got herself into a fuss.

"No idea. My mother also wanted me to look into the open coffin. Totally macabre."

"Really? She wanted you to look at your dead father?" Doris took a sip of her hot coffee and swept her dark hair back so that the young guy on the table next to us could admire her face properly. I noticed that her manoeuver had the desired effect.

"Yes, right there in the room behind the altar. I didn't even want to go into that room. She dumped that one on us like always, without talking about it first."

"I think I would have done it," Doris bit her lower lip.

"What? Thanks a lot. It was just the body of my father and not Stalin or some Egyptian mummy or something." I shuddered with disgust.

"Yeah sure, that's not the same. Not very nice of your mother," Doris said quickly and played around with her teaspoon. She gave the sugar shaker a little dance on the table, then playfully threw her hair back again.

I lamented some more. "She always does stuff like that, you know. Never talks about anything up front."

"I think I would look at the body even if it was my father's." Doris stared dreamily ahead as if she could actually see her father's open casket. "I've never been to a funeral. Wonder if it's like the movie 'Harold and Maude'."

"We can trade places if you like." I waved my hand in front of her face until she focused on me again. "In reality, it's nothing like the movies. That's a real person you are close to... were close to. As if he's still around and it's not even real that he's dead."

"I wonder if the body is still the actual person or maybe the person is no longer inside the body."

Oh dear. Perhaps I should have told Doris about Dr. Albrecht's regression therapy and about reincarnation and all that, but that meant I had a lot of explaining to do and I really didn't feel like doing that right now. I so wished that Dad was up in heaven. A heaven that was just like Masuria with its endless forests full of mushrooms and berries and that had a large lake, where he could go fishing forever.

After we had silently guzzled our piping hot drinks and shared a piece of cheesecake, she asked me, "Have you ever heard of karma?"

"No, what's that supposed to be?"

"That you must answer for bad deeds in life after you die - or something like that. Anyone and everyone must pay for their bad deeds at some point."

"You mean just like in church. You have to answer to God, the judge, and then the good you did is balanced out against the bad things you did. I think I learned that in a catechism."

"Really? I thought that karma-story came from India."

If you speak of the devil: two women in colourful saris and winter coats entered the coffee shop and brought a gust of ice-cold air inside with them. They were talking to each other and I stared at them, but couldn't understand a thing.

The door closed quickly, which set the bell ringing again and they both took off their woollen shawls. The younger woman smiled at me before they both climbed the stairs up to the gallery.

"What?" I looked at Doris.

She had asked me a question. "Wonder how they can bear the cold in such thin dresses?"

"No clue. I'm also cold, come let's go. I'm dog-tired and it's getting dark outside." I counted a few coins onto the bistro table. "Grandma Bertrand is going to worry where I am."

Soon, I had forgotten about the strange song and even the feeling that the funeral celebrations should have been different somehow. At least not because of a non-existing funeral pyre or a procession or cooky stuff like that.

After the funeral, my mother kept yammering on day in and day out. She took some sort of tablets again, but I doubted that they were helping much.

"Why has he left me all alone in this world? How could he do this to me?" She whined. "I wish he'd taken me with him."

"You still have us. What are we supposed to do without you?" Evelyn asked her sadly.

"That you always have to think about yourselves! Why don't you put yourself in my shoes for a change?"

Her words touched Evelyn to the quick and she had tears in her eyes. "Why don't you just go and wallow in your stupid self-pity, then?" I said harshly. "You'll never change anyway."

"I don't have the nerves for your bad behaviour, Isabell. Oh, why didn't he take me with him? Now I have to deal with the three of you all on my own." She was completely serious about that. She didn't seem to care when we were around and we left her well alone.

That's probably why she didn't notice that Paula had changed. She often came home late at night and quickly crawled into her bed, refusing to speak to anyone. Spoilt Paula slowly got out of hand.

Perhaps she suffered in her own way. She had not been allowed to see Dad at the hospital's intensive care unit, because she was only thirteen. No exceptions. Nobody had given her any attention since, while I was able to flee to Grandma Bertrand.

As soon as all the relatives and mourners had left our shores, Mum took my Dinosaur-Granny to task. Apparently, there was no longer a place for her around here. Grandma Bertrand's wealthy daughter Bertha came at the end of the month and took her away while I was in school. All I knew was that she now lived close to Kassel. Our questions went unanswered and all we were told was that our mother had finally had enough of her. I had no choice but to move back home.

Evelyn was a chain smoker now and soon moved in with her boyfriend. She was eighteen and rather pretty but completely lacked self-confidence. Despite being intelligent, she could no longer cope with school and was burning her arms with cigarettes again. Soon, we no longer saw each other. It was a blessing in disguise that I found a room in a commune through the varsity notice board. There it was on a slip of paper right in front of me:

'30m^2, centre of town, 120 Marks/month incl. Tel.: 457 782'

Fantastic. I dialled the number.

"Room's still up for grabs," a physics student by the name of Ingmar said. "It's a large room on the fourth floor. Simple. It has a washbasin. We share a big kitchen and a small toilet. Manfred studies meteorology and is a very quiet guy."

I immediately cycled over to the address and - they accepted me.

My new abode was on the top floor of an old patrician house next to one of the noisiest main roads in Karlsruhe. It was simply wonderful and I hardly even noticed the noise. Both students were rather conservative looking and completely reliable. No trace of hippiedom whatsoever.

Ingmar was a puny physics student in his third semester with big glasses and an even bigger motorbike. Manfred, on the other hand, was broad and boring, but nice enough to let me use the phone in his room. As long as I paid him the amount he'd work out to the last cent every month.

All of a sudden I had two big brothers. Who needed daft sisters if you could have two big brothers?

I was barely seventeen, but my mother had no objections against me living in a commune. I was free at last and felt terribly grown-up. The modest orphan pension I received was just enough for the rent and a little food. Whatever else I earned by tutoring fifth-graders in Latin, I'd spend on books and second-hand clothes. Once a week, I took my washing to my mother's flat and often she wasn't even there.

It worked for me.

Despite its shortcomings like the stinking oil heater next to the wash basin and the leaking roof, I enjoyed my undisturbed existence. Being able to go to parties when I wanted or Renate could sleep over and so on. We studied or listened to music or I could be alone, just as I pleased. After a while, even my mother's critical voice in my head gave it a rest. At last, I could think my very own thoughts.

After a few weeks of blissful freedom, I learned that my younger sister Paula had begun to hang out in dangerous company. She was involved in drugs. At the age of thirteen, she was still too young to move out and live on her own, but she could do as she pleased.

Our mother was oblivious to the situation. When she decided on impulse to invest the first insurance payment in a cruise trip around the Mediterranean, Paula acted all delighted. For three weeks she would have the run of the house! I did my best to keep her under control, but Paula was stubborn and didn't see why she should explain to me where she'd been the night before. She slid through my fingers again and again.

"Who are you hanging out with?"

"Leave me alone, Isabell. You're as dull as dishwater," she would answer. "You must talk! Isabell, the rebel."

I tried to smell her clothes. The sickly sweet smoke gave it away.

"It's none of *your* beeswax, anyway. You are not my mother."

"Yes, thank goodness for that! Are you off to the 'Omnibus Club' again tonight?" I asked and watched Paula slurp her muesli.

"Okay. So what if I am, and the 'One Stop Café' - why?"

"Because I have to know that. You are only thirteen."

"But I look a lot older than that. Everyone says so. Hans even thinks that I should become a photo model." Hans was her latest boyfriend and at least eighteen years old.

"For once try and use your brain, Paula. A model at thirteen? Are you kidding? What the hell does Hans know about stuff like that?"

"He's introduced me to this other guy. He's a photographer and wants to take my pictures and even pay me for them."

"Have you lost your marbles? Did you tell Mum about that? You will under no circumstances go to some sleazy photographer who wants to pay you for photos. Is that clear?!" I gasped helplessly and had absolutely no idea how to keep her from doing a thing like that.

"Oh really? Try and stop me if you can, Mummy."

Of course, Paula went to see the photographer. And he gave her cocaine. That's all she was prepared to tell me.

"Don't you breathe a word to Mum about this or it will be your fault when she has a heart attack," she croaked the next day. Her eyes were still puffy from crying.

"You are damn right I won't tell her!" I barked at her. "Because you'll do that all by yourself. What if you become a drug addict?"

"Oh please! I'm no drug addict. I've also done heroin with Ute that one time. I just smoke a bit of hashish now and then, that's all. Everybody knows you don't get addicted from that." I felt powerless.

At least half of my classmates smoked hashish now and again and I was always the party pooper because I stubbornly refused to do drugs of any kind.

After three weeks our mother was back from her cruise as happy as a clam at high tide. A silk carpet from Turkey and the ceramic vases from Greece made a huge impression on Mrs Speidel from the fourth floor.

"But that must have cost you a fortune…" I stuttered.

"What's it to you? It's my money after all. I've never ever treated myself to anything. Always making ends meet because we had children. Nothing but hard work and raising you children."

"Well actually on that score…" Naturally, Paula hadn't told Mum about her escapades. "Paula bunked school quite often while you were gone. She's always running around with Ute, that girlfriend of hers and her boyfriend Hans. Hans introduced her to a photographer the other day who gave her cocaine. He also took pictures of her and God knows what. Ute is a heroin addict and pregnant and Paula goes to stay with her often in some druggie-commune in the Southend." I took a breath in a hammy way. "I just thought you should know."

"Did you make all of that up?"

"No!"

Her face blushed crimson. "You were supposed to look after her! Can't I rely on you even with something like that?"

She snapped at me and for a brief moment, I actually believed that she would have a heart attack.

"How is this my fault? She is thirteen years old and you were not supposed to leave her alone for that long. I'm only seventeen and Evelyn is god-knows-where."

"How dare you speak to me in this tone? I deserve to have a little time to myself. After all I had to go through, these past few weeks. Can't you show some respect?"

"You have to earn that respect."

"Are you starting again with your nonsense, now that we must all pull together? Do you want me to call the social worker again?" She gave me a threatening stare.

"I wonder what she would have to say about Paula's behaviour."

"Oh that's what it is, so now I'm not good enough as a mother?" What was I supposed to say to that? She was the only mother we had.

After that spat, we didn't speak to each other for a few weeks and, of course, I had to listen to yet another one of Paula's hateful tirades. Nothing new, but it didn't stop there.

One night, a rueful Paula phoned me. She had been gullible enough to take a piece of hashish, hidden in a Nutella glass, to prison on a visit to her drug-dealing boyfriend. Now suddenly she needed my support again.

"Are you totally bonkers?" I yelled at her in desperation.

"Oh Isabell, I was so daft. I should have put pepper into the plastic sachet. Then the sniffer dogs wouldn't have found it."

"Yes, that's the problem. Not that it's a crime to smuggle drugs into a prison. No, being more professional at it would have done the trick. What the hell is wrong with you?"

"Oh, I don't know. Hans told me what to do."

The matter went to court. The judge gave my by now fourteen-year-old sister a strict warning and slapped her with eighty hours of community service at a childrens' home. He also ordered my mother to frigging take care of her daughter who was still a minor after all.

Mum was deeply embarrassed. What were people going to

think - and especially her family? It didn't take her long to decide that nobody was to know about this. Naturally, we weren't allowed to tell anyone, either. Whatever. We never saw much of these 'people' in any case.

One afternoon, when I had just done my washing and wanted to make a quick getaway, I heard my mother stir in her bedroom. Anything was better than to face her now, so I tried to sneak out of the flat as quietly as possible. We were avoiding each other again, so I left and jumped over the cracked step on the second floor, trying not to look directly at a broken glass window. Of course, of all people, I had to run into the arms of Mrs. Speidel!

"Good day." I tried to flee, but that wasn't so easy.

"Good day, Isabellshe, are you still at your Mum's at this late hour?" Mrs Speidel shrilled.

"Yes, I was doing my washing. Must get home and study for a test," I lied. "Bye now."

"I see. How is it going at school? Are you doing your school work as you should?" She squinted at me suspiciously.

"Yes, of course, I am. Bye." I didn't wait for Mrs. Speidel's answer and was out the front door before she had a chance to involve me into a full-blown conversation.

"Tztztz, young people these days…" I heard her complain behind me.

It was for the best not to let her draw me into any kind of discussion. Mrs. Speidel would tell my mother in any case that I'd been back home. Dammit! As if I didn't have enough on my plate already.

In time, I became more independent. I worked, got good marks at school, paid my bills and rather went to Renate's house to do my washing. In spring, I attended a school seminar in the country. My ethics-teacher had put my name forward and there were only three other names on his list. It was nice of him because there were only thirty pupils from our federal state at the weekend seminar.

I shared a room with Kathrin. She was terribly grown-up for seventeen, smoked cigarettes and had a steady boyfriend.

Apparently, her mother was divorced and didn't mind at all.

I thought it was just fabulous. What a modern mother!

We bought a packet of cigarillos down in the village, behind our teachers' backs and puffed away at it in our room. I felt all grown up because of this little secret of ours, although I didn't like smoking at all and cigarillos even less. Truth be told, they made me feel nauseous.

When we returned home to Karlsruhe, Kathrin suddenly wanted nothing to do with me anymore and I never touched cigarillos again because they reminded me too much of Daddy's much-loved cigars.

CHAPTER THREE

There was nothing easy about growing up on my own. Nobody felt the need to explain the world to me, never mind anything to do with boys. But the thing was: boys were beginning to bother me.

Why on earth did they want to go out with me? In my eyes, schoolboys were so darn tedious. They could jump in the lake for all I cared. I decided that it would make my life a lot easier if I just stayed away from them.

I could hardly wait to do my own thing after leaving school and my high-flying plans involved the study of either medicine or cultural anthropology. Due to my lack of enthusiasm at school, I wasn't exactly popular with teachers, but I had a sharp tongue that kept my adversaries at bay. Renate was also a master at this. I still enjoyed a certain grace period, because my father had recently died. Unfortunately, it didn't always do the trick and I was summoned to the principal's office again.

"Miss Bertrand, we cannot allow you to attend ethics classes if you are a Catholic! You must attend your catechism classes and that's all there is to it," Mr. Mandel, the principal, ranted.

"But I don't want to go to catechism. It's worse than boring. Ethics is so much more interesting," I objected.

The principal was not used to dissent. His face turned beet-red and the vein on his forehead began to throb dangerously.

"Why do you always have to revolt against every single rule, Miss Bertrand? These rules exist for good reasons. If everybody here did as they pleased – well, where would that leave us? I run a respectable school here and will not tolerate a scandal of this sort. Do we understand each other?" He stood over me in a threatening stance.

Was it a scandal if someone preferred ethics classes? I considered this for a furious moment.

"Oh, I do understand. Rules, respectable and so on. Just that it doesn't change the fact that I will never go to catechism classes again."

"Don't be so obstinate, Miss Bertrand! We only have your best interests at heart."

"Can I go to ethics lessons when I'm not Catholic, then?"

Mr. Mandel's mouth looked like that of a fish as it snapped open and closed and he had to sit down. "You mean, you want…"

"Yes, to leave the Church."

"You are much too young for that sort of thing to decide on your own and in any case…"

"Actually, I'm old enough. I believe one has to be sixteen and that I've been that for a quite a while now," I said cheerfully.

"Miss Bertrand, I am warning you. Don't make things worse for yourself. This school is a reputable institution. If you dare compromise our good reputation…"

"Good reputation? Why, I thought it was my fundamental right?"

"Don't get all brazen with me, young lady. Leave now, before I lose my last bit of control. But I'm warning you," the honourable principal repeated and waved his arms around. "If you go to such lengths, I will make you regret it."

I turned on my heels, strutted out of the office and past the bewildered secretary. Then I hot-footed straight to the registry office and declared my membership in the Church cancelled.

"That's such garbage. What's Mr. Mandel going to do to you?" Renate asked me later on the phone.

"No clue. Perhaps, he'll have me secretly assassinated by a hitman or he'll throw me to the lions."

"You are not taking this one bit seriously, are you?"

"I'm scared shitless, believe you me, but how can I give in when he's so damn stubborn? 'Not compromising the school's reputation… blah blah…' What has this got to do with reputation? All I want is not having to veg out in catechism, listening to boring old Mrs. Rabe and wasting my precious time."

"Watch out, he might tell the teachers to give you bad marks." I considered this for a second.

"You think, old Mandel can do that?"

"I hope not." Of course, he could, but I didn't care.

Obviously, my mother learned about my misdeed and threw a hissy fit. "How can you do this to me? Where will I bury you now? Not in hallowed ground, that's for sure. You're a heretic, that's what you are."

"Sorry, but in which century do we live?"

She roundly ignored my argument. "What if people should learn about this? I'm dreading the mere thought of it! What about Grandma Heydenreich?" She needed to sit herself down and that's what she did when the storm had somewhat settled. I still didn't care. I thought I was tough as nails, living on my own like that and paying my own bills and stuff.

Just that it was much more difficult to live on your own as a teenager than I was willing to admit to myself. But there was no time to dwell on cumbersome details. I was curious about everything, wanted to know about people and learn about their way of life. For that, the ethics classes were so worth all my trouble.

I moved in larger circles outside of school now. First of all, I met Pam Mayer at a physics faculty party that Ingmar had invited me to. She was British, thirty-three and recently divorced from her German husband. Pam was steeped in contradictions. Self-centred, but generous, open-minded, but nonetheless often depressed. She worked as a hostess in the red-light district because it paid her more to sit around at a bar counter than sitting around at a supermarket till all day.

"How can you work in a bar?" I asked her flabbergasted. "Doesn't that put you off one bit?"

"The men who stumble into the bar, buy expensive drinks and chat my ear off. That's what my job is about. They often can't have a proper conversation with their wives at home and I listen. The owner watches us like a hawk all the time, so nothing untoward takes place in the private booths," Pam reassured me. "They don't play blue movies there and none of the other dirty stuff happens like in many bars."

Apparently, Pam had self-confidence and that's why she could work in this bar. At least, that's what she wanted me to believe.

At first, I stayed well away from her place of work. Then my curiosity got the better of me and I began to visit Pam once in a while after school, in a dark, smoky fish-bar in the centre of town. Every time, another interesting scene awaited me. I even managed to interview a streetwalker on one such occasion. She had a face the texture of puffy dough and had come in for a Coke on her break from streetwalking. The tiara topping her hairpiece looked somehow out of place. Everybody just called her 'The Princess'.

"Did you work in here at some stage?" I asked her.

"When I was younger, I drank all of them under the table. The johns would buy me tons of piccolos. I made lots of money back then." She laughed and leaned over in a conspiratorial sort of way. "I used to wear these shiny high boots and I poured champagne into the top. None of them ever noticed. Then I'd go to the loo and chucked the bubbly into the toilet. There would have been hell to pay if anyone got wind of it."

'The Princess' touched a scar on her chin and pushed the tiara that was sitting askew back into place. "Now nobody will buy bubbly for me anymore and that's why I have to 'walk the streets'. What they want here are spring chickens like those two over there." She pointed to a couple of Thai girls on the other side of the oval bar counter.

I felt like a reporter, researching an article on the red-light district. I liked the thought of it, but I quickly learnt that those weren't the best circles to hang out in. Some of the men were interested in *me*.

Pam had disappeared once again with a customer into one of the dank-smelling private booths and I was waiting for her outside while getting some fresh air. The weather was rather unpleasant, but I preferred to wait on the sidewalk than in the dark, smelly bar.

A man in a black suit and tie stopped next to me in his snazzy car and rolled down the window. "Hey cutie pie, wanna hop in? I'm paying twice your asking price."

Should I be flattered?

"No thank you," I answered politely. "I'm just waiting out here for a friend of mine."

"You're a lesbian then? In that case, you can bring your girlfriend."

"No! Leave me alone."

"Am I not good enough or what?" He attempted to get out of his car.

The entrance to the bar flew open. I turned around and the persistent businessman drove off. It was Pam. "Isabell, come inside. There's this guy here, who says he wants to meet you."

"But… I don't want to meet him… you promised me…"

"He's paying me 200 smackeroos more if I introduce you. You know that I haven't paid last month's rent and also for …"

"Pam, that feels too dodgy! Why the hell did you tell him about me?"

"He saw you inside a bit earlier. Oh come on now, don't be like that. We can share the money. Don't you need some dough?" She pulled her best stunt to persuade me to go with her.

"I'd rather not share the money and I don't even work in this place. Whatever it is that you do in there has nothing to do with me. I thought we wanted to go to the American Carnival together."

"Yes, I know, but it's just this one time. Then we're off to the American Carnival, I promise."

I sighed and went with Pam to the private room. The customer was already eagerly awaiting us inside. He sat at the cheap table grinning like a fat Buddha. We must have been a sight for sore eyes. Pam was a short woman in a mini-skirt and killer heels and I was at least a head taller than her. A schoolgirl with braided hair and dressed in painter's pants that I had dyed myself. My instinct screamed blue murder when I saw the poster above the entrance to the booth. It showed a plump, half-naked blonde in a rather compromising position.

"If this slimeball thinks he can buy me, he's got something coming," I hissed rebelliously.

"Don't be such a prude. All you have to do is be nice to him."

Pam elbowed me in the ribs and smiled so hard that I felt like getting a cramp myself.

"Ah, the young lady is here," the slimeball greeted us.

"You're talking about fresh meat or what?"

Pam shot me a wilting look. Stroppy backtalk was not the way to a customer's wallet.

"Ho, ho, what a belligerent young thing. A challenge for a change." The background music started to get on my nerves. Jennifer Rush and the Bee Gees.

"I love a hot little fox like you. Not taking crap, are we?"

"What's that got to do with me, what you like?"

The man laughed such an oily laugh and then played around with his tongue that I would have loved to zap him one.

"Don't you want to earn some extra bucks?" He whispered to the tune of 'How deep is your love' that blasted from the loudspeaker.

"I'm listening." Pam leaned eagerly forward.

"Your little friend and you can come and meet me by the park when the joint here closes. I pay well."

"How much? Nothing doing under 500 smackeroos. 300 up front and 200 for the other deal." I stared confused at Pam, but she ignored me.

"Ho, ho. This one knows what she wants, hey sweetheart?" I pulled a disgusted face and the slimeball shrank back.

"It's just business, right?" Pam whispered. Then she called: "Another piccolo, Fritz." The expensive bubbly arrived in a jiffy and the man paid without comment. More banknotes changed ownership under the table and Pam stuffed them into her bra.

That's when I left. I jumped onto my bike and cycled alone to the American Carnival. Later, Pam took a taxi and tried to force me to take the money but I heroically refused. She phoned me the following day. I sat down on the floor in Manfred's room. Luckily, he was busy in the kitchen.

"Did you go there?" I asked.

"No way, that guy was way too dangerous."

"But you took his money yesterday."

"So what? That's how the cookie crumbles. He's the one taking a risk. Moron."

"Have you done this sort of thing before?" I changed position because my legs started to tingle.

"Sure, sometimes you get a guy like that. And why not?"

I had difficulty believing that Pam could be this calculating." What if he comes to the bar again and demands his money back? You practically stole it from him."

"Then Fritz will put him straight. I'll give him a story. What he did is unethical, or not?" She said full of conviction.

"And what you did, that was ethical?"

"We all have to survive," she said dryly.

"What about honest work? You could take typing lessons. Or are you just after a quick buck?"

"No of course not, Isabell," Pam sulked. "What do you take me for? We are friends, aren't we? And you just came to my aid a little bit so we could make some money. What's wrong with that?"

I could give her a million reasons why that was wrong.

"Cause I'm not a whack job, that's what. Your boss asked me yesterday in all seriousness if I wouldn't like to work for him once in a while."

"Really, did he now? But you are my only friend in the whole world, Isabell. Don't you like me anymore?"

"I don't like what you're doing, Pam. I want no part of it."

"Don't make such a big thing out of a little molehill."

"Hmm, let's see," I paused for effect. "Oh yes, it is a big thing if somebody beats you up or worse even..."

Manfred came in with a plate of sandwiches and I hung up.

I never heard from Pam again. *Alright then*, I thought, that was quite something and my curiosity had been quenched for the time being.

Soon I returned to the park, my old turf, and met an Egyptian ballet dancer who went by the name of Magdy. I'd seen him around, strutting about in a black cloak just like Count Dracula. He listened to my guitar playing for a while and then asked me if I wanted to do a ballet lift with him right there. I thought the idea was hilarious.

Magdy dropped his cloak to the ground in a theatrical gesture, then lifted me up and onto his shoulder. I was supposed to stand up and balance myself elegantly on one leg. Easier said than done.

"You must hold yourself quite stiffly, Isabell," Magdy said.

I couldn't balance long for laughing and fell after an endless minute. There was applause from the audience regardless.

Something always seemed to be happening in the park. On a warm day in August, I played Frisbee with a group of young Americans on the big lawn behind the castle. That's when Raymond Hewitt caught my eye. He was eighteen and not the brightest boy around. But he was undoubtedly the best-looking one with his short dark hair and astonishing blue eyes.

I must have been staring at him, admiring his languid movements and how he handled the Frisbee so effortlessly. Not only did he look like an athlete in jeans and lumberjack shirt, he had good manners as well. That fact surprised me. Most of the German boys I knew dressed in torn jeans and had long hair and always tried to appear as cool as possible.

We played Frisbee in the sunshine and listened to music by the 'Eagles' in the shade. When his friends set off one by one, taking the tape player with them, only Raymond and I stayed behind. He told me that they were exchange students and had come to Germany for three months.

His German wasn't exactly fluent and my English was far from fantastic, so we talked using our hands and feet. Suddenly it was dark and the gates to the park were being locked for the night.

We had no choice but to lift our bicycles over the wall and to clamber over ourselves. "Careful, here it comes." Raymond pushed my bike over the part of the wall where it was denuded of iron spikes.

"Okay, got it." I pulled the bike down and sat on it, watching Raymond letting himself down with ease. We slowly walked to the tram station.

"Would you like to go for a hamburger?" I asked him, knowing full well that I couldn't afford one.

"I must go to Ettlingen. To host family," he said, carefully pronouncing each word. Okay, no skin off my nose.

"It's quite late anyway and we write a math test in morning," I said.

"Will I see you again tomorrow?" Raymond asked me and pushed his bike into the No. 5 tram.

"Sure, maybe after my school? I am coming often in the park." So we met again.

It was a refreshing experience to go and do stuff with other young people for a change. I even introduced them to Walter, Angie and Tarek, but the more time I spent with Raymond, the less I saw of our clique. A tiny yellow school dictionary went wherever I went and I tried to learn New York slang as well.

"What's up with you and that Yankee?" Tarek asked me sharply as we walked side by side to our visual arts classroom.

"All we do is go out once in a while. Harmless stuff. Why, are you jealous?" I gave a guarded laugh and looked at him sideways.

"Me and jealous? Phew!" Tarek shook himself.

"But you could pop in once in a while and spend some time with us for a change," Angie piped up. "I miss our cooking experiments."

She pushed the heavy door to the visual arts room open and light flooded the dark passage.

"Fine, then let's do it tomorrow afternoon at my place. Is 3 o'clock okay? You can bring whatever you like. Just no meat, please. Then we'll cook like there's no tomorrow." I had recently decided to become vegetarian.

"Meat's too expensive in any case." Angie sat down on my bench.

"Are you sure you want to meet?" Tarek sat down on the bench in front of us. He took pencils and watercolours out of his case and put them neatly on the wooden desk.

"Sure thing," I answered brightly. "We can make pancakes with different fillings again. I thought it went down a treat last time."

"Only if you make the pancakes, Isabell. You have a knack for that sort of thing. We'll take care of the fillings."

"Hey, Angie, no bloody way. It's your turn this time."

"But…"

Mr. Linke came hurrying into the classroom and plunked himself down on his desk chair. So Angie got stuck with the task of making the pancakes. My friends were right, of course. I spent a lot of time with Raymond. He had temporarily replaced them and I just didn't want to admit it.

Despite this, our relationship was almost exclusively platonic. Compared to Werner and Jean-Paul, Raymond was way more experienced when it came to kissing, but that was the extent of it. I think it had something to do with his religious beliefs.

Never mind. Relationships were too complicated anyway and he would soon go back to the States. The boys in his group were a little envious that he had hooked himself a German Fräulein and Raymond didn't see any reason to set them straight. I was knitting a wool jersey for him with a pattern of elks and stars in a procession around the chest. This happened mostly during Mr. Teichmann's math class, where I knitted with about half of my classmates.

Raymond had to fly back to New York at the beginning of November 1979. He was proudly wearing my jersey and offered to send me a plane ticket, so I could come and spend Christmas with him in Albany, NY.

I was delighted. Christmas with Raymond in America!

There was just this eensy-weensy problem: I wasn't eighteen yet and my mother flatly refused to sign the visa application. I hadn't seen her since my scandalous departure from Mother Church and that didn't make things any easier.

"I will not sign this document. That'll be the day! What if you don't come home to finish school? Perhaps you'll want to marry this man," she got into a fuss. "You do know how important it is to finish school before getting married. I had a rewarding career as a nurse when I met your father and earned our upkeep so he could complete his studies. Oh yes, I would have preferred travelling to all that work, but in those days we didn't have the opportunities you have today." I'd had to listen to that a million times before. She didn't know much about Raymond, just that he was an exchange student.

"What has all of that got to do with my trip to America? That might be my only chance to ever go there."

A piercing alarm shrilled in the kitchen. "Oh, I must quickly take the Chelsea buns out of the oven. Surely you'll want to eat one too?"

I had to admit that the aroma of vanilla and cinnamon was mouth-watering, so I nodded. Baking was Mum's latest hobby.

She continued to berate me through the open kitchen door. "Of course you don't care about such things. It gives you pleasure to embarrass me all the time. What are people supposed to think? Mrs. Speidel keeps on and on about your loose lifestyle."

If I had learned anything, it was to ignore provocations like that. All I wanted was her signature. I needed the signature on the application form.

"How is Mrs. Speidel going to hear about my trip? I'm happy if I don't run into her all the time, never mind having a conversation."

"You could at least be more polite to people. It must be that you're the middle child. You have to struggle your way through life. Isn't that right, Isabell?" My mother walked in with a plate of fragrant Chelsea buns and placed it in front of me. "I must not forget to take a plate of buns up to Mrs. Speidel. Her husband is so fond of home-baking."

Mr. Speidel was as round as a ball. We went off subject. *Think, Isabell, think!* I really wanted to enjoy the brief freedom of an American Christmas and all I needed was my mother's signature. That's all there was to it.

"Hmm... these Chelsea buns are delicious."

To my surprise, my mother changed her mind and agreed to sign the application form. She decided to tell 'the people' that I would be going to New York for two months as an exchange student. I couldn't care less.

Naturally, my sisters were jealous. "You always get what you want! How did you twist her arm this time? Do you have any idea how dangerous a trip like that can be? You hardly know this guy," Evelyn caterwauled and Paula also had to give her five cents worth.

"Of course, she doesn't listen to anything we say. Isabell always gets special treatment."

"And why shouldn't I? I deserve some special treatment. In any case, Raymond has already sent me the plane ticket. Don't you want to come with me?" Evelyn hesitated for a second. Then she answered fiercely. "You are totally off your head and I have plans."

"I've also got something better to do over Christmas. Hans has been released from prison," Paula said and winked at us.

We stared at her horrified.

"Whaaat?! It's just a joke," she said. Evelyn and I weren't so sure about that. "And I want to go to at least three parties."

This time I wouldn't be able to keep an eye on her. That was Evelyn's job and already I counted the days to my departure. New York! It was so far away. Nobody I knew had ever travelled farther than Italy or the Costa Brava. Except for Raymond, of course.

After the longest flight of my life, we landed in driving snow at John F. Kennedy Airport.

'Throw all foodstuffs into the provided drums," a loudspeaker barked at the passengers. "...then proceed toward exit D."

Exit D, exit D... another right turn and then straight ahead. I would be seeing Raymond again any moment now. Just through the sliding doors at the other end of the long passage. The passage was endless.

I wondered what would happen to all the apples and

oranges that disappeared into the drums as I added two mandarines. A security officer waved me aside. "This way, please. We'd like to ask you some questions."

"Me?" Had I made a mistake?

Raymond was waiting for me behind the sliding doors. I didn't have the time to answer some questions now.

"This way please, ma'am. Routine check." Routine check?

I had no choice but to follow the officer, who led the way to a glass cubicle. His hair was greasy, a few strands covering a bald spot on top.

They must have discovered the small spray can with CS gas in my handbag as I'd pushed it through the x-ray machine. I knew it was against the rules.

An older security officer with greying sideburns was already waiting inside the glass cubicle, sitting at a time-worn table. He pushed a can with Fanta away from him and studied the pages in my passport.

"Who do we have here? Miss... Bertrand," he mumbled without glancing up once. Obviously bored, he began to rattle routine questions off a questionnaire. His face was tired and puffy and his hands searched his breast pocket for a packet of cigarettes.

"How long are you planning to stay in the United States for?" He asked in a bored tone.

"Just over Christmas and New Year. I'm visiting a friend," I answered.

It was a daunting experience. Was this interrogation going to take long? Hopefully, Raymond was still waiting for me in the arrival hall on the other side of the sliding doors.

"Will you be staying at this address in Albany?" The puffy officer wanted to know. He scrawled incessantly with his pen on the margin of the questionnaire. The security officer with the greasy hair was standing behind me the entire time. The windows multiplied his image and I could see him watching the arriving passengers outside. He moved away from the glass front and sat himself down at the table.

"Very likely. That's why I put it down on the arrival form. My friend lives there." He looked directly at me for the first time.

"Are you planning to get married to this friend of yours?"

Had he secretly spoken to my mother?

"Me? No… of course not," I laughed nervously. "I'm just seventeen and I still go to school. He's just a good friend of mine. An exchange student." I emphasized the word and sat very still, feeling disgusted.

"Believe me, Miss Bertrand, stranger things do happen. You are aware that we could put you on the next plane." He whistled through his teeth and moved his hand in an arc through the air. "Hey presto! On your way home." The puffy officer grinned and took a cigarette from the packet in his breast pocket without lighting it.

They both enjoyed giving me a hard time.

"No, I had no idea that you welcome teenagers who travel alone and just want to visit your country over Christmas in such a way." Had I been too cheeky now?

The puffy one observed me spitefully and read out the next standard question. "Miss Bertrand, is it your intention to murder the American president?"

I gasped. What? Had he really just asked me that? I felt laughter surging up, tickling my throat. Pull yourself together, I reminded myself. I wanted to get out of this glass cubicle, wanted to breathe fresh air and see a friendly face. Raymond's face.

"Why on earth would I do something like that?" I asked with indignation.

"Perhaps it would please you to give us an answer, Miss Bertrand."

"I don't have an answer. I don't even know the name of the president or where he lives. I'm seventeen and just want to visit friends in America to celebrate Christmas. That's all."

"Answer the question." The puffy officer played around with his cigarette.

"No, of course not!" I answered with all the graveness I could muster.

"Are you sure?"

I bit back a sarcastic answer that sat on the tip of my

tongue. "Yes, I'm quite sure!"

"Thank you very much for your time, ma'am. That would be all." I was free. Just like that. I was allowed to stay.

They would not be sending me home on the next flight to Germany and I would not end up in some prison for cheeky teenagers, who were suspected of wanting to murder their president.

I was released from the glass cubicle without further ado and staggered down the dark corridor in a daze all the way to the sliding doors that were ready to rescue me. For some inexplicable reason, I felt guilty. The feeling lasted only an instant.

"Where have you been all this time?" Raymond took me in his arms. "I was beginning to think you were bailing on me. But they told me your name's on the passenger list."

I explained about the glass cubicle and that the security officers had wanted to send me back to Frankfurt in case I was here to murder the American president.

"How do they get the idea that you of all people could be an assassin?" A woman dressed from head to toe in glaring red shot us baneful looks. We continued to speak in German.

"Beats me."

"Maybe they are looking for someone who looks just like you."

"A German school girl?"

"Yeah, sounds a little crazy."

"Exactly. Maybe they just didn't like the way I look."

"Oh well, I like the way you look," Raymond laughed and my dark mood began to lift. "I hereby apologize on behalf of the American people for the inexcusably rude welcome to this our glorious country."

"Many thanks, Mr. Hewitt," I said in the same formal tone and took a little bow.

"Let's get the hell out of here. We must still find a bus tonight that can take us to the Amtrak station."

We collected my tote bag from the luggage carousel and finally left the unfriendly airport. New York had been icy cold, but when we arrived in Albany, it snowed so hard that it was almost impossible to see a thing. The streets were thickly covered in ice and snow and during the ride to Raymond's housing complex on the municipal bus, it snowed even more. Soon, darkness fell. I was hungry and exhausted.

Mrs. Hewitt was a woman of about forty, who lived with her younger children in a large basement flat at the complex and – she hated me.

Raymond's siblings immediately gave me the third degree. 'So, you are not for the Nazis in Germany?' and 'Why don't you have light blonde hair?' How was I supposed to answer that? I tried to explain that not all Germans have light blonde hair and that Nazis were water under the bridge.

"But Germans are always light blond in the movies and ugly and Nazis," Raymond's twelve-year-old brother David insisted.

"Those are just old movies. We have a democratic government in Germany and Germans have all sorts of different hair colours – really."

"Are you sure there are no longer Nazis in Germany? They look so real on TV," the younger Hewitt said and my smile froze.

"What?" I was getting irritated. "How can you take ancient war movies so seriously? They are not real at all." The younger sisters, who sat next to me were flabbergasted.

"David, leave Isabell alone. She's never been to the States – and what is she supposed to think of us if you say stuff like that? My host family was so friendly and not Nazis at all. Honestly!"

During supper, nobody spoke much and the children went to their rooms straight away.

"I'm truly sorry about that," Raymond apologised.

"It's alright, nothing you can do about. And it's not your fault anyway."

"You know what, Isabell? It's terribly cold here in Albany. I was wondering if we shouldn't go and visit my aunt in St. Petersburg. That's in Florida. What do you think? On the way, I can show you a bit of America."

"Sounds great. Florida is warmer than upstate New York, then?"

"Much warmer."

It was so freezing outside that we were barely able to leave the flat, but three days later, Raymond had organised a car whose owner had flown to Miami. All we had to do was drive the car to Miami and pay for the petrol. After delivering the vehicle, we would get even a bit of pocket money. A cheap and comfortable way to travel.

In the morning, we left in a rather new Dodge for the warmer south and I was certain that Raymond's mother was happy to see me leave. She had barely spoken three words to me since we'd arrived.

We drove along the east coast and just before we reached Philadelphia, the weather had improved considerably. The farther south we travelled, the more tropical the landscape became. Gradually, thick jackets, jerseys and heavy boots went into the trunk of the car. America was confusing and big and so amazing. During the trip, I acquainted myself with tuna salad sandwiches, coleslaw and pecan pie. Food was cheap and abundant.

Our first stop was a motel in Maryland. Simple but clean.

"Do you have telephones in Germany by now?" The nosy owner asked me as we signed our names on the register.

"Yes, we do. Why are you asking me that?"

"Everybody knows that Germany was destroyed after the war. We bombed the hell out of the Krauts back then!" Unbelievable! Raymond pinched my arm in warning.

"And?"

"America has phones and appliances like fridges and blenders, but they don't have that in Germany, do they?"

"Yes, of course, we do," I said baffled. "Have you never heard of Bosch or AEG? Germany produces loads of quality appliances."

"Get outa here! And what about —"

"Sorry, we must take our luggage to the room now," Raymond interrupted him. "Can we have the key, please?"

"Which planet is this guy from?" I asked him angrily when we closed the door behind us. "Does he still live in the forties or what?"

There were two beds in the room and a bible on the nightstand in the middle. A typical, standard motel room.

"Don't take offence. There are lots of ignorant people like him who live in the past. I also didn't know that before I went to Germany. Let's get some sleep now. We'll head out again at daybreak."

We slept in separate beds like good kids should. *That's fine,* I thought, *we are not a real couple after all.*

I saw bluegum-trees in North Carolina with bearded moss hanging down from burly branches and a herd of proud chestnut-coloured horses grazing in a paddock next to the country road. I felt a vague longing to saddle up and gallop over hedge and ditch as I looked at them in passing.

The December air in Florida was mild and we drove past many a citrus plantation. We could see large, juicy oranges peeking out from between dark-green leaves. Amazing. In Miami, we delivered the Dodge and decided to spend the night at a youth hostel.

"Why is there barbed wire everywhere?" I asked Raymond as we handed our passports through a small window in the red steel door.

"Maybe they have to protect themselves. It doesn't seem like a good area," Raymond said awkwardly.

"Oh, that's just great."

"Sorry, I didn't know that. Never been to Miami before. But it could be even worse in another area."

"So you still want to stay here?"

"It's not far from the beach, so we should probably stay here for now. We can go down to the beach and spend the day there."

"Did you book the room?" A grouchy voice asked through the small window. We looked at each other frowning.

"Actually yes, I spoke to Marilyn just half an hour ago," Raymond said.

"Okay, then you can come in." The heavy steel door flew open.

"It's only for one night," I calmed myself.

Soon we walked down to the ocean and I had quickly forgotten about all that. It was warm and sunny and I had never seen that many palm trees anywhere. The ocean was so incredibly blue.

"Oh, I'm glad that we drove all the way to Florida," I cried and jumped with enthusiasm into the soft sand.

Raymond looked content as we rambled down the beach. We found sand-dollars and seashells and ate frozen yoghurt at an ice-cream booth. *That's what perfect freedom should feel like: just living in the moment*, I thought. At dusk, we strolled along the road overhead and back to the youth hostel, where a young couple approached us.

"Hi, are you new around here in Miami?" The beachboy in shorts and t-shirt asked.

"Why, are you also on holiday?" Raymond answered.

"No," the girl in her skimpy bikini-top said a tad too quickly. I pricked my ears. "We're from Gainsville. Tim's looking for a job and we'll be here only for a few days. My uncle has a cabin down on the beach." She seemed a bit nervous.

"Alright," I said not really interested and scraped out the last scraps of frozen yoghurt in my pink cup. "That's very convenient."

"Where're you from? You don't sound American."

"I'm from Germany."

"Oh really? My uncle is also German," Tim said quickly.

"I thought it's *her* uncle," Raymond stared at the girl and instinctively took a step back.

"Our uncle. I'm Susie's brother."

"I see."

"It's not far from here, the beach cabin. You can come with us and we'll get takeaway burgers on the way. The sunset's real stunning down there."

A brown pickup truck suddenly stopped next to us. A dark-haired beachboy sat behind the steering wheel. "Come on guys, hop in. We'll drive to the diner and get a few hamburgers."

How did he know about that?

"We've already paid for the... hotel," Raymond said cautiously. "And actually, we're not that hungry."

"You can go back to your hotel later. Let's go to the beach

first. It's a lot of fun there. You can get your stuff later. There's plenty of space in the cabin. Enough space for all of us and it's free."

The look the dark-haired beachboy gave Susie was telling.

"Better not. We still have plans to go somewhere else. Let's go, Isabell, or we'll be late," Raymond declined as calmly as possible.

A broad police car stopped next to us. "Everything alright here, ma'am?" The policeman behind the wheel asked me.

Before I could answer, the blond beachboy, whose name was Tim, said "No problem, officer. We're just talking."

The policeman didn't seem to believe him because he parked his car at a petrol station across the road and kept an eye on us.

"Come on," the dark-haired beachboy said to Tim and Susie. "Let's go. There's a shitload of greenhorns over there."

The three of them left us all puzzled and drove their pickup truck down the long promenade until they were out of sight. The police vehicle followed them slowly.

Back at the youth hostel, we were told that the police had just busted a Miami-gang. They'd been stalking unsuspecting tourists and terrorising easy marks for weeks.

"Really?" Raymond was mortified about the news. We told them what had happened to us on the promenade.

"Goddam luck," Andy, the guy who guarded the red steel door, said. "They lure tourists with stories just like that one to a secluded beach, then rob them blind. They found a young man murdered just the other day. Defended himself, apparently. Drug addicts, of course."

Every paradise had its shady side, it seemed.

We took the bus to St. Petersburg. I couldn't gawp enough at all those big houses and tropical gardens in the suburbs. There were fewer palm trees here compared to Miami, but loads of orange trees everywhere. Raymond's Florida-aunt Molly was plump and cheerful and instantly pressed me to her ample bosom. "Welcome to the Sunshine State!"

She was the polar opposite of her sister Amy in Albany, who was thin as a rake. She congratulated Raymond on his nice new girlfriend – German or not. His last girlfriend had apparently been pretty, but something of a bitch. The memory of her made the good aunt shudder.

"Oh aunt Molly, you mustn't tell Isabell stories like that. I had only nice girlfriends – didn't I?"

Aunt Molly laughed until her tummy started wobbling like jelly. "Yes, of course, my boy, if you say so. Have another piece of pumpkin pie, darling. You're way too thin. Let the poor child get some rest, Ray. To drive down the coast in four days! I bet you had just unhealthy diner-food all the way. Here, put a bit of cream on top." Aunt Molly decorated a good-sized piece of pie with cream from a can and monitored the demolition of her construction. The entire family loved good food and lots of it. I even learned how to prepare pot roast and that the best Christmas turkey filling had to have sweet chestnuts in it.

Christmas was only two days away and the temperature was a warm, 20°C outside, but inside heaters were doing double-duty day and night. I'd never dreamt of ever experiencing Christmas like that.

"Here sweetie, you gotta try my special pecan-pie." Aunt Molly pushed a plate with said pie in front of me.

"The best pecan-pie south of Georgia," her rotund husband Herb agreed and also helped himself to another piece. I must admit that this pecan-pie was simply divine.

For Christmas lunch, we had turkey and corn on the cob, sweet potatoes and cranberry sauce and I ate until I was ready to burst at the seams.

It would have been perfect if it hadn't been for Bullet.

Bullet, the black family cat, had made it a habit to lie in wait behind the bathroom door then ambush house guests with his sharp claws. He got me twice, but apart from that, my food-rich and warm-hearted Florida-stay was turning into a terrific experience.

"Oh, don't mind him, darling. He goes to an animal psychologist once a week because of his bad behaviour," Aunt Molly apologised. An animal psychologist? I'd never heard of something like that. Dr. Albrecht sprang to mind. Was it possible to hypnotise animals?

"Can't you put him outside for a while, Auntie?" Raymond asked.

"Oh no," Aunt Molly said. "Bullet belongs inside the house. He is a true house cat." House cat or not, when Bullet jumped Raymond for the third time that day and dug his claws into his calves, sending a handful of cashew nuts flying against the TV screen, uncle Herb locked the antisocial pet into the broom closet.

From that moment on, we were able to celebrate a claw-free Christmas. Soon it was January and we took the Greyhound bus back to Albany. But it wasn't half the fun riding a bus up the coast than it had been taking a road trip all the way down to Florida.

I flew back to Germany from a New York that was somewhat friendlier than before. Thank goodness , there was no interrogation at the airport this time. My trip ended in jetlag and home-made chocolate chip cookies from a packet that I'd baked at three o'clock in the morning.

Once again, I was alone and it was still another week before the start of school. There was nobody around to talk to and have a good laugh with at all my crazy adventures in America. And I missed Raymond.

He called in February and informed me that he'd decided to move to Germany so we could be together.

"But why now? I thought you wanted to go to college in New York, and we are not exactly a real couple. You never wanted to…" I stammered in confusion.

"I could study in Karlsruhe and work part-time. Of course, we should get married and look for a proper place to live."

That was just too much!

"Oh Ray, wait a minute there. I don't think that would be such a good idea at all. I have to finish school and what about your scholarship? And I'm way too young to get married."

"But I want to be with you," he moaned.

"I don't even know myself, who I am, never mind living with

a man. I don't want that right now, really. I need my freedom."

There was a long pause after that. Did we have a bad phone line?

"Raymond, are you still there?"

"I miss you too much. There's a college here that offers correspondence courses and you'll be done with school this year, right?" He'd planned the whole thing in detail!

"I also miss you, Ray, but we go to school for 13 years here. So, I'll have to stick it out for at least another year. And afterwards, I go to university. There won't be much time for a marriage."

"We'll get it to work somehow. I want to be with you."

"And what if you don't find a job? Then what? I can't afford to make ends meet on my own."

"I can organise a sum of money. I'm sure my uncle will give us some." Ray had a wealthy uncle in New York with shady connections.

"That's still not enough, Ray. Life is expensive. When all the money is spent, then what do we do? We should wait," I said assertively.

"How am I gonna get through this without you?"

"You will just have to."

Of course, Raymond got through it without me. He often wrote letters telling me about his mechanical engineering studies in New York and that he was still planning to come and visit me in Germany. It lasted almost a year, but he never had enough money to come. Later, he moved to Texas and married a nice Texan girl, who appreciated aunt Molly's cooking.

It was fine by me. Actually, I hadn't been in love with Raymond for a while now and I was certain that there had to be another man waiting for me somewhere out there.

Whenever I saw how other girls were battling in their relationships, I was happy to be single for the time being. My sister Evelyn broke up with her boyfriend Marko and moved into a tiny little room in Mühlburg. She'd also stopped burning herself with cigarettes and I was glad about that.

"Anything is better than going back home," she whined

during one of her rare visits. "If you want my advice, stay away from those damn losers. It always ends in disaster." Then she ignored her own advice and wasted her time with even more losers.

Paula had given up her career in drugs and lived once in a while at home with our mother. The rest of her time she split between two boyfriends, who knew nothing about each other. She was fifteen now.

I didn't get off that lightly, either. Rüdiger, a chain smoker in my parallel class agreed to help me not very successfully with physics before a test. Then he wanted to go out with me and ambushed me, while we were chatting downstairs as I was leaving his apartment building.

"No Rüdiger, I'm not into that right now. Relationships are far too complicated for me."

Rüdiger stepped on his third cigarette on the tiled floor and was obviously embarrassed by the whole thing.

"You're so aloof, Isabell," he lamented. "You blow every guy off. Do you think that you are better than everybody else because of your ancestors, these Huguenots, or what?"

"What? No! Who told you about that? Actually, only…"

"Renate knows about it," we said in unison. Well, that was just great! Who else knew about the Huguenots now?

"She didn't tell me directly. I overheard her telling Tarek that your family came from some aristocrats. Besides, you were in America and that's something different for a change."

I sharply drew in the air. That was pretty steep: 'something different for a change!'

"Thanks, but no thanks. I guess I must have a word with Renate, but that's got nothing to do with you. I just don't want a boyfriend right now, okay? I've got enough on my plate."

Understandably, Rüdiger didn't like me much afterwards and I had to find another physics tutor. All the girls jabbered incessantly about their boyfriends, about the pill and relationship issues. It was enough to drive me mad! Even Renate started messing around with a drummer from Atlanta, who'd served in the American army here. This Steve-guy was something else. Their relationship was of a hot-cold variety and Renate told me every little detail, whether I liked it or not. I couldn't understand her. Boys were by-the-way for me and just a stupid distraction.

"Bite me, I'm a late bloomer," I played things down whenever I had to listen to yet another taunt.

Right now, it was far more important that I studied for exams and made preparations for an orderly journey through life. I knew that I wanted to study medicine... if I could manage to survive school at all.

Oh yes, and from now on I would ride the same train as everybody else: finish school, study, work, get married, have children and a pension fund. I also wanted a happy family, just like aunt Molly had. Well, maybe with less food and cooking involved.

It got around that I had spent two months in America and suddenly the popular kids at school showed an unexpected interest in me. Rüdiger probably had something to do with that as I had somehow acquired the reputation of a daring globetrotter: aloof yet no longer invisible.

I enjoyed the attention for a while, then even this phase passed and I stubbornly focused on my school work again. But after a while, riding the same train as everybody else didn't appear so attractive anymore.

I just couldn't help it but go my own way.

By now, Dr. Albrecht and his hypnotherapy were all but forgotten, as were Nusrat and Imran and my supposed life as a Rajput. I did find myself a temp job and was already planning my next trip – to London this time.

Then in the midst of all this, I made the acquaintance of Altaf Khan.

CHAPTER FOUR

I'd noticed that more and more strangers were arriving in town, for the most part at the university campus and in the park. Among them were lots of young people from other cultures. It had become easier for me to make friends and we were heading into the age of Aquarius: peace, love and understanding. That's why it wasn't unusual for me to meet someone like Altaf Khan.

I had seen him a few times in the crowd, and the one time he'd had his arm around a pretty redhead who appeared to adore him.

Altaf Khan stood out: he was tall and handsome with a Mediterranean charisma, had shining eyes, wavy hair and tanned skin. Imagine my surprise when he told me that he came from the faraway country of Pakistan. Altaf was twenty and at a young age, he had signed up as a machinist on a Greek ship in Karachi. He now worked for a company in Karlsruhe that manufactured hot-water boilers. He approached me in front of a department store across from the main post office and I found it amusing that he spoke German with a Karlsruhe-accent.

Our conversation flowed with ease.

"What do you need a slotted spoon for?" I asked him after a short introduction. He held the newly-purchased spoon up as if it was a microphone. "Oh, I need it to fish pakoras out of the boiling oil."

"What are pakoras?"

"Well you know, they are made of cauliflower and other veggies dipped in a curry batter."

"You can cook, then? That's interesting. I also sometimes

cook with my friends from school," I said. "We usually meet at my house because we have a big kitchen. I share it with two students in a commune. Last time we made pancakes with fillings and salad. But at the moment, I don't eat meat. It's too expensive in any case."

"Pancakes? I also share a flat in the Southend with two Pakistani friends. We often cook and make pancakes. They're called chapatis and they are like bread to us. I can show you how to make them."

"Yes maybe. I've got lots to do." I had to think about the pretty redhead who'd clung to Altaf's arm.

"But you also meet with your friends from school and then cook together." Altaf tucked the long spoon under his armpit and rubbed his clammy hands. The day was cold and grey and the pedestrians around us were spreading the wet, grey slush all over the sidewalk.

"Well, we always study afterwards. We are writing our final exams next year," I said with a hint of pride.

"Do you like studying?"

"No, not really, but I don't have a choice in it."

My tram was late and we chatted about this and that until his very polite friend Latif showed up to fetch Altaf. Latif looked just the way I'd imagined Pakistanis were supposed to look. Dark with smooth black hair. *Why do you put people into categories like that?* I scolded myself. Then my No. 3 tram came around the corner with screeching brakes.

Several months passed before I met Altaf again by chance. It was during a faculty party to which Evelyn's new boyfriend had invited me. Altaf introduced me to two engineering students from Nigeria and Afghanistan. Eddie Adeyemu from Nigeria told me that he was about to marry his girlfriend Dagmar.

"We have a six-month-old daughter. Her name is Yemissi. I want to take both of them with me to Lagos so my family can meet them, but Dagmar doesn't want to go. She says that maybe I will behave differently when I'm not in Germany anymore. She doesn't trust me." Eddie had given up with a heavy heart to try and persuade her, so his family in Lagos had to make do with photographs instead.

The other student was Atesh and he was from Kabul. The only son of wealthy and educated parents. His sister Afshan studied medicine in Frankfurt and his mother worked there as a human rights lawyer.

"My father is still in Kabul," Atesh sighed. "But we'd like for him to come to Germany as well. We have an export business there, but since the Russians have invaded Afghanistan, it's become really difficult to live in the city. The resistance is strong and consists mostly of very traditional men from the Hindukush. They still fight alongside the Afghan army but who knows what will happen once the war is over."

"Is Afghanistan close to Pakistan?" I wanted to know.

"Of course it is, we share a border in the east and many of the Pashtun have already fled from the Russians into Pakistan," Atesh said and Altaf nodded his head.

"I see." I neither knew who the Pashtun were nor where the Hindukush was but I felt sorry for Afghanistan. It wasn't until much later that I learned how Atesh's father had been killed during an air raid on Kabul.

After the party, I saw Altaf a few times in town with Atesh. Winter was upon us once again when Altaf wrote his phone number on the palm of my hand. I never phoned him. Not that I didn't like him but it was my priority to find out what it was that I wanted in life. A relationship was still at the bottom of my list.

The next time we crossed paths, he suddenly appeared behind me as I was pushing my bicycle through the pedestrian zone.

"Oh hello, Altaf. Sorry, I'm in a hurry today," I said and thought of a quick getaway. "Must go to a sports class at school just now and... just need to quickly buy something."

He smiled at me charmingly. "Come on, you'll have five minutes for an old friend like me. Didn't you want to give me a call?"

"Yes well, unfortunately, I had to wash my hands and your phone number came off," I said in a snippy tone. Altaf seemed oblivious to the tone. Why didn't he just leave? I still needed a new book and wool for a scarf. How was I supposed to concentrate on wool colours if he kept hanging around, talking? Instead of leaving, he trudged after me into the bookstore and then the wool shop while telling me his life story. There was something innocent and friendly about him and I let him talk. Then I began to listen.

Altaf was from northern Punjab. That meant 'Land of Five Rivers' and I had never heard of it before. He'd had to flee his country before his sixteenth birthday and before he could get drafted into military service.

"At fifteen? Isn't that way too young for the military service? That's a cock 'n bull story, isn't it?!"

"No, seriously! That's what they did after the government was overthrown."

"Okay..."

One of his uncles had organised a forged passport for him with a different birthdate, making him eighteen years old. Then he'd joined the crew of a Greek cargo ship. The somewhat coarse but good-natured captain and his wife had taken him under their wing and he'd learned how to be a machinist. He had also been to Africa and South America several times and suddenly Altaf appeared a lot more intriguing to me. Somebody who'd seen the world! That was far more than I had ever done.

During the next few months, we enjoyed a budding romance that never really came into full bloom. That was okay by me. I accepted that and kept studying for my A-levels.

Altaf seemed to take things more seriously, though. Perhaps his passion was fanned by my utter lack of it. I was still rather inexperienced and thought nothing of his behaviour, although it was remarkable how often we met in town by coincidence. When Renate wasn't with me, we'd go to a pizzeria or eat ice cream or we'd just chat while I studied the shop window displays on Kaiserstreet. After a while, I was convinced that I had gained another brother together with Manfred and Ingmar.

We actually became best friends or second best rather. My

bosom friend Renate was still in place one. The next weekend, her drummer boyfriend Steve was set to play with his band 'Hotstix' at the youth centre in town and I went to the concert with Altaf.

"See over there? The guy in the red jacket, that's Steve," I explained to him as we took up our position in front of the stage.

"The black guy in the red jacket?" He asked.

"Yes."

"She has a black boyfriend?"

"Yes, she does. I'm sure he's serious about her. Renate told me that they are planning to get married as soon as she's done with school. At least that's the general plan."

"One, two, three, four…" the loudspeakers blasted away as the band began to perform their first song.

Yes, Renate was really planning to get married to him, although I knew that there were sparks often flying between them. In the meantime, she earned money waitressing in a pub because she wanted to be as independent as possible of her father's maintenance payments. I also worked on and off in a bookstore whenever they needed me.

Then just before the Easter holidays, Renate and I spontaneously decided to take a trip to London. First by train to Calais and then by ferry to Hull. I felt pretty rough during the ferry ride and was thankful when we finally arrived towards evening. Of course, we hadn't booked any accommodation due to a lack of proper planning. All we had was the address of a youth hotel in the fancy Kensington district.

The youth hotel turned out to be an impressive urban villa and because it was some sort of insider secret and not very busy at the time, we were lucky enough to get a double bedroom straight away. It was awesome.

We joined a group of teenagers and toured London together. Madame Tussaud's Wax Museum, the Tower Bridge and Windsor Castle. We couldn't afford anything but 'fish and chips' for supper but that didn't dampen our mood. We came back in high spirits - and Altaf disapproved of our trip!

"I could have shown you so much more if I had come with

you. I have family in London and Newcastle, you know."

"Sure, but I wanted to go on this trip with Renate."

"It's not exactly safe for two women to travel alone…"

"Oh, why is that? Nowadays it's no big deal and we had no trouble at all."

"But there are plenty of men who take advantage of girls."

"Come off it! We know self-defence and England is not Saudi Arabia or some country like that."

"Of course not, Europe is different."

"Exactly." And that was the end of the matter for me.

We were in a rather unusual friendship, Altaf and I. Almost as if we were actually related. Nothing could keep me from enjoying my freedom in the commune and choosing whether I wanted to spend my time with friends or chill alone. And I had quite a circle of friends by now. They were rather diverse and I thought it was best to meet with them separately. It was also time to introduce them to Altaf.

Doris and Renate were not all that fond of each other (plus, Doris would have been jealous of Altaf), and Angie and Tarek were too sensitive for Renate's pig-headedness. So it was complicated. That's why I introduced Altaf to Renate and Steve first. It went surprisingly well and Altaf quickly got used to the fact that Steve was black and an American.

Sometimes, I would also visit Altaf at his commune. He shared a flat with other young Pakistanis and their commune was completely different to ours. I had already met Latif and then there were also Zaheer and George. George had lived in England for a while and we talked about London for a bit until our conversation ran dry. They often cooked together and invited friends over for a meal. The hot spices gave me terrible hiccups at first and it took me some time to get used to the vast amounts of chilli and garam masala in the food. The guys taught me how to make their special flatbread. One had to shape the dough into small balls and then pat them flat. Just like pizza bases.

"Good job," Altaf praised me. "Now you have to put it in the pan."

The flatbread, they called chapati, was then baked in a flat iron pan and held over a gas flame until it formed a balloon.

"I'll also show you how to make saalen – a type of stew. We won't add so much chilli to it, then you can eat with us."

To tell the truth, I wasn't too fond of saalen, which was a rather hot oily stew made of beef and potatoes. Pakoras, on the other hand, were pieces of vegetables in a curry batter that were deep-fried. They tasted better than French fries.

"Where do you get all the ingredients from?" I asked. "I've never seen garam masala at any supermarket."

"There are many Turkish shops behind the red-light district. They have most of the ingredients we need. They also sell atchar. Look, here on the shelf is a jar of atchar made with green mangoes. And that one is made with lemons." Atchar seemed to have the same status in Pakistan as tomato ketchup in the west.

Notwithstanding Altaf's concerns, I decided to carry on travelling on my own. Even if it was on a shoestring. It didn't bother me that I had no money. All I wanted to do was to see the world!

In the summer, I went back to London and met up with friends from Morocco on an international camping ground for young people. I had made their acquaintance at the Kensington youth hotel over the Easter weekend. Zohra was a dark-skinned beauty with long black hair, while her cousins Hassan and Mohammed looked more like Southern Europeans. Zohra explained to me that they were Berber and one could find a whole spectrum of skin colours within a single family. She couldn't explain to me why it was like that and it didn't really matter.

I practised speaking French and sat in their massive caravan, drinking sweet peppermint tea with them. Other tourists came and joined our little tea ceremony: Tunisians, Irishmen and French travellers to name but a few. Her two cousins kept a close watch on the graceful Zohra because she obviously attracted attention. In any case, Moroccan women were not allowed to travel unless they were in male company, never mind go out on their own. All three of them had holiday jobs at a factory in East Acton. Without these jobs, they would not have been able to afford their vacation. So I got used to heading out on my own.

"It would be so much nicer if we could do something together," I complained after a lonely excursion to the city. "It's boring during the week without you guys."

"But we always do something together over the weekend and in the last two weeks of our vacation we won't be working at all. Then it'll be better."

Zohra suddenly had a light bulb moment. "Isabell, why don't you come and work with us at the factory? It's not difficult work and you could earn yourself some money as well. Pourquoi pas?"

I considered this. "True, why not? Let's see, I could try it for a week or so. What do you have to do there?"

"That depends on the section they put you in. I work with the washing machines on the first floor."

"Washing machines?"

"Yes, it's easy. Maybe we'll work the same shift." Her eyes sparkled.

"Okay, I'm sold," I said.

"Bien d'accord. Monday morning we can take the bus to East Acton together. The factory is close to the station."

The 'factory' turned out to be a huge laundry firm, servicing hotels and restaurants in the area. They sent loads of dirty linen to the 'factory' to be cleaned. It was my job to sort fabric serviettes according to their colour and stain types. Not a very demanding task that paid £ 4.70 an hour. A lot of money for the Indian ladies in my team. The older women seemed to be taken with me and apparently had plenty of unmarried nephews.

"Hey, pretty girl!" Aisha called me over during the coffee break. She was a portly matron and the leader of the brigade. "You must give me your photograph. Ooh, my nephew will like you. He's looking for a wife. He's an engineer, who makes good money. How old are you, Isabell?"

"I'm eighteen, Aisha," I said awkwardly.

"Ah, eighteen. A bit old, but I'm sure he'll fall in love with your picture." She cackled and the others joined in.

"But I really don't want your nephew to fall in love with me. I don't want to get married at all," I protested. Aisha just smiled and waggled her head from side to side.

At first, I thought it was a joke and gave her an ancient passport photo of mine. But before I knew what hit me, I was invited to Southall and an Alu Gobi dinner, where I was introduced to other elderly women. Fortunately, the nephew in question was in India at the time but allegedly, other nephews were also interested in me. That was going too far and I refused to accept any more invitations as politely as possible.

Thankfully, Zohra and I often spent our lunch breaks together, which further limited my contact with the matrons. Then Abdul, a Moroccan chap who stayed at the camping site and was not related to Zohra and her cousins, declared himself my protector for no apparent reason. This led to an instant decline in the fervent interest in my person and I even received my photograph back.

After ten days at the laundry, I began to get bored and resigned from my job. It was far more fun to watch how people in Speaker's Corner in Hyde Park stood on soapboxes and ranted against the government. I also liked to do window-shopping in Southall or Nottinghill.

A few weeks after I'd returned to Karlsruhe, Zohra's first letter arrived. She invited me to come to Morocco for a visit the following year. *Not a bad idea*, I thought and agreed for the time being.

I told Altaf how much I'd enjoyed London and he asked me at once to take a trip to Athens with him at Christmas time.

"In winter it's nice and warm in Greece and it takes only about 24 hours by train to get there." It sounded enticing. "Germany is so horribly cold in winter. My Greek 'parents' - my old captain Costa and his wife Elephteria - live in Athens. Right by the port of Piraeus. I haven't seen them for quite some time now."

Athens! It had always been my dream to visit Greece. The land of Socrates and just about all the great scientists in ancient times. I found it irresistible to travel and see the world and expand my horizon, so I didn't give it a second thought and agreed.

Zohra and I had purchased silk saris in Southall on a whim and I began to wear my sari to school just for kicks. This earned me disapproving glances but I couldn't care less. I liked my sari and was, in any case, already used to being 'different'.

It became too cold to wear the sari in winter and, on a freezing December morning, I walked to school dressed in my cosiest Afghan dress, leather boots and sheepskin jacket. I mentally prepared myself for yet another boring day. Maybe I could convince Doris to go to the 'Krokodil' with me during a free period for a cup of hot chocolate.

Students were standing around with transistor radios in every corner and scowled as if it was the end of the world. I trudged up the broad staircase to the second floor and already felt like returning home and taking a nap.

"Why does everybody here look so depressed?" I asked Doris, who stood waiting in front of the physics room.

"Don't you know what happened? It's all over the news this morning." She looked at me flabbergasted as we pushed into the classroom with the other students. Good, Dr. Mohlmann wasn't there yet.

"What? What's on the news?"

"It's everywhere!"

We sat down in our usual places. One of the boys had brought a radio inside and a few students formed a half-circle around it. I glanced at them with a sinking feeling.

"Alright you got me, I'm a total dunce but what's going on here? You're creeping me out! Did somebody die?" Doris looked away.

"No! Who died? Dr. Mohlmann?" I groaned.

"Rubbish! John Lennon has been shot in New York."

"What?" I was totally thunderstruck. "That's not possible. Stop making stupid jokes, will you!"

Should I burst out laughing? John Lennon was invincible like all the Beatles. He was my idol. He just couldn't be dead.

"Are you nuts to give me such a fright?" I wanted to slap Doris on her arm when I heard a snippet of the radio news: '...*The New York Police Department has confirmed that John Lennon, a founding member of the pop group 'The Beatles' was shot dead last night in front of his apartment building. It is unclear at this stage whether the shooter is...*'

I sat there in a daze and couldn't believe what I'd just heard. They were making a mistake... surely. Things like that simply didn't happen!

"Now I'll never have his babies!" dimwitted Melanie cried. "I want to just die. Oh John, take me with you!"

"Oh shut your trap!" Rüdiger snapped at her crossly. "They just said that the murderer was nabbed by the police and that he's probably crackers. I couldn't understand the guy's name thanks to you."

"He must be totally crackers, shooting John Lennon like that," Tarek said with utter contempt.

"John Lennon was shot last night by a madman?" I babbled.

"Yes, of course."

"Are you sure?" I asked meekly. "Maybe he was just injured." I felt nauseous. It was a good thing that I was already sitting down.

"No, they said it on the news, he's dead!"

"Good morning!" Dr. Mohlmann's voice cut through the awkward atmosphere and everybody began to climb over each other to get to their chairs.

"Enough with the chit-chat. Rüdiger, wipe that hideous scrawling off the blackboard. And turn that damn thing off!" A few bars of 'Yellow Submarine' that drifted through the physics room died down instantly.

I was devastated. Once again I was grieving. And in winter for good measure. The sky outside was grey and it had begun to snow. How fitting. Could things get any worse? Luckily, I could look forward to a two-week holiday in Greece. A welcome distraction. And before I knew it, the Christmas holidays were around the corner.

*

The train left Karlsruhe Station in bone-chilling temperatures and a whole day later, we arrived in warm, sun-flooded Athens.

I was dog tired. We hadn't thought of bringing enough food with us and sleeping on the extendible seats had been sheer torture. Now I found myself standing on Greek ground. Athens was astonishing with all those old-world streets and the drone of the traffic. This language sounded so foreign, the scents of the city, the buildings and the food were so different. Everything was exciting!

Altaf masterfully manoeuvered us through the seething masses and inquired in fluent Greek how to get to the bus station. Our bus stopped directly in front of the house in Piraeus.

Captain Costa and his wife were salt-of-the-earth people and a strange-looking couple at that. The captain was around fifty and bald-headed. He also sported a respectable paunch and one could hear his booming laughter outside in the street. Elephteria, on the other hand, was a nervous, thin, stick-insect of a woman with peroxide-blonde hair and a shrill voice to boot with. Costa endured his moody wife with an indulging patience and his wife tolerated his crude seaman's demeanour and swearing. So their marriage seemed to work for them.

"Efprosdektos, kalosorisma! Pretty girl, elkystiki, eycharisti stim emfamisi!" Her words gushed forth with vehemence when Altaf introduced me. He had to translate this, of course.

"She welcomes us and thinks that you are rather nice."

"Oh, thank you. Eycharisto parapoli!" I answered.

Altaf had taught me basic Greek during the train ride and now I could put it to good use. It seemed to give Elephteria the impression that I could understand her perfectly. She jabbered on vivaciously, while I stared at her not comprehending a word she said.

"Parakalo, parakalo, koritsi." She turned around to her husband and pointed to our luggage. "Ela, to etero mou imisy!"

"She has prepared a room for us," Altaf explained. "Come, it's over here. Captain Costa will bring our bags."

There was a big bed in the room.

One double bed! I didn't know how to react. "But Altaf, we can't sleep in the same bed together. Please tell her that."

"I can't tell her that."

"Why not?"

"She'll throw a tantrum because she thinks that we are engaged."

"And why would she think that? I'm not even your girlfriend," I hissed. Elephteria looked up all confused. Wasn't the bed good enough? Did I need anything else?

Altaf shrugged his shoulders and gave her his most charming smile. I had no choice but to thank her dutifully. Of course, the two of them thought that we were a couple! He must have told them. I was determined that I would not spend my first Greek holiday in a mood, but I always slept right on the very edge of the double bed.

Elephteria made a big fuss of me, Altaf's German fiancée, and wished to introduce me to a whole clutch of relatives. For some reason, this never happened; probably because we were constantly out and about. I wanted to see as much as humanly possible of this city and the country, so Altaf suggested that we should take the ferry to the island of Salamina.

Salamina was one of the small islets closest to the coast and he still knew it from his previous visits. We were planning to spend the night there and to take the boat back to Piraeus the following day. Alas, I became terribly sea-sick during the bouncy ferry ride so nothing came of it. Altaf later told me in not so flattering detail how green I had looked around the gills when I'd begun to feed the fishes.

A young guy grinned at me with a sneering look on his face and I turned and barfed in the other direction. Then I sat down on the wooden bench, trembling.

"Altaf, I feel so terribly sick. What are we supposed to do?"

"I'm sure you'll feel better once we're back on land."

But I didn't feel any better. I stepped off the boat and continued to barf on the rocky beach.

"Come on Isabell, sit down on the stone over there." Altaf gave me some Coke to drink from a bottle we'd bought back at the harbour.

"Oh no, I need to vomit again," I wailed.

"We should go and find the village. It won't be long before nightfall."

Nobody was in sight. Nobody we could have asked for directions to the next inn, so we had no option but to return to the landing and take the last ferry to Piraeus. The very last. My stomach only settled once we were back at the harbour in a bar and with the help of a shot glass of Ouzo. Then we climbed up the street where Captain Costa lived.

The following morning, I was as fresh as a daisy again and Captain Costa had laughed so hard when he learned about my mishap that tears were streaming down his face. Elefteria gave me strong, hot coffee to drink and give me a lecture in brusque Greek.

We visited the Acropolis and the ancient quarter around the temple mound. The entire time, I had an inexplicable feeling of déja-vu as if I'd been there before. We also went to visit Altaf's friend Adil who lived in a village not far from Athens with a long unpronounceable name. Altaf seemed to know people everywhere and had a sizeable network.

Adil shared a modest little house with other Pakistanis. The 'bathroom' consisted of a lean-to shed with a hand pump. My first experience with how to make do without running water.

We spent Christmas in Piraeus in the midst of a spirited crowd outside on the central square. We had calamari, lamb on a spit and there were huge fireworks at midnight. Our two hosts were very amusing and very drunk.

On the morning of New Year's Day, a very special surprise was already waiting for me. Elephteria put a pot with herbal soup on the table. A sheep's skull chopped in half floated in the clear liquid. She handed me a spoon and prompted me with animated gestures to eat the brain of the sheep. A pinkish mass interlaced with darker veins.

"Troo to peridromo, koritsi," she urged me on with an encouraging smile.

I nearly dropped the spoon in horror and declined to eat the pink brain while I tried to smile politely. My stomach simply refused. But I wasn't prepared for our hostess's vehement reaction.

Elephteria cried hot tears of disappointment and called out in a fluster: "Ti krima! I did the best I could. O Theos to xeri. As God is my witness. But it is not good enough. I must be a terrible cook. De ime kalli mayirissa!"

What was I supposed to do?

"No, no, Elephteria, you are a brilliant cook. I just can't, I mean I've never…" The cleaved sheep's head grinned at me. "I mean I'm not hungry," I changed my tune.

Altaf was no help at all. He and Captain Costa had their hands full, trying to calm the offended housewife. She sat on the floor and flailed her arms about hysterically.

"Our food is not good enough for her," she cried over and over. "De ime kalli mayirissa!"

After getting a hold of herself, she held the silver spoon out to Captain Costa. "Here my husband, the honour of eating the first bite falls onto you. To etero mou imisy. And here, another mouthful for my little Altaf. Eat, eat your fill!"

Afterwards, Captain Costa thought it best that we should move into a small guesthouse until we left. His wife was too upset. I felt guilty but there was nothing we could have done. Although our trip ended on a low point, I longed for the warm Greek sun and being close to the ocean when I sat on the northbound train.

As soon as we got to Belgrade, the temperatures dropped. It began to snow incessantly and a white blur obscured the passing landscape. The cold German winter we had left behind had grown into a fully-fledged north pole winter from hell in January.

Karlsruhe greeted us with a thick layer of ice and a flurry

of snow. Our taxi crawled through totally surreal streets and took us to Altaf's flat building in the Southend.

And I immediately came down with the flu. I'd never experienced anything like it, was unable to move or speak and my headache became unbearable. I shivered despite all the blankets piled on top of me and couldn't even think about eating food.

Altaf did what he could and gave me hot tea to drink. The streets were virtually impassable and no emergency doctor would have made it through. As soon as the weather improved a little, he had to go back to work and I lay on the couch all day doing my best to recover. Eventually, I could hold myself upright and managed to phone my mother.

"Where have you been?" She rattled off. "Are you roaming all over the world again and forgetting everything else? Your family, your school… Your principal phoned and threatened to fail you if you don't go back to school immediately. Now you're even starting to skip school …"

My head hurt.

"It's not like that at all," I croaked as soon as I got a word in edgewise. "I've been back in Karlsruhe for days and got awfully ill. It's the flu, probably because of the change in climate. I couldn't get out of bed this entire time. Couldn't even get to the phone until now," I said, ending off with a fit of coughing.

"Oh is that so? You were unable to get out of bed and give your mother a ring? Or let your school know? And where are you if I may ask? Paula went to your room but you weren't there. Why couldn't your fine new friend give me a call?" Luckily, I had taken a headache pill.

"He didn't have your number and I was too ill to even speak to him."

"You seem to have an answer for everything, don't you?"

"It's the absolute truth. Cough. Please do me a favour and phone the school. I'll take a taxi home later."

"Why are you not going to see a doctor? You always do as you please. Where will all this end?"

"I'm too sick to go and see a doctor."

My mother kept kicking up a fuss a while longer before the nurse inside her won the upper hand. "Very well then, go and get to bed. I'll be over at your place as soon as the snow lets up and I will let your school know. That cough doesn't sound good at all."

Cough, cough. "Oh really? I've been practising for days."

Of course, nobody believed my story of coming down with a sudden flu. Who's ever heard of something like that? A nice little cold maybe, but a heavy flu? I was obviously too young for a serious illness. In view of the imminent final exams, Mr. Mandel deigned to let it slide. My mother had probably put in a good word for me.

As soon as I was well enough, I delved into preparations for the written exams. The pedigree of the horse, Cézanne's biography, and I had to remember all of this by heart. Two weeks later, I was fit as a fiddle again. The exams began and everything went like clockwork. Mr. Mandel and Co would be bitterly disappointed. After the biology exam, Altaf asked me if I felt like accompanying him to his *brother's* wedding in Pakistan.

"Farooq has been living in London for years. He works at a chocolate factory in Slough. He's finally saved up enough money to marry his fiancée Nasra. It's a love match. Rather unusual in our family, but they've known each other forever."

"Won't they be surprised if you bring me along? I'm not even your girlfriend."

"Farooq knows all about western customs. He'll understand. Nasra went to school in London and they'll go back to England after the wedding."

"Alright then, but you'll have to tell me exactly what I must do."

First America, then Greece and now Pakistan. I was becoming more worldly-wise by the minute and would probably end up writing a book about globe-trotting one day! Just that I couldn't quite picture this exotic country.

In the end, I convinced myself that it would be great. After all the exertion of the past few weeks, I was in dire need of a break. The orals were scheduled only in May and one couldn't study all the time, right?

"You want to travel where - to Pakistan? Where is this Pakistan, isn't it one of those Mohammedan countries in the Middle East? Are you planning to marry this man?" My mother had to sit down. "Oh no, what will people say?"

"Mum, his name is Altaf. We are not engaged and I will definitely not get married for a long time to come - especially not to Altaf. And I don't want to get married anyway. I'm just invited to his brother's wedding in Pakistan. That's all. And yes, Pakistan is an Islamic country, but between Afghanistan and India. And I couldn't care less what 'the people' are saying."

"Haven't you had enough trouble after playing truant in January?"

She began to mumble again about 'the people' and what they would be thinking. I sighed in resignation. "I didn't play truant. I had the FLU."

"And you are Catholic. Mohammedans are just too different from us. You will not go and that's all there is to it!" She changed the subject. "Here, have another piece of the Russian Cheesecake." I took a piece and she seemed mollified. A good sign.

"You know that I'm no longer Catholic and what does it matter anyhow? In any case, they don't seem to particularly like the Brits, and the Americans even less. But I am German so there shouldn't be a problem. I've already booked the flight. A special off-season price and I saved up the money for the trip. I'm going straight after my birthday in March. Mr. Mandel has also given me his consent."

That was actually true.

I'd explained to the long-suffering school principal that the trip was a unique opportunity and had something to do with the subject I wanted to study.

"So that's how it is, you ask your school principal's permission, but not your mother's? How nice of you. It's all those ungodly influences outside the home. Come to think of it, you should move back home. A young unmarried girl like you..."

"Mum, I'm almost nineteen. Why should I ask you for permission to do anything?"

"No good deed goes unpunished. You don't get this stubbornness from my side of the family! Us Heydenreichs, we are able to get in line. You take after your aunt Bertha. Those rebellious Protestants – always questioning everything!"

"I am not a Protestant. I'm nothing at all."

"That's all I need: my daughter is an Atheist. Your Grandfather would turn in his grave."

I sighed. "Let's rather not talk about that man."

She hesitated for a brief moment. "The other one, of course. What will people think? First, you become an Atheist, then you travel to a Mohammedan country. Good Lord, my own flesh and blood."

"You can tell people whatever you like. You always do that in any case. Mrs. Speidel won't hear it from me, that's for sure."

My mother wove some story for 'the people': that I was going on some course in Bavaria, to prepare for the oral exams. Or something to that effect. Then Mr. Mandel topped even her reaction: he changed his mind three weeks before my flight. I was summoned to the principal's office during the morning break. My written application to have the Easter holidays extended by two weeks lay before him on his massive desk.

"Miss Bertrand," he greeted me with spurious politeness. "Why am I not surprised that we see each other again? What kind of trouble are you creating at my school now? Oh yes, you want to travel to P a k i s t a n." Mr. Mandel exaggerated the word. He wanted to poke fun at me.

"But you did agree that…"

His eyes followed my movements in badly hidden contempt. "You seem to have a distinct preference for gentlemen of foreign origin, Miss Bertrand." I would have loved to slap his face, but of course, I didn't do that and tried to be as composed as I could manage.

"You have been lying to me about a university course…" he said in a chilly tone, "…and for that, you need to prepare with a trip and..."

"Excuse me? What gave you that idea?"

"I just got off the phone with your mother. She kindly told me the whole truth. A wedding."

"The truth? I have no idea what she told you, but I can assure you..."

"Tell me, haven't you travelled enough? And then you want to go to a Mohammedan country. Untenable. And may I remind you that you have already extended your sojourn in Greece without permission? Shouldn't you rather concentrate on the upcoming exams?"

That was pretty steep.

"Mr. Mandel," I began, "... first of all, I'm an adult. Secondly, I had a vicious flu attack after my return from Greece. And thirdly, Altaf is only a friend who invited me to attend his brother's wedding..."

Was there a fourth point? "...and one doesn't have the opportunity to learn about other cultures every day. I've passed my written exams rather successfully and..." Mr. Mandel interrupted me.

Stay calm, stay calm, stay...

"...Miss Bertrand, must I repeat myself endlessly? I've already told you in no uncertain terms that we cannot tolerate such extravagant behaviour around here. You simply don't display the necessary maturity and I have therefore decided to withdraw my consent to let you take this journey."

I stood up very slowly. The chair scratched across the parquet floor. "Very well, I'll have to go without your permission then."

"You won't dare!"

"Oh, watch me," I said and stood my ground.

The vein on his forehead pulsated. "The last word in the matter has not yet been spoken!"

I gazed unflinchingly into his red spiteful face with the pulsating vein on the forehead and closed the door behind me. I'd had enough. Nobody could stop me now.

The preparations for my trip didn't go smoothly, though. I

had foolishly left my keys at Altaf's and turned around halfway back to my place. Altaf had gone out, but after ringing the bell for a while, Latif let me in. He stared at me aghast, instantly dropped to his knees and begged my forgiveness.

"I'm so sorry, so sorry," he kept repeating.

I stood rooted to the spot and watched him bow in front of me, holding his earlobes. A sign of repentance.

"What on earth is the matter with you, Latif?" I snapped at him. "Are you going bonkers or what? I just forgot my keys."

Latif kept on bowing. The whole thing became more embarrassing by the second, but I couldn't leave without my keys. What could be the cause of his behaviour? I pushed past him and walked into the common room.

"Oh, my word." I didn't believe my eyes.

In the middle of the room was a magnum bottle with brandy. Three Pakistanis sat around it with their filled glasses, looking rather squiffy. Latif stood behind me and was still busy apologising. The men gave me wild stares as if they expected that I dropped some pearls of wisdom or would possibly chastise them.

"Latif, all that has nothing to do with me. That doesn't mean you guys shouldn't be ashamed of yourselves." I felt rather irritated by now.

"Ah, but you are like a sister to me. Yes, I am ashamed. I never wanted to drink alcohol but the devil was stronger than me," he wailed.

The half-empty bottle told another story.

"Stop blubbering for goodness sake! Put away this damn bottle or better still, empty it out. Then you won't be tempted to touch that stuff again." I discovered my keys. "Oh good, there they are. I must go now. Bye," I said and was out of the door and down the stairs in a flash.

"I always thought Mohammedans are not allowed to drink alcohol," Walter stated the next time our clique met.

"They often do that in secret," Tarek told us. "The power of the forbidden fruit, I guess. Don't know what's worse: to drink secretly or be allowed to get sloshed publicly in pubs."

"Latif of all people gave me a lecture on how virtuous Muslims are and raved about stuff like that!" I said awkwardly.

"What does Altaf say to that?" Angie asked.

"I'm not sure what he thinks. He shrugged his shoulders and said that nobody was really observing these rules around here. They don't always pray when they are supposed to and you can buy alcohol just about everywhere. He draws the line when it comes to pork, though. He thinks it causes pimples."

"Pimples? I've been a vegetarian for two months now and just look at my skin." Angie touched her face in horror. "Do you think he's acting all virtuous here and as soon as he's in Pakistan, he'll behave differently?"

"No clue. Eddie Adeyemu's wife was afraid that something like that might happen. Then they went to Lagos last year with little Yemissi and everything was hunky dory."

Tarek weighed in again. "I think that when you guys are in Pakistan, he'll definitely stick to the rules when it comes to alcohol and stuff like that."

"I've never seen him drink," I offered a feeble defence.

"That doesn't mean anything," Walter piped up. "If you don't drink alcohol just because you can't buy it - what does that say about you? Poor show!"

"Exactly, you shouldn't do that out of principle, but people like to break the rules." Tarek could be so full of wisdom sometimes.

"Oh really? I'm always punished when I break the rules and I never drink alcohol," I said defiantly.

"That's a different matter."

"How so? Some rules just don't make sense."

"So, what are you going to do?" Angie asked anxiously.

"I can't really back-paddle now just because of something like that. And I'm travelling to Pakistan with Altaf and not with Latif."

"Should we go for a beer?" We glared at Walter. "It's just a joke. Loosen up, haha…"

I could surely rely on Altaf, couldn't I? He was a true friend, had taken care of me selflessly when I had the flu. In Greece he had also behaved himself despite the double bed. Renate had a different opinion on this.

"Are you totally loopy?" She was flaming mad. "It counts for nothing in countries like that. If he's the one paying and you two don't get along, what are you gonna do then? You don't have the kind of money to do your own thing."

Renate and Steve had flown to Washington DC for the Christmas holidays to visit his family. It hadn't panned out quite the way she'd expected.

"I'm a German citizen, right? There's surely an embassy in Islamabad. That's the capital city. It's the eighties after all."

Renate gave me a provocative stare.

"Come on now. Do I look like your typical doormat? There you are. And Altaf is not exactly some macho-pasha thing."

"Where's your self-respect? You're friends here, but don't tell me that you are equals over there."

"Oh, Renate, stop it already. When do you ever get a chance to visit a country like Pakistan?"

"I pass. Do you have any idea what it's like if men and women talk separately all the time?" She rolled her eyes.

"You mean like Steve's family?"

"Exactly. His sisters came to the airport with their hair in curlers. Curlers! We sat around in the kitchen all day long, chatting about cooking and babies and the latest gossip. Me and cooking!"

We laughed. Renate was a scary chef.

"I sat there and didn't know what to say. Politics or books. Phew. No, just gossiping about the neighbours and whoever else. Steve behaved like the worst macho around his family. Afterwards, he kept apologising to me. I should have left him right there and then."

I had listened to the same story over and over and Renate was still hopping mad. Their marriage plans were on the back burner for now.

But the thing with Pakistan was completely different.

"Look, all I want to do is see the country."

"Whatever you say. But you won't let them get the better of you, you hear me?"

"Loud and clear."

Zohra, my Moroccan friend, wasn't half as negative as Renate, but she still gave me a stern warning despite the abysmal phone connection.

"Try not to challenge..... men too much. Crack, crack. Look down when you meet.... in public..... rustle. And cover your hair with a scarf or.... veil.... you are rather blon..." The connection faded.

Zohra was calling me from Hassan's office in Casablanca where she was currently visiting. Hassan worked as an engineer for a French company and seemed to earn a good salary.

"Thank you for the advice, Zohra. I'll give you a call when I'm back."

She tried to say something to me, but the rustling and crackling in the line became too noisy.

Then, of all things, I started to dream of Nusrat. At first, it was just a fleeting feeling. A feeling of pride and duty towards the family. I was proud of my heritage and that feeling accompanied me for a few days. Then slightly longer dreams kept creeping up on me.

Imran would say something funny and I laughed a little longer and louder than necessary. I looked at him openly and he gazed deeply into my eyes. A gaze that touched my soul... It was just too much. I didn't even know who this Imran was and why was he making an appearance in my dreams now.

I gave Dr. Albrecht a ring. "One moment please, I'll put you through." Elizabeth patched me through to him.

"How interesting, Isabell. I've never heard of anything like it," the familiar voice said in a comforting tone. "That's still an unexplored area. We haven't really concluded your lifetime as Nusrat, isn't that so?"

"Yes, but there has to be an explanation why it's happening right now. I just can't dream about stuff like that all the time. It's driving me nuts."

I was doodling pictures on the writing pad in Manfred's room. Triangles with dots around them, flowers with three, four, five petals.

"Something must be drawing you to this lifetime. There has to be some sort of a trigger. We can try and find this trigger and then I'll be able to work with a suggestion to stop these dreams."

I felt relieved. "Yes, that sounds great. Just what I need. When can we start?"

"Stay on the line while I patch you back to Elizabeth. Please make an appointment with her."

"Yes okay. I'll see you soon, then."

It clicked and clacked as the call went back to reception. Elizabeth's voice sounded good-humoured. "Hello Isabell, are you still there? Dr. Albrecht asked me to give you an urgent appointment. I'm looking at his diary right now. Dr. Albrecht is booked out chocker-block. But how about the fourteenth of March?"

Impossible. "Can't we do it sooner? I'm flying to Pakistan on the twelfth."

"No, I'm really sorry. I can put you on the waiting list but I can't do anything about it right now."

"Well then…" I was disappointed.

"I will give you a call as soon as somebody cancels. Patients sometimes cancel at the last minute," she told me.

"Yes alright, thank you."

It would take a few days. Perhaps the whole thing had been caused by exam stress and the dreams would stop all by themselves. Perhaps I should pay my old friend, the park, a visit. The park was already dressed in spring. Flowers were in bloom and the green lawns were more or less dry. *Soon there would be yellow forsythias and blue lilac,* I thought. Hopefully, they had flowers in Pakistan.

I had to write a test when Elizabeth phoned and then I was already on my way to Karachi. There was nothing to be done.

Shortly after my birthday in March of 1981, I was sitting in a Russian Aeroflot aircraft en route to Moscow. My guitar was safely stowed in the overhead compartment above the seats and I was busy writing Urdu and Punjabi terms into a little black notebook. I think we were hovering somewhere above Poland at the time.

"What is 'to speak', Altaf?" I nudged my dozing travel companion. He sat up straight. "To speak is… 'bolt'. You would say 'me Urdu bolti hum', because you are female. A man would say 'me Urdu bolta hum'."

"I see, thank you." I scribbled it down. A Russian stewardess stomped past my seat and the rickety aeroplane started to wobble even more.

In Moscow, we had to stop over for eight hours and waited in the transit area. The queue at the passport control was endless. Just take your time!

When it was my turn, the officer stared at me intensely, copied my passport and studied my face and ears, while I tried to get a grip on a rising urge to giggle. Then he gawked at me dolefully and asked:

"Where are you from?"

Don't laugh, do not laugh! I reminded myself. One could get into hot water by saying or doing the wrong thing. Even doing all the right things. The thought was sobering. "I am from Germany. See there, my passport." I pointed to my travel documents through the thick glass of the window.

Altaf stood in the queue directly behind me, his face serious as if we didn't know each other. Naturally, he didn't want to draw attention to his forged passport. The passport official didn't take any note of him. Instead, he kept staring at me and asked something in Russian. Obviously, I didn't understand him. He noted down my passport number and spoke to someone on the phone. The passengers in the queue started to fidget.

Why do they always have to pick on me? I was peeved.

At JFK Airport in New York, two officials like that had grilled me for half an hour in a glass cubicle. I didn't have the slightest desire being grilled in a Russian glass cubicle now and began to stare ahead expressionless.

It worked.

"Everything in order." The official put my precious green passport back into the drawer and I heaved a sigh of relief.

"Why the hell did he keep staring at me?" I asked Altaf afterwards.

"Perhaps you don't look German enough."

"Why not? I have light hair and light eyes."

"No idea what he might have thought. Do you want something to drink? We still have about two hours left."

The Pakistani airline took us to Karachi via Tashkent. The PIA plane was sheer luxury compared to its Aeroflot-sister. The engines purred softly and the elegant stewardesses smiled behind thin veils.

As we approached Pakistan, we were even served edible food. I had never flown to anywhere this far away! At some stage, I must have nodded off.

I am in Dâkân. In my husband Mansour's Thikana. The roofs of the village are visible in the clear air. I walk to a shrine by the rear garden gate. The horses graze on the paddock outside. The name Pir Panjal went through my mind. Pir Panjal.Then I find myself running around my father's garden. My cousin and I chase each other between the apricot trees. We sit down on a wooden bench and eat the ripe orange-coloured apricots. I can taste the sweet fruit, can smell its aroma...

Altaf woke me up. We were on the final descent to Karachi.

CHAPTER FIVE

A bus transported us the short distance across the tarmac and it became clear that Karachi was a hot and dusty place. The airport building was dimly lit and not very clean. We fetched our luggage from the carousel and waited in line with the other passengers.

A strict-looking official, wearing a headscarf, searched the suitcases with remarkable thoroughness. It was obvious that she disliked my guitar.

The official made sure that there was a musical instrument in the thin cover and not a machine gun. Apparently, proof of this fact wasn't enough to let us go and she made us wait until the last passengers from our flight had been processed and left the checkpoint.

I seemed to be the only European soul in sight. Altaf spoke to the official and the conversation became more and more agitated. There was no doubt in my mind that this woman demanded some sort of payment. All I could understand was 'Dollars, Dollars'. Altaf refused point-blank and asked to see her supervisor. A male official appeared, mediated and found in Altaf's favour. I sighed, picked up my suitcase and guitar from the table and plodded behind him toward the exit. The woman stared at us in indignation but we were allowed to depart. I could see from the corner of my eye how the next load of passengers arrived and made its way to the luggage carousel.

"What did that woman want?" I asked while Altaf tried to wave down a rickshaw. I already knew the answer.

"Money," he said offhand and haggled fiercely about the fare with the streetwise rickshaw driver. We squeezed the luggage and ourselves into the limited space at the back of the rickshaw and the driver took off. In an instant, we found ourselves in the bedlam of intense activity.

A moped clattered past and roaring buses hooted their way past other vehicles. I had never seen buses like that before: decorated with garish, colourful images and hammered tin sheets. There were plenty of rickshaws in every conceivable colour threading through traffic at break-neck speed. Pedestrians and mopeds barged through the melee wherever they could to find an opening. All the women, except for me, wore a Punjabi suit that consisted of wide trousers and a tunic with a thin veil draped across their shoulders.

Our rickshaw zoomed along the broad avenue into the city centre. Billboards brashly advertised Coca-Cola and radios. I closed my eyes and longed for hot water, soap and a clean bed. We stopped in a side road in front of a building that had seen better days. The grimy paint peeled off the neglected façade in long strips and a tattered green flag with a white half moon hung limply above the entrance.

"A hotel," Altaf explained.

"That's supposed to be a hotel?" My mood darkened.

"It's cheap and we'll stay only one night, while I try to get hold of my uncle Chacha Qasim. Apparently, he's moved."

"I see. Why is his name Chacha? That sounds like some kind of dance."

"No, Isabell. Chacha means *uncle*." Altaf had to laugh. "And Chachi means *aunt*. He's moved to some new area that I haven't heard of. This place is, unfortunately, all I can afford right now."

Our room was situated on the first floor. The walls seemed to be made of brown cardboard and brown cockroaches populated every nook and cranny of the room, watching us suspiciously.

It was noisy here. High-pitched songs whined incessantly from a radio somewhere. There was a couple squabbling, which echoed all over the courtyard at the back and through the open window. The windows with the blind glass-panes had to stay open because of the oppressive heat and because of a ceiling fan malfunction. As for ablutions, a rusty tap released brownish water and an open toilet was right in the middle of the room. There were also two single beds that defied description.

"Are you serious?!" I asked in a trembling voice. "This toilet doesn't even have a seat."

"You have to squat down then wash yourself afterwards. I'm sure I told you about that. There, you see? You must use this plastic jug and fill it with water. The soap is over here."

Of course, the jug was a brownish colour.

I hadn't used a long-drop since Grandma Heydenreich installed a flush toilet in her village home some years ago. No, wait a minute, it had been in Greece. There had been a pit toilet in Adil's back garden, but it was a different matter if you couldn't sit down at all. I knew that you were only allowed to use your left hand for this business because it was regarded as unclean. The right hand was reserved for eating and the like.

"But without any toilet paper?"

That, I could not easily get used to. I would have to wash my hands a million times afterwards. What I didn't know yet was that a toilet without a seat was better than no toilet at all.

"Isabell, try and get some rest. Wash up and sleep a little if you can. I'll go out for a short while."

"Sure, having a wash and sleeping sounds good to me, but I'm also getting really hungry."

"Alright then, I'll buy us something to eat while I'm out. I'll be right back."

Altaf locked me into the brown room and plunged back into the tumultuous crowd outside.

I tried to follow his advice and dozed for a while. Then darkness fell and another argument was carried out with renewed fervour in the backyard. I must have read the magazine I'd bought at the airport in Frankfurt at least a hundred times. By the time Altaf finally unlocked the door, I was dozing again. "Isabell?"

"Hey, you said you'd be right back!" I sulked.

"Don't be cross with me. I met somebody I know in the street and we had lunch back at his house."

"Hey, thanks a lot. How could you forget to buy *me* something to eat?"

"We can go downstairs right now and get some food for you."

"You went to get some food hours ago. It's so hot in here and I need to drink something. This brown water is not exactly appetising."

"Oh come on now, let's not argue."

I began to realise why those people in the backyard were fighting all the time. Right now, I felt like doing the same thing.

"What do you expect from me? I've just arrived in this place and have no clue where I am. I don't speak the language, I'm tired, hungry and thirsty, but I mustn't argue when you leave me alone for hours on end in this rat hole?"

"Alright, alright. It's just for one night. This friend of mine, the one I had lunch with, gave me Chacha Qasim's new address."

"Whoop-dee-doo," I grumbled.

Eventually, we went out. At night, the mood of the city changed profoundly. The wild chaos had died down and the crowds moved at a more leisurely pace. The heat had retreated and I was almost at ease as we walked past the many food stalls. I greedily devoured fiery samosas and drank a small bottle of Sprite.

I was hungry enough not to worry about hygiene. Altaf bought a cup with rosewater ice cream and glass noodles and we shared the *kulfi*, which was apparently a culinary speciality.

I began to feel better. A man who was dark from the sun and dressed in only a loincloth deftly turned a large metal wheel with a hand lever. I watched him in fascination.

"What do you need these presses for?"

"They are used to squeeze juice from sugar cane. It's in season right now. See those long green stalks? That's the sugar cane. You can also buy it cut into pieces."

The long stalks reappeared on the other side of the two

massive rollers completely flattened. Altaf paid for a handful of cane pieces and I chewed them while we strolled about the stalls. Some of the people we passed stared at my western clothes: white jeans and a blue-floral blouse. I tried to ignore the stares. The wide trousers and tunics they wore looked like a uniform to me. Here and there, a multi-coloured sari shone through the drab crowd. Perhaps I should have packed my silk sari from London!

"We'll buy you some proper clothes tomorrow," Altaf said.

"I think that's probably a good idea."

We walked past a group of soldiers armed to the teeth who were patrolling the streets. Those were real machine guns and in the dark street, they looked rather dangerous.

"Damn it Altaf, where have you brought me?"

"Sorry, I assumed that you'd heard about the military coup."

"What? What military coup? How am I supposed to know about that?"

All that Altaf had mentioned to me was that some general called Zia ul-Haq had taken power just recently and the president, Zulfikar Ali Bhutto, had been recalled. I thought that's what he'd meant by a coup. Now I learned that the army had toppled the democratic government and that the president and members of the Pakistan Peoples Party had been summarily executed. My eyes popped.

"Now, our hollow-eyed general Zia ul-Haq governs the country. You can see his picture everywhere. There are still occasional riots and that's why the army is patrolling the streets."

"Thank you very much for not telling me sooner."

"Sorry, Isabell. Would you have come with me otherwise?" Altaf gave me his most charming smile.

"Probably not."

"There you go! It's a lot better in the rural areas. You'll see, it's rather quiet in Punjab."

Altaf's home village was in Punjab. A large, rural region in the north of the country. Karachi was in the south on the coast.

"I'm so glad to hear it. I wouldn't enjoy it very much if I

was shot by a gun-wielding soldier during my holiday."

Altaf didn't pick up on the irony. "I'm sure that won't happen," he said with a serious expression. "Please don't speak to Chacha Qasim about politics. He's a big cheese in the army."

"Is that so… does he also carry a machine gun?"

"Not that I know of."

"Good."

I didn't sleep very well on the thin mattress that sagged considerably under my weight. The bed covers were clean but didn't smell all that fresh, and I wasn't used to the noises that startled me during the night. Altaf didn't seem to mind. After all, he'd lived on a ship for many years and this was probably as easy as pie for him.

The following day, our nightmarish state of affairs seemed finally over. We didn't go straight to Chacha Qasim's flat but rather fit in a spot of sight-seeing, while our luggage waited in the locked room.

I found the heat oppressive but we had to stop at a park that belonged to a mausoleum to wait for another bus. No soldiers anywhere. Then we made our way to clothing shops and bought a proper Punjabi suit for me. "My goodness, the air is so humid!" I groaned as we stepped into the street and waited for yet another bus.

"That's because Karachi is on the Arabian Sea," Altaf said. "Some days there is an awful lot of moisture in the air." The bus arrived and Altaf sat next to me in the smaller section reserved for women. Apparently, that was alright but women were not allowed in the main section of the bus where most of the men sat. We drove past a mosque and I admired the magnificent building.

"The day after tomorrow, we can go down to the beach if you like. There's always a breeze."

I wiped the sweat from my forehead. "Can't we go there now?"

"No, we can't. Chacha Qasim and Chachi Sabeda are waiting for us." He had already called his uncle and announced our arrival.

So we went to fetch our suitcases and set out to find the new residential area built for Defence Force personnel. Everywhere I looked I could see dust-encrusted building materials lying around and sometimes a road ending in an open field. The bus stopped right next to a pile of concrete pipes and a spanking new shopping complex. Otherwise, there were only flat buildings still waiting to be plastered.

Luckily, we found the address immediately. A pretty young woman opened the door and greeted us with great exuberance. Chachi Sabeda was Altaf's cousin. Three young children pushed noisily past their mother, who charmingly spoke a few English words. She was obviously delighted to meet a woman from Europe.

"Good morning, good morning! You are Germaan?"

"Yes, yes. Mera naam Isabell hé," I proudly said in Urdu.

She was stunned by that. "Ah, tu Urdu bolti hé?" You speak Urdu?

"Ahó." Yes.

"I want speak Angrezy," the young woman insisted. "My name Sabeda."

"Then it's Angrezy, Chachi Sabeda. We can speak English. No problem." I must say that I was taken aback by this. Auntie Sabeda was everything but the venerable old lady I had expected to meet. She was so young and already the mother of two daughters and a son!

Uncle Qasim's flat was airy, cool and rather spacious. A group of prying women huddled together on the smooth concrete floor in the kitchen. They washed and cut and fried something green while they kept glancing in my direction. The vegetables they cooked resembled small gherkins. Great, gherkins I knew rather well. One of the women served us strong and sweet chai tea. Altaf accepted it graciously with a brief grunt and a flicking movement of his hand.

The inquisitive women chatted animatedly in the kitchen. Apparently, they couldn't believe that my hair colour was genuine. I heard the word 'baal'. Hair. Sabeda gingerly touched my ponytail and nodded approvingly. The women laughed. My hair was real! Soon Sabeda's significantly older husband came home and the mood changed in an instant. The women suddenly disappeared and Sabeda retired to another room with her children. Chacha Qasim was a loud, rough-and-ready soldier with a moustache and a sizeable paunch. The plain girl from Altaf's village had been married off at the age of sixteen to her father's cousin. He was also related to Altaf's father, some kind of a frigate captain and seemed to rule his household with an iron fist.

"Salaam Aleikum!" he roared and slapped Altaf on the back.

"Aleikum e Salam," Altaf answered and grimaced a little.

The uncle bellowed. "So Altaf, this is your finacée from Germany?"

"Yes, Chacha Qasim. This is Isabell Bertrand. Isabell, this is my uncle Chacha Qasim," he introduced us.

"It is my pleasure to meet you," I said and stopped myself from trying to shake his hand. The two of them spoke Urdu for a while before we sat down on floor cushions. The two men and I, the European woman.

Dinner was dished up. A platter with chapatis, a type of goulash, the green gherkin-vegetable and some other dishes. Sabeda was not expected to be present. She ate with her children in a separate room.

"This is karela." Altaf pointed to the green gherkins. "A speciality."

I was proud of how nimbly I mastered the art of eating: tearing pieces off the thin chapati, scooping up goulash with it and putting the lot elegantly into my mouth without getting my fingers dirty. However, Chacha Qasim seemed to take this for granted.

"Why doesn't Sabeda join us?" I wanted to know. Chacha Qasim gave me a puzzled look.

"Our women are well-bred. They don't cavort with men."

"But I'm also a woman," I stated the obvious.

Chacha Qasim laughed. "That's a different matter altogether. European women are like men. They behave like men without shame."

"Excuse me?"

I had to suddenly cough and retch. The green gherkin-vegetable was bitter! Incredibly, unbearably bitter! A hollow-eyed, moustachioed Zia ul-Haq found this amusing in his wooden frame on the wall. I couldn't help but spit out the vegetables I had started eating and tried to apologise while being handed a glass of water. "That is way too …bitter!"

I gasped and took another sip of water.

Chacha Qasim watched me critically and grunted before imparting with his opinion on western women. "So, you are already nineteen and still at school?"

He asked as if I was a little retarded.

"Yes, I would like to study and then find a job afterwards."

"I would never allow my wife to work," he said while chewing. "Women who work sooner or later have sex with the men at their place of work. They are expected to do so and it doesn't matter whether they are married or not. We also watch western TV shows here. J.R. Ewing, Dallas."

I nearly choked again. "It's not at all like that in the West. TV series exaggerate things like that to get people to watch them."

Chacha Qasim laughed at me and slapped at a mosquito that had landed on his hairy forearm. He called for insect spray and Sabeda came running into the room at once with a spray can.

"I don't just know this from TV shows. I have first-hand experience," he declared proudly. "The women we encounter in western harbours have no shame at all. They try and have sex with men as quickly as possible."

I was considerably shocked that he spoke to a young woman like me about such matters. But I wasn't a proper woman in his eyes after all. I was shameless like a man.

Could someone of his age really be this vulgar and naive at the same time?

"That's probably because they are prostitutes, who sell themselves to the sailors," I said sharply. "Are there no prostitutes in harbours here in Pakistan?"

"These damned mosquitoes," the uncle bellowed and sprayed all over our food. I suddenly lost my appetite. Altaf put his hand on my arm and I swallowed a stinging remark.

Altaf was rather silent during this peculiar conversation. Chacha Qasim was the uncle who had provided him with the forged passport. He owed the man a certain degree of loyalty.

"We don't have something like that here in Pakistan. Women must be pure and faithful to their husbands. Pak means *pure*. Pakistan is 'the land of the pure'," he lectured me.

Chacha Qasim concluded his diatribe regarding western women and seemed rather content with himself. What was I supposed to say? Of course, he was lying. I was sure of that. Surely there were prostitutes everywhere. I struggled to keep my mouth shut. Chacha Qasim was our host and an influential military man and he was certainly not the kind to invite opposing opinions.

After dinner, I was at long last able to wash with hot water and soap in a clean bathroom that I could lock. Even if the hot water was in a pot and the cold water in a plastic jug that I refilled from a tap. Clean, with my hair washed, I fell asleep on the sofa, despite the heat.

In the morning, I dressed in the wide trousers and light blue tunic, we had bought the previous day. Sabeda fastened the matching veil with a loose knot on my back. The veil was called dabatta.

"This should be fine here in town. If somebody stares at you, just pull the dabatta over your hair. Look down when a man glances at you. It's best if they cannot see your blue eyes."

Altaf had to translate what she said. Zohra had given me similar advice. Sabeda took me into a small storeroom that housed her entire dowry and gave me an olive-green Punjabi suit embroidered with silver sequins along the hemline.

"Here, I want to give you that," Altaf translated. "Put it in your suitcase."

I was grateful for her gesture. "Thank you very much, Sabeda. Shukria merbani," I stammered, touched by her kindness.

"Don't tell my husband about it," she said through Altaf. "He is a good man, just uncouth at times. Don't take offence when he speaks about women like that. I do like you," Sabeda said. She'd been eavesdropping, of course! This woman was anything but a submissive doormat. She had an opinion of her own.

"When we're alone, you can tell me about your life and I will tell you about mine. Altaf won't breathe a word." Altaf winked at me.

"There is something else," she continued. "You brought a guitar with you and I would love to hear you play. Can you play a song for me?"

Her nosy neighbours, the Mrs. Speidels of Karachi, were nowhere to be seen. I was relieved and would not have wanted to sing in front of Chacha Qasim either. He might think that I was a notorious singer from some honky-tonk in a western harbour.

But I didn't mind doing Sabeda a favour and I even enjoyed losing myself in the familiar melody. Sabeda's face brightened as she sat down and listened to my own version of 'Yesterday'. Then she ran off to find her squalling son.

"Come, let's go," Altaf urged me. "We want to see Karachi before evening. First, we go to the mosque in town and then it's off to the beach."

"We also have to send some postcards. Atesh wanted a picture of the border with Afghanistan."

"We can do that in town. There are loads of shops selling postcards. You must send them as soon as possible or we'll be back in Germany before they arrive."

The Memon Mosque, the paved squares and parks of the city were too beautiful for words. I liked that everything was kept clean and admired the intricate design of the buildings. We also saw many more poles topped with the typical white half moon on green flags. I wasn't allowed to set foot in the mosque, so we bought a snack and sat down on a bench outside. I watched the motley crowds and thought of our short visit to Athens.

"You know," I said. "It's not that different here compared to Athens. I mean the traffic is even more chaotic and people dress differently, but I also can't read the street signs here and I don't understand the language. And there are just as many tourists."

"What did you expect?"

"Probably... something totally different. Well, I'm not sure, actually."

"So, you like it here then?"

"What I don't like is that all these beggars have to sit on sidewalks in their filth. Many of them have hands or feet missing. I feel sorry for them. I wonder why everybody tells me that Pakistan's the land of the pure."

We'd pushed a few Paizas into the odd outstretched hand. Not all of the beggars had both their hands.

"According to Islamic law, if they nab you for theft they cut off your left hand. When it happens again, your right hand, then the left foot and so on. Only the most serious crimes justify an execution," Altaf explained.

"You can't be serious!"

"But that's how it is around here. Some of these people are so poor that they mutilate themselves in order to arouse pity."

I observed the forecourt of the mosque then I looked closer. One of the policemen who took care of law and order, swung a long, thin stick, taking a swipe at a lonely beggar who sat on the square.

"Did you see that? He's beating that man!"

I couldn't just sit around and watch. Altaf couldn't believe his eyes as I quickly made a beeline for the moustachioed policeman.

"You cannot do that! You cannot just beat people like that!"

I was mighty upset. The policeman gave me a puzzled look and forgot for a fleeting moment that he was supposed to be the one representing authority here.

"Stop it at once. I mean it! I don't want you to whip this man." I pointed to the impeccable mosque. "This is Allah's house. A divine place. I don't believe for one moment that

Allah wants to see you doing that in front of his house."

The jaded policeman lowered his stick and looked contrite. "I'm sorry, madam, I have my orders that no beggar is allowed to sit on the square in front of the mosque. They harass the tourists." He was truly sorry. The beggar took the opportunity and made a run for it.

"But do you think the tourists want to see something like that? Please find another way to do your job." I looked the man straight in the eye and what I saw was respect.

By now, Altaf had caught up with me and some of the passers-by gawked. He spoke to the policeman and seemed to explain something. The policeman bowed slightly and slunk off.

"Are you nuts? You can't speak to the police like that!" He scolded me.

"And why not? You can't treat people that way. It's simply wrong! And it went alright, didn't it? At least, he stopped hitting the beggar."

"And what if he'd arrested you? This is not Germany, you know."

"Why would he arrest me?"

"That can happen quicker than you think."

Then Altaf told me what he'd said to the policeman. In a society steeped in tradition like the Indian one, one could never be sure who was standing in front of you. A simple woman in the street would never have dared to speak so boldly. That's why the policeman naturally thought that I must belong to a rich and influential family. Altaf hadn't objected to that.

"Please, never ever do something like that again. You have no idea what trouble it might cause. They abuse people in prison here."

He shuddered and I looked straight at him. Had Altaf spent time behind bars before? His mood lightened once we sat down in the rickshaw and were on our way to the Marine Parade.

The coast was covered in mangrove swamps and the breeze was heavenly as we strolled along the ocean beach. I squeezed wet sand with my toes and then let seawater run over my feet. Just as I had done back in Miami.

"It's too hot for this time of year," Altaf apologised for the hot weather. "We should leave Karachi as soon as possible. We can stop at the railway station on the way back to the housing complex and buy tickets to Lahore. From there we will take a bus to Jhelum. One has to reserve a seat on the train as early as possible."

"Okay, let's do that." I watched a group of women, dressed in saris, as they waded into the water until it came up to their tummies. They splashed each others' faces with water and laughed gleefully.

"Why are they not wearing swimsuits?" I asked.

"That would be unseemly. Women are not allowed to show their bodies in swimsuits in public."

"That's why they go for a swim with their clothes on? Isn't it rather unhealthy to walk around in wet clothes all day?"

"Ha, and what about the heat? Saris dry quickly. Why don't you go and have a swim in your clothes?" Altaf chuckled.

"Me? No thank you very much. But what about you?"

We had a lark, splashing each other with seawater and chasing along the pebbly beach until we were out of breath.

A stern-looking man in a long robe scowled at us, which made us laugh even more.

It should remain the most carefree day of my trip to Pakistan.

At the station, it was virtually impossible to get through the crowd to the ticket counter. I had never seen so many people in one place and they all pushed and shoved each other relentlessly. At least, I didn't draw much attention to myself in my shalwar-kamise, as Sabeda called the wide trousers and tunic. Just as I thought that I couldn't take any more of this pushing and shoving, we suddenly stood in front of the ticket counter.

"He says that first class is booked out," Altaf informed me at the top of his voice. "We can still get second class. Then at least we'll have upholstered seats."

"Oh, that's nice."

"Well, if we travel in third class, we won't get much sleep

at all. They'll have first class again only in a week or so."

Altaf bought the second-class tickets to Lahore and was immediately jostled away from the counter. Sweat ran down my back and I struggled to breathe.

"Come this way!" Altaf yelled and we shoved forward along with the rest of the crowd. Somehow we got through the throng and back to the entrance. I took a deep breath and wished that I could just board a train right there and then and leave this suffocating place behind. That's exactly what we did the following day.

The local dress was comfortable and I had practised with Sabeda how to hold my trousers up when tying and untying them. Otherwise I would struggle with it when I had to use the toilet on the train. That's because I had to use the toilet all the time.

"What's the matter with me Altaf? I must have eaten bad food," I complained.

"You just have 'Karachi Belly'," Altaf laughed. "Here, Sabeda gave me tablets for you." Of course, he didn't have any problems with *his* digestion. I secretly praised the prudence of this young woman. I washed the tablets down with Coke and at first, they didn't seem to help one bit. The swaying of the train didn't help either when I had to squat on the steel floor of the toilet and simultaneously hold up the wide trousers.

The long train journey was just as hot and dusty as I had expected. The seats in the long compartment were packed with people and many sat atop their luggage. Chickens in a cage clucked away, children cried and men chatted noisily from one end to the other.

"It'll get better once we're out of the suburbs," Altaf said and he was right. Once we'd left the suburbs behind, the number of passengers decreased dramatically and the trip started becoming more bearable.

At every stop, food vendors walked up and down the platform and yelled: "Lassi, lasseee, lassi, lasseee." Many passengers bought the refreshing yoghurt drink.

"Would you like a glass?" My travel companion asked.

"No, not really. I'd rather have a Coke or Sprite. I'm terribly thirsty and my head hurts." I'd thought the 'cockroach hotel' was the worst thing that could happen to me on 'Planet Pakistan' and now I was sick.

I didn't want to complain endlessly like a spoilt brat, so I slept most of the time leaning against Altaf's shoulder. Hours later, we arrived in Lahore and made our way to the bus rank where we had to wait around for quite some time standing in the red dust right next to some big monument.

That was no cakewalk for me in the hot sun. I waited alone guarding our luggage, while Altaf bought us food and something to drink.

I couldn't help but notice the stares in my direction. None of the other women was as tall and light-skinned as I was. Once my veil slid down and the crowd murmured. I threw it back over my head with a practised move and the murmuring stopped.

"Am I glad you're back!" I whispered when Altaf stood next to me again. He held a bag with samosas and Coca-Cola bottles.

"Why, are you feeling that ill?"

"Yes, but apart from that, people here are eyeballing me."

"Of course they are. When do they ever get to see a woman like you? They probably think that you're some kind of film star. There are quite a few light-coloured members in my family but they usually don't take the train or bus."

"How do *they* travel?"

"They usually fly and a car comes to fetch them. But the likes of us are too poor to buy air tickets all the time." He opened one of the Coke bottles for me.

"I wish the border with India was open, then we could go and do some sight-seeing on the other side. But our governments are at loggerheads again and the border is closed."

"I'm too tired anyway," I sighed, "and too hot."

I felt a bit unsteady on my legs and had to sit down on the red suitcase. I bit a piece off my second samosa and chewed it listlessly while I watched the over-the-top decorated buses.

They were even more colourful than the buses I had seen in Karachi.

Soon, a whole lot of these buses came rolling into the square, enveloped in a red dust cloud and hooting like mad. We boarded a bus bound for Jhelum and our luggage was stowed away on top of the roof of the bus.

I kept my guitar with me, because who knew what would happen to it on top of the bus in between all those suitcases and boxes? Again, we spent hours sitting down but I was in luck: my tummy behaved itself this time. People weren't as exacting in the overland buses when it came to separating men and women and I sat on a normal seat next to Altaf.

"Does the music have to be that loud?" I grouched.

"Yes, otherwise, all you hear is hooting." That was true, as the bus drivers seemed unable to manage driving without using an arsenal of hellish klaxons.

"Why do they have to hoot all the time?"

"That's just how it is. I think the bus drivers want to show off how important they are or just say hello to each other."

"How cute."

Whenever the bus came to a halt at a stop along the tarred road, enterprising men climbed aboard and peddled their wares. They got off at the next stop and the bus driver received his cut.

A Chinese dental practitioner demonstrated his services with a range of false teeth, pliers and mirrors. They were neatly exhibited on a vendor's tray, covered in red felt. He handed out pamphlets that I was unable to read. At the next bus stop, pieces of luggage were hurled down from the top right into the dust. Somebody called: "Lassi, lasseee, lassi, lasseee!" and money and glasses were exchanged through open windows.

In the aisle, the usual commercial scenarios played out. A boy carried something on his shoulder that resembled a tiny human with a shaved head. "Look at that!" I nudged Altaf in the ribs.

It was a completely shaved monkey, dressed like a human, wearing a collar and chain around its neck. The boy held onto the chain while the little guy climbed back and forth between the boy's shoulders.

The monkey did little tricks but, most of the time, stood on two legs while the boy walked up and down the aisle to collect money from the passengers.

"Give him something!" I urged Altaf.

"Alright, here's one rupee. That's enough." He waved the boy over and pressed a banknote into his hand. The tiny ape embraced the boy and gave him little kisses on his forehead. I watched the two of them how they climbed down the steps and disappeared into the next bus.

"It's quite an ugly brother he's got there," Altaf said dryly.

"Oh come on that was a monkey, wasn't it?"

Altaf just grinned. The bus driver hooted and we carried on along the bumpy westbound road.

"Are you hungry?" Altaf asked and held out the oily paper bag with the samosas he had bought in Lahore.

"No thanks, I'd rather have another Coke. It's so stifling and hot in here." Then in the blink of an eye, I fell asleep again.

"Wake up, Isabell, we're almost in Jhelum."

"Are we there yet?" I yawned all confused.

"It's still quite a way until we get to Khadriala."

The bus stopped at the edge of town and I got off the bus on wobbly legs as our luggage was carefully handed down from the roof. We stood in front of a row of small shops and I was eating a samosa. We walked into one of the shops to buy something to drink. It was time to take one of the tablets that Sabeda had bought for me back in Karachi.

A few giggling children stood in front of me and pointed at my hair. I fastened the dabatta around my head and turned away. The children began to pluck at my sleeves.

"He, chalo chalié!" Altaf cried and the children ran away. He was already speaking to one of the rickshaw drivers outside. Apparently, there was no bus service to his village and we had no time to waste.

The sun was already low in the sky and sinking fast.

"We must leave right now. The rickshaw driver refuses to

drive back into town in the dark."

"Okay, then let's hurry up," I said weakly and sat on the back seat one moment later.

Altaf hadn't said much during our train trip but as we sat in the back of the rickshaw, wedged between our suitcases, he became more talkative. The rickshaw huffed and puffed along a rough dirt road that took us through wheat fields and past a herd of goats. Then we continued along a broad canal. The goats held us up for a while and the driver yelled and waved at them impatiently.

"The canal is there for the irrigation of the fields. They divert the water from the Jhelum river. My village is pretty close to the river. It's huge and sometimes floods the entire area, but there is a deep moat around the village and a thick wall to keep it at bay."

"Really?" I said and took a sip from my Sprite bottle. The sun slowly disappeared behind the trees and the rickshaw driver raced down the road as if the devil was chasing after him.

"I'm sure that Chacha Qasim has called them already," Altaf said. "There are no telephones in Khadriala but my uncle in Jhelum has a phone at work and he probably sent somebody home with a message. They will be expecting us."

"As long as I don't have to walk a mile…" I was tired but with all the rumbling it was impossible to get some shut-eye. The driver was very annoyed when we had to make a brief stop so I could disappear in the green wheat field. There just hadn't been any time for this business in Jhelum.

We didn't make it before nightfall. The rickshaw driver stopped about a kilometer from the village and refused to continue another inch. Altaf wanted part of his money back and the two of them argued. The argument ended with the driver pushing our suitcases onto the ground.

"What's the matter?" I asked faintly. I couldn't really understand what they were fighting about.

"He wants to go back to Jhelum and doesn't want to return any of the money I've already paid him to take us all the way. Now we must carry our suitcases to the village."

I looked at him aghast. "How far is it?"

"Twenty minutes, perhaps."

"What?!"

The rickshaw had already turned around and soon we heard only a faint humming in the distance. Altaf lifted his fist and swore like a sailor after this heartless man.

"Maybe I should stay here and you go and fetch somebody who can help us carry the suitcases," I suggested.

"That's not safe. We'd better start walking."

"But I'm so exhausted. I've lugged the red suitcase this far."

"Wait, I'll take your suitcase. It's heavier than mine."

What choice did I have but to pick up the bag and the smaller suitcase, the guitar on my back and stumble after Altaf through the near-darkness? I kept an eye on the red suitcase until I could barely see it anymore. Just when I thought I'd be unable to take another step, the outline of a high wall came into sight just behind an earth mound through which the narrow trail cut its way.

"That's it. That's Khadriala. Here, sit down, I'll get somebody to come and help us."

"Thank goodness, I'm totally beat," I moaned, sat down on the red suitcase and held my guitar in a tight embrace while waiting obediently in the silent darkness. On my own. Only a few sleepy cows mooed softly.

Khadriala seemed to be encased in a very high and very thick wall and not even the roofs of the houses inside showed. I could feel something wet on my hand... like a snout! I froze. Were there stray dogs around here or even prowling tigers?

The thought frightened me. I'd heard absolutely nothing approach! One glimpse was enough to confirm that just a damp flower that had touched my hand. The sky grew pitch dark and I began to contemplate whether it would be a good idea to just lie down and go to sleep. No, stay awake, I cautioned myself.

After what seemed like an eternity, torches flared up. I saw a massive, iron-bound wooden gate open. A drawbridge was lowered. *A drawbridge? That's just like the Middle Ages*, I thought. Then the villagers came darting towards me along the footpath. Relief. Hands helped me stand up and some boys carried our luggage across the wooden drawbridge into the fortress. "Salaam aleikum," I heard voices all around me. "Salaam aleikum."

"Aleikum e salaam. Shukria merbani," I thanked them.

We reached the gigantic gate and I found myself inside the fortress, walking on rugged cobblestone roads. The narrow roads were framed by housewalls, illuminated by torches in sturdy iron rings. Their light shone the way to Altaf's house. Small girls walked next to me and each wanted to hold at least one finger of my hand. I pulled back instinctively.

"Don't worry, let them hold your hand. You're the first white woman they've ever seen. That's something special here in Khadriala."

"Excuse me, they've never seen someone like me?" I marvelled.

"People don't get out much."

An older woman moved towards me, indicating that she wanted to put a flower garland around my neck. I had to bow my head as I was much taller than the village-women. Then she greeted me with a festive speech I did not understand.

"Shukria, shukria merbani," I thanked her and the chatter around me rose again. Altaf also had a flower garland put around his neck and it looked as if we were in Hawaii. I was completely unprepared for such an enthusiastic welcome.

"You never breathed a word that I would be something so special around here. My goodness, they make me feel like some celebrity!" My energy was on the wane and I was longing to just sit down. Instead, I stumbled along the cobblestone roads and smiled into beaming faces. Hands were reaching for me, steadying me.

"Who in God's name are all these people?"

"Family. I'm related to almost everybody in the village," Altaf said.

"The whole village?"

"Yes."

It was a surreal experience yet somehow it seemed all familiar to me: the greeting rituals, the torches and the garlands. Just a little different.

We walked past illuminated house walls and wooden gates until we were led through an open doorway. This had to be Altaf's home, his parents' house. A dark roof-covered passage lay ahead of us and behind it a dimly lit inner yard.

"Are we there at last?"

"Yes we are, come this way. Do you see the door here on the right with the steps in front?"

The door was right by the gate. "Yes."

"That's the guest room and we have to go inside."

I gave the inner yard one last glance but I couldn't see much apart from a few doors. Then I entered a whitewashed room through the green double-winged door. There was a bed in the middle of the room that was pushed against the wall at once. Directly underneath the grinning, hollow-eyed president of the country.

"Go, sit on the bed," Altaf told me.

"You don't have to tell me twice." All I wanted to do was put my head on a pillow and close my eyes. But that didn't happen.

"Hey, you can't go to sleep yet. First, we must greet all the visitors outside," Altaf cried.

"Why must we do *that*?" Visitors in the middle of the night! I couldn't understand why Altaf hadn't prepared me for this.

"It's the custom around here."

"Can I at least have something to drink?" I begged.

"Mushtaq!" A boy of about fifteen instantly appeared in the doorframe.

"This is my youngest brother, Mushtaq," Altaf introduced him. The boy grinned and looked shyly to the side.

"Please bring us some chapatis and chai."

"Yes, big brother."

He had to fight his way through a crowd trying to push into the room. This, I found scary. "Are you serious? What do they want from me? Can't we greet them tomorrow? Why does it have to be now? It's getting late."

"The people are curious. We have to at least greet the elders. That can take a while and tomorrow morning, we'll receive the others."

"Oh no! Can't I at least freshen up a bit? I also have to go urgently… well, you know what I mean."

Altaf called a young woman by the name of Shireen, who accompanied me through the dark passage to a dark room with a water pump. She put the lamp on the floor and left the room. I assumed that this was the bathroom. It was equipped with a cement floor and a handpump, that was it. Shireen waited outside. I made an attempt at washing myself in the dim light of the lamp. The dirty water ran into a gutter that led outside.

Shireen held the lamp up as I opened the door, and stared glumly at the gutter. She went to fetch a bucket and rinsed the unspeakable into the street. Apparently, one wasn't allowed to answer the call of nature in here. But if not in here, then where?

"Here, have something to eat and drink," Altaf said as I sat cross-legged next to him on the bed once again.

There was no time to ask him any questions. Masses of people who filed past us asked him one question after the other and gave me furtive glances.

I understood nothing and wearily ate a piece of chapati. Cups with strongly sweetened chai were poured and put on a small decorated table. I drank thirstily and was introduced to yet another group of elderly villagers.

"Salaam Aleikum."

"Aleikum e Salaam." I smiled like there was no tomorrow and endured their curiousity. At some stage, I was unable to keep my eyes open, placed my head on a pillow and drifted off into a deep, dreamless sleep.

CHAPTER SIX

"Morning!" Altaf was already up. Somebody had tucked me in and he had fallen asleep on the bed right next to me.

Strange, I thought. At uncle Qasim's flat, we had slept in separate rooms, because moral customs were rather strict and we weren't married. Was this any different in the country?

In the daylight, I saw that the guestroom had small windows facing the street, and that a stack of framed pictures was hidden behind a chest of drawers by the windows.

"Oh, that's got to do with politics," Altaf explained. "The pictures only come out when it's absolutely necessary. How are you feeling today?"

I listened within for a moment. "I think I feel better. I'm thirsty, though. Could I perhaps have something to drink?"

Someone brought us breakfast. Then the first visitors of the day began to hammer against the door.

"Savaar. Salaam Aleikum."

"Aleikum e Salaam."

As was to be expected, I didn't understand any of the conversations.

Mushtaq ushered one group out and the next group already pushed into the room. He went and fetched more tea.

"Shouldn't I, at least, introduce myself to your parents?" I asked and downed my third cup of chai. The black tea was boiled with milk, sugar and cardamom and I slowly got used to the taste.

"There's no rush. Plus, they saw you last night."

"Really? I don't remember meeting them," I said. "Why do all these people have to see us so urgently? I feel like a politician on a state visit or a circus attraction or something."

"They think that you are special."

"You're kidding, they're not all here just because of me! I thought they wanted to come and visit *you*."

"Why not? I explained it to you yesterday," Altaf said with pride and added, "I'm sure there are not that many of them left."

But the stream of visitors continued until late morning. In between seeing groups of people, I somehow managed to go to the bathroom. In the end, Altaf's mother, a corpulent matron with gentle eyes and a firm voice, sent away the last of the villagers and the queue outside gradually dissipated.

A few older men looked offended but Amma's authority extended even to the old men. "Vaqt hé, chalo. Time to go."

I immediately took a liking to her. When she laughed, little apple cheeks appeared on both sides of her fleshy nose. Amma loved to laugh and did so heartily. She closed the red curtains and two giggling girls brought in a bowl with hot water. Altaf left the room. I smiled thankfully at the girls, which made them giggle even more.

Had I fallen asleep again?

Imran and Nusrat race each other into the copse outside the village wall. 'I can aim much better than you,' she cries, takes an arrow from the quiver and sends it into a slender tree. 'Well done, Nusrat, now it's my turn…' I slowly opened my eyes and dozed off again from sheer exhaustion.

"Hey Isabell, wake up, it's getting late."

The room was bathed in a gentle, red light and was completely quiet. Hard to believe that there had been a continuous stream of visitors not too long ago. I sat up with a start. "What time is it?"

"It's three in the afternoon. You must get out of bed now. Hakim is here," Altaf announced.

"Who is Hakim?"

"He's a bit like the village doctor and he'll give you something for your tummy problem. Amma summoned him."

I quickly got dressed in the green suit Sabeda had given me. There was a soft knock on the door. "Atcha!" Come in.

Two girls entered with a serving tray laden with chapatis

and chai, and a metal bowl full of steaming water. One of the girls was not particularly pretty with her moustache and coarse hair was welling up from under her veil. She stared grimly ahead and put her tray on the small table.

"Salaam Aleikum."

The girl darted an adoring glance at Altaf but he didn't pay any attention to her. Then she gave me a look filled with hatred. I flinched.

"Shertan!" She hissed. "Shertan!" I knew that word. 'Shertan' - devil!

"Shukria merbani," I thanked her uneasily. This was obviously a mistake because it produced an even nastier stare and a flood of fiercely angry swearing. Where had Altaf gone to? Amma opened the green double-winged door. "Hai, Saïda, chalo!" She brought the village doctor with her.

Saïda stared at me one last time before both girls covered their hair with veils and crept out without another word. I drank a little of the chai and could only hope that the irate Saïda hadn't spit in it.

To me, Hakim didn't look at all like a doctor. He was bald and had jet black, cunning eyes that quickly took in all the necessary facts. His earlobes were incredibly elongated and he wore heavy metal rings at the bottom of the long slits.

Altaf came back into the room and interpreted for me.

"When did the problem start?" The village doctor wanted to know.

"Three days after my arrival in Pakistan."

"Ahó, and was there any vomiting?"

"No, only diarrhoea."

"Where does it hurt?" I showed him where I was feeling pain. He didn't ask me to undress and at no point did Hakim touch me. He contemplated the symptoms for a moment then spoke rapidly to Altaf and his mother. They both nodded and gave him the required information. Hakim said goodbye and left.

"That was it?" I asked in surprise.

"He will send some medicine for you later. It needs to be

freshly prepared but I'm sure it'll help you."

"Nothing poisonous, I hope."

"No, Hakim is an excellent healer, otherwise he would have been kicked out of the village long ago. I've known him since I was a little boy."

"What did he say?" I wanted to know.

"I can't explain it to you."

"Okay, well I think it's time for me to brush my teeth." I jumped up from the bed. "Good, my tummy is giving me some peace."

"Alright, I have to go now anyway. See you later," Altaf said and was about to take off again.

"Hey, wait a minute! What was going on with this girl Saïda just now? Why was she so angry at me?"

"Ah, just ignore her."

Before I could ask him any more questions, Altaf had already disappeared through the gate. I groaned in frustration but what was I supposed to do? I brushed my teeth and decided to go out myself. The big gate to the street was wide open. Perhaps it was a good idea to take a walk and have a closer look at the village. I carefully stepped into the cobbled road. On the other side of the passageway, I could see the inner courtyard, framed all around by doors to longish rooms. Amma had to be somewhere inside the courtyard.

A few women sat around an open fireplace and made chapatis in flat pans. One of them ladled clarified butter from a large tin into a cooking pot. I had already learned that this *ghee* was used for cooking. Watching them use so much butter alone made my arteries clog up. I plucked up my courage and walked towards the group.

"Salaam Aleikum."

"Aleikum e Salaam," a choir of friendly voices greeted me back. The unfriendly girl who obviously couldn't stand me sat leaning against the back wall. She kept quiet and just stared at me as if she was ready to throw stones.

Shireen jumped up and spoke with me in broken English. She had a friendly, round face and her eyes twinkled intelligently from under long lashes.

"Oh hello Shireen, we have already met," I greeted her. "I'm Isabell." She smelled of jasmine-scented hair oil. Sweet and intense. By now I was able to distinguish it from a whole array of strange smells.

Shireen looked slightly confused. "Yes, Isabella. Not Urdu…? I can English. We speak."

"Thank you, that's nice of you. Unfortunately, I can speak neither Punjabi nor Urdu," I replied.

"Oh thank you, yes." She said and seemed to reflect on something. "I want to go to London."

"To London?" I was taken aback.

"Yes, can you help me... go to London?"

"I… believe, I can't. Why would you want to go there?"

"I want to see the world... like you. Before I get married."

I didn't quite know how to respond to that. "Don't you want to introduce me to the other women here?" I asked. The women stared at us, enthralled by Shireen's language skill. She was able to communicate with the stranger! Saïda grumbled something and was summarily ignored.

"I am saying names of woman here," Shireen declared.

She introduced me to the other women but it wasn't easy for me to remember all their names. Even though I repeated every single one of them, I forgot the names rather quickly.

I had already made the acquaintance of Amma, Altaf's mother, then there was the stout Meera, Altaf's sister-in-law with her young daughter Miri. Next were three women whose names I simply couldn't memorise no matter how hard I tried.

"Meera is married to Altaf's older brother. He is a captain in the army. Comes for shaadi – wedding, on special leave," she said.

"I see, is he on his way?"

"Yes, he comes from army. They have a room here." Shireen pointed to an entrance right next to the passage. One could hear a baby cry and Meera disappeared inside. She returned carrying her baby son.

"His name is Farooq like his father," Shireen explained

but we were still busy with introductions. It was the ill-tempered, moustachioed girl's turn.

"This is Saïda."

I already knew that. "Hello Saïda," I said in a friendly tone but she didn't seem interested and avoided my gaze. The women were embarrassed and I asked myself what could possibly make Saïda behave this way. Perhaps, she just didn't like Europeans?

Shireen was already pointing to another young woman who came walking towards us from the passage, holding the hands of two little boys.

"This is Mandira and child. She is wife of Altaf's cousin. She stays in our street." Shireen pointed to the gate.

Mandira resembled Shireen with her friendly, round face but she seemed bashful and barely dared look my way. Her boys had remarkably blue eyes and dark-blond curls.

"This is Altaf's father, Babu," Shireen finished her introductions.

I hadn't noticed the man before. Babu sat quietly in the shadows by one of the doors on a bed frame with a surface of woven strings. He was very thin and looked like a much older version of Altaf. And he seemed to be in his own world.

"Salaam Aleikum. Mera naam Isabell hé," I addressed him politely. Babu fixated me with a vacant stare and said nothing. Later, I would learn that he'd been arrested after Altaf had left the country, and had come back a changed man. The women laughed. They tried to pronounce my name.

"Isaba, Isa, Isabella,"

"Yes, close: Isabell," I repeated.

The women laughed themselves silly. Even the sullen Saïda couldn't help but crack a smile.

"You have beautiful hair. Chubsuret," Shireen blurted out and the women started giggling again. Saïda returned to her glum expression. *Chubsuret* meant beautiful. I had learned that word back in Karachi.

"Why do you cut your hair?" Shireen wanted to know.

My hair was far from short, falling over my shoulders, but

in Pakistan, it couldn't compete with the magnificent long hair most women preferred. Even Shireen's hair came down to her hips.

"It isn't short where I come from," I answered.

Shireen translated what I had said and the women oohed and aahed about this new way of styling ones hair. They soon took turns in touching my hair. Miri brought a hairbrush and two plastic clips and proceeded to pin up my hair. I didn't mind that, even if she pinched me a little.

"Your eyes are blue."

"Yes, I know. But I've also seen people with blue eyes and blond hair around here."

"Yes, but your hair and your eyes are European. From far away. Chubsuret," Shireen said and smiled.

"Thank you so much. Do you think I could freshen up a bit? I'd like to have a look around the village just now."

Shireen was simply overwhelmed by this flood of words and I had to repeat what I'd said at a slower pace.

"Ahó, to wash…" She took me to the big window-less room with its cement floor and water pump. "You can wash here."

"Isn't there a loo somewhere nearby?"

"Loo? No." She had to laugh. "No loo. You do Number One here…" She pointed to the gutter that ran into the street along the house wall and underneath the stairs to the guestroom. "Number Two outside in the field. This evening it's women's turn."

Oh dear! The fleeting image of village women queueing in front of a pit latrine crossed my mind. In Germany, in the Middle Ages, it had probably not been much different.

"This evening?"

"Yes, always like that."

"My tummy."

"Still aching?"

"No, but I have no tablets left."

I gesticulated and Shireen understood. "Wait." She ran back into the yard and chatted to Amma. On her return, she said: "Make fresh. We go walk."

I followed her out of the yard and into the narrow street, through the village and then through another iron-plated gate towards the river.

"Go this way. I will guard." Just as the previous day, I went into the green wheat field that offered scant privacy.

"Better?" she asked when I re-emerged from the plants. "Yes, much better! Shukria merbani."

We walked back along the path towards the gate when I saw a rather old man enjoying the afternoon sun, sitting cross-legged on a bedstead made of woven string. This was an excellent vantage point. The old man had a henna-red beard and looked rather frail but his white suit was impeccable. We greeted each other with a smile. "Salaam Aleikum."

"Aleikum e Salaam, Batshi." He called me little daughter. I had the curious feeling as if I knew him from somewhere.

"Who is that man, Shireen?" A horde of curious children began to follow us. The girls wanted to hold my hand.

"Oh, we just call him 'Baba Ali'. He sits every day and waiting to die."

"He's waiting to die?" I was surprised.

"Yes, he is old. His wife die long ago. He wants to die," Shireen said as if it was the most natural thing in the world.

In the following days, 'Baba Ali' and I became friends. Sometimes in the afternoon, we sat on the bedframe and chatted, even though we couldn't actually understand what we were saying. Despite this obstacle, we understood each other on a different level that had nothing to do with language.

Why are you so worried? He seemed to ask, *you'll see everything will be alright.* The villagers just shook their heads when they saw us but we barely noticed them. We just understood each other. When his youngest son came at nightfall and carefully picked up 'Baba Ali' to carry him home, it was also time for me to leave.

Here, nobody was neglected, not even in their ripe old age. They even took a picture of us sitting next to each other on the bedstead. I sat next to 'Baba Ali' and the old man had an otherworldly smile on his face just like a saint...

When Shireen and I returned to the yard, Amma showed me a small, corked glass bottle. Hakim had prepared the medicine and sent it over. The powder inside the bottle looked greyish-brown and tasted hideous. I was told to take it twice a day with water.

I immediately swallowed the first dosage and my tummy recovered with astonishing speed.

With one problem solved, the next dilemma was just waiting to happen. There were no longer special favours for me as the bathroom was strictly reserved for Number Ones. I was expected to fall into line with everybody else in the village. And they did it not in a latrine pit but directly onto a fallow field outside the medieval village walls.

That's where the men went before sunrise and the women after sunset.

"Come, Isabella, we leaving," Shireen said and I looked up from my magazine. "Outside to make toilet."

We used the same path through the iron-clad back gate we had walked through in the afternoon, then joined the throng of women who also headed out to the toilet. I only realised what that meant when we stood on the field and the first lot of wide trousers dropped to the ground. The field was about as private as a bus stop in town.

"I'm supposed to do that?" I asked Shireen but she was already busy squatting next to Meera. That couldn't be true! But I had no choice. Either now or after nightfall tomorrow. I found a spot as close to the edge of the field as possible and hurried through the process.

Thank you, Altaf, thank you very much! I thought angrily. Where had my host disappeared to again? I hadn't seen him since Hakim's visit.

I felt incredibly embarrassed by the whole thing. The fact there were toilet rules of this nature had never crossed my mind. I gave it some thought and came to the conclusion that the good old Bertrands had probably done it just like that on their country estates in France. I realised how spoilt I was: enjoying the daily luxury of running hot water from a tap on demand, toilet paper and toilets one could sit on.

Altaf came back hours later. Two village girls were busy brushing my hair while I wrote in my notebook. Before that, I had played a song for them on my guitar. They giggled when Altaf walked into the room and left hurriedly.

"Where have you been all this time?" I berated him. "It was sheer luck that Shireen speaks some English otherwise I would have been in a fix."

"I had stuff to do. Aren't the girls looking after you? You know that things are different here: men and women don't spend that much time together."

"Is that so? Shireen was nice enough to take me to the village toilet."

"Well, then you have everything you need," he said without missing a beat. "Shireen's my cousin. She went to school in Jhelum and that's why she can speak some English."

"Oh, did she graduate from high school?"

"No. She'll soon get married to my cousin Zaheer. The family council decided that she'd been in school long enough. Zaheer lives on the other side of the village. They are no longer allowed to see each other until their wedding," he explained.

I didn't get it. "Who decided that she'd been in school long enough?"

"The council of family elders. They decide on things like that."

"And she had no say in the matter?"

"She likes Zaheer."

"Mhmm. Another marriage out of love, then?"

"So to speak, but the elders must arrange it."

"If they do all that, do you have any choice in the matter? What if Shireen changes her mind?"

"I don't know." He seemed to lose interest in the topic. "What have you been doing with yourself today?"

I told him that Shireen introduced me to his father and the women in the yard and about me meeting 'Baba Ali'. There was a knock on the door and Mushtaq carried a metal tray with food and chai into the room. *I'm sure my stomach can take normal food by now*, I thought and began to choke on the spicy saalen. Meat and potato pieces swam around a very oily sauce that was red with chilli powder. Altaf gave me water to drink until I could breathe normally again. I should have known better.

"Eat some yoghurt with that, it mellows the heat of the food."

"I thought it was used as a spice but this is devilish," I wheezed and took another sip of water for good measure.

"That's how we eat in Pakistan. Sabeda was cooking extra mild food for you, also because of the children. They often can't take all that chilli."

"That was mild? Why on earth do you need so much chilli in your food?"

"We are just used to it. Maybe you should eat something else."

"Like what? I don't want to be the spoilt brat who wants special treatment all the time. My tummy is much better now."

"Then the girls can wash off the meat and potatoes. That'll take the heat away. They also do that for the little ones."

"Okay, if it doesn't make any trouble. I don't want everybody to look at me like Saïda did today."

Altaf seemed embarrassed. "Sorry about that. I'll have a word with her."

I devoured a piece of chapati. "Why does she call me 'devil'? Does she also think that Western women are all prostitutes - like Chacha Qasim?"

"Don't let her upset you. I'll talk to her," he repeated.

"Good."

There was another knock on the door. Altaf's brother Mushtaq entered with a friendly-looking man who was introduced to me as Chacha Sardar, an uncle on their father's side. He had just arrived from Islamabad for the wedding. Chacha Sardar was around fifty and sported the most sizeable moustache so far, just like the Rajput nobles I'd remembered. "Salaam Aleikum."

"Aleikum e Salaam."

Altaf probably explained to him why my eyes looked so

teary and why I was gasping because he asked: "What do you normally eat?"

Whoopee, somebody else who spoke English.

"Oh, definitely not spicy food like that," I answered. "We don't eat much chilli at all. I often eat bread with butter and honey."

Chacha Sardar gave Altaf a deprecating look. "I could try to get hold of my brother and ask him to send us some honey. His farm is not far from Islamabad where he has bee hives and surely enough honey for your needs. There will be more relatives arriving for the wedding and I'm sure that somebody can bring it with. Mushtaq, can you ask the women to churn some butter?"

"Aho, Chacha Sardar," Mushtaq answered obediently. Mushtaq was shy but his smile was just as radiant as Altaf's. I knew that he was learning English at his boarding school in Jhelum but he didn't have the courage to speak to me. He had been granted a few days off for the wedding.

"Chacha Sardar is a civil servant in Islamabad," Altaf put me in the picture. "He works for the armed forces."

"That's interesting," I said. "But I must say that I find soldiers rather scary. Like the ones we saw in Karachi."

"Patrols are unfortunately necessary in the name of law and order," Chacha Sardar said. "My job is not very interesting. Only desk work." His eyes were gentle and had a glow about them, just like Altaf's eyes.

"Uncle's wife died last year and they had no children. Now he's a bit lonely all on his own in Islamabad. He's planning to move back to Khadriala after his retirement."

"I don't believe that this young lady is interested in matters like that, Batsha." He called Altaf little son. "It's time for me to visit the rest of the clan and I'm sure that your wife would like to go to sleep."

"I'm not his…" Altaf interrupted me with a flood of Punjabi words and involved the uncle in a discussion as he led him and Mushtaq outside.

He seemed displeased when he returned. "You can't tell

anyone that we are not married, Isabell!"

"What, you told your family that we are married?" I couldn't believe it. "In Greece we were engaged and now we're already married? That's why they let us sleep in the guest room. Why are you lying?"

"You don't understand things like that," he said sheepishly.

"Exactly! I don't understand it at all."

"No, You don't understand why I said that."

"Very well, then explain it to me. Explain to me why you make up stories about me and you," I demanded.

"Men and women who are not related can't just travel around the way we do. You would have to sleep in the big room at the back of the yard with all the unmarried women. We'll be reassigned to other quarters soon enough when Nasra, Farooq's bride, arrives in a few days. I thought it would be best for you to live this way at first," he explained.

"You could have at least told me about it. Getting married is a serious matter." It was hard to admit but I could understand his point of view.

"Yes, I know. I'm really sorry. Please don't be angry with me. Things are different here. Can you forgive me?"

"Alright. Forgiven," I said with some trepidation but decided to be understanding. I was about to find out how *different* things really were.

The following morning, my supposed 'husband' left the house early and returned later for breakfast. Monotonous singing that came from creaking loudspeakers had woken me up but thankfully the noise had soon stopped.

"Okay then, what is planned for today?" I asked enthusiastically.

"I thought you wanted to get some rest."

"I'm feeling better. If I do nothing but sit around, I'll get cabin-fever. Are you still busy or can you get away from whatever you are doing?"

"We could take a walk to the river," Altaf suggested. "There's often a cool breeze down there."

Again, we walked along the streets past the façades of

village homes and through the back gate. It was only late morning but the promise of a hot day already hung in the air.

"My mother wants me to buy some fabric and have a light shalwar-kamise made for you by her tailor in Jhelum. If you like we could go into town on Zaheer's motorbike." That was going better than expected.

"Oh good, then I get to see a bit of the area."

"Yes, last time it was way too dark."

We walked down the same path, Shireen and I had taken the day before. 'Baba Ali' wasn't at his usual place at the top by the gate yet.

"We can go to the fruit trees over there," Altaf suggested. "I want to show you something." The fruit trees were planted in orderly rows close to the Jhelum river.

We ambled along the path between the trees. Altaf broke two green twigs from one of the young trees and peeled the bark off one end. He gave me one of the twigs and began to chew on his.

"Why are you doing that?" I asked him.

"It's like a toothbrush. Toothbrushes haven't been around for that long. This is how people have always cleaned their teeth."

"Really, with twigs?"

"Yes. We have special trees for that but fruit trees also do the job."

I chewed on my twig until the one end was all fibrous while watching the expanse of the broad river. The other shore was so far away that you couldn't see it. "This river is huge," I marvelled.

"Yes, during the monsoon season, it becomes a problem. Luckily, the village was built on a mound and the moat fills up with water from the river when it rises."

I could barely imagine a rainy season like this monsoon. It was way too hot and dry for that right now.

"I hope I'm no longer here when that happens. We have enough rain back in Germany. Sunshine is much nicer when I'm on holiday."

"I'll see what I can do for you, madam."

We continued along the path between the fruit trees. It was peaceful by the river and the air was cooler. "What kind of cows are those?" I asked and watched the herd of animals a cowherd had led to drink by the river. Their horns were massive and they had lappets hanging from their necks.

"They are Brahmans. As far as I know, they are more buffalos than cows."

"I wouldn't want a lone encounter with them in the field."

"They are actually quite tame."

We passed a couple of huts outside of the village walls. Women were squatting atop the flat roofs and shaped flat cakes from a pile and slapped them onto the roofs and walls.

"What are these women doing?"

"They are making pats from cow dung, then dry them in the sun. They are used as fuel in the hearth fires. We don't have a lot of wood for that."

"They touch the cow dung with their bare hands?" I shuddered.

"Of course, that's how it's done around here. They naturally wash their hands afterwards." Altaf had to laugh at my ignorance. A woman walked past us with a bundle on her head.

"She looks very poor, not like the other women in the village," I said.

"Even here, we have poor people. They look after the animals and work in the fields. They work for the villagers."

"Do Muslims also have a caste system like the Hindus?"

"No, but some people are wealthier than others."

"Are there Hindus around here?"

"Not many. When India and Pakistan were separated, almost all of the Hindus went to India and the Muslims went to live in Pakistan and Bangladesh. We had civil war back then."

"Genuine, civil war?"

"Yes, didn't you know that?"

"No, it's impossible to know everything. I've heard about Mahatma Gandhi, and that Britain was occupying India at some stage but that's about it."

"Yes, India wasn't exactly a peaceful country back then. At

the moment, both governments are arguing again. Sometimes, war breaks out between the countries."

"Not right now, I hope."

"No, you can relax."

We walked past huts that huddled close together. Tangy-smelling smoke rose from the huts; probably burning cow dung. Another village came into sight far in the distance and a long, slender tower.

"What kind of a tower is this?"

"It's a mosque. Muezzins sit right at the top and sing and call the people to prayer. I've been there a few times since we arrived. The village over there also belongs to our family, by the way. But it is not so nice. We come from Muslim and Rajput stock and they are just Muslims."

I pricked my ears. "You also have Rajput ancestors?"

Altaf hadn't heard the *also* part.

"Yes, that's a long time ago. We are Muslim now."

So, hundreds of years ago, the noblewoman Nusrat was not allowed to marry outside of her caste and now, there were actually clans that had Rajput and Muslim ancestors! Of course, Altaf knew nothing of my regressions with Dr. Albrecht. I didn't really want to share this with him. He would probably just have laughed at me.

The droning singing in the morning had come from the muezzin on the tower then who called on the people to pray. After a while, I got used to the background noise but I was never invited to go and pray with the others. Only once did I see a group of men through the open door, how they sat on small carpets, bowing all the time.

An hour later, we sat on the borrowed moped and were on our way to Jhelum crossing the farming area. We rode along the canal again where an inevitable herd of goats blocked our way. Altaf called out to the goatherd and the man herded the animals to the side.

I was glad that Altaf was able to spend some time with me. That was more like it. Soon the wedding would take place, then we would do some sight-seeing and would be on our way back to Germany. Luckily, I hadn't listened to Renate's warnings and had travelled to Pakistan regardless.

"What happens during the wedding?" I yelled into Altaf's ear and held onto my green veil that threatened to slide off my head.

"Everybody comes to Khadriala for a few days to participate in the ceremonies," he called back.

"What ceremonies?"

"The Barat and Dholki before the actual wedding. Drumming and singing. Nasra probably has a henna-ceremony... for the women... and Farooq, well, he'll have ceremonies for the bridegroom."

Did he expect me to know what a Barat and Dholki were? But it wasn't exactly easy, having a discussion about things like that on a moving motorbike.

"In the end, the actual wedding takes place in Nasra's village."

"Is that around here somewhere?"

He turned halfway around and yelled against the airflow. "No, we have to take rickshaws."

"You better look out for those sheep over there," I laughed light-heartedly.

After my seclusion in the countryside, the town seemed incredibly lively. We visited one of Altaf's aunts in the hospital and took a look around the bazaar. At the fabric shop, I chose two thin cotton fabrics from large piles of rolls.

We took the package to the tailor who measured me in wide-eyed astonishment because I was taller and had broader shoulders than the average woman. We sauntered about the market stalls and waited for the Punjabi suits to be sewed.

"Look, there's a shoe shop. The slippers over there, the embroidered ones in silver, try them on. When you have proper shoes you won't have to walk around in sneakers anymore."

The slippers were surprisingly comfortable and would match the new peach-coloured and violet suits nicely. We ate a mild curry in an air-conditioned restaurant and when we went outside again, unpleasant hot air hit me.

"Why are people staring at me like that?" I wanted to know. "I'm wearing my dabatta like a good girl." I had also followed Zohra's advice: to always look at the ground and not into people's eyes.

"Your hair is visible through the dabatta."

"But there are other blonde women around here. Why don't they stare at them?"

"They are well-known in town and usually come from good families. That's why nobody gapes at them."

"Right, and I'm the strange woman on show, or what?"

"Just ignore them. They will get used to you after a while. Perhaps it's a good idea to buy you a tjunee, that's an opaque piece of fabric you can use to wrap yourself in."

"You mean a like a shador?"

"No, a shador looks more like that." I saw a woman in a brown floor-length sack with a latticed piece in front of her eyes.

"Let's have a look here. They have tjunees in this shop." Altaf pointed to yet another fabric shop. "We'll just buy you one now. You can pick one."

I didn't exactly like the idea but wrapped into the long, printed piece of cloth, it was definitely easier to disappear in the crowd. We stopped in front of a stall that displayed mountains of colourful powders. "They have spices here. My mother wanted us to buy cinnamon and chilli powder." The red powder was scooped from the open sack into a small paper bag.

"Oh no, not so much of that hot stuff," I moaned. "I'm already suffocating just watching this!"

"We just like it hot. That's how we're used to eating our food. Without chilli, it tastes just bland and boring." Obviously, I had no say in the matter when it came to cooking. I saw another interesting stall.

"Just look at the jewellery over there. I think I'm going to buy some gifts," I said cheerfully.

"It will be best if we tell them that you come from Kashmir, then they won't overcharge us." Altaf had taught me in Karachi how to bargain – and I bargained like there's no tomorrow. The salesman seemed in awe of the strange woman with the strong accent and gave me everything at the price I fixed. A bracelet and a broad necklace made of polished agates in cheap metal fittings. I was rather proud of my accomplishment.

"Isabell, you must be fair and not push the price down too much," Altaf cautioned me.

"I thought that's the whole idea," I said bewildered.

"Yes that's true but it has its limits."

We paid a more appropriate price for the cake slices topped with wafer-thin silver leaf after that. When we returned in the afternoon cheerful and weighed down with brown paper parcels of clothes, spices and gifts, a group of grim, hirsute men was already waiting for us in the guest room.

Shireen took me aside. "Come with me, Isabella. You can help me cook." She looked rather worried.

Saïda pushed past me with a triumphant expression, carrying chai she intended to serve to the men. "Shertan!" She hissed in passing.

"Who are these men?" I asked Shireen. Was Altaf getting arrested?

"Saïda's father, uncle and brothers. They here from their own village," she said.

"She doesn't live here?"

"No."

"What do these men want?"

"Saïda is supposed to get married to Altaf. For long time... betrothed. They are furious. You are here. You are first wife."

"They are angry because of me?"

"Yes, now elders must speak and do something."

Oh boy! Now I realised what complications Altaf's lie was causing. Was I here to help him wriggle out of an arranged marriage?

"I had no idea," I said awkwardly. "Altaf hasn't told me about that. About Saïda." Of course. That's why this moustachioed girl had been so peeved with me. Her long-time fiancé had rejected her with my help. That's why she'd called me 'devil'. She was engaged to Altaf!

"He not say anything?" Shireen tried to clarify the matter.

"No. I had no idea."

"But you are married. He no longer wants Saïda, not even as second wife. He doesn't like her."

"But why…"

"I also like you better," Shireen confessed when she pounded a chapati into shape and threw it nimbly onto the heated pan.

I wanted to tell her the truth: that Altaf and I were only friends and that he'd only invited me to his brother Farooq's wedding. But, apparently, that was impossible in Pakistan. Everybody was either related or engaged or married. Loud voices issued from the guest room. Angry voices. That was just great, my presence was causing a family feud!

The silent women around the fire pit seemed to get nervous and Saïda was nowhere to be seen. I tried to distract myself by shaping a chapati in my hands. What did I get myself into? Renate had warned me about exactly such a situation. I could just imagine what she would have to say about it. The negotiations in the guestroom carried on for the better part of an hour.

"What are they talking about all this time?" I asked Shireen.

She tried to explain and I understood that it was about restitution for the jilted bride. And suddenly all of that had something to do with *me*!

When the glowering men were ready to leave, they sneaked a few glances at me. Apparently, they took Saïda with them because I never saw her again. The men of Altaf's clan held a much calmer discussion afterwards. It was obvious that they were backing him up. The women stayed out of it.

I heard steps and looked up.

Chacha Sardar came personally to give me the honey in a big glass bottle, he'd mysteriously procured. Perhaps he wanted to cheer me up.

"Shukria merbani, Chacha Sardar," I thanked him. He called out to Meera and she handed him a small bowl with almost translucent butter and a plate of freshly made chapatis. Chacha Sardar carried the lot in front of me into the guestroom that was once again empty.

"Khao, Batshi. Eat, little daughter," he coaxed me.

And so I ate chapatis with butter and honey under his watchful eye.

"Thank you, Chacha Sardar. That tastes really good."

"It's my pleasure, child. Now you won't starve on my watch." I was moved to tears about his caring gesture.

The wedding was around the corner and there was much busy hustle and bustle outside in the yard. Relatives from the entire region arrived for the nuptials and had to be taken care of. Chacha Sardar needed to greet his relations and left the room. At some stage, Altaf returned and this time, I reproached him for his actions.

"Give me one good reason why I shouldn't pack my things and go home this very minute? You only think of yourself, don't you? You wanted to get rid of Saïda. That's why you've been telling everybody that we're married. So you won't have to marry her anymore. Am I right?"

He looked at me with guilty eyes. "You are right but that's only part of it. Can we take this somewhere else, please? The walls have ears around here and that could become embarrassing."

"Embarrassing? How do you think I feel about this? And we speak German in any case. Nobody here can understand that."

"Anyway. I'd rather speak to you in private. All the relatives are arriving. I don't want to dampen their joyful anticipation."

I was so furious that I'd completely forgotten about the wedding preparations. Of course, I didn't want to put a damper on the happy mood on my behalf. I'd already caused enough trouble. At dusk, we took the moped down to the canal. Hopefully, we were out of earshot. I had to express my frustrations and didn't need witnesses for that.

Altaf parked the moped at the side of the road and we sat down on the embankment. "Okay, what the hell were you thinking?" I attacked him at once.

"I'm terribly sorry," Altaf began. "The council of the elders had decided on the betrothal when I was on my way to Venezuela aboard a cargo vessel. They just decided it and I could hardly say no. All I had was a picture of Saïda when she was still very young. When I saw her for the first time, I couldn't for the life of me imagine marrying her."

"My goodness, I can understand why she's not exactly your dream woman but that doesn't explain why you had to drag me into this mess. Couldn't you resolve it some other way? I was so stupid to trust you and I thought we were friends." I was huffing with anger.

"You're not stupid and we are friends. I'm glad that you came with me to Pakistan and met my family. You know why I had to say that we are married." There was a pause. We should have left it at that but my anger was far from over. "Without telling me the truth upfront?"

"I was afraid you wouldn't come with me if I told you the truth. I just couldn't tell you."

"Damn, I'm sure I would have come anyway. We could have devised a plan together but you had to use me!"

"I didn't mean to use you. I love you."

"What did you just say?" I was taken aback.

"I love you. I want to marry you and not Saïda." That was getting better by the minute.

"We are just friends and friends don't get married. Where do you get off thinking that I would do something like that? Perhaps you should have asked me first what I was thinking."

Altaf chewed on a blade of grass.

"You are my friend. My best girlfriend. I've never been so close to a woman as I am to you. In order to have a happy marriage, it's not necessary to be in love right from the start," he said. "Look, it's like a pot of water: if it's cold when you put it on the stove, the water begins to boil. If the water is already boiling and you put it on a cold stove, all it can do is cool off."

"Hello! You're talking about me, Isabell. I'm a European

woman and want to finish school and then study. I have free will and that's what I want to do for the next few years at least. I want to fall in love first and then get married. Later. Nobody decides my fate. I'm nothing like Shireen who has to leave school to get married."

"Shireen wants to get married."

"Aah, but that's not the point! The point is that the only person who decides what I do with my life is me. Not you, not your elders or my mother for that matter. Nobody else but me!"

I'd worked myself up to such an extent that I would have loved to give Altaf a sound slap. I took a deep breath and continued on a calmer note. "I'm just cross that you didn't talk to me first. You've planned the whole thing without talking to me. I trusted you." Renate would have rejoiced. Then suddenly, Altaf began to cry.

"I'm such an idiot. I made a big mistake. I thought that if I got you to come with me, you would love me back. I thought…"

"But I'm not in love with you. Nothing can change that. Why on earth did you think I would love you if I came with you to Pakistan?"

"You are so different to other girls. Strong. And beautiful. I'd hoped that…" I felt almost sorry for him. "Okay then – sob – there is no reason for me to keep on living. Why not end it all right now? You couldn't care less whether I live or die," he howled.

"Don't talk such rubbish! You don't kill yourself because of something like that." I rolled my eyes at him.

"And why not? You don't love me."

"What a performance! Just don't lose it in the middle of Pakistan. You are trying to put pressure on me, right? That'll be the day!"

Wild thoughts of running away shot through my mind, how I would pack up my things and leave in a rickshaw. But go where? Go to Islamabad and the German embassy? That was hardly realistic. Better to calm him down somehow.

"I will drown myself. Right here in the canal," he cried.

"You're off your rocker!"

But he seemed serious about it. Altaf got onto the motorbike and slowly drove down the sloping embankment. A half moon shook its head at the bizarre scene and retired behind pale clouds.

"Stop it already. Are going bonkers or what?" I screeched.

The irrigation canal was obviously way too shallow to drown yourself in and the moped's front tyre got stuck in the mud. Altaf sat down on the shore and carried on wailing. I let him be for a while then helped him push the moped back up the wall. Somewhere a donkey brayed its hacking eeyore, eeyore. *Keep it together*, Isabell, I thought in desperation, *you must keep it together*.

"You know what… I will stay here for the wedding. I won't tell anyone about your lie. Things would become too complicated anyway. Then we could take a trip to Islamabad and go on an excursion to Kashmir," I said in a cool tone. Much calmer than I felt on the inside. "You got what you wanted: a reason to not marry Saïda. And I want to see this country. Shouldn't we help each other out?"

A sobbing little boy sat in front of me who couldn't get what he wanted. Somehow, I felt sorry for him. He was stuck between the strict rules of his culture and the desire to live a western lifestyle. But I couldn't let him spoil my trip to this fascinating country.

"Yes, sure if that's what you want. Forgive me, Isabell. I am weak. You make me weak."

"Hey, don't you dare make me responsible for the mess you've created!"

"We are friends, right?" There was a shimmer of hope in his eyes.

No! I wanted to shout. *How can I still be your friend after you used me like that? No trust, no friendship.* I said out loud: "Of course we're still friends. But never ever do something like that again, you hear?!" Altaf promised and calmed himself down.

People in the village were already wondering where we'd vanished to. The bride had arrived shortly after we'd taken off. Nasra stayed – as tradition demanded - with the family of her future husband. She had moved into the guestroom in the meantime and gone to bed.

Without further ado, I moved into the dormitory for unmarried women. Here, I shared a large room with five young women and I didn't mind one bit. During the night, I had another dream.

I ride on my stallion Kalyan's back. My steed gallops down the slope and I lie down flat against his muscular neck. The wind rushes through my hair. When we approach the villa, he slows down to a trot. I jump off his back and throw the reins at the groomsman. I feel free. Happy and free.

The following morning, I decided to take a walk down to the river. Just the way I had always done in Karlsruhe when I had gone to the park by myself. Some gentle exercise couldn't harm and I would be back in the yard by breakfast. My new clothes made the morning heat almost bearable.

I walked through the rear gate and down the pathway to the river, stopped on the shore and took a deep breath. The grey expanse flowed leisurely before my eyes and there were some cows taking a rest on a sandbank. Bliss. My solitude didn't last very long.

"Isabellaa, Isabelaa!" I turned around. Mushtaq, Altaf's younger brother came running after me.

"Isabella, you cannot leave the village all on your own. That is not permitted," he said, catching his breath. It was the first time, he'd addressed me directly.

"And why not? I just want to be alone for a while."

He shook his head in helpless disapproval. "Being alone is not right for a young woman like you."

"I have to be alone to think, whether I'm a young woman or not." I turned around again and faced the river. Mushtaq pondered my reaction for a moment.

"Then I sit here while you think. Not long! I'll wait." It was a compromise.

I tore a twig off the nearest fruit tree, just as Altaf had shown me, and cleaned my teeth with it. I walked along the edge of the water and dipped my toes in, thinking my own thoughts. Then I was ready to go back to the village.

Mushtaq followed me the whole time at a safe distance and disappeared once we'd reached the house. Amma was already waiting and read me the riot act. The nice old lady stood with her arms akimbo and Shireen who appeared behind her had to translate what she said.

"She says you cannot just leave the village. You are a young woman and must ask Amma if okay."

Amma's hands fluttered through the air like two fidgety birds. All the excitement, having a foreign visitor in the house and the extensive wedding preparations must be putting quite a strain on her. I understood.

"Please tell her that I'm grateful for her hospitality but if I need to be alone and want to take a walk down to the river, then that's what I will do."

Amma seemed displeased with my answer. She waggled her head and uttered a short sentence.

"You are a young woman. Men will like you. Alone. That's a problem: men like young beautiful women."

"That's not exactly what she said, is it?" I was skeptical.

"No, but I tell you so you know."

"But I'm not a Pakistani woman and I want to be able to go for a walk when it suits me," I answered stubbornly.

Shireen gushed forth a few quick sentences and it was doubtful that she was translating what I had said. Amma looked way too complacent and waved for me to enter the yard. A young man I hadn't met before, walked through the gate and Shireen rushed into one of the rooms bordering the yard. "Salaam Aleikum."

"Aleikum e Salaam."

"I'm Zaheer, Altaf's cousin. Nice to meet you," he greeted me and I understood. Shireen was engaged to him and was not allowed to see her fiancé before their wedding.

The girls here seemed way too involved in this whole

marriage-thing! I saw how Shireen climbed onto the flat roof next door and from there onto the village wall. There she stood and secretly watched her betrothed.

I was told that all the girls were doing that. I also climbed onto the wall but I found the view far more captivating than the young man who chatted downstairs to his cousins.

"This is Mandira's husband." Shireen pointed to a stocky young man with short, blond hair.

When I stood on level ground again, I met Farooq, a worldly-wise man who had travelled all the way from England. The bridegroom who was staying with an uncle in the village looked handsome and spoke in a soft voice. And he looked nothing like Altaf. Older by a mere two years, he had gone to England at the age of twenty.

Farooq was, without the shadow of a doubt, very much in love with Nasra. His face lit up every time his eyes randomly searched for her. He had eventually earned enough with his job in a chocolate factory to be able to buy a dowry for Nasra and to build a small house in Khadriala.

Bride and groom were also not allowed to see each other during the preparations and Farooq soon left. Then I met Nasra at last by the fire pit where she was being fed lunch. She looked firmly into my eyes and smiled. I thought it best to introduce myself.

"I'm Isabell from Germany. Nice to meet you."

"My name is Nasra and I'm the bride. Come sit here with me then we can talk for a bit." She spoke English with almost no accent. I sat down on a low chair with a woven string-seat and was also given a plate with food.

"What's the matter with Amma?" She came straight to the point.

"You're not the type to beat around the bush, are you?" I marvelled. Nasra and Renate would have gotten on like a house on fire.

"Well you know, I've lived long enough in London. That's where you learn that sort of thing."

I sighed. "The thing is, I wanted to go for a walk but

apparently you're not allowed to do that as a young woman. Mushtaq came running after me and Amma was rather cross."

Nasra giggled. "Ah, don't take it the wrong way. The story with Saïda put her a bit on edge and the wedding, the 'shaadi', is always exhausting for the family."

Clearly, Nasra was a feisty young woman who knew what she wanted. We bonded immediately. She was not exactly beautiful with her hooked nose that was too big for her delicate face and her pointy chin. But Nasra had spunk and spoke her mind.

"All these people," Nasra groaned and poured a cup of chai for me. "I've already had it up to here. I have to constantly greet somebody and most of them I don't know to save my life."

"Were you also beleaguered in the guestroom?"

"Yes, as soon as I arrived yesterday."

"You are the guest of honour. Isn't that exciting for you?"

"Honestly? I can't wait for this whole thing to be over," she said with a mischievous smile.

Nasra stood up to greet an elderly couple and their son. She sat down again and said: "Yes, I'm the guest of honour at my shaadi. The 'dulhan' – that's what the bride is called. I have to change my clothes all the time. My red and pink wedding saris are embroidered with gold thread and so scratchy and I have to model them for everyone to see."

"You look very beautiful in those saris."

"Thank you. Your violet Punjabi-suit is also not to be scoffed at."

My own wedding had been a different affair, it flashed through my mind. I had been wearing a Kanchi-Kurti, the ceremonial dress of married women. Modest, with a long skirt, a blouse and vest and topped by a half-sari. It had been green. A green, embroidered sari...

I shook myself, shook off those strange thoughts.

"Why are you shaking your head, Isabell? Don't you like your suit?" Nasra asked.

"Yes, I do…it's just a fly…"

"You're right, there are lots of flies in the village. You're not used to them." We chatted for a while longer then somebody came to fetch Nasra for some ceremony.

She had many duties, like accepting presents or letting Amma rub her with a yellow paste. Or having her hands and feet decorated with dark-red henna patterns. In between, there was little time for us to talk.

"I can hardly wait to move back to London," she told me in confidence. "We'll be on a plane back to England right after the wedding and already have the tickets. We have loads of family in London, you know. I used to live for years with my rich aunt in Slough."

"Why did you come back to Pakistan if you prefer to live in London?"

"The elders decided that I should get married. They chose my cousin. I didn't particularly like him and avoided him whenever I could. Just like Altaf and Saïda, I guess. Then I met Farooq and the engagement was off." She smiled tenderly. "Farooq is different. He's a modern man and will help me with the babies. We've already agreed on that. Don't you want children as well?"

"Yes, later maybe. I need to finish school first and then study."

"You have courage, Isabell. I wish I could go and study but I think that ship has sailed."

Nasra had many questions about Germany and I told her all about my boring life and my wanderlust.

"Have you ever been to London, Isabell?"

"Yes, twice already. Once with my girlfriend Renate. I'm sure you'd like her. And the other time, I was alone on a camping site. It rained nearly all the time and I would wake up in the morning with my tent being flooded."

"Oh yes, the English weather! That's obviously the only draw-back but we have monsoon seasons here that are a knock-out."

She glanced at me admiringly. "I wish I could be as free as you are. When I have daughters, they will also be allowed to do as they please. Studying, travelling."

I took Nasra into my confidence regarding Altaf's

behaviour and how he'd got me into a tight spot. She contemplated this for a moment.

"Look Isabell, he's not a bad guy and he made a mistake. I'd be beside myself if Farooq would do something like that." She grunted in contempt. "I will also remain his only wife. Give Altaf another chance. I mean you can stay friends, just don't tell anybody else about this."

"What will happen to Saïda?" I asked.

"They will conspire with some other family to get her married off."

I was really glad that the surly girl had left Khadriala. I could only hope that nobody else would shoot hateful looks at me or hiss insults.

Soon, Nasra was off to yet another ceremony and Shireen taught me how to squat properly when a sobbing Mandira came running into the yard.

"What's the matter with you, Mandira? What happened?"

"She doesn't speak English," Shireen reminded me with some pride in her voice. She was obviously more educated.

Shireen and Mandira had a discussion. What transpired was that Mandira's mother-in-law had beaten her because she didn't like the food that Mandira had cooked.

"Her mother-in-law just beats her? What does Mandira's husband have to say about this?" I was flabbergasted. A brief exchange of words resulted in even more tears.

"Her husband says that she must respect his mother. Mother is right," Shireen said.

"Bloody coward," I blurted out. I felt hot anger rise up inside me. Beatings were just not on. I needed to help Mandira somehow.

"Blood? Coward?"

"Ah, forget it. Where does Mandira live?" I wanted to have a word with this coward of a husband. This blond and blue-eyed husband of hers. Mandira and Shireen showed me how to get to a stately home. The largest in the village. I learned only later that it was the house of the village elder. The patriarch of the Khan-family.

I didn't find Mandira's wimpy husband in the reception room but just an old woman who lay on a raised couch in an elegantly furnished living room. A young girl reverently served her a cup of chai. When I walked in, she looked up with a bored expression.

Mandira and Shireen were running for the hills and I was suddenly left without an interpreter! I studied the woman who must be Mandira's mother-in-law more closely.

She had probably been quite a beauty in her youth but her face was hard and arrogant.

Her eyes were blue and the tightly combed-back hair must have been blonde at some stage. Just like 'Baba Ali', the woman no longer had her teeth but she was big and robust. There was no doubt about it that she thought of herself as a woman of consequence.

Oh well, now that I was here I couldn't just leave again. I knew that she spoke some English.

"Where do get off beating your daughter-in-law?" I railed at her. "You cannot just do as you please!"

The old woman stared at me awe-struck. I could be reasonably sure that nobody had ever dared to speak to her in such a tone. And now this complete stranger came waltzing into her home and held her accountable. She barked at the cowed girl and after a couple of minutes, Shireen appeared in the doorway. Apparently, she hadn't quite understood all I had said to her!

Shireen gazed stiffly at the painted cement floor and didn't quite know what was expected of her. I continued instinctively, had to use the momentum I had accidentally created.

"I really don't care what you think of me," I said with all the authority I could muster. "There is no reason good enough to hit someone like Mandira. You should be ashamed of yourself. She is the mother of your grandchildren and a grown woman."

Shireen stuttered something. The old woman was sitting up and listened how I gave her a piece of my mind. It was bizarre. The blue eyes didn't know where to look but my eyes were locked on her. There was no turning back now.

"If you want to be respected, you must respect others first." Shireen seemed to struggle a bit with the translation of what I was saying. Especially with the insults.

"That's all I have to say to you. I don't want to hear that you lay a hand on Mandira again. Chudafiss, goodbye!"

The spell was broken and I marched out of the expensively decorated living room. I had violated all the rules of politeness and not cared a hoot about the consequences.

Oh dear. I had no idea what consequences my impulsive behaviour entailed. All I could do was hope that the mother-in-law didn't take it out on Mandira. But I was nevertheless in high spirits as I rushed down the street.

"Isabella, Isabella, wait!" Shireen caught up with me and we walked silently back to Altaf's home. "You have courage like man," she whispered.

The other women who were busy with food preparations didn't speak to me. Perhaps I had fallen from favour for breaking the unbreakable rules.

I didn't want to just sit around and began to sew a golden border onto my new peach-coloured silk veil. Meera couldn't bear the sight of it and said something in a firm tone. She took the needle from me and had the border sewed on in no time at all. I noticed that the other women gave me sidelong glances as I sat there watching Meera sew.

"Isabella, why you go to wife of *Agoo*? You very angry," Shireen began.

"Well, I know. I wanted to have a talk with Mandira's husband about her treatment. Beating someone is just wrong. You have to treat people well."

"But he was not at home."

"Exactly. I didn't mean to cause trouble but once I was there, I had to say something to someone."

"You're like a man, Isabella. Why not like woman?"

While she spoke, Shireen patted perfectly shaped chapatis and baked them in the pan. Meera chatted with her briefly and Shireen seemed to explain to her what we were talking about.

"Meera is asking why you were so angry. You don't even know Mandira." That was, of course, true. How was I to explain that I hadn't been able to help my sister when I was a toddler but now as an adult I could do something?

"Well you know, women in Europe are just different," I answered simply. Shireen translated and Meera gave me a doubtful look. She obviously didn't want to ask any more questions. I might get angry again.

"Do you want to say sorry to wife of *Agoo*?" Shireen asked me and the freshly baked chapati slid onto a plate.

"You think I should apologise? But she hit Mandira." I didn't understand. Because of their customs?

"I cannot explain very well, but yes."

"No, I will not apologise." Shireen didn't understand what I had done but she later told me that Mandira was no longer abused. At least for the time being.

It didn't take long for Nasra and Altaf to get wind of the scandal. I didn't see Altaf often because he had to help his brother with all the wedding-ceremonies as his best man. I didn't mind because I hadn't quite forgiven him yet.

"What were you thinking, shouting like that at the wife of the village elder?" He wanted to know when we saw each other.

"I actually wanted to speak to your cousin but only his mother was there. I simply can't bear it when people are beaten." How often did I have to explain that? Nasra nodded in approval.

"It's just rather unusual to do something like that but I think you'll be forgiven. It's not your fault if you don't know how things are handled around here. A woman from the village would never have dared to put the wife of the village elder in her place."

"I agree that it wasn't exactly diplomatic but wrong is just wrong. That's how I see it."

Altaf didn't seem to agree with me.

"You must try not to see everything through European eyes," he tried to get his point across. "We live differently here. It could mean a lot of trouble if you just do whatever you like."

"You think it's only here like that? In Europe, it's also often the problem and I already told you that I was planning to speak to Mandira's husband. Plus, if people just stand by and never do anything nothing will ever change for the better. We don't live in the Middle Ages, you know!"

"Mothers who have sons are very important here. If a woman doesn't have a son, it's a problem. If her own mother-in-law didn't treat her well and she's now more important, a woman will treat her daughter-in-law the same way."

"But that's not right. And the vicious cycle is never broken. Mandira has sons, so what's your point? Not that I believe this sort of thing should matter at all!"

"Well, that's just how things are," Altaf said.

CHAPTER SEVEN

From now on, the wedding preparations went into high gear, which distracted me somewhat from the strange incident by the canal. I had come to Pakistan for the wedding, after all.

By now, I almost exclusively wore Punjabi suits, which made the heat during the day more bearable, despite the prescribed length of sleeves and trouser legs.

But in Amma's eyes, my appearance still begged perfection. Since I wore no jewellery at all, that state of affairs had to be changed at once!

A travelling salesman who sold glass bangles in all colours and sizes was summoned to help me and Nasra get equipped accordingly, befitting to our station. The poor guy had his hands full with me - so to speak — because my hands were more muscular, and thus, larger than those of the local girls.

He massaged Vaseline into my skin to make it more supple and pressed my palms together until he was able to slide the glass bangles on. As part of the deal, he palmed off cheap necklaces and elaborate earrings made of violet glass on Amma.

Only after that procedure was I declared properly adorned.

From now on, I no longer had peace and quiet. The sound of clinking glass bangles accompanied me wherever I went, no matter what I did. I had to be careful not to bump against anything or they could break. The village itself had become a noisier place.

Traditional drum processions were the order of the day, walking up and down the streets, accompanied by the same repetitive rhythms over and over again: Tomtomtomtom

Tom Tom Tom Tomtomtomtom. The drummers marched all day, followed by a group of children. At least two of the drummers carried their drums horizontally on straps over their shoulders and worked them incessantly with hooked sticks. Whenever they met at some place in the village, they performed a solo each before they carried on marching past one another in opposite directions.

They went into the courtyards and more and more children followed them out into the street as if they were some sort of pied pipers. I followed with some of the other girls and the little ones clung to every finger of my hands. I sang along to the best of my ability: "Oh shaadi-i-i, oh shaadi -i-i, oh shaadi -i-i."

Then it was time for the bridegroom to officially hand over the dowry to the bridal family. Farooq rode formally into the village on horseback, a veil of golden lametta covering his face and a curved sword in his hand. It was rather obvious that Farooq wasn't exactly accustomed to such gallant pursuits and he needed his brothers' help to get out of the saddle.

Yet another procession of guests, led by the drummers arrived in the yard, where they awaited the bridegroom's arrival. Everyone sat in a circle around blankets on the ground where the dowry was laid out.

Every single sari, every bangle and every bar of soap was shown to the crowd and accurately recorded in a notebook. Family members pinned bank notes to Nasra's Sari. The bank notes were later counted and the amount entered into the notebook as well. The entire time, Nasra sat with feigned indifference under her gold-embroidered veil.

It had been just like that at the time of my own wedding, I thought. Only that the riders had been experienced warriors and my dowry had been far more exquisite... Oh come on, nonsense, I scolded myself, *I'm neither married nor do I have an exquisite dowry.* My imagination was running wild again. In any case, should I ever decide to get married, it would certainly not be anything like this spectacle around me. While I was lost in thought, I instinctively avoided Altaf's glances as much as possible not to encourage him. Right at the end of the ceremony, the most valuable pieces of dowry were shown off to the guests: an entire set of jewellery made of gold and rubies. An elaborate necklace, earrings, a nose ring on a chain and heavy bangles! The valuable pieces were handed around on pieces of dark velvet for everyone to admire.

"That's so different from the Hindu tradition," I whispered in Shireen's ear. "Why does the bridegroom give her such expensive jewellery?"

"Bride is worth so much. She keep jewellery when divorce happens."

"Really?"

"Yes, really."

After the lengthy ceremony, we followed the drummers on foot along random paths across the fields and to a neighbouring village, while the bride was cleansed and anointed by female relatives back at the house.

"We collect more family," Shireen explained.

"There is more?" I asked in an astonished tone, but she didn't hear me.

We arrived at the village and the women began immediately to dance with large tin vases on their heads to the rhythm of the drums. I was given one such empty water vessel and, despite my protests, I had to perform a dance in the middle of a circle of clapping village women.

"You not bad," Shireen praised me and laughed.

"Oh yes, I was bad," I also had to laugh.

The drummers led us back into Khadriala through the back gate where musicians, fire-eaters, an elephant and a camel were already awaiting us.

Young people took turns climbing onto the backs of the patient animals and - before I had a chance to object to such an exercise - I was lifted onto the neck of the elephant. I nearly died of fear when the animal rose slowly to its feet. I was higher up in the air than I could have imagined looking up from the ground. The elephant flapped its large ears and shifted its weight from one foot to the other until I began to feel dizzy. When it went down on its knees again, somebody had to help me slide off the leg that was as thick as a tree trunk.

The entire following day, the drummers were still entertaining the villagers of Khadriala and there was no escaping the constant noise. Nasra's big day - the Nikah – would soon arrive. Then, on the eve of the wedding day, Shireen came running to me all excited.

"Isabella, the Agoo wants to see you. Alone. You must... go... now."

Oh dear! That didn't sound like a pleasant visit. Perhaps the leader of the clan wanted to read me the riot act for being disrespectful and giving his wife a piece of my mind. Perhaps, he would ban me from the village altogether right before the wedding.

"Why only me?" I asked cautiously. "Can't Altaf come along?"

"He didn't say why. Only, you must come alone."

"Should I be worried about it?" I asked Altaf. He seemed embarrassed by the whole matter. Apparently, I was having a negative effect on his good standing in the village.

"I can take you there. Go and see what he wants. He's the most important man here in Khadriala."

"What if he wants me to leave the village for causing too much trouble? Or maybe he wants to tell me to stay out of his family's affairs."

"I don't think so." But Altaf didn't look at all convinced.

I mustered all my courage and walked behind Altaf through the streets to the impressive building I already knew. Then he left me there in the street in front of the large wooden gate. I knocked.

The confident Agoo himself opened the gate and walked ahead of me into the living room I already knew. I faintly remembered having seen this impressive man of about 60 years of age: he had been among the throng of visitors on our very first day in Khadriala.

Tall with broad shoulders and dressed in a high-necked suit, he cut a dignified figure. In the light of the gas lamps, his bearded face seemed noble and wise. It wasn't hard to see why this man had become the leader of his clan. There was nobody else in sight and I expected the worst.

"Please take a seat," he offered in impeccable English. I sat down on the stool he'd pointed out. "Chai?"

"Yes please." The village leader poured from a decorated silver jug. It was rather unusual for a woman to be served by an older man. Up to now, I had only seen Chacha Sardar do this for me. I waited.

"A little bird told me about the incident with Mandira and my wife," he began. Oh my! But at last, he would tell me the reason why I had been summoned here. "I was on a business trip at the time. And I can tell you that nobody has ever dared to speak to my wife like that. Not even I."

I could see myself packing my suitcase and leaving the village in a state of disgrace. Perhaps they would let me stay in Nasra's village...

"I am very sorry," I apologised before he could continue with the dressing-down. "I never had the intention to treat her with disrespect. I actually wanted to speak with your son and tell him to stand up for his wife. I simply cannot tolerate violence."

"I'm not here to reproach you," the Agoo said. It took me a moment to understand that he wasn't about to punish me for my behaviour.

"I must honestly say that I admire your courage."

Our conversation took an unexpected turn.

"You do?"

"Senseless violence destroys the soul. Mandira is unable to defend herself and she is the mother of my grandsons. I am not always around to know what is taking place in my house but from now on, things will change. I've seen enough violence in my lifetime to know what I'm talking about." There was a moment of silence. The Agoo seemed to collect his thoughts.

"In the last days of the Second World War..." he continued, "...the British arrested a large number of young men on trumped-up charges. You must have heard that India used to be a British Protectorate and Pakistan came into existence only at a later stage?"

I nodded silently.

"They forced us into the military. We had the choice to either languish in a British prison here or fight against the Germans. As cannon fodder! We had no reason to fight the Germans but what choice did we have? Most of us decided to go into battle alongside the British." The village elder sighed. "We barely knew what this war was about. Before I knew what was happening, I found myself being shipped off to Europe."

"You were in Europe?"

"Yes, I was even in Germany."

Oh no, was he about to accuse me of being a Nazi just like Raymond's little brother had? But the Agoo did nothing of that sort.

"The Germans were good to us." I looked at him in surprise. "We were captured almost immediately," he continued, "and didn't even get a chance to do battle. I spent the remainder of the war in a German prison."

"I'm very sorry about that…"

He interrupted me. "The prison warder treated us well – and he gave me German food to eat: fried potatoes and goulash for example. He turned out to be a good man."

I just sat there with my mouth open. This noble man had met good Germans - during the Second World War!

"I have a surprise for you, Isabell." The Agoo stood up and walked over to a cooking plate in the corner of the room. He lifted up two pots and placed them on the low table in front of me. Then he took off the lids just like a magician would have done.

When the patriarch saw my astonishment, his face lit up. There were fried potatoes and goulash inside the pots! Obviously without crispy bacon but there was hardly anything more German to be had in Pakistan than the food right in front of me.

"I made the fried potatoes myself," the village elder announced proudly. "And also the goulash."

Never! A Pakistani man in his position? Not only wasn't he going to throw me out of the village. He had cooked me a meal all by himself!

"I don't know what to say, Mr. Agoo," I said a little awkwardly. "It's simply extraordinary! Thank you so much. I'm very impressed with this!"

"I've waited a long time to pay for the good treatment I'd received in the past. Now I have the opportunity to serve a German food from her home."

I was absolutely speechless. This was totally unexpected.

The village leader seemed to enjoy the effect his surprise had on me. This pillar of the village community who was served left, right and centre all the time, had prepared German food for me. The fact slowly sank in.

We ate together with knife and fork and chatted about England and Germany and Pakistan. It was obvious that this worldly-wise man was incredibly proud to be a citizen of Pakistan. He was also a fan of the Pakistani cricket team and couldn't understand why I had never even heard of this sport before. He urged me to get seconds and spooned more of the goulash onto my plate.

"You know, Mr. Agoo," I said. "You are quite astonishing. I was worried that something else would happen because I had violated your customs. And now you are so friendly to me and cook food from my home country for me. I'd like to thank you for that."

He inclined his head in a benevolent gesture. "We lead simple lives here in this rural area but I didn't want to let you return to Germany thinking that we are a cruel and backward people."

"I certainly wouldn't think that."

"Our branch of the clan is descended from two noble lineages you must know: the Moghuls and the Rajputs," he continued. "Now we lean more towards the Muslim faith but my grandfather always quoted a verse from the Mahabharata: 'There is nothing in all the three worlds that lies outside of the reach of the courageous man'. And you are courageous, Isabell."

I had never heard of the Mahabharata but thought that the quote was quite cool. The Agoo was a truly remarkable man. He had even paid me an unusual compliment. Whoever this German prison warder may have been during the last days of the Second World War, at that moment I felt nothing but gratitude for him.

Later, during the night, I dreamt of a wedding that had taken place a very long time ago. The colours and smells and even feelings were so real: it was as if I was there myself and the dream went on and on.

I am supervising the servants during the preparations for my eldest son's wedding. He is about to marry a beautiful girl of pleasant character from an old Jammu clan. She is perfectly suited to be his wife. I am dressed in a jade-coloured sari and look down at my new gold-embroidered slippers. The horoscopes of the two youngsters were favourable and the most important ceremonies had already taken place. Now it is time for my son to arrive in a golden cloak, riding on the back of an elephant, holding up a sword. His bride is wearing even more jewellery than he does: a golden, jewel-encrusted necklace, golden bangles and rings, golden hair ornaments and earrings and toe rings. She must be the most beautiful Rajput-princess Dâstân has ever seen.

The Dholan musicians arrive. Our servants run this way and that and add finishing touches to the 'Mehfil' on the closed-off terrace that is reserved only for us womenfolk. Here we would congregate in the evening, dressed in our beautiful robes to enjoy the dance and music.

The food is waiting on platters in the kitchens. Vegetarian and non-vegetarian dishes. The aroma of Alu Gobi and Dal-bati, made of lentils, and dumplings with preserved berries, roasted lamb and various fish dishes.

It is a banquet befitting the status of our family. Mansour is still in his rooms to work on his paperwork. I feel happy and a deep joy. There would be grandchildren at last. At last!

My husband's grandmother comes from far to be here. Her snide remarks hurt me but I would not argue with her. Not on this wonderful day. Her undesirable presence had to be borne with stoic forbearance. We were warriors. Strong and courageous. And forbearing.

I awoke briefly. It was still dark in the room. The woman in the bed next to me snored softly. Help! I'd never had such a long and detailed dream! *C.G. Jung, Sigmund Freud and Dr. Albrecht. Where were all the qualified psychologists when I needed one?* The fleeting thought came and went and I fell asleep again.

Early the next morning, we got ready, took rickshaws and minibuses to Nasra's village that was about an hour's drive away. I still had this gloomy feeling towards Altaf and rather sat next to Shireen. His family probably assumed that we'd had a minor marital tiff. At least, they let me be.

"What did the Agoo want from you yesterday?" Shireen whispered into my ear.

"He was nice and gave me dinner," I whispered back. The Agoo had asked me to keep quiet about our conversation and the German food he'd cooked himself. Word of it could undermine his authority.

"Really? Not too much chilli?" Shireen played her astonishment down.

"No, no chilli."

"That's very nice of him. Mandira cooks very well."

"Yes, she does."

We were approaching the village. Nasra's home was a lot grander than her future husband's. The entire village was grander than Khadriala.

"Nasra's family is very wealthy," Shireen had explained during the ride. "Her father is a government office."

"Government official?"

"Yes, government official. We are not allowed to play music or dance. No drums also," the young woman sighed in resignation.

"But why not?" I didn't understand. In Khadriala the mood had always been so joyful.

"The army has forbidden."

"What does the army have to do with music?"

Shireen shrugged her shoulders. "I cannot explain."

The bridal guests were already seated in the garden and enjoyed an elaborate meal. There were large platters with tshawel – spiced rice with pieces of meat – placed on the long tables. Nasra had gone inside the house to change her attire. I was sitting down on the bench when Shireen came running. "Nasra wants you to come inside," she told me breathlessly and walked behind me, carrying my plate.

The bride sat on her bed without a veil under the disapproving stare of president Zia ul-Haq, in a generously-appointed room. Her arms and hands were covered in dark-red henna patterns. Nasra's mother and her sisters smoothed down their dresses, did their hair and put on more make-up in front of a dressing table mirror. The women ignored me roundly and I took in the scene in fascination.

"Why don't you come outside?" I asked Nasra innocently. "Farooq is sitting at the table all by himself."

One elegant, younger sister obviously understood what I had said and snorted with disdain. "She is not even Muslim," she hissed and pointed with her chin at me. "Why is she allowed to be in here? Just look at the rags she's wearing."

"Asma! She's my guest," Nasra reprimanded her curtly. "Behave yourself. I'm sorry, Isabell, my sister is forgetting her manners again."

This was the first time that I had been exposed to this kind of cultural hostility. Asma bowed her head and withdrew.

"You know, Isabell, we do things differently here. I'm not yet allowed to officially see Farooq and that means that I'm not supposed to celebrate outside with the guests or him. We only just signed the marriage contract."

"For real, you are not allowed to celebrate with us? It's your own wedding." This was rather different from what I had envisaged.

"We've already celebrated quite a bit in Khadriala, haven't we?"

"At least there was a lot of music," I said. I must have said the wrong thing because the women in the room suddenly held themselves very stiffly. Had I put my foot in? Nasra didn't seem to care much either way.

"Khadriala is in a more liberal area compared to this one. That's why things are a bit different when it comes to celebrating," she said frankly.

"Oh, I see. When is the ceremony, then?"

"There won't be a ceremony. All we do is sign the contract in the presence of witnesses. Male relatives on both sides. It's called Nikah-Naama. Just to make sure that the marriage wasn't entered into under duress. Now I'll stay inside the house for a while until the celebrations are over. Then we'll simply return to Khadriala." She applied some red lipstick.

"That's all, no ceremony?" I was disappointed. The other expensively dressed women withdrew visibly.

"Yes, isn't it the same where you come from?"

"No. We get married in white dresses in church or at the registry office. And then we celebrate big time for what it's worth."

"Hmm, I think it's the same in England. But I was never invited, just saw it on TV a couple of times."

Nasra's mother seemed out of patience. Her body language spoke volumes and she began to throw clothes around. That was a clear sign.

"Okay, perhaps I should go outside and see what the others are doing…" I said unsure of whether it was the right thing to say or not.

"Thank you for coming, Isabell. Truly," Nasra said and I left. Outside I sat down next to Shireen, feeling confused. She had filled another plate with rice and meat for me. I had forgotten my other plate inside the house.

"Why are these women so hostile toward me?"

"Hostile?"

"Yes, you know - unfriendly."

"Oh yes. That's just Nasra's family. They are better than us. They think. Much money and in government. Mother is unhappy that Nasra marry into poor family."

"They think that Nasra is marrying down? How arrogant of them."

Shireen gave me a puzzled look.

"They are not nice," I explained and she nodded.

My admiration for Nasra grew by the minute. What a strong character she had! It had to be even more difficult for her to put her foot down in the face of such resistance.

"No, but Farooq and Nasra are very happy."

"That's the most important thing. I just wish there was music and dance here just as we had in Khadriala."

"Yes." Dessert was now served and Shireen got stuck in. Small white balls decorated with green pistachio nuts and an orange latticed confectionery made of deep-fried dough. After some time, the bride appeared outside wrapped into a gold-embroidered long red veil with her head bowed.

She walked right up to Farooq and sat down on the bench next to him. Her mother opened the dabatta so everybody could see Nasra's face. Farooq's face underneath the silken turban beamed with pride. Then the guests made ready to hit the road.

The wedding had ended abruptly and Altaf walked up to me. "Come, Isabell, we must accompany the bridal couple."

"Where to? What's happening now?"

"We accompany them out of the garden and into the road," he said. "Then the two of them will take a minibus back to Khadriala. We're all leaving now."

"Already?" I asked surprised.

"Come on, we must hurry up."

Farooq and Nasra already stood in front of the house and somebody held a book above the bride's head. Then another man held the book and gave a brief speech.

"Altaf, what book is this?"

"That's the Quran. They are praying that Nasra will become a good Muslim wife who abides by the rules of the Quran."

"So they do hold a ceremony."

"Just a tiny one. It's rather strict around here. It's better if we leave quickly now. I don't want Nasra's brother to start an argument with me."

"Why, don't you like each other?" But Altaf had already stopped one of the rickshaws and waved for me to come over. We climbed in and I sat the entire ride squished between a fat woman and Altaf. I'd already forgotten about the problem with Nasra's brother.

We didn't see much of Nasra and Farooq in the days that followed the wedding and I began to miss the conversations I'd had with the feisty young woman. Altaf stuck to our agreement and was making plans for a trip to Islamabad, Rawalpindi and to Murree in Kashmir.

"Chacha Sardar will come to Islamabad with us. We can stay with him at his flat. He is still on leave for another week and wants to take us on some excursions. I also have an aunt in Islamabad but she's already gone home and I didn't see her before she left."

"You'll organise things for us, I'm sure and I can't wait to see more of the country at last. How far is Islamabad from here?"

"Almost a day's journey to the West. We'll leave early on Monday morning. We can stop on the way at the new Tarbela Dam and have a look at it. Chacha Sardar is rather proud of it."

Monday was in two days.

"Sure why not? I can have a look at the new dam."

On the weekend, Altaf told me that a group of young people wanted to go and watch the horse races nearby and that we were invited.

"Mamu Ashraf is my mother's brother and shareholder of the racing club. The club is having a horse race just outside of Jhelum. It's a formal event and we must dress up for the occasion. It's going to be fun, you'll see. Nasra and Farooq are also coming."

It was the first time the newlyweds were showing themselves in public and I was looking forward to it. Nasra was wearing the compulsory red for a newly-wed bride and lent me one of her many saris. A rose-coloured sari blouse and a long baby-pink length of fabric, embroidered with a silver border.

"How do I wear this best?" I asked her and eyed the length of fabric suspiciously.

"First you must put on the blouse and the petticoat." Nasra helped me to get into these articles of clothing then took the soft baby-pink fabric.

"Look, you must wrap the fabric over your hand back and forth just like that, to make the folds," she instructed me. "No, you must hold them together like that. Then you tuck the pleats into the front of the petticoat. Here, fasten them with a large safety pin. Yes, just like that."

"Nasra," I said as she knelt next to me with the safety pin in her mouth. "Can you imagine Amma ever hitting you?"

She took the pin out of her mouth and burst out laughing. "No! Amma is just about the nicest mother-in-law you could wish for. Why are you asking me that?"

"Oh, just a thought I had. Do you believe that your mother would treat a daughter-in-law badly?"

"I even know it. My mother treats her daughters-in-law well but my brother's wife doesn't have an easy life... enough now with all that morbid talk. Come, you're ready. The others are surely waiting for us."

At first, I felt a little awkward in the Indian wrap-dress. Shirt and slacks were way better for me. The saleslady in London had also demonstrated the wrapping of the sari differently on me and Zohra and the end-piece was worn over your head just like a veil. But I got used to it after a while and I felt quite feminine wearing a sari.

"Oh Isabell, you look just like one of our women here," Altaf praised me.

"And you are wearing the turban – just like a Rajput." I was beginning to feel more comfortable around him again.

"A Rajput?"

"Yes, I remember seeing a picture once," I promptly lied.

The men had spruced themselves up as well and looked

elegant in their white Punjabi-suits, dark waistcoats and turbans with a fan in the front. When we arrived at the race course in our rickshaws, Mamu Ashraf proudly showed off his white stallion.

"His name is Prïnda." The stallion nodded his head up and down.

"See, Prïnda, you know your name, don't you?"

"What a beautiful animal! He looks just like a Marwari breed." I'd made an ill-considered remark.

"You know about Rajput horses?" Mamu Ashraf asked.

"Just a little bit. My horse Kalyan…" I began proudly and stopped in my tracks. Had I had just said that? The men looked at me in astonishment. How was I supposed to explain to them what I meant?

"Oh, nothing. Prïnda must be one of the favourites today." I changed the subject. Mamu Ashraf glanced at me a moment longer and then my puzzling remark had been forgotten. The Marwari stallion put his delicate nostrils in my hand and Mamu Ashraf handed me a piece of sugar for him.

"He seems to like you."

"Yes, Prïnda is such a beautiful animal. Aren't you just, Prïnda?"

"You'll bring us good luck during the races, Isabell," Altaf laughed. "Come on, guys, we can stand over there by the balustrade. I think the first race is about to begin."

The horsemen pointed their lances to the front and were off the mark on command. Nasra and I laughed in excitement when the magnificent horses stormed past us in full gallop. How I would have loved to ride with them! *Just as I have done so many time before*, I thought. But I, Isabell, have never sat on a horse! The men inspected the horses before the winners of the race were paraded around. Prïnda was one of the winners.

During the interval, Nasra and I were standing in the shade, leaning against the slats of a wooden fence, drinking Coke and eating snacks.

"I wanted to ask you something," I blurted out.

"Yes?" Nasra took a pakora from the paper bag she was

holding.

"Why are there blond people here in Punjab?"

"You mean like those two over there?" She covertly glanced at a group of men and quickly looked away.

"Yes like that, and the Agoo's wife for example. I've also seen others like that in Jhelum," I said.

"Good question. Some people think it has to do with the Englishmen. But older people say that it was the Greeks that settled in the North."

"The Greeks?"

"Yes, soldiers or merchants. Nobody can exactly say why. There was a lot of contact with the West because of the Silk Road. That was ages ago."

"Really, the Greeks?" I repeated baffled.

"Maybe. The Agoo's wife is from Kashmir. From Jammu. Some family connection of his. My brother has reddish hair, by the way." There was some food for thought.

We spent the entire afternoon at the horse races, having fun and returned to Khadriala in high spirits. I was dog-tired and went to bed early.

"Isabell, Isabell, wake up! Sleepyhead, it's time to get up." I needed a while before I got my bearings and realised that I was no longer sitting on the back of my horse, riding through the hills of the Pir Panjal back home. Home?

It slowly dawned on me that I didn't own thorough-bred horses and wasn't the young noblewoman Nusrat. Only the German Isabell Bertrand on holiday in Pakistan; and that Farooq's wife Nasra was the one who was shaking me by my shoulders, trying to wake me.

We quickly said our goodbyes as I would only be gone for a short week. A duffle bag was all I needed for the trip. My suitcase and guitar remained in Khadriala. Altaf, Chacha Sardar and I took the rickshaw that had been ordered in Jhelum and when we arrived there, I stood around waiting on the sandy ground by the bus stop for the two men who had gone to buy food.

A circle of curious people formed around me and I began

to feel nervous. I pulled the tjuni over my face and looked casually at the ground as if nothing was wrong. Women often wore their veil down on their shoulders when they were at home but I had learned not to do that in public. Women also wore long garments and dark burkhas with crocheted windows in front of their eyes to be able to see. Some children suddenly stepped forward and touched me. One of the boys even pulled on my tjuni. What on earth was I supposed to do?

"Ho, Chalo chalié!" I heard Chacha Sardar call out. I heaved a sigh of relief. The uncle shouted a good deal of other things I didn't understand but judging by the tone of his voice it seemed clear that he was used to being obeyed. The people grovelled and retreated, letting him through. He carried a sandwich bag with boiled eggs and chapattis that he had brought with him from Khadriala. With the other hand, he cleaved a way through the crowd.

Chacha Sardar led me away by the arm into the shade in front of the store where Altaf was still paying for more food and Sprite and Coke bottles. The crowd dispersed.

"What do all these people want from me?" I asked rather shaken.

"One of the girls thought you were a popular film star."

"A film star? Will they do that wherever I go?" I sighed.

"I hope not. We should keep an eye on you at all times."

Altaf joined us and handed me a bottle of Sprite so that I could take Hakim's bitter medicine. "Must eat something," he said in a caring tone.

"Perhaps later. I'm too nervous now."

"Alright, then drink at least. It will be hot today." I took a sip from the bottle and swallowed the medicine.

"What should we do if people want to touch me again?" I asked.

"If somebody asks, we just say that you are from Kashmir. That's what we did at the bazaar, remember? Everyone will believe that. There are quite a few people from Kashmir around and it's not unusual to look like you in the city. We can speak German and explain that it's a dialect where we come from if somebody asks."

"Okay, I see you gave this some thought. At least we have a plan. As long as they don't keep touching me, I'll be fine."

"You can take off the tjuni when we're on the bus."

"Are you sure?"

Altaf nodded. Chacha Sardar pointed to one of the buses that were parked in orderly fashion next to each other in the sand. "Look, our bus is just coming in. Let's go before the good seats are all taken," he said.

We travelled at a leisurely pace on the country road westward to Islamabad. The usual dentists and beggars did their rounds through the bus but I didn't find them as interesting as I had before. The bus suddenly stopped on the side of the road when we weren't far from the next village.

"What's the matter? Is it time for a toilet break?" I asked sleepily.

"I don't think so. Two men came aboard at the last stop and started fighting with the bus driver. Maybe it has something to do with that," Altaf answered. Chacha Sardar leaned across the aisle to speak to Altaf. "There is a pickup truck in front of the bus," he said with a troubled expression. Since I had the window seat, I couldn't see a thing.

Two more men pushed the door in the front open and a few women screeched. I got up from my seat and saw through the windows that a man on the back of the pickup truck held up a cricket bat.

Our bus driver was pulled through an open window and thrust onto the truck. The passengers began to panic. They screamed and cried and utter chaos ensued. The doors opened and many of them jumped off the bus only to stand at the side of the road while the pickup truck drove off.

"Isabell, stay here!" I sat obediently down next to Altaf.

"What was all that about? What just happened?" I couldn't comprehend what I'd seen.

"Stay here," Altaf told me calmly. "It is too hot to stand outside in the sun - and it isn't safe."

"What are we going to do now? What if they also attack us?"

"They are having a problem with the driver, not with us."

"What will they do to him?"

"I don't know. They will probably beat him up."

"Beat him up? But why?" My tummy ached.

"I couldn't understand what they were talking about," Altaf said.

He turned to speak to his uncle and they had a conversation in Punjabi. The bus windows were wide open to let in some air. I leant back in my seat. *Breathe, Isabell, breathe.* I tried to calm myself but that was easier said than done. I just wished it wasn't so hot...

Smack. My behind hurt. Somebody's hand had hit me through the open window! I flew around furiously and saw two young men run to the front of the bus. They looked back at me and grinned in triumph.

"Hey, you assholes!" I yelled at them and was about to run after them for a good old confrontation. But Altaf and Chacha Sardar held me back.

"What happened?" Altaf wanted to know.

"Those two bastards outside... one of them hit me on my backside. Through the open window," I reported all upset.

"Please sit down," Altaf warned me and took a look outside. "Please."

"Why?"

"It's not safe," Chacha Sardar said. "They are so hyped up, who knows what else they are able to do."

"I cannot just let this go, can I? " I started up.

"Believe me, it would be for the best," Altaf implored me. What choice did I have but to swallow my pride? I didn't feel like being beaten up with a cricket bat and thrown on the back of a pickup truck myself.

"Perhaps we should turn back? There are buses passing us in the other direction all the time," I said later, having downed a bottle of Coke.

"We should wait here."

Maybe I should have stayed in bed this morning, I thought with resignation. We were only halfway through the day and things were going all wrong.

The day didn't improve much. As the glistening sun rose higher in the sky, I sweated profusely and waited inside the bus with all the patience I could muster. What if no other bus stopped for us and we had to spend the night next to the road? I shuddered, just thinking about it. It took another hour or so before our patience was rewarded.

"Quickly, come Isabell. Another bus is taking us," Altaf urged me and took my bag. I trudged outside after him and Chacha Sardar.

The stranded passengers were helped to lift their luggage onto the roof of the new bus and off we went to Islamabad. I sat next to the window again. Fresh, cool air at last! The remainder of the road trip was peaceful until the bus turned into a broad avenue in Islamabad. A VW-Minibus drove slowly up alongside our bus and a man began to curse the bus driver rather aggressively. Right next to my window.

This put me over the edge!

"What the hell is the matter with you?" I yelled in German through the open window. At once, the cursing badass youngster looked a lot less self-assured. "If you are thinking of giving us trouble, think again! That'll be the day that you spoil the last bit of my trip!" I was just warming up. "Will you just sit down in your damn car and drive off?!"

Altaf pulled frantically on my sleeve. "Isabell, stop it, please! It's too dangerous to say things like that. Please sit down."

But I was so furious that I carried on scolding the baffled men a while longer in English and German before they actually drove away. Away from this crazed woman who was obviously no Pakistani and had no idea how to behave in a well-mannered way.

Very well, I thought and sat down. Some people started laughing and some applauded. I simmered down, but Altaf didn't think there was anything funny about this. "Are you totally nuts?" He scolded me. "What you did was so damn dangerous! That could have ended badly."

"Badly? You want to see badly? You knew exactly how bad things get around here, but you brought me to Pakistan anyway. And now you expect me to just sit down like a good girl and let everybody walk all over me? Why did you not say anything to them if I may ask?"

"That's not done around here. What if they lay in wait for us at the terminus? You saw what the others did to the bus driver. Do you want to get the police involved?"

I hadn't thought of that. My anger blew over. "If that gang had wanted to make trouble, the police would have come in any case," I said stroppily.

Chacha Sardar stayed out of our argument. I had the feeling that he was on my side but perhaps he just didn't understand us. We were speaking German after all. Nobody seemed all that bothered by these incidents. It was quite obvious that such confrontations were the order of the day.

The bus took us blithely past modern buildings and manicured lawns with fountains. There were even people around who wore western clothes and tailor-made suits in Islamabad!

The city bore all the hallmarks of a modern metropole. This was in such glaring contrast to what we had experienced today that it made my head hurt. For a fleeting moment, I considered the possibility to seek out the German Embassy that had to be around here somewhere. Then my sense of adventure won the upper hand again. It was a decision that I should later regret.

We approached the bus terminus.

"My flat is quite close, so we can walk from here," Chacha Sardar informed us and so we trotted down the road, passing a number of shops. A butcher worked in a space that was open to the road with a large round chopping block placed right in front of the entrance. Pieces of meat hung on large hooks from the doorframe and inside in an unappetising, smelly display. The chopping block was encrusted with blood and covered with flies. I hurried past the butchery.

"I really wouldn't like to eat meat from this place," I said.

The mere thought was nauseating.

"Why not? All butchers work in the same way."

"Are you telling me that I have been eating meat from a butcher just like this one all the time I've been here? This dirty?" I shook myself.

"Not in Khadriala but definitely in Karachi."

"Oh yuck, disgusting. That's so unhygienic!"

Altaf gave Chacha Sardar a look that seemed to say: 'We're stuck with this spoilt brat from Germany! There's just no pleasing her.'

I was tired of arguing with Altaf and kept my peace. I'd had enough excitement for one day and didn't want to risk insulting Chacha Sardar.

His flat was on the second floor of the most modest-looking building in the neighbourhood. The place was small and clean and even had a proper bathroom! I was assigned to the guest bedroom and Altaf would sleep on the sofa. Did the uncle know the truth about our relationship, then? Minutes later, I enjoyed the luxury of a shower.

Hot water, soap and some time to myself at last! I made the solemn promise to myself, to never complain about anything at home again that I had taken for granted! I got dressed in my new Punjabi suit with the peach flowers and killed time by jotting down the incidents of the day in my little notebook.

Altaf knocked on the door. "Isabell? Chacha Sardar is making us something to eat. He says that we should go for a walk while he's busy preparing dinner in the kitchen."

"There is a park around here?"

"Yes of course, just across the road. You can find loads of nice parks in Islamabad."

He turned to leave the room. "Wait a minute, Altaf. I'm sorry that I was so impulsive earlier." My apology didn't come easy but I thought it appropriate under the circumstances. "I was just angry at those guys and didn't consider that you have a forged passport and all that..."

"Let's talk about that later in the park."

Night had already fallen when we hastened across the busy main road. A well-kept park was right there in front of us and I was duly impressed with it.

The moon bathed everything in its silvery light and illuminated pruned trees and hedges. It was a magical sight. Gurgling fountains and sculptures shone brightly in the light. Oh, just to be in a park again! I realised how much I had missed the castle-park in Karlsruhe.

There were several families and couples strolling blissfully along the paved paths. Judging by today's events, I had serious doubts.

"Is it safe to go for a walk in the dark?"

"Chacha Sardar says it's safe. The police are keeping a close eye on things. Many foreign diplomats live in the area."

"Oh I see, the police, your special friends."

Altaf looked rather serious. "Isabell, I must talk to you about something."

"No please, I can't take another unpleasant surprise today." I was hoping that he wouldn't ask me again to marry him!

"I'm serious, I have to tell you the truth about something. Because you don't know the whole truth yet: the reason why I had to leave Pakistan at the age of fifteen and all that." I stopped abruptly in front of a long-stretched sculpture of a bird ready to take off. A bearded father pushed a twin-pram right past us.

"Really, and why is it that I don't know the whole truth yet?"

"Because I didn't want to worry you." Altaf stared sheepishly at his feet.

"Well, I think that train left the station a while ago. All those lies you dished! First, you made everyone believe that we were married, then you are suddenly engaged to Saïda, then you get it in your head that you want to marry me for real. And I'm the fool who knows nothing about the truth..." I couldn't stop myself using a sarcastic tone with him. What could Altaf possibly throw at me now that would blast my socks off?

"Alright then," he said. "Here goes the truth: It all started when I had a fight with the son of an army general. He's from Nasra's village and a close friend of her brother's."

"I see, that's what was behind all that underlying hostility when we were at the wedding."

"Yes, well that's not all. We didn't stay there very long because I couldn't risk anyone in his family recognising me."

"Then you killed that guy or why is it such a big deal when two teenagers have an argument?" Altaf gave me a defiant look.

"He'd insulted my family and I took a swipe at him. It turned into a major punch-up. He fell and injured his head. That meant I had to quickly disappear or his father would have done me harm. My family moved in to protect me and that's why my father was arrested. Chacha Qasim managed to organise the new passport so I could leave the country."

"No way! Now that – I didn't expect of him." I couldn't think of anything else to say.

"Family comes first."

"Was he badly injured, the other boy?"

"He was in hospital for two weeks. In a coma."

"And then?"

"He recovered and everything is okay with him now – I think. But his father is still a General and the son is now a Colonel in Rawalpindi. The father has a lot of influence and still bears a grudge against my family. Khadriala is also too unconventional for their liking."

"Unconventional? I thought it was very traditional."

"Politically speaking. My brother is in the army and other relatives as well, but we don't actually support the military government and their rules."

"What could this General still do to you after all these years?"

"We're not sure. When they couldn't find me at the time, they threw my father into prison. He didn't tell them where I was and they tortured him."

Altaf spoke rapidly and even in the moon light, I could recognise the torment he must feel. I kept listening to his shocking account of events.

"That's the reason I was unable to return home for so

long. It's the first time in a long while that I came back to Pakistan. Even now, it's somewhat of a secret that I'm here. The Agoo took care of things."

"I'm so very sorry about what happened to your father. But doesn't everybody in Khadriala know the truth? And now your finacée Saïda has every reason to snitch on you."

"Yes, Saïda's family is really miffed but they belong to our clan. They won't snitch on me. When it comes to Nasra's family, it's a different story. But Nasra's honour is at stake whether they like it or not. That's why it took them so long to give her permission to get married to Farooq in the first place."

"Nasra seems to have her family nicely under control."

"Yes she does," Altaf laughed. "She told them that I'm a distant cousin by the same name. After seven years, nobody can remember how exactly I look. It seems that I look more European now."

"Really, more European?"

"Yes." We walked for a while without talking, while the moon hoisted itself higher up the night sky.

"But what happens when someone smells a rat? Will you have to go to prison?" I asked. "You are taking so many risks. Honestly! Why didn't you tell me about all this right from the start?"

"Then you would not have come for sure."

"So what?! It's my life after all."

"I'm sorry. I had to come to Farooq's wedding and we are doing everything so that people won't find out. And I have you with me. What could possibly happen to me when you're here? You know that I love you."

I studied the sculpture of the large bird. "Don't start with that nonsense again! Now that we are getting along." This whole issue seemed to me like a tedious marathon with no end in sight!

"Would it really be so bad if we got married?" Altaf asked enticingly and touched my arm. I had to think on my feet so there wouldn't be a repeat of the pathetic scene by the canal.

"Please… you are just infatuated, aren't you?" I said and

shook his hand off. "But you are like a brother to me. A rather annoying brother. Not my kind of husband material. Why don't you try for once to understand that from my point of view? I'm not ready to get married to anyone anyway and that's it! You weren't even able to tell me the whole truth until now."

I quickly walked on and Altaf tried to catch up with me.

"But now I have told you the whole truth. I don't love any other woman the way I love you. We could get married and then live together as friends."

"What? That's a fantastic plan," I said snappily. "How often must I tell you? Brothers and sisters don't get married. I still want to do so much living on my own. Study and work and travel. I don't want to get married and I don't want to get married to you." I felt another headache coming on. It had been a bit much for one day.

"Perhaps you'll change your mind once you get to know me better. I promise that I would never marry another woman, ever, if I marry you."

"How generous of you! None of the men I've met so far had more than one wife. Even the Agoo." Now I had opened a can of worms!

"There's a man in Khadriala with two wives because the first wife was unable to have children."

"And, I hope they're very happy together."

"His second wife only had daughters and she is ashamed of it."

"Goodness, enough of that! I have no desire to even talk about marriage – anyone's marriage. Or marrying more than one woman or whatever else has got to do with it!"

"I agree that it's not the best of times to discuss this issue. Oh, just smell that," Altaf said suddenly. We stood in front of a large bush, densely dotted with white blossoms. The flowers gave off a wonderful strong scent.

"That's jasmine. Chimelli. Exactly like you. You are my Chimelli."

"Bloody hell! Stop it already! Saying things like that is so inappropriate. Have you even heard a single word I said?" I got seriously ticked off.

"Yes, yes of course I did," Altaf rushed to assure me.

"Then let's talk about something else now."

"Alright, if that's what you want."

"Yes, that's what I want," I said curtly. "Enough already." He could be so high-maintenance. I changed the subject. "What's the description saying under the bird statue?"

"'Nusrat', " he said. "It means 'Victory'."

"Really, 'Nusrat'?" Could that be a coincidence?

"Yes, why?"

"Oh nothing," I said. "Chacha Sardar is probably done with cooking by now. It wouldn't be very polite to make him wait. What if he calls the police if we are not back soon."

I couldn't help but enjoy a little sarcasm. Altaf winced at the mention of the police. I could only hope that he'd be less troublesome from now on. We'd soon left the Nusrat-Moonlight-Park and returned to the flat.

"You aren't cross, are you? I mean that I didn't tell you all those things before..." Altaf wanted to know.

"If you ask *me*, nothing much surprises me anymore. It's your life after all. Would it have been better to just come out with the truth? Sure, but that's got nothing to do with me. All I want is to get home in one piece. And in the meantime, you better behave yourself."

"I will be a good boy."

Altaf didn't say anything else but I could feel that the chapter wasn't closed by a long shot.

"I still have a few days' leave," Chacha Sardar said during dinner. We had a mild chicken curry. No beef. "Why don't we all take a day trip to Murree?"

"Where is Murree?" I asked with a full mouth.

"Murree is in Kashmir. We should be able to make it in a day by bus and even fit in a visit to the Tarbela Dam."

I had totally forgotten about the dam. There hadn't been any time on our way to Islamabad.

"I think it's an excellent idea. I didn't know Kashmir was so close by... but what if our bus is attacked again?"

"That's unlikely. I've never experienced anything like it. And then twice in one day. But you showed those thugs in Islamabad."

The dignified Chacha Sardar began to giggle and I had to smile. "With my luck, nothing would surprise me."

"I don't know what those guys in the first bus wanted. They spoke a strange dialect. Perhaps they knew the driver," Altaf added his five cents.

"And the second time around?"

"The driver in the sedan wanted to change lanes and the bus was in his way. He and his chums didn't like that very much."

"And that's why they caused such an uproar? I don't think something like that would happen in Germany. People here behave so differently."

I couldn't believe I sounded like my mother right now.

"Are you sure about that?"

I pondered the question. "People at home aren't as aggressive but who knows..." I had to think about all those friendly and peaceful people I had met in Altaf's village. Perhaps with the exception of the village elder's wife.

"Okay, then it's a done deal. We'll take a trip to Kashmir tomorrow. I'm sure it'll be really interesting," I said cheerfully.

So, we started out in the morning in a great mood when it was still blissfully cool. No dream or snoring aunt had disturbed my sleep and I felt rested and relaxed. Not a single problem in sight.

First, we took the bus in a north-westerly direction to visit the famous dam. Chacha Sardar was very proud of his dam. "A marvel of technology", he translated the text on a plaque by the viewing platform.

"This dam was completed in 1976. It was the result of the 1960 Indus Waters Treaty between India and Pakistan. The dam wall is 143 meters high and stretches almost 3 kilometres across. With its total capacity of 106 million cubic metres, it is one of the biggest artificial lakes in the world... the power stations generate a significant percentage of Pakistan's hydropower," Chacha Sardar read.

"This lake is so huge." I surveyed the reservoir in wonder. "What does the sign over there say? The writing doesn't look like Urdu."

"It's in Arabic. A quote from the Quran: *'And HE hath made the rivers for service unto you'.*"

"Mohammed was a modern man."

The two men had to laugh. "Mohammed wrote this more than 1300 years ago when he was about my age," Altaf chuckled.

"That long ago?"

"Yes, it's been a while."

Chacha Sardar moved towards the edge of the viewing platform. "Khadriala also has access to electricity now," he said with pride.

"It's becoming quite normal to have electric light," Altaf added. "We just don't have a lot of appliances yet. They have exactly one television set in the village. But I want to buy a refrigerator for my mother."

"Well, that's a good idea. I don't know what we'd do without electricity in Europe. We are so used to things like that."

I admit that it must have sounded a bit boastful. A new group of tourists pushed onto the platform and we took the next bus north. After viewing the dam, we travelled to some kind of marketplace or bus station. Here, we waited for a minibus that would take us to the resort town of Murree. High up into the Himalayas!

"We'll be taking the Simly Dam road to Murree," Chacha Sardar said.

"Another dam?"

"Yes, the Simly Dam. It is much smaller than the Tarbela and only about 30 km east of Islamabad. The view of the mountains from this road is just wonderful."

"I always thought Kashmir was part of India," I said.

"Kashmir is divided between Pakistan and India. Murree is on the Pakistani side of the mountains."

"Kashmir is divided?"

"Unfortunately, yes. Would you like something to eat?" Altaf asked in a caring tone. He tried to be nice.

We shared samosas from a bag and waited in silence. I watched a few tiny clouds drift across the sky. The marketplace consisted of army-green tarpaulins above and between the market stalls.

I noticed that one of the men was staring at me. I pulled the tjuni over my face so my hair wouldn't show and looked down at the ground. Earlier, in the women's section of the city bus in Islamabad, a man had ogled me the whole time. Ignoring Zohra's advice, I had stared back at him. Thankfully, the man and his wife had disembarked soon after. "Shouldn't people here be used to Kashmiri-looking women?" I asked.

"Why, is somebody gawking at you again?" Altaf asked.

"Yes, one of the salesmen over there."

We moved further inside the tent-market and Altaf stepped protectively in front of me. While we waited inside, the sky seemed to grow darker by the minute. One gas lamp after the other was lit and a cool wind began to blow. Although it was only early afternoon, it could have been the middle of the night.

Altaf nudged me and I saw that, at last, the minibus to Murree was ready for boarding. We sat tightly squeezed in the minibus. There were probably more people inside than was officially permitted. Nobody seemed to give a hoot about little rules like that. I was lucky enough to sit next to the window with a superb view of the scary, dark cloud cover.

"It looks creepy, Altaf," I moaned. "Is that normal?"

"We're likely in for a monsoon rain soon."

"A monsoon rain?"

"Yes, it normally passes rather quickly."

"Terrific."

The minibus pulled up the hill constantly avoiding potholes on a rocky tar road. When we were negotiating one of the many steep bends of the road, I saw the marketplace below that we had just left behind. The wind set the many gas lanterns under the roof swinging.

A mighty gust of wind caught in the tarpaulins and they ballooned outward. One of them tore loose from its pole and flew away. Then another one followed the first. By then, we were further up the serpentine road and all I could see now were rocks towering in front of us. On the other side to our left, stretched a yawning canyon.

At that moment, our jaunty excursion to Murree didn't seem like such a good idea anymore. Rain began to bombard the windows of the van and it was impossible to see anything but pouring water.

A heated discussion inside the minibus ensued. The driver stopped on the side of the road and there was nothing else to be done but to tensely wait out the downpour that was lashing out at our small vehicle.

"How long do you think will it take?" I asked Altaf in a soft voice.

"What?"

"How much longer do you think this will take?" I cried over the drumming noise.

"Can't say exactly, but the driver says we can't go up the mountain in this rain. The water comes rushing down the road like a river and could carry us off the road. We might even have to turn around."

"Sounds rather unsafe."

"It could turn into a dangerous situation."

Altaf said these words as if this was quite normal. But I had never experienced such heavy rainfall. We had to open the misted-up windows a crack for the many passengers to have air to breathe. It was quite cool outside and my shoulder under the tjuni got wet.

We waited.

The place where the van was parked turned to sludge and we slid down a little along the gravel. Panicked murmuring arose inside the vehicle and my tummy ached. The driver took the bus further up the road and parked on a narrow stretch of tar.

"He knows what he's doing," Altaf said with respect in his

voice.

"Thank God!"

It took the better part of half an hour for the sky to clear up as quickly as it had released the rain. We finally drove on and after a while, one could even see through the windows again. A cloth was handed around, for us to wipe the windows. The road was a messy sight but the driver knew his business.

Wonder what happened to that marketplace down there, I thought. It wasn't long before we'd reached the top of the next snake-like bend and passing minibuses started a gleeful hooting concert to greet us. I felt cold and wet under my wrap but then it gradually grew warmer. The sun reappeared and shone as if the monsoon rains had never happened.

We passed colourful carpet displays and were in for a simply breathtaking view of the valley and the mountains. There wasn't much time left to explore Murree before the last minibus left for the valley. We took a walk through the narrow streets of the small town, strolled over a broad bridge swarming with tourists and enjoyed the fresh mountain air.

"There are many holiday cottages around here where people can stay," Altaf said. "It's very pleasant here in summer."

"We should have a look at the English Theatre," Chacha Sardar suggested. He'd bought us another snack. "I'm sure that Isabell will be interested in that."

The English Theatre was a properly old-fashioned building complete with carved wood, painted in gold, and a red velvet curtain. Stunning. Then, before I knew it, we were seated in another minibus and on our way down again. We arrived back in Islamabad late in the evening.

"Tomorrow we'll take a trip to Rawalpindi," Chacha Sardar said, his eyes gleaming adventurously. "After this weekend, I must go back to work and I won't get another chance to take you there."

"Where is Rawalpindi?" I asked. "Is it far from here?"

"No, it's very close to Islamabad but completely different in character. Much older and, for a long time, it was the seat of the Moghuls. We could also go and visit the great Raja-Bazaar. That will be a feast for the eyes."

"That sounds nice. Perhaps, I could buy a few gifts there."

"Don't you have enough gifts yet?" Altaf acted all indignant.

"Men don't understand things like that," I answered in the same tone.

"Best we go to bed early so we can leave when it's still cool and before the morning rush hour."

In the end, it turned out that we were too early. The bazaar was still closed. So was anything else of interest, but Rawalpindi was, indeed, of a completely different character.

The streets around the Raja-Bazaar were covered in a thick layer of dirt and rubbish that forced us to use the elevated sidewalks. If you could call it that.

There was almost no traffic and I couldn't understand why Chacha Sardar had made such a big deal of it. Soon, I regretted my premature judgement when traffic turned into the same chaos as the traffic in Karachi.

"Best to go to the bazaar later," the uncle said. "We still have the whole day. Let's rather start with the tourist attractions."

We boarded a city bus that lacked the simplest of decorations and once again I settled into the women's section in the front. Only two long benches on either side.

A man sat down right across from me and his gap-toothed wife cowered next to him. He stared persistently at me. Not again, I thought, but this time I looked straight past the man and through the window. We passed an old castle and Chacha Sardar waved for me to get off the bus. Relieved, I left the gawper and his wife behind.

"Come, Isabell, I'll buy you a packet of sweets. They are called jalebees. I'm sure you'll like them." Chacha Sardar was as generous as ever. The castle turned out to be some sort of mosque.

"There are so many mosques and parks in the city," Altaf said. "It's hard to decide what to visit first."

"We should stay in the centre of town, otherwise we'll

struggle with traffic to get to the bazaar."

Chacha Sardar knew what he was talking about, of course. The place was swarming with tourists. I wished we could have taken in the unique sights of the Taxila ruins outside of town, but instead, we took a rickshaw from the Army Museum back to the Raja-Bazaar.

"That was really nice, uncle," I thanked him. "Now I'll have much to talk about when I go back home."

"We will miss you, Batshi," Chacha Sardar said and I knew he meant it. We searched for the entrance to the bazaar along the dirty street. The traffic was bad, which didn't make it any easier.

"Where was the entrance to the Raja- Bazaar… I haven't been here for a while. My wife loved to shop but I don't need that much for myself," Chacha Sardar explained sadly. The entrance to the roofed-in bazaar was well hidden between grey walls and metal gates, but we found it. One of many - and jumped into the fray.

Altaf's plan to introduce me as his young cousin from Kashmir seemed to work brilliantly. A few cunning traders didn't believe the story at first and spoke to me in some Potohari dialect. At least that's what Altaf called it. I was supposed to look clueless, which wasn't even an act.

"No, she doesn't understand you," Altaf lied for all he was worth. "She comes from an area further up north." We then said a few words in German to prove his point.

"I just hope nobody here speaks German or we're done for," I said. Up to now, our little trick had worked just fine.

"Isabell, let me handle this, and when they start haggling, I'll haggle the price down."

We got a good price again and again and my two companions helped carry the many plastic bags with fabrics, spices, fashion trinkets and khol. We even purchased a painting. It was stifling hot inside the roofed-in bazaar and I felt thirsty.

"We can buy something to drink just now. They have Coke at the stand over there," Chacha Sardar said.

"That's a good idea. It's so hot in Rawalpindi. I wish we were back in Kashmir!" I sighed. "Murree was so much cooler."

"True, the air is nice and fresh there," Altaf agreed. He had turned into an exemplary host and our arguments were a thing of the past.

We passed a stall with carpets on display. "Oh look, what do you think of the carpet over here? Isn't it just the most beautiful carpet you've ever seen?" I stroked the soft woollen pile with delight.

"Women..." Altaf groaned and rolled his eyes.

The carpet salesman immediately zoomed in on us and extolled the benefits of owning such an outstanding, valuable product. In Punjabi, of course. I smiled blankly and Altaf translated.

"He says that the carpet comes from Kashmir. Hand-knotted." Much of what we'd seen in the bazaar was from Kashmir, allegedly.

"The birds look so life-like and just look at those colours, Altaf." Perhaps, I should show more restraint. It wasn't a good idea to be too enthusiastic when haggling for a price.

"It's much too big to take with us on the plane. You've already got this picture here to stow away." He held up the painting of a young Kashmiri woman that he had just bought way below the asking price. I knew he was right but I kept stroking the carpet just a little longer.

"Kinnaa?" Altaf asked the sly salesman. How much?

The man named his price. Judging by Altaf's upset expression, the price was way too high. They had words. After some declining gestures and contemptuous grimaces by both Altaf and Chacha Sardar, we walked on.

"What did the guy say?" I wanted to know.

"He said that you are not from Kashmir, that you look too European. He asked for the normal price, he would usually get off foreigners. Seems to think that we're rich or something..."

"Pity," I said and already eyed a stall on the other side of the aisle with plenty of silk fabrics.

I was beginning to understand my mother's compulsive

shopping streak on her cruise to the Mediterranean Sea. Soon, I would be on a plane back home and this was my last chance to do proper shopping.

At least I could afford the prices here. But as much as I admired carpets and brass vases, those things were far too big and heavy to take to Germany. But this jade-coloured silk fabric would look so pretty on Renate; *Oh, and just look at these chandelier-earrings for my sister Paula*, I thought and, despite Altaf's warning, delved into my next haggling attempt.

"Can we please buy something to drink now?" Altaf complained. "Then we should slowly get going. It's getting late."

"Let's go over there," Chacha Sardar suggested.

"We can have something to drink, then we'll get some fresh air," I agreed, wiping the sweat on my brow.

As we strolled along the aisles, our beverages in hand, two bearded men in white robes walked towards us.

The older one of the two wore a crocheted skull cap, the other one had reddish hair. I quickly looked down and saw from the corner of my eye how the skull-cap-man grabbed with lightning speed between my legs. I was shocked but before I could say something, they had both disappeared in the throng of shoppers.

I stood stock still.

"Isabell, what's the matter? Come, let's go," Altaf urged me on. He hadn't noticed a thing.

"The one guy... over there... just grabbed me between my legs... as he went past us," I stuttered.

"Are you sure? Perhaps it was by accident."

"That was not by accident!" I glared at him. "How often does something like that happen to you?" What did I have to do around here to be taken seriously?

"I'm sorry. Of course, it wasn't an accident. Where is this guy now? Do you want me to read him the riot act? No, that's probably not a good idea. We're not in Germany after all." I'd heard that tune before.

"He went off in that direction." I pointed to the spot but of course, the men had disappeared in the crowd.

"He's gone."

"I can see that. And his friend is gone as well. That one had red hair," I said grumpily.

"What are we supposed to do now?" Altaf asked his uncle in English.

"It will be best for Isabell to walk between the two of us. Then she should be safe from such harassment. I thought it's a rumour that this bazaar has become dangerous for women. But apparently, there's something to it."

"Make sure that your hair is covered by the tjuni and don't look directly at anyone," he advised me. How often had I heard that piece of advice?

"How am I supposed to see where I'm going if I'm not supposed to look around?" I asked him.

"Just don't look at the men. Islamabad is rather modern but here in Pindi many people are still quite old-fashioned."

"I'd rather go back to Islamabad - as quickly as possible."

"We are on our way now. Men are not supposed to harass women but what can we do about it? We just have to be careful until we sit on the bus again," Altaf said.

"If you just knew," I said and thought of the men who had eyeballed me in the women's section on the city buses.

Chacha Sardar wanted to quickly buy some Pindi-sweets before we left the bazaar. In a corner not far from the entrance. I stood close to him with Altaf by my side when suddenly the lights went off. For a brief moment, the corner where we stood went pitch dark.

I panicked and grabbed Altaf's hand. When the lights came on again, I had a major scare. Looking up, I saw straight into the grinning face of the skull-cap-man who had felt me up in passing.

"There, Altaf, there he is again," I cried and trembled. "It's the same man who groped me!" I pushed quickly between Chacha Sardar and Altaf.

"Where, where is that man?"

As I looked up, the man was gone. Again. "He was here, right in front of me. I swear to it! The guy with the crocheted cap and the beard. He was directly in front of me."

"Are you sure?"

"What a stupid question. Of course, I'm sure. How do they do that? Disappearing so quickly?"

"They know this place. We should go." Chacha Sardar left the sweets he wanted to buy and we made our way towards the entrance. Just as we stepped outside into the street, the two same men approached us.

"Do you believe me now?" I wanted to run away but Altaf held me back by my hand.

"Stay calm and let Chacha Sardar and me handle this."

The bearded men involved my escorts in a conversation. About money. About me. That much I could understand. The ginger guy pointed to me and waved his arms around. Suddenly, the skull-cap-man disappeared again. A proper Houdini, this guy.

"Nejé, Nejé," Altaf said repeatedly seemed to get rather upset.

I hid behind him as much as I could and saw that Chacha Sardar's face was quite serious. He was quiet and pointed to the other side of the road. To a policeman who observed the traffic from the sidewalk.

Without another word, Chacha Sardar hurried across the road, carrying the painting of the Kashmiri woman under his arm as well as various plastic bags. He spoke to the policeman and kept pointing toward us. The ginger didn't seem to notice him.

Altaf said something. "Ahó, ahó," the other man grinned, climbed into a waiting rickshaw and off he went.

"At last. Hopefully, they're gone for good," I sighed with relief. Altaf waved for his uncle to come back. But the uncle still spoke to the policeman and didn't see him.

"We must go," Altaf insisted, "and quickly now. This guy wants to buy you, this scoundrel! For his boss. He says he's going to get the money then come back. He thinks he struck a deal, but I had to get rid of him somehow. I'll quickly go and get Chacha Sardar. Stay here where I can see you."

"What money? Don't leave me standing here all alone!"

"We'll be right back."

I didn't want to run after him and instinctively retreated into a recess to the side, grinding my teeth. From here, I could see how Altaf pushed his way through the kamikaze-rickshaws.

He'd soon reached Chacha Sardar and spoke animatedly with him. He waved, probably to reassure me. Altaf, Chacha Sardar and the policeman stood on the edge of the sidewalk, ready to cross as soon as they found a gap. I moved forward, wanted to meet them half-way. Better than waiting for them here by the bazaar.

Suddenly I was afraid for my life.

It all happened so quickly. Somebody held me by my arm and I wanted to spin around. A rough cloth was pressed over my face, covering nose and mouth. A nauseating hospital smell.

Then there was only darkness.

CHAPTER EIGHT

Airplane, guinea pigs, pecan pie, Athens, hospital smell...
I sighed deeply. Such a stupid dream.

Muffled voices and rancid body odour all around me.

Did I get seasick again on the ferry to Salamina? My brain
switched on again. I tried to open my eyes. Not easy at all.
The room seemed to be small and dark. I sweated and the
wool blanket I was lying on felt scratchy. Where was I?

Somebody coughed softly next to me and a muffled voice
said something. I couldn't understand a thing. There were
other girls in the room with me. Was I in the dormitory for
single women in Khadriala? Or in Dâstân perhaps?

"Shireen, is that you?" I whispered. "Nasra?"

Giggling. A bit louder this time. What was going on?

I sat up abruptly. Oh no, I felt nauseous! I tried to breathe.
The air was hot and humid. It was I who smelled of hospital!
Was I injured? *Just don't start vomiting now*, I thought.

A small tilted window let in a little moonlight and air
somewhere above my head. There were faint noises outside
in the street. Apart from that, it was quiet. I saw a door on
the far end of the room.

I threw off the blanket and it landed on the floor. I
ignored the timid, urgent whispers. *I must reach that door*, I
thought. On my way there I steadied myself against bed
frames here and there. The door was locked. Why?

I had to get out of here! I beat against the door, hammered
against the large wooden board that separated me from the
street and the outside world. Hammered and hammered!

"Open up! Open up! I need to get out of here!"

There was no answer and nobody opened the door.

Nobody.

I grew tired and sank to the floor. Tears were running down my face as the other girls led me back to my blanket. Somebody lifted it from the floor. Why was I here? A hand held out a glass of water and I drank thirstily.

"Shukria," I mumbled weakly. Thank you.

Altaf and Chacha Sardar and policeman on the other side of the road. So much traffic. A hand touched my arm. Did all of this really happen? Where was Altaf? And Chacha Sardar?

Altaf didn't want to let me out of his sight. If I was at a hospital, why was the door locked? Too many questions. Clear thoughts eluded me. For the first time since embarking on this trip to Pakistan I felt alone. All alone.

I put my aching head on the mattress and covered myself.

When I woke up again, daylight brightened the wall above. A key turned noisily inside the lock. The girls sat up sleepily.

"Chalo, chalié! Ho chalo!" Rough male voices cut through the quiet of the morning. So it wasn't a hospital. I stood up on wobbly legs. Acidic nausea rose in my throat.

One after the other, the veiled girls stumbled out of the dark room into the dawn. I wrapped myself tightly into the tjuni. *Cover your hair*, I thought. The air felt much cooler than it had the day before. I looked around. Where was this place? Somewhere behind some shops.

That much seemed clear.

Was this still the Raja Bazaar? Hard to tell. What did these people want from me? Was somebody searching for me?

Two Land Rovers waited around the corner. In a dark alley. Not the latest models but what the hell did I know about cars anyway?

My head was filled with cotton wool. The pressure in my stomach rose up in my throat. I bent forward and vomited right next to one of the armed men. I felt so dizzy that I almost fainted. The guy with the weapon swore at me. He made a move as if he wanted to push me away with the butt of his rifle because I had smudged his boots. A sharp command and the armed guy stepped aside.

There were more words, then one of the girls knelt beside me. She gave me water from a tin cup. I still retched a little. Then I rinsed my mouth with the rest of the water and stood up bravely.

To attempt an escape at this stage would have overextended my strength. Apart from that, I couldn't even find my way around the maze around the bazaar, never mind out here. Despite those obstacles, I would have loved to just run away, rather than climb after the others into the parked Land Rover. Or scream for help. Just that it was doubtful that anyone would have hurried to my aid.

The connection to Altaf and Chacha Sardar was disrupted. How were they supposed to know where to look for me?

Perhaps the police were searching for me in a completely different place – if they were looking for me at all. And where was I supposed to run?

I was no James Bond, who got zapped and managed to still save the world straight after. No maze would be too complicated for James. He'd balance his way out across rooftops or race hand-cuffed on a motorbike through shops and stuff like that. But I was no James Bond.

The weapons the men brandished, were the first ones I had seen since Karachi. They were machine guns. The mere sight crushed the last remnants of my bravery. The other girls sat crammed together on their seats, their faces hidden by tjunis and dabattas.

Had they been abducted in the same way that I had been grabbed? Abducted?!

How could Altaf bring me to such a place? He had broken his promise to me; the promise he'd made in Jhelum. I was angry, but what was I supposed to do with all my anger?

I wanted my freedom back! That's why I had to keep a clear head about me – if this was at all possible. My early survival training as a child kicked in. *Pull yourself together and wait until an opportunity presents itself.*

I had learned to switch off my feelings. Just like that. I didn't have to give it a second thought. And I was sure that opportunity would present itself. Soon.

We hit the road, drove right, then left, then right again through the dusty, deserted streets. I tried to memorise the route until it became too complicated.

Perhaps this was due to the after-effects of the Chloroform but I still felt woozy. The sun was rising to the right. That meant it was East, right? The main roads looked familiar. A second Land Rover directly in front of us. We were heading out of town and were soon in the country. For the first time, I realised that I could be in actual danger.

We were not even half an hour on the northbound country road, when I began to try and persuade the men on the front seats that they should let me go.

"I am a tourist from Europe," I tried to explain the facts in English. "Please let me get off somewhere. I'll find my way back. Over here would be a good spot." I was ordered to shut up and sit down. Now! Could they even understand English?

"We are going to Peshawar. Peshawar." That much I understood.

Where on earth was that? Up north, of course, stupid question. We were travelling due north most of the time. I hadn't seen the ginger and the guy with the crocheted cap since yesterday. They had probably done their job.

Why did these villains think that it was a good idea to kidnap a German tourist?

Then it dawned on me: of course, they didn't know that I was a German tourist. Altaf and I had had the splendid idea to introduce me as his cousin from Kashmir. Dammit! Just to save some stupid money. Now I was in a nice pickle. But that wouldn't get me down.

All I had to do was keep myself from thinking about all the things that could happen to me.

I was unable appreciate the beauty of the passing landscape. Here I sat on my seat and screamed inside my head: I want to get out of here, right now! My stomach did somersaults.

Who was the patron saint of young women travelling

alone? I had no clue. Grandma Heydenreich would have known for sure. Never mind. Whoever you may be, get me out of here, do you hear me?!

After a while, I just sat there wallowing in my gloom, waiting for the hours to pass. The Land Rovers drove on and on, jolted by the rocky side roads the human traffickers used to take us to Peshawar.

I sat with my chin resting on my hand, looking out of the car window, when I saw a small brown beetle crawling along the rubber seal outside. I envied this little beetle its freedom. It could just fly away when it had enough of crawling and continue on a bush or rock of its choice.

I, the mighty human, had to sit inside a Land Rover with other people I didn't even want to know. Ironic. I closed my eyes. My head ached from all this thinking. The little bug was carried away by the air stream. At least it was free. I sighed unhappily and sat brooding in a morose mood.

There was no hope for a quick escape. In my imagination, I would have loved to just jump out of the slow-moving car. Not very realistic, judging by the machine guns and the hardened faces of our guards.

Patience, I reminded myself and leaned glumly against the accursed bench inside this accursed car that carried me farther by the minute, away from Islamabad and my idea of normal. It was hot and dusty. They gave us girls water and something to eat and we were even allowed to have a toilet break. When we were ordered back into the Land Rover, I became more talkative.

"So, you just sit here and put up with all this. You know this place and you speak the language. You could escape, but no, you prefer being kidnapped!"

Some of the girls looked up with tears in their eyes. Of course, they didn't understand a word I said. We shared the same space in the car and that was the end of our similarities. There was a huge abyss between us. Despite all that, it felt good to say something and hear myself talk.

"I have no idea why I'm here or who these nut-jobs are," I

blabbered. "I'm a tourist from Europe and was visiting the bazaar with my friends. No, actually we were about to leave the bazaar. And these bastards drugged me and dragged me away, just when Altaf and Chacha Sardar weren't looking. Those two were supposed to take care of me."

I stared out of the window again in resignation. It was ridiculous to speak to myself like that. I wondered how late it was? Midday, perhaps?

"The heck with it. You can't even understand what I'm saying." I challenged the girls with a long stare.

One of them looked me directly in the eye. She was very pretty with her translucent, light brown eyes in a dark face. There was a hint of intelligence and something like - courage. Strands of dark, glossy hair had worked themselves out from under the tjuni and onto her forehead. Her mouth was resolutely compressed.

"Some of us here do understand English," she said sadly. "Most of us just a little bit. What is your name?"

I gave her a baffled look. She spoke excellent English.

"My name is Isabell," I breathed.

"Isaba. Issabéel."

"Isabell," I repeated firmly.

"Isabé. Strange name." She cracked a smile. "My name is Shabnam Choudhury, but everybody just calls me Banu. The others here are Lalli, Schabila, Nivin, Tarub…"

She pointed from one of the four other captives to the other. They sat cowered in their seats and looked up in awe when she said their names. I was of average height, but in comparison to them, I must seem like a blonde giant. The girls looked at me furtively and giggled.

"Nice to meet you, Banu. Salaam aleikum. I wish we could have met under different circumstances but here we are. I come from Germany."

"Oh really, from Germany?" Banu seemed shocked. "I heard their leader Bakhri-Shah say that you are Kashmiri." She quickly glanced at one of the men who sat in the front.

This Bakhri-Shah sat next to the driver. He wasn't very

tall, had light skin, a reddish-brown moustache and wore a felt cap on his round head that reminded me of a double pancake. The surly expression around the corners of his mouth made him look uglier than he already was.

I knew that 'Bakhri' meant 'goat' and wondered how had this unlikeable man had received his rather unfortunate nickname.

"No, I really am German. I was invited to a wedding in a village near Jhelum. That's why I took a plane to Pakistan. We wanted to travel around a bit afterwards so I could see a little of the country. He only acted as if I was from Kashmir, so the sales guys wouldn't pinch such high prices from us. We were at the Raja Bazaar when I was abducted. I think they put me under with Chloroform."

"That is very bad. I'm so sorry for you."

I didn't know what to expect or why I was telling Banu all of this fresh off the press. She was in the same position as me after all and unable to help me in any way.

"Well, I will split as soon as I can. That's for sure," I said defiantly.

"Ai, ai, ai. I don't think that's so easy. Did you see their weapons? Some of the men are Pashtun, I think. My aunt told me," Banu whispered.

"Your aunt?" I asked flabbergasted and tried to ignore my recurring headache. I could vaguely remember that Atesh had once mentioned the Pashtun.

"Yes. I cannot understand them all the time but sometimes they speak a mixture of Punjabi and Urdu."

"How come your aunt knows? What has she got to do with them?" I whispered back.

At this point, Banu told me the whole story; how her great-aunt, related by marriage, had persuaded her to move to Islamabad to live with her and to study at a private college. Banu came from a remote town called Lalamussa and that her family was rather traditional. Her father had made an exception for his youngest daughter.

"I rejoiced because I didn't want to live in Lalamussa. I

love to study, you know. But then everything changed overnight," Banu said with a sad tone in her voice.

We had to whisper so the men on the Land Rover's front bench couldn't hear us. The other girls were also joining in now and the men didn't seem to mind our whispered conversation.

"Chachi took me to the bazaar to buy new clothes," Banu gnashed her teeth in despair. "She told me, by the way, that she'd sold me to these people from Peshawar. As if I was a buffalo or a sheep!"

"Your aunt sold you?" I asked aghast.

Banu nodded. "They look for pretty girls and sell them as brides." Up to now, I hadn't thought much about the purpose they had in mind for us. Selling us as brides? That'll be the day!

"All I ever wanted was an education and then to get a job. To be independent before I get married. That's not for women, Chachi said. She will tell my family that I met a young man and eloped with him. She knows very well that I will be disgraced. My family wouldn't believe it if I could tell them the truth."

"Imagine, your own aunt!"

I had tears in my eyes. Tears of commiseration. Banu's story was heart-breaking. But actually, I wasn't in a better position right now. Then a thought flashed through my mind.

Was it possible that Altaf was involved? In the kidnapping? Had he known the men at the bazaar? Had he sold me to them as well?

The flash waned. No, definitely not. Altaf didn't have a reason to do such a thing and Chacha Sardar…never. The son of the General, perhaps?

"How dreadful. Why wouldn't your family believe you?" I asked quickly.

Truth be told, my mother hadn't believed me either when I had fallen so ill after my trip to Greece. It was the first time in a while that I had any thoughts of my mother.

"Chachi is one of the elders in the family and the wife of

my late grandfather's brother. But her love of money is greater than her love of me. Otherwise, she would not have done this, right?" Banu wiped a tear away. "I can never go back. Because of all the lies she'd spread about me. I cried and screamed at the bazaar. Then I tried to run away – but nobody was prepared to help me." Banu looked down at her clenched fists.

"They found me of course when I tried to hide in a shoe shop. Chachi beat me. They told everybody that I was her niece and tried to run away and live with my American lover. After that, nobody would even listen to what I had to say."

"Was that yesterday?" I asked her softly.

"Yes, yesterday. They have a carpet shop at the bazaar. The storeroom where they kept us also belongs to that shop. It's on the other side of the road, to the left of the bazaar."

Banu pointed to her left as she saw everything before her inner eye. Just that here, there was nothing to see but the hills and fields.

Oh dear, the carpet shop! This had to be the same stand where Altaf and I had been admiring those beautiful, expensive carpets. And I had nearly bought that carpet with the pretty birds I'd liked so much!

"But if your family believes all that talk, that means…"

"Yes, it means I can never go back. They are more concerned about my reputation. Oh, how I wish I could speak to my father and explain everything to him."

"One day perhaps…"

Banu changed the subject and pointed to a petite girl who sat silently on the other end of our bench, veiled in a black cloak. I gave her a closer look. The girl had Asian features.

"Her name is Nuwa. I feel very sorry for her," Banu said. "She comes from a place close to Gilgit. That's on the border with China. She doesn't understand any Urdu, only Balti and Chinese. She speaks to Tarub, who can understand her."

"On the border with China?" I asked flabbergasted. That far away?

"Yes. Her parents lost their lives in a landslide in their

village. Some guy picked her up when she tried to find survivors in the hills. The gang here bought her from that bugger for next to nothing. Tarub says that they want to sell her to a 'house of ill repute'." I stared at her and Banu gave me a resigned smile.

"What about your family, Isabé?"

Right, what about my family? That seemed such a very long time ago. I tried to remember. "Oh, my father died two years ago and I still have a mother and two sisters. Back in Germany. They have their own lives and don't care much about what I do."

"They have their own lives?" Banu asked.

"Well, you know… their own stuff. My youngest sister is almost sixteen and still lives with my mother. My older sister and I moved out a while ago."

Banu couldn't believe her ears. "You moved out? You mean, you live on your own?"

"Well yes, that's not unusual where I come from. I used to live with my Grandmother. That was before my father died. It was unbearable at home. Especially because of my mother," I tried to explain. But we were worlds apart.

"Your mother?"

I had no intention of thinking about such things, never mind talking about them. The 'state' of my mother's mind, the hidings... that was just too close to the bone. That's why I just said curtly: "Well, she isn't quite right in the head, doesn't behave all that motherly." My new friend gazed at me. Uncomprehending.

"But you cannot live on your own, Isabé. That's too dangerous. And what about your reputation? What does the rest of your family think, your grandparents, uncles, cousins?"

Strangely, I had always felt safest in my room under the roof. And who cared about my reputation anyway? Banu thought it was dangerous to live on your own, but it had been her own aunt, one of the elders in the family, who had sold her to the human traffickers.

"I like it. It helped me learn self-reliance. I barely know

everyone in our family, I could care less about them. They feel probably the same."

"I cannot believe that you live like a man – so free. And your family isn't worried about your reputation?"

"Well, that's how it is. Life is quite different over there."

I noticed that the other girls were all chatting away animatedly, except for Nuwa. But we were probably getting too noisy. One of the guards in front turned around and hit one of the girls, who sat closest to him, over the head with the flat of his hand.

She screeched in surprise and the offending man barked a warning. We fell abruptly quiet. The girls moved closer together and out of the man's range. My head was throbbing. I leaned against the dirty window pane and must have dozed off into a dreamless nap shortly after.

The Land Rover began to rumble over an uneven dirt road and I was shaken out of my sleep, sweating and thirsty. Luckily, my head had stopped throbbing somewhat. Banu was staring gloomily ahead. I glanced outside. We were driving through a sea of grey tents.

"Where do all these people come from?" I asked amazed.

"A refugee camp. Refugees from Afghanistan. The Russians started a war over there, you know. It's becoming too dangerous in the villages in northern Afghanistan. In the mountains. That's why they are coming here over the border into Pakistan."

The light-coloured round tents were strewn all across the plain. In between them, there was an eager hustle and bustle. The women's clothes and tjunis were dirty and they carried unwashed children on their hips. They had probably been forced to give up the battle against the dirt due to a dire lack of water.

Many of them were unveiled. The hardened features of the Afghani people were completely different to those of the Pakistanis I had seen so far. There were no bright colours anywhere in sight, everything was a dirty grey. The men wore untidy turbans or felt hats that looked like thick pancakes.

Just like the hat of the guy on the front seat.

"But there is such an enormous number of refugees," I whispered.

"Yes, and there are often problems. Lack of food and not enough water. These people get sick. The men don't want to hand in their weapons and the locals accuse them of committing crimes."

Small surprise then that Atesh had fled Afghanistan for Germany! A group of ragged boys came running towards our vehicles and begged. Our kidnappers yelled at them and waved their arms around. The boys hung back and the Land Rovers drove on at a slow pace.

"Maybe we should jump out of the car here, They have to drive so slowly," I said.

Banu seemed terrified. Not the reaction I had expected. "And then?"

"I'm sure they have Red Cross or UN workers around here. We just run and you ask your way to them."

"Here? They will catch us immediately. We can't get through that crowd. I can't see any UN vehicles and the 'Red Cross' is called the 'Green Half Moon' around here. All I can see are Afghans. All they need here are even more newcomers. They speak another language I don't understand. I'm sure they won't be prepared to help us."

Oh no! I watched the milling crowd with a feeling of longing and discouragement at the same time. The Land Rovers continued to crawl through the crowd. I scanned the plain but Banu was right. There were no official vehicles or tents in sight. Only a sea of grey.

Then we suddenly left the refugee camp behind. We were back on the country road and I was forced to abandon my wild escape plans for the time being. We had almost reached our destination.

The destination of the human traffickers, not mine.

Peshawar was about the size of Rawalpindi. At least as far as I could tell. The town seemed rather primitive and not as civilised as Islamabad and Rawalpindi. In my eyes, this town resembled a vast village. There were no buses around here and no parks. The sounds were muffled and the smells different. I couldn't detect any Europeans and there were hardly any women in the streets. Most of the men had hatchet faces with hooked noses under their pancake hats and looked just like the Afghani refugees in the camp.

When we passed rows of one-storey buildings on the dusty roads, the muezzins began their calls for prayer in their long towers at the same time. I tried to memorise the route we took and any kind of landmarks. Everything seemed to be under a layer of dust, even the curtains in front of the doorways and the carved wooden covers in front of the windows.

We drove to the edge of town. The Land Rovers turned into a large yard and came to a halt. We were allowed to visit a latrine while most of our guards headed off to prayer. A woman covered by a black burkha brought chai and chapattis for us.

Then we were joined by more bedraggled captives. A few veiled girls climbed reluctantly into the other vehicle. These gangsters were so sure that we wouldn't try to run away that they simply locked the cars and walked off. We waited.

Two more four-by-four vehicles drove into the yard and parked on the other side next to a few dented cars. Most of the girls dozed.

I watched how a number of men began to carry brown-paper packages from those vehicles to a thatched roof and to stack them underneath. One of the packets tore open and a flat cake that looked like brown tar peeked out.

The man who carried the cake covered it roughly with the paper and put the package on top of the pile. I almost fainted when I heard an English male voice.

"F*** you! Be careful you moron! That goes over there, you damn hairy lummox. Wrap that properly and fasten the tie around it! Do you want it to fall out and right into the lap of Interpol or what?"

The English-speaking man came into sight. He seemed to

be a bearded Englishman with a broad floppy hat – or was his accent Australian? A genuine Indiana Jones. What the hell was he doing here? Searing hope suddenly shot through my veins. I jumped up. This man was my salvation. He simply had to rescue me!

"I must speak with this man!" I hissed in Banu's ear. "He will help me. He'll take me with him…" Banu pushed me down by my shoulders.

"Isabé," she whispered excitedly. "Stay here! They are all in cahoots. He won't help you. He's a drug dealer. They will put you in shackles if you try to run away. What good will that do you?"

Of course! That's what was in those packages. A bunch of drugs! My sister Paula's dealer-boyfriend would have been delighted.

"Oh my word," I flopped down onto the hard seat. "You are right. Oh no!" I cried in disappointment. I suddenly hated this Indiana Jones.

"Isabé, you must stay strong. Trust in God." That sounded like senseless chatter.

"No, Banu. It's all useless. They will flog me off to some old and ugly gnome in the mountains. Then it'll be too late," I sobbed.

"Allah will protect us. Allah u Akbar. Don't give up hope."

Banu was right: I couldn't allow them to get to me, had to prevail against the odds. *Pull yourself together for goodness sake*, I scolded myself.

"Where exactly is Peshawar, Banu, and where are we?"

"It's on the border to Afghanistan. In the Hindukush. Part of the old silk road from China to Europe," she said softly. "I'm sure the Pamir Mountains are visible from here in the West." I had totally forgotten how educated Banu was.

"Do you think they will take us across the border into Afghanistan?"

"I hope not. There is war in Afghanistan. You know that. All those refugees just now —"

The image sent shivers down my spine but I had no time

for politics and stuff like that. I had to come up with a plan and quickly. Under no circumstances would I let them take me to Afghanistan.

The men in the yard seemed to celebrate something. The Indiana Jones-guy held up a bottle of whisky and poured it into tin cups for each of his pals. They yelled something, held up their tin cups and knocked back their tipple as if it was water.

I observed the hullabaloo with great contempt from behind the edge of my tjuni. The foreigner had put on the regional costume and a flat turban. You could barely tell him apart from the other bandits.

Soon, a few vehicles left the complex and when I looked up again, the pile of brown packets had disappeared. In their place, rifles leaned against the wall under the thatched roof and in front of them were weapons that I couldn't even name. And wooden boxes.

I was getting tired of watching. Perhaps it wasn't such a bad idea to try and doze. The sun began to set when we were finally on the move again. At least it was cooling down. Again, we drove north along dusty streets past dusty shops.

When we were back on the country road, Banu nudged me. "Just look over there to your left. Do you see the Hindukush?"

"Yes." There were stark mountains as far as the eye could see.

Probably the Pamir mountains. Not far from us, men with heavily laden donkeys in tow struggled up a narrow path toward the border, followed by women with bundles on their heads and babies on their hips.

"That's Afghanistan. The Khaiber Pass is about here," Banu pointed to some spot between the mountains.

"Those poor people! That must be hugely exhausting."

"Yes."

"Where are we going now? I thought we were staying in Peshawar."

"No, I heard them say that we will carry on via Mardan all the way to Dargai. That's further up in the North. A small place. They seem to have their headquarters somewhere around there. At least the head of the gang is waiting there for us."

"That's just peachy; the head of the gang. I can hardly wait to meet him." Perhaps it would be possible to negotiate with him. Along the way, we saw more refugee camps with outlaws who stared at us in despair but also full of pride. But none of the camps was as large as the one we had seen right before we'd reached Peshawar.

Here and there, dark guns could be seen strapped to the grey backs of the men. We drove through a grey town until we arrived at a cluster of houses. Not much more than a small village.

The cars pulled into a large courtyard, again framed by buildings. This complex was protected by a high wall – and by armed men in Afghani clothes. How was I supposed to escape from here? The Land Rovers came to a halt next to each other in front of the far wall.

The first thing I saw was a group of men to the right side of the courtyard. I shuddered when I caught sight of a groaning man with his shirt ripped off. He was tied to a wooden frame in a corner of the yard. His back was crisscrossed with long red welts. I tried not to look at him. I had my own problems!

A low wall shielded a few rooms to the left of the courtyard. Darkly-veiled women squatted there around open fireplaces. To the right was a convoluted complex of buildings. We had to get out of the cars and line up not far from the cooking fires. Then I made another shocking discovery: the head of the gang was a woman!

Every man behaved in an exceedingly respectful manner in her presence, grovelling even. The coarse, stocky woman, they were calling Sadu-zai, appeared to be middle-aged.

The embroidered veil had slipped off her grey head and onto her shoulders. She had a few gold teeth that gave her light-coloured face that was a network of thin wrinkles, a look of wealth. Sadu-zai was surrounded by an aura of unassailable authority as she inspected us – the new merchandise.

When it was my turn, the leader poked me here and there in the arm and my back, which irritated me greatly. She held up my chin and peered at my face and my teeth. I would have loved to bite her but I resisted the temptation. Then she ran her beringed fingers through my hair. Perhaps she was looking for lice. I hated it when somebody touched me like that. I was no horse or prize-winning dairy cow!

"Hey!" I shook myself instinctively.

"Qashang dokhtar," she said approvingly and whistled through her gold teeth. Didn't she speak English?

"I am a German national and I demand to be released at once," I said impassively. "You have no right to hold me captive in this place."

I had learned rudimentary Urdu but I wasn't going to make an effort for these bandits. Here, I would speak only English. I didn't see why I should adjust to their needs. I wanted to remain as foreign as I possibly could.

The hard-nosed Sadu-zai was unimpressed. And she understood.

"Ah, you speak English! Qashangi," she cackled. "Good education! A good body and good teeth. Bright eyes and fair hair. They are genuine. And she speaks English!" Sadu-zai looked around and the men began to laugh as if she had cracked a great joke. The woman spoke a passable if somewhat halting English.

"We will find you a rich husband. You are worth every Rupee, Qashangi."

"I wouldn't be so sure," I baulked. "I am German and my name is not Qashangi!"

"German, he?" She knitted her brow.

"Yes, of course. My name is Isabell Bertrand and you will release me at once," I insisted loudly. The more people heard my name, the better. *Maybe there is a police mole around who could forward the information*, the James Bond in me thought.

"Ho, ho. Getting cheeky, are we?! The little one is feisty. Why would we release you, of all these girls here? We could demand a pretty ransom for you. You will understand that

I'm a businesswoman. All this here costs a lot of money. The family costs money. My children must eat. You don't want my children to starve now, do you?"

"My family doesn't have money."

"Aaah, but your government. They have loads of money. Germany is a rich country, is it not?"

The shrewd businesswoman winked at me with her light-coloured eyes.

Perhaps, that wouldn't be the worst option. Better than ending up in the harem of some rich, lecherous man. Just the way I judged Sadu-zai, she'd probably try both. But what if the German government refused to pay the ransom? Better not think about that. "Will you keep me here?"

"Hmm, hmm, hmm, let me think about it, Qashangi. We must keep you safe. Safe from the eyes of men with bad thoughts… hahaha." Her laughter had a vicious undertone. A few of the men cringed.

I had, by chance, blundered into her sphere of power but I'd cork-screw my way out again at some stage.

"They will find me no matter where you hide me."

"Oh, my pretty one, nobody will find you where we will take you. I promise you that," Sadu-zai said full of irony. Her breath reeked of garlic and goat's cheese and tooth decay, as she stood so close to me.

"Where will you take me?"

"Wouldn't you like to know! You will go with the other girls. I'll send you into the mountains until the dust has settled. I can think of a number of good buyers who would give half a fortune for a little woman like you. Such a little hot-blooded racehorse. Hah, hah!" She gleefully rubbed her rough hands.

Sadu-zai wore a thick gold ring on almost all of her swollen fingers and chains around her neck and large earrings decorated with jewels.

"Yes, half a fortune. Or the Germans will pay for you. My people in Rawalpindi did a good job. What good fortune!" She clicked her tongue and laughed. What a lark.

She was probably already counting the money she would get paid for me. *Don't crow too soon*, I thought grimly.

All that jewellery did nothing for the beauty of this woman. It had surely been bought with the money she'd made with the sale of young women. Or that of weapons or drugs.

I found her disgusting but if I wanted to survive, I couldn't lock horns with their commander in chief. She prodded me with her finger into my shoulder and waved for me to go and join a group of girls around Bakhri-Shah. Banu was diagonally in front of me, wrapped tightly into her grey tjuni, staring at her feet.

"Here is another one for you, my son." Son?

"Ta dza!" Bakhri-Shah yapped at me impatiently and waved impetuously. I was supposed to step forward. I was peeved by his surly expression. I shot my most venomous look at him and didn't move.

Sadu-zai clapped her hands and snapped "Sabadana. Samhal!"

Bakhri-Shah shrank back. I concluded that she had reprimanded her son. Perhaps she didn't like that he treated us so roughly. Expensive merchandise, money, lots of Dollars...

I moved forward next to Banu and copied her stance. She moved slightly in silent support. I then observed from under my eyelashes how Sadu-zai inspected the remaining girls and put them into groups.

"Ta dza!" Bhakri-Shah ordered one after the other.

Two of the girls were led away. They lamented vociferously. One of them was sturdy and the other one rather small. I didn't know them. Banu later told me that they lacked physical appeal and were sold right here as household slaves. Now there were only five of us in our group and three in another. Apparently, we were the girls who were 'more marketable'.

"Kashar ror. Idris." Bakhri-Shah called a young man who was busy saddling horses. Beautiful chestnut-coloured horses.

The young man looked up reluctantly while slowly lashing

down a leather strap and calming the mare. I hadn't paid attention to him until now. This Idris didn't seem very fond of Bakhri-Shah. We should get him to join our club!

"Ahó."

"Prede shabâne." Idris took his time before answering.

"Ahó."

Then I glanced at him unobtrusively. I felt confused. I knew this man. How come I knew this man? He was one of the Pashtun-bandits; just because of that fact, it was completely impossible that we had ever met before.

This Idris looked very different compared to the other bandits; not as sinewy and half-starved like most of the men or stocky and thick-set like Bakhri-Shah. He was tall and muscular and had light-brown hair. I suddenly hit me. He resembled Imran - in Nusrat's life.

I tried not to stare at him. *Rubbish*, I scolded myself, *you're imagining things! He cannot be this Idris. Your imagination is playing tricks on you. All these wacky dreams from Nusrat's lifetime are going to drive you insane!*

I was pretty sure that this Idris had bright eyes. Almost green. Imran's eyes had been brown, right? There you go! My imagination had played a trick on me again.

We were taken to the rooms behind the low wall. Four girls to one room. There was even a washroom with a hand operated pump that we were allowed to make use of.

One of the women gave us a change of clothes. Just like the clothes that had been fashionable at Nasra's wedding. We had to change into them. My suit was a fuchsia colour and the gold embroidery was scratchy.

They also fed us again. Tea, chapatis and stew. I had to think of the story of Hansel and Gretel and how the evil witch had fattened them up. But I was hungry. The chilli wasn't so bad and I drank a lot of water with it.

"Idris is Bakhri-Shah's half-brother and the two of them can't stand each other," Banu whispered in my ear after she'd had an extensive conversation with Tarub.

And Tarub had heard it from one of the deeply veiled

women who'd put the food in front of us. Tarub was fluent in Pashto amongst other languages. She must be a real linguistic genius.

"I see." I acted as if the whole thing with Idris didn't interest me.

Inside me, however, my thoughts were running riot, zig-zagging and became entangled. He is the son of the chief of the bandits, I thought in disappointment. He is not Imran and he was not trustworthy if Sadu-zai was related to him. What reason could he possibly have to help me?

"What's that floating in the sauce?" I changed the subject and remained as composed as I was able to. "Is that supposed to be meat?"

I had been forced a while ago to give up on my vegetarian phase. "That here is… brain and the other stuff…"

"Brain?" I had to think of the sheep's head cleft in half that Elephteria had prepared for New Year's Day in Piraeus. Suddenly, I didn't feel that hungry anymore.

"Yes, tastes nice, or not?" Banu looked at me askance.

"A year ago I wouldn't have eaten it if you beat me." I pulled a face.

Banu said nothing and kept eating.

"What did the half-naked guy do, the one we saw in the yard?" I asked her after a while. If anyone knew, it was Banu.

"He'd tried to get it on with one of the pretty girls from Peshawar. He was caught and punished. Sadu-zai then inspected the girl's virginity and sold her to the next willing buyer posthaste."

Oh dear. I was silent for a moment. Only for a short moment. Banu kept eating hungrily. She gestured with her chin: she wanted me to keep eating as well. "We must keep up our strength."

"In case we get a chance to make a break for it?"

"I don't think they will give us a chance to do that," Banu sighed. "The complex is well-guarded. They would catch us before you know it."

"Then we have to wait for a chance, like when they take us

into the mountains later."

"Oh, Isabé, You think just like a man! Here, you should rather eat your food." She gave me a big piece of mutton and took the brain off my plate.

"You should eat that yourself," I protested.

"That's alright. You need your strength. I don't have the courage to run away, but you do."

"Oh Banu, don't say things like that. We will run away together."

Banu just shrugged her shoulders and kept eating in silence. Then I had an epiphany. "I wish I could get hold of a knife or a pair of scissors."

"What do you need a knife for? Do you want to fight your way out?"

"With a knife? Against all these heavily-armed men? Don't be silly. I'm no *Indiana Jones*."

"*Indiana Jones*? Who is she?"

"That's not important, Banu. No, I want to cut off my hair."

"Cut off your hair? No, you can't do that." Banu was truly shocked. "Your hair is beautiful. Just like a Kashmiri. Here, they all say that."

"Exactly! If I'm that valuable to them because of my hair, then they might let me go if they can't sell me anymore. What man will buy a woman with hacked-off hair?"

Banu contemplated this. "It won't work."

"Why not?"

"They are treating you well because you have light-coloured eyes and hair. If you cut off your hair, they will beat you and then wait until your hair has re-grown. Then they can sell you again." She shook her head and continued to eat.

"What? And feed me the whole time?"

"You would have to work, of course."

Perhaps my plan wasn't as brilliant after all. I had to think of something else!

That night, I had another dream. *I ride on Kalyan's back and feel free. So free.*

We stayed in Dargai for two days. The treatment wasn't

bad but there was no chance of escape. It was all I could think about. At night I dreamed about Nusrat fighting with a sword. First with her teacher then with Imran. I was the one fighting in her stead. The dream gave me a feeling of great power. I couldn't just give in!

"What happens if they still take us across the border," I asked when we were in the laundry room, lathering our old clothes. Outside, the sun was shining but my thoughts were dark.

"I don't think that it would be a good idea to put us in such great jeopardy," Banu said resigned.

"Why should they care where the money is coming from if they can sell us off to a bunch of Russians."

"You must not even think such a thing, Isabé," Banu cried and the other girls looked up at us. She quickly regained her composure and carried on scrubbing away at her trousers.

"You are right. They wouldn't have given us those wedding outfits. Russians wouldn't give a hoot about that," I thought aloud. "But on the other hand, they seem to be Pashtun, which means they are likely to have relatives in Afghanistan."

"Yes, but they could have relatives everywhere around here."

"They probably help them to smuggle the drugs. I saw last night how they piled packets of that stuff again into one of their Land Rovers."

Banu glanced at me nervously. "It's better not to speak about such things to anyone. Act as if you were simple-minded," she whispered. "Sadu-zai is roughshod and primitive, but stupid she is not. She only cares about profit. If she knows that you see what's going on here —"

"I understand. But didn't she tell us that they will take us up into the mountains? What mountains are they?"

"She must have been talking about Kashmir. The Karakorum Mountains are somewhere East of here."

I had to think about our day trip to Murree. How carefree we were when we had strolled around the narrow streets of the resort town. This time it would be a different story. The gang was going to offer us up for sale. "Is there some war going on in Kashmir?"

"I don't believe so."

"Then it makes more sense. At least we know more or less where we are if we fly the coop there."

"Oh Isabé, your thoughts are dangerous."

"This whole situation is dangerous," I started up. "I will never be a slave, Banu. Never ever. I must do something." Shabila and Nivin looked up with an admiring expression.

"Sshht. Be careful," Banu in a whispering tone. "If Sadu-zai learns about this, there'll be hell to pay. She is a cunning one."

"Yes I know, you said so before. She won't know a thing if we use a code word. Forget about drugs and weapons —"

Banu looked around alarmed.

"If I want to speak about 'escaping', I will say from now on instead —" I looked down at myself. "Kneecap." Stupid word but off the cuff, I couldn't think of a better one.

"A code word, alright… but why kneecap?" Banu didn't seem to be all that impressed with my brainwave.

"Why not? Kneecap is as good as any other word."

Banu pondered this for a moment. "Yes, okay," she said simply.

"Brilliant." I beat the fabric enthusiastically against the washboard as if all our problems had now been resolved by the mere existence of some code word. Then I thought of something else. "Do you have a clue what Sadu-zai means or is it just a name?"

"I think it means something like tribeswoman or so. Why do you ask?"

I just wanted to imprint it on my mind. Sadu-zai. Perhaps from the tribe of the Pashtun. Were there other tribes in the area? Why didn't I ask Atesh more questions about his country when we were in Karlsruhe?

"No particular reason. We just have to stay a few steps ahead of this Sadu-zai," I said and vigorously worked on a stain on my peach-coloured trousers. I wanted to take clean clothes with me. Cleanliness was important. As a reminder of civilisation. And those clothes would come in handy for sure.

I scanned the sunny courtyard. Idris was working on a car. His legs in blue pants stuck out from under one of the Land Rovers. I was sure that everything was in peak condition if he was responsible for the repairs. Despite his high status, Imran had always lent a hand. But what was he doing here?

Idris ignored us girls as much as possible but I noticed here and there when he glanced in my direction. He was always busy with something else when I looked up.

Once, our eyes had met when he wasn't careful. They were full of compassion and hidden anger. He hastily looked away but we seemed to have an invisible connection afterwards. Should I try to speak to him? No! He was Bakhri-Shah's half-brother. The brood of the criminal Sadu-zai. Why then did I feel this connection to him?

Concentrate, I warned myself, *all you want right now is to get back your freedom, understood?! He is not Imran!*

My flight from Karachi to Frankfurt was booked in ten days and I didn't want to miss it. That was my goal! I couldn't allow anyone to draw me into their stuff, even if this Idris reminded me of Imran. And I hadn't even met him yet. Oh dear, what a complicated situation.

Then early one morning, we decamped rather abruptly. There wasn't much to pack. Only our half-dried clothes. And it began to rain again. Can't you take notes for once, stupid weather? Rain at night and sunshine during the day! This heavy rain was going to drive me nuts. It had worked just fine back in London.

A slippery layer on the steep tar road slowed us down quite a bit. We drove in a north-easterly direction. Into the Karakorum Mountains, then.

But I didn't want to go north! I wanted to go back in the opposite direction. Back to Islamabad. Perhaps it would be possible to think myself away... I watched my reflection in the car window.

Okay – that would have been too easy. It was the third day of my abduction. No wait, I hadn't counted the first night. My thoughts were busy doing their own thing again.

Should I ever get out of here, I'll make peace with my mother and my sisters, I thought. In case we should never see each other again, would our endless squabbling be all they remembered?

The farther we drove into the mountains, the more depressed I felt. I was beginning to sketch wild escape routes, always when we came out of the next curve. Over there, between the rocks, would be the perfect hiding place ... before we had passed the spot. Perhaps over there, by the clump of crooked trees... and then along the rocks away from the road...

In case, nothing worked, I could still throw myself off a cliff. There were more than enough of those around here. At least then I wouldn't be forced to live with a complete stranger and his other hundred or so slave women, for no other reason than that he had the money to buy me. But wait – it would never get to that point! It was just a question of time until an opportunity presented itself.

We passed a police roadblock unhindered. What? The vehicles weren't even stopped! Banu had to caution me to stay calm.

"Later, kneecap, later," she whispered.

The two Land Rovers pulled off the road, something that disrupted my grim thoughts. The bandits wanted to take a rest in a gorge that was hidden from the road. It no longer rained and the ground was much drier around here.

One of the women from Dargai, an elderly widow who never smiled, had come with us as our chaperone so to speak. If you could call it that. She never said much to us and we just called her Dosti. Woman friend. Rather ironic.

A young shepherd passed us with his woolly, baahing herd. He briefly glanced at the weapons and the vehicles that stood parked in the shade and hurried on.

The girls settled themselves in the shade of an overhanging rockface and began to braid each others' hair. At least there were no mosquitos around here. I kept wriggling around when Lalli and Banu got to work on my hair. I kept fidgeting this way and that. Dosti gave us pakoras and water and the men mooched about the rocks, chewed on grass blades and entertained themselves with some sort of board game. All of a sudden, there was a commotion.

One of the girls tried to skedaddle and Bakhri-Shah personally charged after her. It was a bizarre scene. The girl's name was Faridah. She had joined our trek in Peshawar and had always kept to herself like the Balti-girl Nuwa.

Maybe she had hoped to catch up with the shepherd and his clan. Truth be told, I had also kicked that thought around for two seconds or so.

Faridah didn't stand a chance. Her courage was punished immediately. Bakhri-Shah had gotten hold of her soon and beat her angrily with a thin switch he had broken off a nearby bush. His flat felted hat had slid off his head treating us to a glimpse of his red, wiry hair and a large bald spot.

His rough companions just watched and laughed. Faridah cowered screaming on the ground and held up her arms to protect her head. It was too much. This I could not watch!

I jumped up. "Stop it this minute! Have you gone insane? Stop it," I yelled at the leader of the band. "Na kotak zadan!"

I had no idea that I had cried words in Pashto.

Banu told me later. How was I supposed to know that language? To my utter surprise, the hideous slave trader stopped in his tracks.

Faridah crawled away crying and was led away by the other girls. Bakhri-Shah turned around and gave me an incredulous stare. "So, you aren't German after all, Qashangi," he croaked and planted himself in front of me, dripping with sweat from the exertion. I stood a hand's width above his head. "I've known all along!"

He noisily drew in the air between his teeth and gawked at me pompously with his light-coloured little piggy eyes. Then he did something I had not expected at all. Bakhri-Shah slapped me across the face. "That's for lying," he growled.

I stood rooted to the ground. Lalli and Schabila, who stood right next to me were slapped as well. Just for good measure for watching. They slid to the ground and started howling. "Ai, ai, ai."

So, it was that easy. Slap, slap and then shouting a little and his male pride was restored. I bestowed the most venomous look I could manage on Bakhri-Shah and he shrank back with a confused expression.

"I am lying then?!" The German words whirred straight at him like pointed arrows. I spat on the ground. "You can slap me as much as you like you slimy bastard. You will not get to me. I won't do you that favour!"

From the corner of my eye, I saw how Idris and the black widow stepped next to him. reinforcement or what! My cheek smarted hotly but I would not back down an inch. I wanted to burn Bakhri-Shah to a crisp with my contempt. Perhaps he had felt the heat through his thick exterior.

He turned around abruptly and strutted away without another word. The switch he had used to beat Faridah, landed in some bush.

Banu hurried up to me. "Are you alright, Isabé?"

I hated the fact that tears shot into my eyes. Nusrat would not have shown weakness like that. But I wasn't Nusrat, just Isabell.

"No," I panted out the words through gritted teeth. "But he picked a quarrel with the wrong woman." I plunked myself onto a rock. Banu sat down next to me and looked at my face.

"It doesn't look too bad," she said, "just a little red.

Idris approached us. His right hand was clenched in a fist and he rubbed it against his left palm. His expression was furious. Was he about to give me another drubbing? But he didn't seem angry with me. Idris waved Banu aside.

She stood up with a reluctant air and sat down with the others. Idris sat down on the rock next to me and held me back by my arm as I started to jump up.

"We must talk." He relaxed his fist.

"About what? There is nothing to say. You have no right to me."

"I know."

"You know that? Why don't you let me go, then?"

"It's too dangerous for a woman to battle her way through the mountains all by herself. We must wait for an opportunity. I will help you." His voice was barely audible.

"Oh really. And why would you do that?"

"I know you somehow from somewhere." Idris shrugged his shoulders.

"That's impossible," I lied and held my chin high.

He put his hand on mine and pulled it back at once. "It is possible," he said softly. My façade began to crumble. "I know. I also know you," I admitted in a whispered tone. "But I don't understand how."

Idris' face lit up. "Not important. Allah is trying to let me know that I must give you back your freedom. He's been trying to tell me for a long time now that it is wrong to belong to this gang." So, he had no clue that I reminded him of Nusrat. Perhaps it was better that way.

"I hate what my mother has been doing since my father died. She wants me to take over all that from her one of these days. Not Bakhri-Shah."

"And what is it you want?" I asked.

"To study further in England. I must go now." He stood up abruptly and walked away.

I could see that one of the guards stared in our direction. It would remain the last time that we could speak to each other.

The Pashtun slave-traders took us afterwards to a deserted house in the mountains. The roof above the remains of a room was leaking down the back wall. The only thing that had not yet collapsed. The Land Rovers were parked behind the house.

Why they even bothered to hide the cars was a mystery to me. There wasn't a soul in sight. I wished I could hide in a cupboard somewhere. Anywhere, far from this absurd situation. *To be alone with myself*, I thought longingly.

But of course, there was no cupboard anywhere and I could only dream about being alone somewhere.

The men leaned their weapons against the inner wall and

rested on the broad stairs leading up to the room in the front. Dosti, who had travelled ahead in the second Land Rover, had kindled a fire under one of the overhanging tin roofs. Hot water was already boiling in a saucepan. There would be tea and something warm to eat later.

Us girls were taken to the room at the back. Dirty mattresses were laid out along the inner walls. Small puddles had formed underneath the two barricaded window openings.

It was almost dark in here. The wooden planks let in just enough sunlight and fresh air.

We clung to each other underneath the woollen blankets but we were trembling despite the little warmth they offered.

It was a much-used hide-out of this gang; that much was clear. They had probably passed several loads of fresh female cargo through this place.

Soon, the smell of food wafted through the house and the aroma of hot chai. Dosti gave us two aluminium pots with the chai and we took turns slurping the brownish drink from a ladle. I began to feel warmer and threw off the blanket.

The girls murmured amongst themselves and loud laughter could be heard from the large entrance hall.

When Dosti let us go outside into the field, I could see that Idris had turned away from the others and was leaning against a pole.

"Chalo, chalo…chalié!" We were driven back inside the ruined house when the first raindrops began to fall.

Idris stood there in the same position when we trudged back into the back room. I wanted to speak to him - to discuss a plan. Of course, that was quite impossible.

The wind howled through the cracks and rain began to whip the leaking roof by the time we were given some food at last. Two metal bowls with rice and a hot meaty sauce were placed on the floor in the middle of the room.

The girls couldn't wait to lay into the food. I could eat only a little myself and washed my hands straight after with the water that was dripping down by the windows.

I would have loved to use a toothbrush or a a fruit-tree-twig at the very least to brush my teeth with. Even the private washing room in Khadriala would have been a sheer luxury in this place. I washed my face and gargled as much as possible.

Should I be found or managed to get away, then at least, I would feel clean.

Soon, we crawled exhaustedly back under the thin blankets but I was unable to find peace of mind. My thoughts went round and round inside my head.

This Idris – was he serious about helping me to escape or had it been just idle talk? What would happen if I escaped? Not in this rain, of course.

Were there people living around here who could notify the police? Oh, I felt so impatient!

Tarub, our language-expert, had managed to draw Dosti's attention to us up front and we were allowed to answer the call of nature one more time behind some bushes. Luckily, the rain was letting up.

Afterwards, most of us had fallen asleep, leaned against each other's backs and shoulders. The rain drummed monotonously onto the metal roof and I must have just dozed off when I heard shrieking and shouting. It wasn't even possible to sleep around here!

Those hard-boiled gang members were barking at each other like angry fighting dogs. Who cared why they were fighting? *As long as they leave us alone. Maybe I should take advantage of the situation*, I thought. But I was too exhausted for that.

A male voice intervened in the confrontation, calming the brawling men. It was Idris. Then a sharp command from Bakhri-Shah and they were instantly quiet. I hated everything about Bakhri-Shah, even his croaking voice.

Meanwhile, more water was running down the wall in a thin stream and washed across the dirty floor right down into the front room. Right where we could hear the bandits rumble about.

A little clap woke me from a fitful sleep. I had just taken a ride on my stallion Kalyan through the countryside. I'd been free, free like a bird.

"Isabé," Banu whispered.

"Yes?"

"The men are fighting again."

"Why are you waking me up then? Let them fight for all I care," I said sleepily. "Hopefully, they'll kill each other off."

"But we need them to protect us."

I snorted in disdain. To protect us! "In case they don't succeed in shooting each other, I'd love to do it for them. I would rather starve in freedom and I'd rather protect myself in a... a cave or something like that than have these stinking slave traders protect me"

I could only guess how much of my speech the other girls undestood. I perceived a wave of fear in the group. The foreigner was going bonkers: she wants to take care of herself and starve in freedom? Even Banu seemed to distance herself a little from me.

"You can't think like that, Isabé. You will not starve. We will be - okay."

"Maybe it's not enough to just be okay. To be the property of someone who calls himself your husband and has the right to do to you whatever he feels like? Just because you were sold to him by a handful of criminals who have no right to you in the first place?" I was just getting fired up.

"In exchange for what? A roof over your head and a little food? Is that supposed to be - alright?"

"No, that's not what I meant."

"Oh." I didn't want t get into an argument with Banu. It was enough that those hot-headed firebrands outside were screaming at each other.

Unfortunately, the brawl slacked off quickly. No dead bodies. Well, at least I was getting some shut-eye. We slept until early morning. Next to the house was a handpump and we could wash with the help of empty tin cans. We were even allowed to spend a few hours in the sun, albeit under heavy guard. The girls braided each others' hair again.

"I miss my mother," Banu sighed.

"I wish I could play my guitar. That always makes me feel better," I said.

"Oh, you play the guitar?" she asked.

"Yes, but I left it back in Khadriala. I wish I could sing a song and accompany myself by strumming the guitar."

"I'm sure the girls know one nice song or other."

"Better not. Who knows if these guys will get angry if we make too much of a noise."

"Yes, better not." The light in Banu's eyes faded.

She wrapped the tjuni tightly around her slim body and leaned against Fahrida's shoulder. It gave her a start and Banu scooted over to Lalli and leaned against her. I felt sorry for Fahrida because of the shackles she had to wear on her ankles and all that.

"What a waste of time to sit around here. All the things I'd be able to do instead," I complained. How I would have loved to write into my little notebook. But I had left it behind in Islamabad.

"Try and get some rest, Isabé. You must stay strong." Banu had her eyes closed and her face was relaxed.

If I was a boy... I hummed the popular German hit in my head,... *everything would be just half as tough.*

We stayed for two days in the dilapidated house. On the last morning, we were allowed to stretch our legs for a bit. Unfortunately, it was impossible to find a hiding place anywhere around.

That didn't keep me from making use of my brief freedom and forge out a plan. A very simple plan. All I had to do was stay alert and wait for the right opportunity. Soon. It would be time for it very soon.

If we arrived in the place where the gang was going to sell us – wherever that may be – then what? Perhaps it was a marketplace for trading slaves in the Himalayas. But when I managed to escape, how was I supposed to find my way back to Islamabad? What made it even more difficult was the fact that I didn't have any papers on me. None.

You can cross that bridge when you get there. First things first.

You have to get away from here. But what about Banu? A little voice in my head asked.

I stood atop a cliff and had a look at the hills sparsely covered in grass. In the distance, behind the plain, the snow-covered peaks of the mountains glowed. *A well-known, familiar view. I feel like standing by one of the large window-openings between the red pillars and the silk curtains, as I look out and survey the green valley...*

Giggling pulled me back from my reverie. I turned around and saw a little bunny sitting next to a rock, pricking its ears. Brown and grey and at home in these mountains. It scampered here and there and hastily chewed on the hard grasses.

The girls took joy in watching the little animal. Nuwa tried to bait it with a bushel of grass.

Bang! A shot momentarily destroyed the carefree mood and the bunny zig-zagged its way to freedom. One of the ruffians, they were calling Shabir, had taken aim at the rabbit. And missed. He could have hit one of us instead! Nuwa was in shock and stayed down.

After a horrifying second, the girls started screaming in fear and ran into separate directions, just to re-assemble by the ruined house. The bandits began immediately to fight again among each other.

An infuriated Bakhri-Shah ripped the rifle from Shabir's hands and roared like a berserker. His gold-tooth flashed. The others got involved.

"What a smart little rabbit," I praised. "Those idiots can't even hit a bunny. Pshaw! Let's scram from the circus show."

I helped Nuwa up and walked with her back to the group. Our guards were busy carrying boxes from the ruin to the cars.

"What's going to happen now?" I asked Banu." Are they taking us to the slave market at last? I can't wait to meet my future husband."

"Isabé, no, don't make jokes about that! We have to leave now. Nivin says that there's a problem."

"What kind of problem?"

"No idea. Perhaps the police are looking for the gang."

"You mean those clowns at the roadblock yesterday?"

"I will ask her again." Banu quickly chatted to Nivin.

"Isabé, the police are looking for you. Nivin says, maybe also the army."

"For me? It's about time!" It was possible that Altaf had notified the embassy. Or Chacha Sardar had pulled a few strings.

"Yes, it was on the radio, that a German woman had been abducted. Somebody came to tell Bakri-Shah. The police are requesting the population to participate in the search. No ransom."

"Oh, that's just brilliant. What are these criminals going to do now?"

"They want to go higher up into the mountains."

"Then I have to make kneecap as soon as possible or I'll never see Germany again."

"Be careful. You saw what Bakhri-Shah is capable of."

Yes, I had seen that. So what?! "You'll come with me, of course." Banu hung her head. "Oh, I don't know."

"No backchat. You cannot say with these guys!" I whispered before we had to climb back into the Land Rover.

After a good while along the rather steep road, the gunslingers took another break. I sat down, as far removed as possible from the rest of the group by a slope.

I scanned the area. With a jerk, I understood why all this seemed so familiar to me. We were in the vicinity of Dâstân. The place where I had lived after Nusrat got married! I knew my way around!

I didn't care whether it made sense or not.

Idris way lying underneath one of the Land Rovers, repairing something or other. Actually, he could have helped me but I had to make do without him. My thoughts raced. What about Banu? She was too far away and didn't look in my direction. Nobody was looking in my direction.

What a great friend you are, I scolded myself. But unfortunately, that couldn't be helped.

If the path was still where it had always been, I knew

where it would lead. The path on the slope would take me past the hero's shrine and then along the wall into the village of Dâstân. Whoever was now living in our former villa or nearby, would surely want to hide me.

The veil was in my way and I tied it around my waist, then I climbed up the slope without looking back and as fast as my legs would take me. The path was still there where I remembered it. After all this time! There wasn't much undergrowth but I tried to hide behind rocks and earth walls wherever I could. Below me, the voices grew louder. They had detected my escape!

Soon, I ran around the wall and saw a house before me that hadn't existed during my time. I rushed towards it. A woman was standing in front of the house, pumping water into a bowl.

I tried to enter the house but the woman kept me from doing so. I just couldn't understand why she did this and what she was saying to me. Then I tried to communicate through hand movements. She pushed me back onto the footpath. I glanced over my shoulder and felt that something about this wasn't right.

This was not what I had thought would happen. Bakhri-Shah came running as fast as his bulky mass allowed. Idris followed on his heels. Why on earth didn't this stupid woman help me?

"Get out of my way," I yelled. "How dare you? You are going to deliver me into the hands of these criminals!" Of course, I couldn't think of anything to say in Pashto when I really needed to.

Instead of helping me, the old hag called out to Bakhri-Shah. It almost seemed to me as if the two of them knew each other. Oh no, the woman was an accomplice! Bakhri-Shah suddenly stood in front of me, huffing and puffing and gave me a triumphant look. At that instant, he looked just like his mother. Idris had almost caught up with us.

Bakhri-Shah raised his hand but Idris pushed him aside, which made his half-brother stumble. I screamed and held my arm over my face. The blow broke only several of the thin glass bangles.

Blood dripped from superficial cut wounds but I barely noticed it. I kicked Bakhri-Shah between the legs, as hard as I could. Just the way I had learned to do it in the self-defense class. It did the trick. It took him by surprise and the man winced with pain. I felt a certain satisfaction.

Bakhri-Shah snorted in anger and was about to push past Idris, ready to attack me. They could barely contain him but Idris managed to restrain him with the help of one of the other men who'd arrived out of breath. The old woman ran wailing into the house. "Ai, Ai, Ai!"

Bakhri-Shah blustered and cursed. He threatened me with his fist but fortunately, I didn't understand any of it. I still stood in attack pose, ready to defend myself.

When one of the other bandits had caught up with us, Idris wanted to lead me away by my arm but I shook him off and did not deign to look at him.

Clearly, I had overestimated Idris. He was no different to the other bandits otherwise he would have helped me escape and not stopped me.

"What were you thinking, Isabé?" Banu asked me in a soft voice when I sat down next to her in the Land Rover.

"This is my village. My Dâstân. This damned woman didn't recognise me. She helped these bandits to catch me again. She could have offered to hide me in her house…" I choked and tried not to break out in tears.

"Why is it your village? I don't understand," Banu asked and seemed bewildered.

"Oh, forget about it. I can't possibly explain this to you," I grumbled.

Banu moved away from me ever so slightly. I felt so incredibly furious that I was ready to burst, but that couldn't be changed. The guard on the front seat gave us a warning stare. I challenged his stare. It was better to die fighting than to carry on living as a coward. One of the bandits approached with shackles.

"Oh no, you will not dare touch me!"

The man said something. "Bakhri-Shah has ordered him to put them on you," Banu said.

"What of it?" I hollered. "Take your dirty paws off me!"

Idris intervened. He gave me a compassionate look then barked an order at the man and he plodded off. Bakhri-Shah ranted and railed at his half-brother but Idris kept him at bay with a warning.

I was furious with everybody around me just because they were there and because Idris was not the ally I had hoped for. Even if he apparently protected me right now.

I was furious with the girls because they were so passive. But most of all I was furious with myself. How could my escape have failed so dismally?

I should have planned my strategy much better! What if this was my last chance of escaping?

I had no choice but to push all my angry energy into a large angry ball and tucked it away. I sat there, sulking. *Kneecap*, I thought in desperation, *damn it all, kneecap*!

There would be another chance of escape – there simply had to be! But believe it or not, when this chance came along, I almost failed to recognise it.

CHAPTER NINE

I spent an uncomfortable night, leaning against Banu's shoulder. In my unhappy dream, Nusrat had met Imran in the garden again.

'Then I will have to challenge Mansour – to a duel. I will not give up on you. Not for a man you don't love.'

I was startled. 'No, Imran, Mansour is a good man. They will kill you. And that will cause a blood feud. Is that what you want?'

'Then I will have to leave and die of loneliness.'

I shivered under the damp blanket and realised that it had just been a dream. *I'm done dreaming about Imran, stop it already…* I was thinking, half-awake, before I fell asleep again.

Dosti woke us up at daybreak. We were allowed to do our business behind the rocks under Bakhri-Shah's strict watch. How embarrassing. But there was nothing we could do about it. The air was rather cool and a white mist hung sluggishly between the hills.

If there had been any chance at all of getting away, I would have bolted right there and then. Alas, the mist was too thick and I would have probably stumbled or fallen off a cliff. After the morning-chai we had to get back onto the vehicles straight away and set off again, driving on eastward on the uneven road. As before, Idris was in the other vehicle. It was probably for the best.

The blankets weren't much help when it came to keeping us warm but an hour later, the growing heat of the sun made them unnecessary. Nevertheless, even during the day, it was cooler in the mountains than in the plains below. After taking a rest around lunchtime, clouds moved in again and the sky grew overcast. The grey of the heavens just deepened my dark mood.

Oh, please let something happen already - anything. Before I go nuts here! I begged.

A police roadblock appeared in front of us. Had somebody heard my plea? Apparently, Bakhri-Shah was as surprised as we were and was all in a fluster as he chatted to the driver. The man swore and brought the vehicle to a halt with screeching brakes.

That's it. At last! Please let that be it!

The driver gesticulated wildly as he spoke to the two policemen, who stepped up to the window. All I understood were words like 'shaadi' and 'Kashmir'. The guardians of the law were probably told an improbable story of a wedding we were expected at.

"Kneecap, Isabé, Kneecap…" Banu whispered into my ear through the thin veils. She remembered our code word. But if things carried on like that, nothing would come of it!

I spontaneously leaned forward and let the fuchsia-coloured veil slide over my shoulders. One of the policemen seemed to notice my hair colour. He pointed at me and asked questions. That was about time!

"Neyé. Neyé. Family hé," Bakhri-Shah insisted.

"Please help me, I'm from Germany. They kidnapped me in Rawalpindi. Please!" I was so flustered that my voice grated. They were about to rescue me, would get me out of this Land Rover prison and take me to the nearest police station!

Bakhri-Shah shot me a look that would have easily slain a dragon. The policemen looked at each other. Oh no, that couldn't be true – they didn't understand English! Bakhri-Shah leaned over the driver and jabbered for what it was worth. He did his utmost to be convincing, laughed and gestured excessively.

The policemen were speechless.

"Weschta chubsuret hé," one of them said shakily. Pretty girl. The rough guy in uniform winked at Bakhri-Shah. Oh no, no, no – He'd managed to convince the policemen! I shuddered when he gave me a lecherous look. Bakhri-Shah laughed and kept chatting as if the policemen were his best pals. He probably wanted to distract them from the merchandise that was meant for wealthier buyers.

If the policemen had seen the weapons at the back, it would have been a different story altogether. A wad of banknotes was greedily received and after some backslapping, the police let us pass.

That just couldn't be – another failure!

Banu told me that he had introduced us as his family, that we were on our way to a wedding in the Nanga-Parbat district. The fair one, although pretty, didn't have all her marbles. That must have sounded credible to the inexperienced policemen. In any case, a man's word superseded that of a woman many times over. The men had come to an agreement. There was nothing that I could have done to change it.

"It's all Altaf's fault," I mumbled angrily.

"Why is that?" Banu moved closer.

"He is the one who invited me to Pakistan. All of this would not have happened if I had stayed in Germany," I grumbled.

"But you wanted to come. It was your decision, or not?"

"You don't understand that…"

"Okay." She leaned her head against the window.

I was even done speaking to Banu. She had obviously accepted her lot. I wanted to be mean - angry. The angrier the better. It kept me from feeling so defeated. I stared out of the window.

Dark clouds were moving in over the mountains. Bolts of lightning illuminated the landscape from behind the cloud cover. Then, all of a sudden, it grew pitch dark. The rumbling thunder came closer and a sizzling lightning strike cracked nearby. Then another one right after.

Raindrops began to splatter onto the road and against the roof of our vehicle. The wipers could no longer cope with the amount of water running down the windshield, which made it impossible to see anything in front of us. Everyone instinctively ducked at the first loud thunderclap. Pieces of tree bark smashed into our car. A tree in the field flared up like a huge torch. The next thunderclap had the girls in a state of panic and they began crying. The stench of burning wood reached my nostrils. Then the blaze was quickly extinguished by the rain.

"Tufaan!" the driver yelled over the drumming noise. He swore extensively and steered the Land Rover abruptly to the side of the road close to the rockface. The car continued to crawl up the mountain. The second Land Rover, with Idris aboard, crept up the road right behind us.

Then we suddenly lurched to a standstill. I managed to hang onto Banu and the back seat just in time. The driver rammed into a massive rock that had toppled down onto the road surface.

The car skidded in the mud, slid to one side and crashed into another rock. Swearing and screaming. Then there was an even stronger impact. The second Land Rover had crashed into us from behind. A shot was fired and I could hear myself scream.

Lalli scuttled over the seats in a panic and kicked somebody in the face. Banu and Tarub had been wedged into Nuwa. Banu had her eyes closed and seemed to be unconscious.

"Banu, Banu." I shook her by the shoulder. "Banu, kneecap. Banu, get up. Kneecap!" She didn't move. I somehow had to drag her out of the car! Carry her if need be. But my arm hurt and my head ached even worse. I could move my arm, so it wasn't broken, at least. I desperately pulled on Banu's sleeve with my other arm. It turned all red and sticky.

"Haussa billa hé…" Schabeela began to pray somewhere underneath us. Doors were ripped open and hands began to haul us up. I felt the seam of my kamise tear. It didn't matter. This was my chance. Maybe it would be my last. I could only hold onto one thought: get out of here!

So I climbed out of the Land Rover and found myself

standing in the deafening rain, fiercely determined. I could barely see for the pounding rain. The rockface towered darkly above me and streams of rainwater streamed down the slope. My head hurt, and my arm. What should I do next? Where should I run? A hand pulled me around.

No! I would kick and bite and fight my way to freedom.

Then I saw Idris's wet face right before me. His eyes seemed so big and unreal, they begged me to keep quiet. He dragged me with him. I ignored my injured arm. He pushed me into the other Land Rover. It was empty and only somewhat dented in the front. I let him push me in, climbed onto the front seat and slammed the door shut. Idris turned the key in the ignition.

Please start! Please! Please! I was ready to howl with relief as the engine turned and began to rumble. *Kneecap*, the thought shot through my head. Was I growing insane? *Kneecap!*

Before the other human traffickers realised what was happening, we had already left the first bend in the road behind. Somebody came running after us but Idris kept going without turning around. Shots cracked. The road was slippery, otherwise the man would have surely caught up with us. The shots didn't find their mark. Right now, the pounding rain was our best friend.

With every serpentine bend, we moved farther from the grotesque scene, and finally, left it behind. The slippery road was difficult to navigate, although the rain was letting up now. We were steadily driving down into the valley.

I clung to the dashboard and prayed. No, really. I prayed like I'd never prayed before. *Oh please, get us safely out of here!*

There was no turning back now. Freedom at last! It shot through my veins like a drug, kept me wide awake. I didn't dare look at Idris. Didn't want to distract him from driving safely. We had become a team. He had kept his word after all and was different to the barbaric bandits! He was different from Bakhri-Shah, different from his mother. He had become more like Imran, even if he wasn't aware of it.

I cannot say how long this breakneck drive lasted. Once, we had nearly skidded off the road when Idris had to swerve around two lost sheep that suddenly emerged behind a curve.

The soaking wet shepherd stood terrified on the side of the road. He was an older man. I could see us plummeting right past him and into the muddy field.

Idris swerved the steering wheel around and gained control over the vehicle. He couldn't completely avoid one of the sheep and brushed against it with one of the mudguards. We lurched from side to side and drove on the wrong side of the road for a while. I prayed even harder when we narrowly missed a pile of mud and rocks. If it hadn't been for those stupid sheep, we would have hit it head-on. The rain regained its strength as we zoomed down the mountain.

"That could have gone so wrong. Inshallah. Allah u Akbar. God is great." Idris bellowed out the words through the splashing noise. Those were the first words he had spoken since the accident. I still couldn't look at him.

"Yes, thank God, you know how to drive." I wiped my dripping wet forehead. There was blood sticking to my hair!

"The faster we can get out of this rain, the better. But we want to arrive alive, right?"

"Absolutely." Idris decelerated.

I believed him and we both calmed down. Then it hit me. I had to think about Banu again. Had there been blood on her arm? Was she injured or...? Oh, why hadn't I been able to take her with me? I felt a stab in my heart. What choice did I have? Everything had happened so fast. My arm hurt and I leaned back to find a more comfortable position.

When I came to, I heard agitated voices outside. Had I fallen asleep? Had the slave traders caught up with us? I picked myself up. My ragged clothes and tousled hair were fairly dry by now but I had lost my veil during the escape.

But there were soldiers standing outside, talking to Idris. The Land Rover stood next to a boom gate. In the twilight behind it, I caught sight of uniform prefab buildings. Two soldiers escorted my rescuer to a car and drove off with him.

Had he been arrested? Why didn't they let him go? Idris had risked his life to take me to safety!

The passenger door flew open and I was forced out of the car and accompanied to an office building. Somebody spoke to me in English. I answered in a slurred voice. They gave me something to drink. A paramedic treated my arm and my head. Women helped me to wash and get dressed. Sleep.

There was a vehicle. Please take me to my friends. I gave them the names and the address in Islamabad. My memory of how I finally ended up there is still sketchy. There was an official from the embassy, in a dark suit. No thank you, I'll manage on my own...

*

I sat on Chacha Sardar's couch, there was the smell of the polished linoleum floor. I tried to listen. I couldn't remember how I had arrived at the flat. Chacha Sardar had given me a fatherly hug and Altaf touched my bandages. I winced.

He blamed himself that he'd left me standing outside the Raja Bazaar to fetch Chacha Sardar on the other side of the road. At least that was something.

"I turned around and you were gone. Why didn't you scream? I would have come running back immediately. The policeman also immediately called for reinforcements but you were gone. As if the ground had swallowed you."

"How do you scream when you have a cloth soaked in Chloroform in your face? There was nothing I could have done."

"I managed to get those men to leave and organise money. They wanted to buy you from me." His face grew dark. "It was the only thing I could think of. I was convinced that we'd had enough time to hail a rickshaw and get out of there. But they must have had accomplices."

"It's okay. They are professionals at this," I said in a resigned voice. "Those guys were only the scouts. There is a whole gang behind the operation. And I wasn't the only victim. There were many of us."

"That is not okay." Altaf swallowed his tears. Seriously?

I said nothing but began to unfreeze slowly. Especially

255

when I saw how he showed emotion.

"We were told that you were wearing a wedding outfit."

"Well… that was part of the plan to masquerade as a wedding party. The other girls and I were destined to be sold at some auction as brides to the highest bidders. They were hiding us in the mountains. In some house. I lost my beautiful Punjabi suit."

Had I really spoken this much? I had tears in my eyes.

Banu.

"Don't worry, we can buy you new clothes," Chacha Sardar said reassuringly. "It's not that important."

"Are you sure you're alright? They didn't touch you, did they? I mean …you know…"

"What? No! I mean… that's none of your business,…" I snarled. "You said you didn't want to let me out of your sight. Now you want to know stuff like that."

"Oh, it is none of my business. I am so sorry. I'm glad you are back safely," Altaf stammered.

"Really?" I asked warily.

"Of course. I barely slept a wink these past few days."

"Right. Thanks by the way for asking how I feel."

"Sorry." I scooted to the other side, didn't want to be too close to him.

"Altaf, give Isabell some space. She has endured this ordeal and needs to take a bit of a rest," Chacha Sardar reprimanded him.

But first, I had to speak to the police.

Three policemen came strutting through the door. The detective began with some pleasantries. "I would like to express in the name of the Pakistani government how very much... I regret this... abduction, while you were visiting our beautiful country…"

"Thank you," I said. Could I really trust them?

He asked me about all sorts of details and I gave him the information to my best knowledge. More or less where the room next to the bazaar had been in which we were kept. How the members of the gang looked, their names and the stops on the road; how long we had spent there, the names of the girls, where exactly Idris and I had left the others behind after the accident…

"We found the damaged Land Rover next to the road… just as Idris Shah had described it to us," the detective said in his guttural tone. "But nobody to be found far and wide. We must assume that some people were injured and we are still searching the mountains - and you say that the head of the gang was a woman? A woman by the name of Sadu-zai?"

There was the same question again.

What did this guy want from me? I'd already told him where in Peshawar I suspected the headquarters, where more or less the long towers had been between the two mosques. One was blue and the other one pink. Had given him a description of the buildings and the courtyard.

"Yes and her son's name is Bakhri-Shah, I must have told you that as well," I said stroppily.

The two policemen who had made themselves at home on the couch across from me gave me a mischievous grin. Their peaked caps were sitting jauntily on top of the coffee table between emptied chai cups and notebooks.

The detective didn't miss a beat. "These questions are purely routine. We have to compare Idris Shah's statement with yours. He never mentioned these persons."

Of course not, they were his family! "Really? Perhaps I didn't always understand properly. I'm not exactly fluent in Urdu."

"I see. Which role did this Idris Shah play in the gang?"

"None. He repaired the cars. I had the impression that he was forced to be part of it because he is related to someone in the gang. He always tried to protect us girls."

"Yes – why did he only rescue you and not the others, Miss Bertrand?"

"How am I supposed to know that?" I groaned. When would he stop with the questions?

"It was all a big confusion. Most of the girls in our vehicle were either injured or unconscious. I'd only knocked my head and was already standing outside in the road. He just wanted to take somebody with him and not flee by himself."

I'd tweaked the truth somewhat but it was none of the nosy policeman's business that Idris and I had this rather special connection to each other. From another lifetime to boot with; as Nusrat and Imran.

Giving more details would just create more trouble for him. That's why I kept quiet.

"Were you and Mr. Shah in a relationship?" The detective lunged at me like a snake in the grass. I recoiled.

"No, of course not. I just told you that it was pure coincidence. Shouldn't you be out there, looking for this dangerous gang instead of peppering me with outrageous questions?"

"We are busy with that, Miss Bertrand, we are busy with that. Apart from Mr. Shah – how many men were in the cars?"

"There were three armed guards in our Land Rover. Including the driver. There were sitting in front. And there were four in the other Land Rover. Then, there was also Dosti, the black widow. She was our 'chaperone'." The policeman scribbled down my answer.

"And was Mr. Shah also armed?"

"No. When we escaped, the others fired shots at us," I said.

"But you weren't hurt?"

"No, it rained so hard that one could barely see anything." Weren't we done yet with all the questions?

"But Mr. Shah could still see enough to drive down the road?"

"Yes, well obviously. Everything happened so fast…"

"Mr. Shah has also not been injured?"

"How am I supposed to know. Why don't you examine him?"

"Oh, believe me, he is being examined." He sounded so smug that I became suspicious.

"Please don't hurt him. He saved my life, after all. "

"Why are you so worried about him? He was one of your kidnappers." Was that a trick question?

"He had absolutely nothing to do with my abduction. They probably just took him with them because he could repair their cars." I changed the subject before I started prattling away. "Have you found any of the other girls? There was this girl, Banu… she was unconscious."

"No, not yet. We are still searching for them."

"Isn't that much more important than to accuse me of having something to do with this gang?" I was upfront. The man began to irritate me.

"You are worried about the girls?"

"Yes, of course, I am free and they are not. We were friends."

"I see, your friends… I see."

"NO, you don't see. I want them to get out of this unharmed," I barked at him.

"So, and you have nothing else to do with these people, you cannot speak Urdu or anything else? You just want these 'friends' - and Mr. Shah – to get out of this unharmed?"

Chacha Sardar looked at the man with a frown. Altaf had left the flat with a mumbled excuse. He was probably scared that they could focus their attention on him and that he might be arrested.

Meanwhile, all the attention was focused on me.

"What are you trying to say?" I hissed at the sneering face. "Why do you keep repeating my answers in your questions? I barely know that man. He protected us from the others or he tried to, at least. And he risked his life to get me to safety. Why the hell wouldn't I want him to be treated well?"

"We are just doing our job, Madam." The policemen were mildly alarmed by the intensity of my hissy-fit. One of them fidgeted back and forth on his seat. The other one lit a cigarette.

"Oh really?" I fixated the detective with a venomous stare that had done the trick with Bakhri-Shah. "You call that doing your job? The policemen in the mountains were all just doing their jobs as well, then? Where on earth is that man from the German Consulate?"

His eyes twitched. "Please remain calm, Miss Bertrand. If you answer our questions, we'll soon be done here." It was grating on my nerves by now; the way he rolled his 'r' and the way he ended his sentences on a high pitched tone.

"I have answered all your questions. That's why we've been sitting here for the best part of an hour!" It was probably the fact that my answers were becoming monosyllabic that prompted the detective to cease the interrogation for the time being.

I felt battered and dog-tired.

The official from the German Consulate arrived just as the policemen had squeezed out of the door. Altaf came sneaking back inside behind him. Coward, I thought.

"The driver couldn't find the address that Detective Tahir had provided," the pink, sweating man who was almost bald, complained. "Turns out that the street name wasn't …"

"The interrogation is finished," I said flatly.

"You were supposed to only speak with the police in my presence."

"Well, I guess it's too late for that now."

Why didn't this guy just leave? All I wanted was a hot bath, to change my clothes and then sleep for an eternity. Perhaps one last effort…

"I'm sorry, Mr., Mr.…"

"Wiederhofer." His nostrils appeared much lighter than the rest of his face and so was the skin around his eyes, almost like a pair of goggles.

"…Mr. Wiederhofer. I am really far too tired to have another conversation now. Please leave; we can talk tomorrow."

"Yes, but what about my report…"

"Please!"

The pink man left. Peace at last.

Chacha Sardar had prepared some food. I wasn't very hungry and took a few bites for the sake of Chacha Sardar. Altaf had disappeared once again and I sat alone at the dining room table with the kind-hearted uncle.

"Thank you so much, Chacha Sardar. I think I would like to go to sleep now. Can I please continue to eat later?"

He looked at me all worried. "Did the kidnappers treat you badly, child?"

"Sometimes."

"I'm so sorry. Your trip was meant to create good memories," he said as if it was his fault.

"There is nothing we can do about it. I will always remember all the good things that I experienced once I'm back at home. Not just the bad ones."

"Thank you, Batshi. We also won't forget you."

"Perhaps I should eat a little more." I perked up again. It was probably the adrenaline.

"But of course, it's all still warm."

"Chacha Sardar?" I asked as he heaped the food onto my plate.

"Yes?"

"May I ask you a question?"

"But of course, child. What is the matter?" he answered gently.

"Have you ever heard of a place called Dâstân?" I had no idea why I was asking him that question. I just wanted to talk about my bygone home in the Hindukush. The uncle pondered this. "No, where is this place?"

"We were there with the bandits. It's a village in the mountains."

"Oh is it? There are so many remote villages. The bandits must have thought that nobody would ever find them there."

"Yes," I said a little disappointed. "Chacha Sardar, do you know the Pir Panjal?" That had slipped out with an unintentional impulsiveness. Chacha Sardar dropped his spoon. "What makes you think of that?"

"It just popped into my mind. There was a programme on German radio once. A report about Rajputs and thoroughbred horses and things like that." It wasn't easy for me to lie to the good uncle but it was less complicated that way.

"Yes, I do know the Pir Panjal."

"Honestly?" I nearly fell off my chair. I hadn't seriously expected that answer. I began to feel all hot inside but I kept my composure.

"The Pir Panjal was a beautiful valley. Villages, Rajput-palaces. We had a lot of cattle and thoroughbred horses. A few Moghul-families that had come from the west had settled there after the invasion of Babur."

"How do you know all of this, uncle?" I asked softly.

"My father grew up there. He was a blacksmith in his village. We are still able to speak Farsi. That's a Persian language."

I was too fascinated to ask any questions and the uncle continued. "The war made a mess of it all. We moved away. To the South. To Khadriala. Part of our family lived there already. When the reservoir dam was about to flood the region, the others followed."

"The reservoir dam?"

"But of course. Didn't they mention that in the radio programme you listened to? The valleys were flooded. The Pir Panjal now rests at the bottom of the reservoir lake, together with many other villages and valleys."

"No. Oh no, that… is so… awful." I was shocked.

The fields, I had gone for a ride with Kalyan back then. The apricot trees in my father's garden. The house… all of this was at the bottom of a lake?

"Yes, it was hard for my father. My grandmother cried incessantly when we heard about it. I can barely remember our home, but sometimes I would like to just go and see it again."

How could that be a coincidence? How could Chacha Sardar know about this? About Pir Panjal, the home of my youth – Nusrat's youth? My heart beat fast. I would have loved to tell him about my memories and described to him the beauty of the valley that was the connection between us. I almost did, but then Altaf walked into the room.

"Where have you been so long?" I wanted to know. The moment had passed.

"I took a walk outside and went to the park. Wanted to make sure that the police had truly left the flat."

"They pumped me for information, squeezed the orange dry. Were you scared that they'd recognise you? I don't think they would have. We started eating without you. It tastes really good."

"Would you like a plate?" Chacha Sardar asked.

So we sat together and had a good old chat about everything. The bazaar and how I had suddenly disappeared. How the police had searched everywhere and had not been able to find me. As if I had vanished from the face of the earth. I, in turn, told them about Banu and the other girls and my constant plans to escape.

I thought to myself about Nusrat and Imran, and where they had grown up. It was difficult to get used to the thought that the Pir Panjal no longer existed.

It would have been wonderful to be able to travel there and satisfy my curiosity about the valley of my 'childhood', which had actually existed.

On the other hand, I had been to Dâstân! The place where I had been so happy with Mansour. It had not been a figment of my imagination or a dream. It must have really happened!

Perhaps that's what I had come to find out — that there was a bond between me and the people in Khadriala; to make peace with my dreamed-up memories.

Soon, Altaf and I were on our way back to Khadriala. Our return was already expected in the village. I was hugged by everyone and Amma gave me a once-over, checking that I was unhurt. My arm still hurt a little, otherwise everything was still in its place. Hakim, the medicine man, was called nonetheless and gave me a strengthening tonic.

"Baba Ali died while you were gone," Shireen reported. "He fell asleep. On his bed outside. After the sun… set?"

It made me sad that I had not been able to say goodbye to the old man.

Hopefully, he had found his wife again in the hereafter. Wherever that might be. The news that Farooq and Nasra had left for London a few days before didn't come as a surprise.

"Farooq didn't have any more leave left and had to go back to work at the chocolate factory in Slough. They had to take their plane to England and will soon move into a new house. Nasra couldn't wait to see all her relatives in London," Altaf told me later. He had been told by his mother.

I had the strong desire to be alone and the best place to be alone was the dark washroom. I latched the door from the inside and washed my body thoroughly, dried myself and dressed in a clean suit. The purple one that I had found on my bed in the women's dormitory. The crack under the door let in only a little bit of light. That was good.

I squatted and leaned with my back against the hand pump. Hot tears ran down my face. I just let them run, didn't know why I felt the urge to cry, but it made me feel better. Somebody knocked on the door. "Are you alright?" It was Shireen.

"Yes, I'll be right out." I sniffled.

"Good, the food is ready."

"I'm coming."

I spent two restful days in the village and Amma kept all excitement far from me. I was even allowed to sleep by myself in the guest bedroom and she didn't try to stop me from taking walks by the river. Mushtaq watched out for me from a distance.

Altaf was busy with his own stuff again and this time I didn't even mind. What was the point of talking in depth about all the things that had happened to me? I even gave a short concert for the men in the village. I had no idea why the women were not allowed to be present and didn't ask questions.

Shortly before I left for Karachi, the village elder demanded to see me one last time. Alone. Shireen took me to the impressive house and walked away trembling. Perhaps she was worried that I would be punished for causing so much trouble since my arrival two months ago.

"I am truly sorry that you were treated so abominably at the hands of our countrymen," the proud man apologised instead. "I sincerely hope that your image of our wonderful land is not suffering too much damage."

This time, the Agoo had not gone to the lengths of preparing a meal. An ewer with chai and two cups were on the carved table between us.

"All that counts is that I have my freedom back. Strangely, I have made friends as well. The other girls who were abducted, for example, and a young man who rescued me. That, I will never forget," I said.

"Sure. I have received the information that this young man is in custody. But they will likely release him as a witness for the prosecution. Many of the criminals have been arrested, based on his statement. This is astonishing because family ties are the most important thing for the Pashtun. They are now awaiting the trial in Islamabad. I wouldn't want to be in their place. There is still no trace of the other girls."

I was relieved for Idris - and I could have cried at the same time. Banu, Tarub, Lalli, Shabila, Nivin and Nuwa. Where are you? I hope you are safe and that nothing bad happens to Idris.

"Thank you for telling me all this. I wish I could do something to help find them again."

"That won't be necessary. The tribes of the Pashtun impose their own rules in cases like that. The girls won't be harmed. Too much attention by the army is undesirable," the Agoo said with confidence.

"I can only hope that they will be found very soon."

As long as they will no longer be sold – or worse.

The following day I said goodbye to the villagers and gave Amma a brooch I had originally bought for Doris. She said a short farewell speech in Urdu and pushed a lunch packet into my hand.

Altaf carried the well-wrapped painting of the Kashmiri woman under his arm and took my red suitcase so I could carry my guitar. I had stuffed some of the things into the cover to save space in the suitcase.

Some people had tears in their eyes. Shireen looked sad. She accompanied us to the railway station with Altaf's brother Mushtaq and kept grabbing my hand. Mushtaq proudly helped to carry our luggage.

This time, we took a train to Islamabad, where Chacha Sardar went with us to the airport.

The train ride would have taken two days and I no longer

had the time for that. Altaf accompanied me on the flight from Islamabad to Karachi and it was so much more comfortable. The soft seats were sheer luxury and the friendly treatment was a balm on my soul but I didn't manage to get rid of my inner languor.

I was still too involved in all that had happened to me in the days before. Altaf said goodbye at the airport in Karachi. He was staying in the city for a few days to take care of some obscure matters and then return by train to Jhelum.

"Take care of yourself and don't let the police catch you," I said and patted him on the shoulder.

Hugging was not allowed.

"I won't. See you in two weeks. In Karlsruhe."

"Yes, see you then." Of course, I didn't tell him that I was relieved that I would not be seeing him for two whole weeks. I walked through the passport check without looking back.

"Ah, Miss Bertrand, you are a Muslim?" The veiled woman behind the counter asked and stamped my passport.

I was wearing my white jeans and the light blue tunic I had bought right after my arrival in Karachi. I had covered my hair with the matching dabatta out of habit.

"No, I'm not. I just got used to dressing like the locals," I said in a friendly tone.

She gave me a scrutinising look but this time I was let through the checkpoint without difficulties. No glass cubicle, no interrogation, no prolonged staring and definitely no request for a bribe. I wouldn't have had the energy for something like that in any case.

I walked along the passage next to the airfield. A man was in a mad rush and stormed right past me. I stood still and saw my reflection smiling back at me from one of the enormous glass windows, when I turned to observe the aeroplanes take off and land.

Was this really the same Isabell Bertrand who looked back at me? The adventurous student who had taken a trip from Karlsruhe to Pakistan? Or was there somebody else in my skin as well? The Kashmiri woman Nusrat perhaps or Isabella or Isabé, the victim of a kidnapping? The face stared back at me with a very serious expression now.

Oh dear, I'm going to develop schizophrenia, I thought and straight after that: *Bloody nonsense, pull yourself together!*

I was good at pulling myself together.

Our flight was announced. I watched myself closely for another long moment in the large, dusty window. Then I took a deep breath and joined the seemingly endless throng of airline passengers.

CHAPTER TEN

"Why didn't you listen to me when I told you that it's too dangerous to travel to a Muslim country? They are so different from us. But no, you were hell-bent on getting your way again…"

My mother was just getting going with her I-told-you-so speech. I let her rant.

"All that stress you are causing me will kill me one fine day… other children do normal things because they are well … normal. But no, not you. You go and get yourself kidnapped. Oh, what will people say when they read about it?"

She referred to the short little article that had made it into our provincial newspaper today. The headline read 'Kidnapped Woman from Karlsruhe, Back Home Safe and Sound'. They were unable to print much more because they didn't know much more about it.

"You should have given an interview, then there would have been a picture in the article, at least. Of the whole family."

My sister Paula struck a pose and twirled a light-blonde strand of hair around her finger.

"No way, that's out of the question! Anyway, I didn't get myself kidnapped on purpose. Seriously. Who would get kidnapped on purpose? We were walking around the bazaar and those guys put me to sleep with Chloroform."

I looked at my mother but couldn't detect any trace of compassion in her eyes.

Both my sisters were present for a change. Because of all the drama and because of the cake my mother had baked. And this time, they were even almost on my side.

"Cool, Chloroform. Just like the movies," Paula marvelled.

"Yes, I even met Indiana Jones in Peshawar. A real bootlegger, smuggling drugs," I showed off a little.

"That wasn't really THE Indiana Jones, right?"

"Don't be daft, Paula. That's just a movie anyway. I believe this guy must have been English or an Australian."

"Cool."

"Where is Peshawar, then?" Evelyn wanted to know.

"On the border with Afghanistan. There were loads of refugees because of the war in Afghanistan. They are constantly crossing the border and are put up in tent camps."

"War?"

"Yes, with Russia. I also didn't know much about it before I went there."

"You shouldn't have gone there in the first place and that's it - period! And what about your exams?" My mother blustered on for good measure. "You look completely starved," she said on a finishing note. "Here, take another piece of cheesecake. I've tried a new recipe. Just now, I'll take a few slices up to Mrs. Speidel; her husband just loves my cheesecake ..."

I bit back one of my usual ironic remarks. We had reached a state of truce and that's the way I wanted it.

"Here, I got you some gifts." I proudly took the presents I'd bought out of my bag. "The Sari is for you, Evelyn." I gave her the dark-red sari, I had purchased in Rawalpindi. Just before... I chased the memories of that dark day away. "And the embroidered veil is for you, Paula." Paula was so eager, she almost ripped the veil from my hand.

"What's that sari supposed to be?" Evelyn eyed the dark-red fabric with suspicion before she accepted it.

"You wear it together with a petticoat and that blouse over here. The material is wrapped in a certain way. It's just like a dress," I explained.

"I see." Evelyn's face spoke volumes. Perhaps, she would use the sari rather as a curtain across her window.

"I can show you how it works if you like."

"Okay."

"Violet is so not my colour," Paula complained and held the veil up against the light.

"Be grateful that you got a prezzie at all," I whinged back.

"Thank you for the floral silk fabric, Isabell," my mother quickly interceded. "I will give to my seamstress and have her sew a nice dress with it." She seemed content with her present. Good.

All in all, my mother had become more tolerable.

Once in a while, she still relapsed, like now, but if there was any truth to my sisters' story, she wasn't quite as neurotic as she used to be.

It helped that Paula was no longer involved with people in the drug scene. And the new medication also seemed to do her some good. There was also a new boyfriend in Evelyn's life and they had moved in together. Apparently, marriage was on the cards.

"My pleasure. I'd bought the gifts before this happened... well you know."

I just couldn't talk to my family about those fateful events. How were they supposed to understand what I'd been through? Apart from that, it wasn't exactly easy discussing them with my friends, either. They usually didn't have a clue what to say.

To me, it seemed as if I'd walked through a door into a strange world. The door was tightly shut now but nobody could really imagine what things were like behind that door, no matter how well I tried to describe my experiences. I was simply expected to pick up where I'd left off.

Obviously, I hadn't believed that I was entitled to a medal or something from the Queen but nobody seemed truly interested. The world behind that closed door remained too strange, too foreign for them. I wanted to speak to Atesh and pepper him with questions about the Pashtun. Just to make better sense of things. But Atesh was currently visiting his uncle in Chicago.

I cycled back to my commune. Ingmar and Manfred had been content with a brief description of my trip and then went back to minding their own business as always. It suited me fine. I wanted to be left alone and just retreat into my own room. It was worth a mint. I had slept a lot in the past few days but wished I didn't have to think non-stop about Nusrat!

After my return, the odd dreams from this previous lifetime had started bothering me again: how Mansour and I were sitting on round floor cushions at a low table, eating our lunch together, for example.

I'm pregnant with my second child. It's unusual for a married couple to have a meal in such an intimate setting. Mansour feeds me delicacies: pickled berries, roasted nuts, little mushroom dumplings. His loving gaze warms my heart.

I awoke with a start. The dream unsettled me. Oh, why didn't these damn dreams stop already? But at least, I was back home and safe. Perhaps, all I had to do was wait a little while and they would fizzle out.

I pushed the dreams aside and rode my bike to the park, to inform my old green friend that I was back in town. I was also meeting Doris at the lake. Summer was on its way with fresh new leaves that were peeking out from bushes and trees. The castle lake gleamed in the distance.

"And they didn't touch you or anything like that?" Doris asked as we took a walk between the lake and the Botanics. I pushed my bike and enjoyed the bright new green around me. The lawn was still too wet to sit down.

"No! I already told you they didn't," I flared up. "Only that one time when the overseer clocked me. And he stopped immediately. Fahrida wasn't so lucky. He kept hitting her with a switch…"

"Wicked…" Doris said excitedly.

"… and Idris, Sadu-zai's other son, gave him quite a talking to," I continued with a sigh. "Their customers wouldn't pay much money if the merchandise was anything but undamaged virgins."

"They would have been shocked in your case," Doris grinned.

"Yes, probably." I laughed half-heartedly. Thank God,

Doris didn't know me that well.

"Man, that's smashing. Just like the movies! It's the bomb."

Yeah, yeah, just like the movies, I thought to myself. As so often, Doris stared into the distance. Probably imagining the whole scene in large Hollywood-format. I waved my hand in front of her face.

"Hi, I'm still here!"

"Hey, I knew that." She gave me an accusing look. "Why don't you let me day-dream a little?"

"The whole thing wasn't like a daydream for me. I thought I was losing my mind when they took us into the mountains," I said. "I can't believe that I'm actually back home and here in the park! As if things were the same as before." I took a deep breath. "Sometimes, I still wake up at night because I can see that tree in front of me, how lightning strikes it and all that. I don't know what would have happened without that horrible storm…"

"Well, and then? You would be a lady of some harem in Kashmir or so," Doris said and grinned. She probably thought it would be something sexy.

"Who knows."

"Cool." Doris made moon-eyes at some long-haired guy who sat with his friends on a blanket close by.

"I don't think that's cool at all," I scolded her.

"Sorry. Naturally, it would have been awful if…"

"Of course it would have. My mother started throwing her toys out when I told her what had happened. And she doesn't even know the half of it. Typical," I grouched a bit.

"Actually, I have no idea what my mother would do. She always reads so many books about this and that. But if something like that should happen for real… I don't know. So tell me the story again with this Altaf of yours? Did he really try to throw himself into the canal? Just because you refused to marry him?"

"He isn't my Altaf…"

Despite that, Doris wanted to hear the highlights of my trip again. As if I was telling her about my latest favourite movie or something. How was I supposed to explain to Doris that all my experiences had been real for me? Not a movie at all but... serious stuff?

It was probably too much to expect that anybody was capable of walking a mile in my shoes. Mr. Mandel, my mother, even Tarek, Angie or Walter. I would just have to deal with it by myself, then. But lucky for me, there was still my friend Zohra!

We had spoken on the phone recently. There had been the usual crackling in the line but we'd managed to forge out a plan all the same. It was as good as a done deal that I would visit her in Morocco after my exams. Zohra would understand. She was Muslim after all. And truth be told, I longed to travel to a country like that again. Without all that drama of a kidnapping and the whole shebang. Just going on holiday. And why not? But I thought it better to keep my thoughts to myself.

Our clique met at the pub in the evening. "No thanks, I'd rather have a Coke," I said to the waitress.

"What, no white wine? You always drink white wine," Angie said with big eyes as if my preference for one drink or another was cast in stone. "Are you sick? You're so different since you came back."

"'Course she is," Tarek came to my aid. "Anybody would be different."

"I must still digest the whole thing and I don't like the taste of alcohol right now. Maybe, because I'm still on quinine-tablets. You know, as a prophylaxis against malaria. I just feel like drinking Coke today."

"I'll also have one," Tarek said.

"Me too," Walter supported us.

"Then it's three Cokes and one white wine." The waitress wrote the order on her notepad.

"So, I'm the only one drinking wine here? Is that becoming the new fad?" Angie sulked.

"Perhaps, but suit yourself." Walter grinned and winked at me.

"Are you all becoming Muslims now, or what?"

"Do you have to become Muslim just because you don't want to drink wine?" I asked in a peeved tone.

"No. But you used to be so different before."

"Before? That's not even two months ago."

Why did everybody drone on about me being so insanely different all the time? They were just imagining things. I was still the old Isabell for sure…

"Hello!" All of a sudden Renate was standing behind me. "Are you dreaming about a handsome Pakistani muscleman?" I was startled.

"Hey… don't talk garbage. I'm just tired. Maybe I should go home and get some sleep."

"Yeah, sure…" Walter stretched the words in his particular way. "You do nothing else but sleep these days."

"You would probably feel the same," Renate answered in solidarity with me. Yesterday, she'd accused me of exactly the same thing.

"What about the Coke you ordered?" Angie asked piqued.

"Renate can have it."

"Okay, no problem. You go home and have a rest. We'll chat some other time. I'll give you a ring." Renate sat down on my chair and made herself comfortable. In the past, she would have followed me out.

I didn't particularly care for the smokey pub air and even less for the drumming music. How were you supposed to have a conversation with all that noise? And the people inside were so loud and obtrusive. I had kittens from the thick cigarette fog alone.

"Hah, get outta here!" Some moron roared next to me.

I missed the smell of fires burning wood and cow dung. Missed the peaceful silence in Khadriala and going down to the river…

"In any case, I'm writing Biology on Monday and have to cram the whole book into my head." The excuse was totally acceptable.

"Whatever's not inside your head yet, you won't cram in by Monday," Angie lectured me.

"We'll see about that."

"I'm glad that it's not me who has to write Biology," Walter said with a sigh of relief. "Sunday afternoon, they show the football final on TV."

"Oh, men are so predictable. Alright then, we'll see you next week," Angie dismissed me graciously and sipped on her white wine.

"Okay. Bye for now."

I put on my jacket and felt somehow naked without a veil. At least, I had my colourful scarf with me. It was cool this evening.

"Oh, Martina is sitting over there." Renate pushed her way to the other side of the pub to say hello to her friend.

Very well. I paid for the Coke and hugged everyone in my group goodbye – and yearned to breathe fresh air outside. *I have to earn money somehow before I travel to Morocco,* I thought as I stepped down the narrow stairs into the wet road. It must have been raining again.

"Hey, aren't you Isabell, Altaf's girlfriend? The one who's just come back from Pakistan?" The accent was undoubtedly un-German. I turned around and saw two Pakistani men whose broad grins seemed to compete with each other. It was nice to see somebody in Punjabi-clothes again. But I had never seen those two before.

"Who wants to know?" I asked grumpily.

"Oh, my apologies. I'm Moh from Jhelum and that's my friend Assaf."

"Good day, Moh from Jhelum and Assaf."

"Would you like to come to a pub with us or go for a walk in town?" Meddlesome, those two. Was he just doing his best to be friendly? In Pakistan, a woman would have taken offence at such a proposal. But this wasn't Pakistan. I didn't want to be rude and decided to show them some civility. "I must take the tram. You can accompany me if you like."

We trudged along the wet roads side by side to the Main Post Office. It began to rain again and we ran for cover under the awning in front of a flower shop.

"So, you went to visit my hometown," Moh from Jhelum said eagerly.

"That's right. Did you hear the drums all the way to Karlsruhe?" He didn't seem to understand the joke.

"Are you going to marry Altaf Khan?" Now that was a step too far!

"Excuse me? What has that got to do with you? I don't even know you," I put him in his place.

"If you don't want to get married to him, we could go steady," Moh said.

"I see. So that's how the cookie crumbles! And why should I go out with you of all people?"

"I'm a better boyfriend than Altaf and you are *chubsuret*. Very pretty." His tone became more demanding. Great. He was making a pass at me and apparently I had a bad reputation to boot with.

"You know something, Moh from Jhelum, you better piss off before I forget myself. You don't talk to women that way. Not in Pakistan and certainly not here in Germany. I would never go out with you. Not in a million years. Got it?"

Moh still grinned like a Cheshire cat and I wanted to get him off my back.

"Altaf will not like it very much that you are making a pass at me. He'll be back in Germany next week."

I couldn't think of a better comeback. Naturally, I didn't mention how Altaf had behaved in Khadriala but this Moh-guy was getting on my nerves. Then I said to his friend Assaf in my best Pashtun, "Haga bad xrab sare de." He is a bad man. The two of them shrank back.

Tarub had often called Bakhri-Shah that. Admittedly, I hadn't expected them to understand it. Not bad at all!

"Oh, sorry, sorry. I didn't mean it that way." Assaf rubbed his earlobes between thumb and index finger. It was as good as an apology.

Come on, Number 5, come on, I thought impatiently.

"As long as we understand each other. Oh, there is my tram, the number 5. Chudafiss." I ran into the rain.

The Number 5 screeched around the corner and stopped in front of me. The doors flapped open and I climbed in. Relief. Had I given off the wrong signals or were people just gossipping behind my back? *Ah well, whatever*, I thought, *who knows what's going on in the minds of men.*

Life would be so easy if I knew the answer to that question. On the other hand, I felt that it was my duty to defend Pakistan's honour at times.

Against Mrs. Speidel, for example.

"So Isabellshe, they wrote about you in the newspaper!" I heard her voice shrilling in the stairwell above me, just as I was jumping over the broken step. I had been at my mother's flat, doing my washing. Just like old times. Should I ignore the chatterbox?

"Huhu! Isabellshe," she called in a grating voice. "Wait a little while." Then she was already on my tail.

"Good day, Mrs. Speidel," I said lamely. "So sorry but I have to get going now."

"Ah, you're always in such a hurry. You can spare a short little minute, can't you? The newspaper said that you were kidnapped! In Pakistaaan. Your poor mother must have been so very worried about you, I'm sure," she kept on fishing and I decided not to bite.

"Yes. Well, I have no doubt my mother has already told you all that. The whole long story before the article was printed. Worse things happen at sea. Please excuse me but I am really in a rush."

However, I couldn't shake off Mrs. Speidel that easily.

"That must have been so terribly dirty there, in Pakistaaan. Did they touch you, those kidnappers?" She shook herself at the mere thought of it. "One hears about so many things that happen. They are not as civilised as we are, those people. And they said in the news the other day…"

"You do hear many things, to be sure. And you talk about even more things. You'd be surprised how much more civilised many Pakistanis are compared to some Germans I've met."

"Oh, you don't say?! Who would have thought? Frau

Pfeiffer from the top floor has told me only this Tuesday…"

"As I said, I'm very much in a rush right now. Have a good day, further."

I managed to escape down the stairs and out of the front door before she had another chance to talk more rubbish and irritate me to the point of snarkiness. The bicycle lock just wouldn't open.

Dammit, was I using the wrong key? The heavy entrance door opened the very moment the lock finally pulled apart. I jumped onto the bike and was on the street where I narrowly missed the rubbish bins that stood lined up in a neat row by the sidewalk.

Then, there was this thing with Rüdiger, the same guy I had let down easy before. Now he started his nonsense again.

"Hey, Isabell," he purred charmingly when he bumped into me on the way to History class. "There you are again."

"Yes, here I am again." I quickly climbed up the stairs to the visual arts room on the third floor. Rüdiger caught up with me.

"Say, that was quite something you experienced there in Pakistan. I read all about it in the newspaper."

"You shouldn't believe everything you read in the newspaper," I tried to shake him off. There were still two tests I had to study for. Art and History. And I'd be damned if I did Mr. Mandel the favour and flunked my final exams just because I didn't get the credits I needed. The last thing I was in the mood for was Rüdiger, chatting my ear off.

"I thought it would be nice if we could go out tonight. Just for a beer or two. Then you can tell me all about it yourself."

"I don't have time to go out. I still have to prepare for the last test in Visual Art, day after tomorrow, and then the exams start shortly after. Pity, really."

"Ah well, then we could go to Café Wolff and spend a free period there. Or I could come and visit you at home for a cup of coffee."

"That'll be the day. Please leave me alone. What I need to do is concentrate on studying. We can have a chat some other time, but definitely not now. You'll have to bear with me."

"So that's the treatment I get after we nearly went steady," he snapped at me. A few fifth-graders sniggered.

"We never ever had anything going, you and I. Never," I cried in disgust. "You helped me with Physics once and that was it. Thanks, by the way."

I rolled my eyes at him and saw Walter standing by the classroom door. Walter also rolled his eyes and opened the door for me like a gentleman. Rüdiger shrank back. "You are always so stuck-up. Just like before. You prefer those Pakis to us German guys, don't you?" He fired off another barb. "You have no idea what you're missing!"

"Aaahh!" I slammed the door shut right in front of him.

"Keep your tail up," Walter said docilely. "You are some kind of celebrity at school right now and he's just giving you a hard time. You know him."

"I sure do. Famous for all the wrong reasons. What gives idiots like Rüdiger the idea that I want to date them? The other day, it was Stefan who wanted to flirt with me," I complained. "Just that he wasn't quite so persistent."

"Just ignore them. School's nearly over and done with."

"I can't wait," I moaned. "We are nearly done, just four weeks and three days. And then – it's freedom at last!"

Two weeks later, the exams were done and dusted. That called for a celebration at the 'Krokodil'. The whole group showed up and this time, there was no dumb discussion about alcohol.

"When do they give us the marks for the written exams?" Tarek asked.

"Next Tuesday. At least, Mohlmann said that yesterday."

"Tuesday. That means we're moving towards the final sprint and the oral exams. Can't hardly wait."

"I don't have a good feeling about English. I probably should prepare for the worst and study," Walter groaned.

"Don't drive yourself around the bend. Rather wait for your marks. There will be enough time to prepare." Tarek ogled his Cola Corea. Coke with red wine. He still drank very little if at all.

"What are you doing Monday, Isabell? Should we meet at your place to cook something or are you not in the mood? We could give a Pakistani dish a try," Angie changed the subject.

She wore the earrings I had given her as a present. "I'm in dire need of some change. How do you spell chapatti? I only know this Italian flatbread called ciabatta. Is that something similar?"

A vision of chapattis and curry with garam masala passed my inner eye. I could even smell the spicy aroma. Was there such a thing as an inner nose?

"I don't think so... ciabatta is more like pita bread, isn't it? Chapatti is also spelled differently. With a 'p'," I answered. The similarity between the two had never crossed my mind. "Renate comes for a visit on Monday. We haven't had a proper chat since I got back."

Actually, I had been avoiding Renate more or less on purpose, ever since we saw each other at the pub. I didn't fancy another I-told-you-so speech. Renate had been against my trip to Pakistan right from the start.

"How is it going with that in any case? With all that stuff you experienced in Pakistan, I mean. Do you still get nightmares?" Angie asked on a note of empathy without mentioning the word *abduction*.

A Fleetwood Mac song came on, blaring from the speakers at such high volume that I had to move closer to her. "No, not actually. I mean, I still feel a bit funny. As if everything wasn't quite real – or something."

Angie looked at me with big eyes. "Seriously?" She hollered over the loud music. It was sheer impossible to discuss things like that in a pub.

"I'll get over it. But I really can't stand school anymore." A quieter song was doing the shift in the loudspeakers.

"First, old Mandel was hostile like hell and felt the need to splatter me against the wall in front of everyone. Then, when the article appeared in the newspaper, he strangely praised me in front of the whole class and said that he admired my courage, my endurance and crap like that. Real grotty. Doris could barely pull herself together for giggling."

"You should be grateful! Doesn't that mean he's giving up his crusade against you? As long as he leaves you alone, good riddance."

"I wouldn't count on it. I'm just glad to have that hypocrite out of my hair." My Coke and French Fries were brought to the table.

"You could go and see a psychologist to talk about everything. I mean to get over the shock you had and all that," Tarek piped up.

Not half bad that idea... Dr. Albrecht perhaps...

"For sure. But at the moment I don't have time for things like that."

Angie sighed deeply. "And what are you guys planning to do after graduation? I, for my part, will take a trip to Italy. To Lake Como. My uncle owns a holiday flat there. I really need a holiday. Give me two weeks and I'll feel like a new woman."

"My father wants me to visit him in Hamburg. Apparently, they have the best art academies there. I'm supposed to inspect them all. You know that I want to study Design, right?" Tarek cut in again. He told us a little more about his plans and about Hamburg.

"Hmm, I'd also be interested in something like that," I said. "Walter, what are you going to do? Are also taking a trip somewhere?"

"Me? No. I don't feel like doing anything. I'll just laze around for a while and then I'll see what comes my way." Walter yawned as if his statement needed extra emphasis.

"My friend Zohra has invited me to Morocco," I mentioned. "She lives in Rabat. So I'll take a trip there. I think she gets the whole thing with the Muslim culture and can explain things that I don't quite understand yet."

"Aren't you fed up to the back teeth with travelling to exotic places?" Walter asked puzzled.

"Great, I wouldn't mind coming with you," Tarek said. "Then I could take a detour to Algeria. I also have a thing for

Moroccan tiles —"

"What is it that you don't quite understand yet?" Angie asked me. I pondered this for a moment.

"For example, why do mothers-in-law have to be so ugly to their sons' wives, even when they were pushed around themselves as young women."

"But that's not exactly a Muslim problem, is it? Mothers-in-law are known to be like that all over the world," Tarek said.

We jeered. "Why, do you have practical experience with it?"

"Haha, very funny."

It did me the world of good to simply chat about unimportant stuff for a change, instead of constantly having to speak about such heavy subjects as school exams and abductions in Islamic countries.

On Monday, Renate arrived for a visit. She was in a bad mood and went straight to the point. "What a shitty day! I'm telling you, any more days like that and I'm going to leave my job," she snarled.

"Don't you want to come in before you get going? What's the matter?"

Renate threw her jacket on my bed and sprawled onto one of the three small horsehair mattresses on the floor that served as a temporary lounge suite. "Do you have some juice for me?"

"There's orange, I think."

"Orange is splendid."

I was pouring two glasses for us in the kitchen when Renate suddenly appeared next to me with a cross look on her face.

"So, what was going on at work today?" I asked her again.

"This old geezer in the pub just now," she grumbled. "He kept staring at me the entire time. Then I had to walk past him and he leaned against me - can you believe it - and pinched my bottom. I nearly dropped my tray with those empty glasses."

"What? That's pretty steep! What did you do?"

"I put down the tray and wallopped the blockhead."

"Bravo! He was probably stunned." Good going, her

anger was directed at the blockhead. Not at me.

"Well, he complained to my boss about me." Renate took another sip of her orange juice.

"Such a jackass!" I said.

"But I refused to apologise. What do I care if that boner comes back or not?" Renate began to calm down.

"Excuse me, your boss asked *you* to apologise?" I was incredulous.

"Mhm."

"Will he kick you out?"

"Nah, he needs me. I work all sorts of shifts, especially when somebody doesn't come to work. Happens all the time."

"Otherwise, you'll just look for another job."

"Precisely. Yesterday, I worked Daniela's shift. Then this woman swans in with her screaming brat. Two, three years old. The little darling didn't want to stop hollering, no matter what she tried. People got up from their tables and stormed out to get themselves neutered."

I had to giggle. That was so typical for Renate; that dry humour of her's was legendary.

"That's my sad little story. What's yours?" She asked abruptly. Dammit.

"Are you talking about Pakistan?"

"What else?"

"Well, I don't know where to start."

"At the beginning would be best."

So I began with the beginning. Told her the whole story. About the so-called hotel in Karachi, Chacha Qasim, Khadriala and Saïda, Altaf's behaviour, the sensation I'd caused in Jhelum, the bus trip to Islamabad and how I'd been kidnapped at the Raja Bazaar.

Then I described the whole experience with the gang of criminals, about Banu and how Idris had rescued me during the random storm. What I didn't tell her about were the dreams that still plagued me. And that I had recognised this guy Idris as Nusrat's old flame Imran.

I'd never seen Renate keep quiet for such a long time. And

what was even better: she spared me the tedious I-told-you-so' speech. We had finished our orange juice ages ago when she put down the photographs of the wedding that Nasra had sent from London. Nobody else had laid eyes on those pictures yet. Nasra had written 'Come and visit us soon'.

"Great stuff, those clothes and all that. They get married with all the bells and whistles, it seems," Renate marvelled.

"Would have been a great experience if it hadn't been for the kidnapping," I said. It was an attempt to apologise for my impetuous decision to take this trip.

"Man, that's something... that Altaf had to drag you into his mess like that." It was Renate's attempt at showing me goodwill.

"I know. But Banu was right: it was my own decision to travel to Pakistan. Just sometimes, when we were chauffeured around the mountains in that Land Rover, I couldn't help but think that I was in the wrong movie."

"With Indiana Jones…"

"Exactly." We laughed. "And the fact that Idris got me out of there. That was something else." I unconsciously touched my arm that was as good as healed.

"I'm just glad that you're back in one piece. So, this Idris, hmm? And what about Altaf?" Renate asked without looking at me.

"What about him? At the moment I'm just glad that I don't have to see him anymore. Such drama, just because he had this crazy idea that I should become his bride." I rolled my eyes. "I should have known better."

"How were you supposed to know what was lying in wait for you?" *Really, is she still not reproaching me?* I thought in astonishment. "Well, not everything was bad. Mostly, it was terribly interesting. Completely different from here. I'm sure you would have liked Nasra. She's taking nobody's nonsense. At some stage, I will remember only the good things."

"Good resolution. When I was in Washington, I could have killed Steve. But it wasn't all that bad in hindsight. Especially when I hear what you had to go through in

Pakistan. We'll probably move to Hanover. I can study Biology there and he wants to start a new band. Steve has been in touch with a few other musicians."

"Hanover? But that's so far away. What am I supposed to do here without you?" I was dismayed.

"You'll survive. And... you can come to visit me anytime you like."

"Alright." Renate and I had been best friends for such a long time. I couldn't imagine the world without her funny, cynical remarks. "I'm not sure yet what I want to study or where," I continued. "At the moment I've enough on my plate to worry about things like that. Plus, I made it through six long weeks in Pakistan without you."

"There you go. Of course, things would have been different, had you taken me with you."

"Of course, quite different."

The phone began to ring and wouldn't stop. That's how I knew that Manfred wasn't at home. I fumbled for the key to his room from under my books that were lying all over my desk.

It was Zohra, who just wanted to touch sides with me.

"Oh bonjour, ça va?" I greeted her. Renate stuck her head through the half-open door. *It's Zohra*, I mouthed. Renate answered in sign-language: *I must go now, anyway*. I got up. The cord extended only as far as the door. *What must I do?* I gestured. She blew me a kiss and had already disappeared down the stairs.

That night, I had a visit from yet another Nusrat-dream.

We are going to a horse race together. My husband and I. We are dressed in fine attire for the occasion... the people in the village should look at us with pride. He secretly presses my hand while he performs his official duty. I feel very happy.

The following morning, I'd finally had it with those unwanted dreams! Having to remember Nusrat's life all the time – that was just more than I could bear. Between work, my studies and the preparations for my trip, I barely had the time to squeeze in a session with Dr. Albrecht, but was lucky to get an appointment. As was to be expected, the good old doctor was bowled over by the adventures I had encountered in Pakistan.

I'd just finished telling him the gist of my kidnap-story. Of course, he hadn't read the article in the paper.

"Fascinating! That you had to go through something like that. How are you feeling now, Isabell? Do you still suffer from nightmares or panic attacks?"

"I think so... which is why I'm here. Those dreams are driving me out of my skull. It helps to take walks in the park, though. I believe that it's still the best place to work through everything that happened to me. I'm also planning to go to Morocco for a few weeks to visit my friend there. I want to discuss everything with her because here nobody here seems to understand what I'm going through."

"That's why you wanted to make an appointment back in March. Because you still had memories and dreams of Nusrat, didn't you? And somehow everything conspired against the appointment."

"I constantly dreamed about Nusrat. Even when I was still here. And now I just can't switch it off. I feel like I am Nusrat and I'm thinking her thoughts. I even recognised one of the kidnappers as Imran —"

Dr. Albrecht gave me a quizzical look.

"The man I spoke to in the garden..."

"Oh yes." He studied his notes and scribbled something down.

"The name of the place where Nusrat spent most of her life is Dâstân, by the way. It's a village in the Himalayas. I was there – with the kidnappers."

Everything came just bubbling out. The more I said, the bigger Dr. Albrecht's eyes grew and he even forgot to scribble down his notes.

"Fascinating. I must have made a mistake somewhere along the lines. My apologies. I'm still right at the beginning of exploring the world of regressions." I waited. Just now, he would pull off the feat and release me from my unpleasant dreams.

The doctor mumbled something to himself. "Wakeup

phase. Better suggestion at the end of the session." He looked up at me. "And those daydreams you are talking about - they came spontaneously and were random?"

"It was more like this wedding that I was attending triggered something in me. It reminded me of my own wedding as Nusrat – if I can put it that way - and suddenly I felt like I was Nusrat. She just took over... freaky somehow."

"That is… simply fascinating, Isabell," the Doc mumbled and wrote something down. This favourite word of his seemed to express everything. I could only hope that he was taking me seriously.

"Idris was Imran and I recognised him. He was the same man and then again, he wasn't. Idris is not as hot-headed as Imran. We spoke very briefly but he seemed to recognise me as well. Somehow."

I told Dr. Albrecht all those things I could still remember. It wasn't exactly easy for me as some memories were a little blurred.

"That's quite normal, " he said matter-of-factly. "Your brain is trying to protect you from the trauma you must have experienced. Perhaps there is still something lurking in the background that we haven't detected yet. We should start with the hypnosis if you feel ready." He checked his watch. "We'll take all the time we need."

"What I want is for these dreams to stop."

"I'll do my very best," Dr. Albrecht assured me and switched on the tape recorder. "Lean right back into the chair. Yes, just like so. You are safe here. The chair feels warm and soft. You sink deeper and deeper into the soft, padded chair. You are safe. There is nobody here who can harm you in any way. Warm and safe." I felt warm and safe.

Then I had to push my hand down against his hand. He suddenly let go and said firmly, "Sleep!" And I fell asleep.

Later, I heard myself in the recording, how I spoke about the kidnapping and how Nusrat would have behaved. Then I was suddenly carried back hundreds of years into the past. "*I am in Dâstân. My mother-in-law is so mean. Oh no! She beats her own daughters. I am scared of her but Mansour doesn't allow her to treat me poorly!"*

"Move on to next important event. You can remember everything," Dr. Albrecht instructed me gently.

"The wedding… my husband… he is so cheerful… they perform the Samaj sword dance. You have to be rather nimble. I would love to participate in this. The food is so good. Mansour's mother dies shortly after the wedding of some disease. I'm secretly glad about it," I said truthfully. *'I must no longer bear her vicious moods."*

"And how do you feel about it now?"

"One must never wish another's misfortune. Karma will take care of them and their sins in time. My Rajput-mother beams when she sees me."

"Do you know your own Rajput-mother?" This question related to my current life.

"No," I answered sadly, "I don't know her."

"Is there any other aspect of your life as a Rajput woman that we have not yet explored? An important matter that's still unresolved?"

'I have explored everything that's important in that life.'

"That life is in the past. You will no longer dream about this previous lifetime unless you wish to do so. You will now awake and feel fresh and rested.," Dr. Albrecht's voice hummed.

As I woke up, I felt more rested than I had in a long time - and there was something else I could remember.

"My mother-in-law. I believe that I know her – no, I'm quite sure of it," I blurted out and had a feeling of dread.

"Fascinating. We must have done something right. Who do you recognise today as your former mother-in-law?"

"It's my own mother."

I was shocked by that revelation and had to take a moment to recover. Elizabeth brought me a glass of water and I drank it slowly.

But that wasn't all of it. "There is also this servant of my father's - Pratap. He had always been so kind when he took care of me as a young child. I felt safe with him all along –

with Pratap."

"Right. And do you recognise this Pratap?" Dr. Albrecht asked.

"I believe that he is my grandmother, Grandma Bertrand."

"Your father's mother?"

"Yes." Another piece of the puzzle fell into place.

"Fascinating."

After this mammoth-session, I left the practice with a renewed sense of hope and with a copy of Dr. Albrecht's book that still had the fresh smell of the printer's press. I appeared in the book as a case study. The title was "Many Dreams – Many Lives". My name in the book was Michaela and my age was18. As far as I could tell, everything else was authentic. I put the book into my bag and decided to read it later. Dr. Albrecht wanted me to give him feedback. Pity, that our session today wasn't in the book.

"No problem, Doc," I had said. "And thanks."

Luckily, his suggestions had the desired effect. At last, the Nusrat-dreams no longer troubled me and I had my own life back! The life of Isabell Bertrand. Here and now and in the present. I just wouldn't be visiting my mother for a while until I had come to terms with our previous connection. The holidays were just around the corner when Zohra's phone call came in. I sat on my roommate Manfred's floor as I spoke to her one last time.

"I'm sure you will like my mother," she said. "She is very nice. We will eat much tagine. Only at night, of course. It's Ramadan, the month of fasting. There is something else… can you bring me some fabric?"

As always, there was a crackling sound in the phone line.

"What? Fabric?" The art of sewing was a book with seven seals for me.

"Yes, fabric!" Zohra yelled over the crackling noise. "4 or better 5 metres… peach skin. I think 6 metres will be best."

"Peach skin?" I had no idea what that was supposed to be.

"Yes, then I can have a wedding dress made from it."

"A wedding dress?"

"Yes, yes. Didn't I tell you? I'm engaged to my cousin Hassan." Crackle, crunch.

I was gobsmacked. Peach skin? Wedding? "No... I didn't know about that," I stammered.

"Oh, I'm sure I wrote it in my letter. And I put some pictures in it. It's probably still on its... way to you ..." Crunch, crunch, crackle. The telephone line was going haywire again.

"Congratulations, Zohra! How exciting! When are you going to get married?" I asked her.

"What?"

"When will you get married?" I bellowed into the receiver and Manfred looked up from his desk with a puzzled expression.

"We don't... know yet. Next... maybe." Crunch, crunch.

"I can barely hear you. I'll bring you that peach skin if I can find it."

There was no answer.

So I trotted off at the next opportunity, determined to find peach skin fabric somewhere. The best time for shopping was during my lunch break. I had to work every day now because travelling didn't come cheap. I had already organised the journey to Spain. Heinz and his girlfriend Nelly were driving to Avignon and would give me a lift. From there, I wanted to take the train. The ferry to Tanger left from Malaga.

Everything was sorted. Just that the saleswoman at the fabrics store had never heard of such a thing as peach skin before.

"An apricot colour is similar to a peach, isn't it?" She said. I allowed myself to be convinced. It was a beautiful, flowing fabric. And as far as I could tell, perfect for a wedding dress. I stepped out of the fabric store with my purchase and bumped straight into Altaf.

Altaf! He seemed somewhat less amazed than I was, which took me off-guard. "You are back in Germany!"

"Came back yesterday," he laughed. "I tried to call you but nobody picked up the phone."

"Manfred is in Stuttgart and Ingmar went to Italy on his motorbike. He has a new girlfriend who is Italian, and I have to work and go shopping."

Altaf looked up in surprise. "In a fabric store?"

"Yes, that's for Zohra. She asked me to bring fabric with me."

"You are going to Morocco? When?"

"Next week. For two weeks. Perhaps, I'll stay in Spain for another week or so. I've heard that they have great youth hostels there," I explained my travel plans to him.

"Then we still have some time to meet and chat. What about right now? Let's go and have coffee. We should also meet with Atesh and Eddie Adeyemu. Amma has given me a few things for you and everybody sends their greetings…"

"Okay, okay. Slow down. First of all, thank you very much for the greetings. And why would she give you things for me? Let's meet at the weekend. I really haven't got the time right now."

I checked my wristwatch. I had another five minutes. "Saturday would be best, breakfast at Café Steinreich. I must beetle off and get back to work now. My boss doesn't like it when I come back late from my lunch break."

"Alright, deal. See you Saturday."

We met as planned. For an hour. I could take no more than that. Altaf spent most of the time assuring me that the problem with the army general and his son had been resolved.

"…by the way, the 'Agoo' gave me a message for you that the girls have been found. The leader of the gang hasn't been found, though. She will probably be punished by a tribal court of the Pashtun. It was impossible to find out exactly what happened," Altaf said.

Then he told me every little bit of village news. I swallowed hard because I'd nearly asked him about Idris. Amma had sent an embroidered tablecloth. It rested neatly folded next to my breakfast plate. On top of the tablecloth was a stack of brand new colourful glass bangles. My feelings were all over the place.

"What will happen to the girls?" I asked him. "They can't

really go back to their families."

"I have no idea. The 'Agoo' didn't say anything about that."

Ah well. I was grateful to the 'Agoo' for his message. Altaf promised to tell him that and express my gratitude for the tablecloth and the glass bangles to his mother. He wanted to get in touch as soon as I was back from Morocco. Not a word about wanting to get married to me. Wonderful, the old Altaf was back!

At last, the following week we received the results of our exams. I could hardly believe it: I had passed with flying colours!

I was delighted. "13 points each for Bio and for Ethics. That's an *A*. English 12 points, a *B*. There, take that, Mr. Mandell!"

"Dammit, now I have to go for an oral exam after all," Angie sighed. I stood in the passage with Tarek and Angie outside the staff room.

"So do I, in French. Cakewalk. Then we just have to endure the graduation ceremony - and we are done!" Tarek jubilated.

"I'm not going," I said. Short and sweet.

"But Isabell, you have to come! They'll give us our certificates. And there will be free food," Angie whinged.

"I don't care a hang about that," I persisted. "I'm done with the whole kaboodle. This moron Mandel no longer has any power over me or to fail me or tell me what I can or cannot do. I'll be on my way to France with Heinz and Nelly that day."

"You can't do that to us. Everbody is going." Angie was horrified.

"They can shove it. I'm sure that the teachers are just as happy as I am if they don't ever clap eyes on me again."

"Why don't you leave after the ceremony?" Tarek made a last-ditch attempt to change my mind.

"Because I don't feel like it. Besides, I'm going with Heinz and Nelly and they want to leave on the same day."

"Always banging your head against a wall, right? Then we'll just have to meet again when you're back from

Morocco." Angie seemed content with this solution.

"Exactly."

"But I'll be in Hamburg until the end of September," Tarek said.

That couldn't be changed. At school, the most diverse characters were cobbled together and afterwards, everybody simply went their own way.

On the morning of the graduation, I was already on my way to Spain. This time, I didn't have to feed the fish during the ferry ride to Morocco.

The fresh smell of the sea was just wonderful and I enjoyed the view of the softly moving waves, glittering in the afternoon sun. How much better was that, compared to the boring ceremony where my friends were languishing just about now!

I found the Mediterranean Sea fascinating and Morocco even more so. The hustle and bustle of Tanger, the landscape I admired during the bus ride to Rabat. Everything.

The interior fittings of the buildings and the colourful tiles that had Tarek in a tizz. The food. Everything was so different compared with Pakistan. And yet similar somehow. The hospitality of the people was especially impressive.

"Marhaban, marhaban. Salaam Aleikum!" Zohra's mother greeted me warmly and laughed with delight at the sight of the modest gifts I gave her.

Unfortunately, I had bought the wrong fabric because I hadn't heard during our telephone conversation that the peach skin fabric was supposed to be white. Zohra quickly got over her disappointment. Her aunt Fatima would then simply have to bring the correct fabric for the wedding dress with her from London.

"Sorry, I don't know fabrics to save my life," I apologised awkwardly. "I thought that the apricot colour would do the trick. That's what they told me at the fabric store. Apricot is almost the same as peach, isn't it?"

"Never mind. I'll do something else with this one. Don't worry, I'll still show you how to draw henna patterns on your hands," Zohra laughed. "Afterwards, we'll go to the Hammam."

"The what?"

"La maison de bain. The bathhouse, of course. It's best if you wear my mother's old jellabah. You can't just walk around the streets with me like that. Especially not during Ramadan. We still have to go to the market and buy rassoul. That's the grey lava soil that we use to wash our hair," Zohra explained when she saw my baffled expression.

We threaded our way through the stalls before Zohra had found the right product.

The Hammam was outside of the massive city walls. Just like the area where Zohra lived. The large square next to the marketplace was surrounded by countless street kitchens. Here at night, delectable meat skewers were grilled on large grids over glowing coals. At night, because it was Ramadan. And at night, there were also all sorts of acrobats and fire-eaters performing in the square.

During the day, nobody was allowed to eat or drink until the half-moon had been sighted.

At the Hammam, we sat by a fountain like all the other women, and talked about Pakistan while 'washwomen' scrubbed us clean. They fetched one pail of hot water after the other and the scrubbing continued. Apparently, each pail of hot water was charged for separately. I'd never felt this clean in my entire life.

Zohra spoke mostly French with me, which turned out to be somewhat tricky. My French was far from perfect and I kept changing over to English. At least, we weren't constantly interrupted by a crackling telephone line.

Despite our challenges with the language, Zohra listened patiently and understood me better than anybody else so far. "D'accord, Isabell. We also have tribes in the mountains who follow their own rules. Many of them are Berber. My family is also Berber," she explained. "Us Berber are different from the Arabs. Our women have more rights and freedoms. Particularly here in in the city, we are rather liberal. We are not required to wear veils and wear the jellabah only so that nobody harasses us."

"You don't say? Do they also kidnap women here?" A shiver crawled up my spine. My back was being massaged at the moment and the feeling quickly subsided.

Zohra's eyes flashed. "Not that I've heard of. At least not tourists."

There were a good many tourists in Morocco. But women were neither required to wear veils nor did they have to endure bothersome ogling from men. Even in conservative Rabat, they were simply tolerated. How different two Islamic countries could be.

Before I knew it, the two weeks were over and I was once again on a ferry, making my way back to Malaga. I'd given Zohra's mother a hand-mirror that I had bought at the market in Rabat as a parting gift for all her hospitality. The good-natured woman reminded me a lot of the motherly Amma back in Khadriala. She even resembled her.

"You must definitely try and come to our wedding," Zohra said. "Next year. I'll send you an invitation when I know the date —"

Another wedding! That would surely be quite different from the wedding I'd attended in Pakistan. Morocco was much more open-minded. That was a fact and I had just experienced it.

The breeze played with my hair. Perhaps it was time for me to spend some time thinking about what I wanted to do with myself in the near future. Studying sounded good. Anthropology seemed quite interesting or Ethnology. I checked the time on my wristwatch. Another half an hour before we were docking in Malaga.

I leaned over the ship's rail and watched the softly undulating waves. The warm air caressed my face and carried my thoughts gently here and there. Then, for the first time in months, I was thinking about absolutely nothing. Silence. Nothingness.

"Excuse me please, I believe you left your bag on the bench

over there," I heard a friendly male voice say behind me.

I turned around abruptly.

A young man with brown hair, tousled by the wind and with a winsome smile, held out a rather familiar green shoulder bag towards me. My passport, all my money, all the tickets and Dr. Albrecht's book 'Many Dreams – Many Lives' that I had read halfway through were in this bag.

I felt a sense of shortlived panic rise up inside me and I gave him a fleeting glance. His light-blue shirt was clearly one size too large for him.

"Oh dear – thank you," I stammered. "My word, how scatterbrained of me! I must have started daydreaming, watching the sea like that. Thank you so much, again."

I took the bag off his hands. It was the beautiful, hand-woven bag I had bought in Greece. Should I make sure that nothing was missing? I gave him a closer look. No, he looked nothing like a pick-pocket to me.

"Nothing wrong with daydreaming," the young man said smiling and little wrinkles appeared around his clear eyes. "I see that your palms have henna patterns on them. In India, women also decorate their hands and feet with henna like that. I just came back from a 3-month- trip to India."

He had beautiful teeth. His remark left me a little bashful and I tried to hide my hands behind the bag that I still held like a shield in front of me.

But he sounded nice. Very nice.

"You're kidding. I came back from Pakistan a few months ago. I was invited to a wedding there. What I mean is… I wasn't just at a wedding… ah never mind. This is the artwork of my good friend Zohra in Rabat." I contemplated my left hand. "I've been visiting her for the past two weeks."

The young man fell silent for a moment. "Tell me, don't I know you from somewhere?" He suddenly asked.

Oh please, not again one of those lame chat-up lines, I thought.

In France, a wannabe gigolo had pestered me on the train with a similar routine. But the man standing in front of me sounded more surprised than obtrusive. For the first time, I looked directly into his eyes. My heart skipped a beat. They were blue now instead of brown but I was definitely not imagining things. I knew these eyes. Knew them well. Would recognise them anywhere.

"I... I don't think so," I stuttered and smiled bravely.

It wasn't easy to hide my confusion. Could it be true? I studied his face for an instant then quickly looked away. There was no doubt about it!

I could feel myself turn red, felt myself moving differently now. My movements becoming more swaying as if I was in Nusrat's beautiful, well-rounded body, had her bejewelled arms...

The young man smiled back at me and said spontaneously, "Well, then I must be making a mistake. Do you feel like grabbing a cup of coffee? Then we can chat a bit about our travel experiences. I've always been interested in Pakistan. By the way, my name is Magnus Lundgren." He bowed slightly. "I'm from Copenhagen and on my way back from visiting my sister Agneta in Casablanca. Her husband has been working there as an engineer for a few years now."

"I'm Isabell Bertrand from Karlsruhe in Germany."

I tried not to stare at him while we shook hands. Then I gave a little sigh and waved my hand invitingly at the coffee bar. We walked towards the shabby counter where a few passengers were already standing in a queue. The wall clock above the bar had stopped working and the short hand on the clock face had gone missing. The bartender seemed to be bored as he was pouring the coffee from a steaming pot into cups.

I could feel Magnus walking behind me, could feel the warm familiarity with this man I had only just met. Could it be a coincidence? But I certainly knew these eyes. There was no doubt about it.

They were Mansour's eyes!

The End

<u>Glossary of terms in the Hinustani languages</u>

Urdu/Punjabi:

Shukria merbani = thank you so much
Mera naam = my name
Rickshaw = motorbike taxi with a passenger cabin
Chubsuret = pretty
Shaadi = wedding
Nikah = signing of the marriage contract
Salaam aleikum = good day
Chudafiss = goodbye
Neyé= no
Aho = yes
Savaar = morning
Shalwar = wide trousers
Kamise = long tunic
Dabatta = veil
Tjuni = big piece of fabric
Burkha = Shador-like coat
Urdu bolti hum = I speak Urdu (for females)
Vaqt hé, chalo = It is time to go
Chalo, chalié! = Come now, let's go!
Pakoras = deep-fried vegetables in a spicy batter
Lassi = a yoghurt drink
Chai = spiced tea
Ghee = clarified butter
Chapati = flat bread
Saalen = a hot meat stew
Samosas = filled, fried dough-triangles
Chacha/i = uncle/aunt (on the father's side)
Mammu/i = uncle/aunt (on the mother's side)
Agoo – village elder
Shertan = devil
Kinnaa = how much?

Rajput:

Sabadana, jawo! = Go, look after yourself!
Vamsh = Rajput Clan
Chandra = moon
Kul = family branch
Moghuls = Muslim invaders in the Middle Ages

Paschto/Farsi:

Qashang(i) = pretty(one)
Dokhtar = girl
Kashar ror = little brother
Haga bad xrab sare de = he is a bad man
Ta dza! = Go!
Weshta = hair

THE AUTHOR

Evadeen Brickwood grew up with two sisters in Germany and studied cultural sciences and languages. As a young woman, she travelled extensively and many of her books are inspired by her experiences abroad.

Feeling adventurous, the newly qualified translator moved to Africa in 1988 and worked for two years as a secretary and language teacher in Botswana.

The author eventually settled in South Africa, where she got married and raised two daughters. In Johannesburg, Evadeen Brickwood studied computers and management of training and worked as a corporate software trainer, professional translator and lecturer at WITS University.

In 2003, she began her writing career with youth novels in the 'Remember the Future' series about adventures in prehistory.

Book 1, the award-winning 'Children of the Moon', has been published twice in South Africa and translated into German. The author now self-publishes and other books in the time travel series are released on a regular basis.

Her works include the novels Singing Lizards' and the crime-mystery 'The Rhino Whisperer' and four of her books have been translated into German.

About Writing This Book

Isabell Bertrand and I have much in common. I grew up in Karlsruhe and, just like her, was often gripped by an insatiable wanderlust. I would call 'A Half Moon Adventure' the most autobiographical of my novels to date, although some passages in the storyline were plucked from my fertile imagination. In real life, I did travel to America and all those countries I mention, and yes, I was invited to a wedding as a teenager and spent almost two months in the rural district of Punjab.

It was one of the most pivotal experiences of my life. Back home, it turned out to be difficult to share these events with others, even with my closest friends. Much later, people still didn't believe me and many thought I was making up the whole story of travelling to such an exotic country. But that's exactly what happened and I hope that the book turned out as gripping as I remember my trip. So I guess, this book is personal. Some things did actually happen and some of them... well, they didn't. I've never been hypnotised, for example, but wouldn't mind giving it a try.

On the flight from Moscow to Karachi, inside a wobbly Russian Aeroflot-machine, I started my travel diary and continued to write down what I heard people say. These words sounded rather foreign to me and spelling them out was difficult but I've done extensive research before I began writing.

Luckily, we now have the internet to fill in the gaps and you will find most of the translations in the glossary. What you don't find on the list, I've explained in the text. It makes me sad to see how Pakistan has changed over the years and now presents itself to the world in such an unflattering light. The country I knew was different and the memories, good and bad, will always stay with me.

Evadeen Brickwood

This print book is available from all good bookstores and the e-book can be purchased from major online stores, such as Smashwords, Kobo, Tolino, Kindle, Apple i-Store & Neobooks.

The author's websites are:

http://www.evadeen.wixsite.com/novels

http://www.evadeen.wixsite.com/youngbooks

http://www.evadeen.wixsite.com/charlieproudfoot

She is looking forward to your mail and can also be contacted on social media, incl. Facebook, Twitter, Instagram, Pinterest, google+ and Goodreads.

Discover other novels by Evadeen Brickwood

This adventure mystery tells the story of 22-year-old Bridget Reinhold who is not exactly the adventurous type, but when her sister Claire disappears in Southern Africa, nothing can hold her in England. Bridget launches herself into the search in Botswana and encounters obstacle after obstacle. She learns the basics of the native language and culture and soon moves to the capital city of Gaborone. Soon, her mission is plunged into turmoil as everything seems to be going wrong. Just coincidence or is there something more sinister at work?

Another mystery novel set in modern South Africa. This time, the murders of a ranger and a rare black rhino in the idyllic Shangari Safari Park rattle the local community of Rutgersdrift. Sofia Helenius from Finland lives at the lodge with her boyfriend Tom Rutgers, the owner of Shangari. Sofia is tormented by a secret she yearns to share with Tom, but the cruel events grab the limelight and put everything else in the shade. One of the native Khoi-San families is known to communicate with wild animals, but what if the criminals get wind of this gift?

When another murder happens in the city of Johannesburg, smouldering secrets begin to unravel. How are the murders connected and will it be possible to halt a relentless crime-syndicate in order to save an African paradise?

www.ingramcontent.com/pod-product-compliance
Lightning Source LLC
Chambersburg PA
CBHW010441100726
47904CB00008B/2431